Also by Emma Wildes

Our Wicked Mistake
My Lord Scandal
Seducing the Highlander
Lessons from a Scarlet Lady
An Indecent Proposition

**More Praise for the Novels
of Emma Wildes**

"A luxurious and sensual read. Both deliciously wicked and tenderly romantic. . . . I didn't want it to end!"
—*New York Times* bestselling author Celeste Bradley

"This wickedly exciting romance will draw you in and take hold of your heart."
—*USA Today* bestselling author Elizabeth Boyle

"Regency fans will thrill to this superbly sensual tale of an icy widow and two decadent rakes. . . . Balancing deliciously erotic encounters with compelling romantic tension, and populating a convincing historical setting with a strong cast of well-developed characters, prolific romance author Wildes provides a spectacular and skillfully handled story that stands head and shoulders above the average historical romance."
—*Publishers Weekly* (starred review)

"Wickedly delicious and daring, Wildes's tale tantalizes with an erotic fantasy that is also a well-crafted Regency romance. She delivers a page turner that captures the era, the mores, and the scandalous behavior that lurks beneath the surface."
—*Romantic Times* (4½ stars, top pick)

"Emma Wildes has thoroughly enchanted e-book readers with her emotionally charged story lines. . . . [A] gem of an author . . . Ms. Wildes tells this story with plenty of compassion, humor, and even a bit of suspense to keep readers riveted to each scandalous scene—and everything in between."
—Romance Junkies

continued . . .

EMMA WILDES

His Sinful Secret

NOTORIOUS BACHELORS

A SIGNET ECLIPSE BOOK

SIGNET ECLIPSE
Published by New American Library, a division of
Penguin Group (USA) Inc., 375 Hudson Street,
New York, New York 10014, USA
Penguin Group (Canada), 90 Eglinton Avenue East, Suite 700, Toronto,
Ontario M4P 2Y3, Canada (a division of Pearson Penguin Canada Inc.)
Penguin Books Ltd., 80 Strand, London WC2R 0RL, England
Penguin Ireland, 25 St. Stephen's Green, Dublin 2,
Ireland (a division of Penguin Books Ltd.)
Penguin Group (Australia), 250 Camberwell Road, Camberwell, Victoria 3124,
Australia (a division of Pearson Australia Group Pty. Ltd.)
Penguin Books India Pvt. Ltd., 11 Community Centre, Panchsheel Park,
New Delhi - 110 017, India
Penguin Group (NZ), 67 Apollo Drive, Rosedale, North Shore 0632,
New Zealand (a division of Pearson New Zealand Ltd.)
Penguin Books (South Africa) (Pty.) Ltd., 24 Sturdee Avenue,
Rosebank, Johannesburg 2196, South Africa

Penguin Books Ltd., Registered Offices:
80 Strand, London WC2R 0RL, England

First published by Signet Eclipse, an imprint of New American Library,
a division of Penguin Group (USA) Inc.

First Printing, November 2010
10 9 8 7 6 5 4 3 2 1

For Dick Leakey, who no doubt has many sinful secrets. I suspect I am much too innocent to know about most of them. You are one of my favorite friends.

ACKNOWLEDGMENTS

I would like to thank Heather Baror for all she does as a foreign-rights agent extraordinaire. The support of my friends is another invaluable asset. In particular I would like to mention Monica Burns, Kerin Hanson, Laura Kubitz, and Sandy James. You cheer for me. Thank you, ladies!

Chapter One

I t was a fateful miscalculation.

The light gloss of moonlight gave an indistinct outline of the shadowy figure as he turned one second too late to completely avoid the blade. Michael Hepburn felt it slice through his fine brocade coat and the cold bite of steel on his flesh. Pain shot through him even as he lashed out with one foot in reflexive self-defense and heard the satisfying *thud* as the kick connected. His assailant grunted, staggered back on the greasy cobblestones, and then caught his balance and lunged forward again.

Fortunately, this time Michael was a little more prepared.

He dodged backward and let his attacker's momentum bring him close enough that he landed a solid blow with his right fist. It was too dark to really see properly in the confines of the narrow, ill-smelling alleyway, so instead of hitting the man's chin, he caught him in the side of the neck with a sickening sound. A low whistle of agony echoed and Michael pressed the advantage by kicking out again, aiming for the stranger's groin.

Fighting fair was for those who could afford to lose.

He'd learned that back in Spain. Dying an honorable death was all well and good, but living was even better in his estimation, and being assaulted out of nowhere in some squalid London backstreet was about as sordid a demise as he could imagine.

The man managed to deflect the blow—showing he'd been in a dirty brawl a time or two himself and had anticipated it—but he slipped on the slick surface underfoot and went down like a felled ox. The knife skittered away and Michael bent to retrieve it, only to see the burly figure scramble up and turn to run. The retreating sound of pounding footfalls was overshadowed by Michael's harsh breathing.

Had it not been for the warm, sticky feel of the blood soaking his clothing he might have even given chase to get a few answers.

"Damnation," he muttered, pulling open the slashed jacket to peer at the damage. The white linen of his shirt was already bright scarlet. Whoever the bastard was, he'd been intent on doing real harm. The blade must have glanced off a rib, and Michael, though bleeding profusely, didn't think the injury was serious. He'd been wounded enough times before to know that singular feeling when it might be *the* one.

But the timing just couldn't possibly be worse.

He pulled out his pocket watch and squinted at it in the meager illumination, trying to ignore the stench of refuse around him. It was damned late but he could hardly go home as he was, just in case someone was still awake. The huge house was crammed with assorted relatives and guests.

Luckily, he had other options.

He walked the distance to where he'd paid well to have a hired hack wait. Bringing the ducal carriage to this location, past shuttered, shabby businesses and sleeping houses, the sloped roofs and sagging doorways indicative of the seediness of the surroundings, would have attracted far too much attention. There was no doubt he was a little light-headed by the time he reached his destination.

The driver, a small man with a narrow face and scruffy beard, looked alarmed at his appearance. "I say, guv. Trouble?"

"Was it the blood that gave it away?" Michael asked cynically. "Footpads are bolder with each passing day."

To his credit, the man did not point out the disreputable neighborhood and the late hour.

A nice tip would hopefully make him forget he saw anything at all. Michael gave the address and climbed into the creaking vehicle, gingerly settling on the cracked seat. The ride was a bit jarring but thankfully not too long as they passed out of the seamy neighborhoods and gained a more fashionable—and safer—part of London. The address was expensive but discreet, just outside of Mayfair, and to his relief, there was a light in one of the upstairs windows. He alighted with murmured thanks and added a handsome amount to the fare. "Myself and the incident are both forgotten, if you please."

There was something in the little man's expression that said he thought the eccentricities of the aristocracy to be puzzling but profitable, and the cabbie nodded and clambered back up on the seat to cluck at his rawboned horse. The clatter of departing wheels rang out.

The door of the elegant town house was answered by a young man with a scarred face and impassive expression, despite the midnight call. He wore a dressing gown and his dark hair was tousled, indicating he'd already retired. They were nearly of a height, and though his tone was always deferential, there was nothing but measured assessment in the way the other man looked Michael in the eye. He moved back in invitation. "My lord marquess. Please, come in."

Michael stepped past him. "Sorry to roust you out of bed, Lawrence."

"No apology necessary. I assure you."

Had it not been for the droplets of blood that dripped on the polished black-and-white marble of the foyer, they might have appeared to just be conversing in a polite exchange of pleasantries. But while they were colleagues, they were not precisely friends. "Is Lady Taylor . . . occupied?"

"All alone this evening, my lord." There was a slight hint of irony in the tone of Lawrence's voice, and he eyed Michael's slashed coat.

"Very good." At least he wouldn't be intruding on a personal interlude. Antonia rarely mentioned her private entertainments and he didn't ask. Michael suspected she and Lawrence shared a closer relationship than majordomo and mistress, but if so, it wasn't his affair and neither of them had confided in him, which was all to the good. They were business associates—albeit with closer ties than most—but still Michael believed in keeping personal issues separate from his duties. "Perhaps you could let her know I'm here."

"She'll be delighted to receive you, I'm sure. She always is."

Despite his wound and the disastrous implications, Michael had to lift a brow in amusement at the slightly insolent tone of the young man as he left. Lawrence hadn't even blinked an eye over a bleeding man arriving in the middle of the night, nor had he asked questions about his wound. He wouldn't, of course. He'd seen worse, and he knew how to keep his mouth firmly shut.

Yet the hint of antagonism spoke volumes.

Minutes later Antonia hovered over him, a silk wrapper framing her voluptuous body, her mouth set in a line of grim reproof. They were in her bedroom, though she'd set a blanket on the floor so he wouldn't bleed on her expensive carpeting. Pale gold silken hangings framed a tester bed, and the windows were open to the back gardens. She'd dragged the gilded stool from her dressing table over on top of the protective blanket and fairly shoved Michael down to sit on it.

"I believe," she said as she tugged his shirt from his breeches, ignoring his wince, "I told you to be careful."

"My source said he had information on Roget so I took a chance and agreed to the meeting. Besides, I wasn't attacked there. It happened as I was walking back to the hack, through not the finest neighborhood in London."

"Does that surprise you? The finest people usually are not the ones who have firsthand knowledge of murderers and traitors."

"True enough."

"And the information . . . tell me, was it worth your blood?" The question was almost lethally soft.

"No."

"I see." She shrugged as she undid his buttons, but there was still a gleam of disappointment in her dark eyes. "A pity."

He eyed the jagged cut with resignation as he leaned forward to help her slide his slashed shirt off his shoulders. The wound was nasty and at least six inches long, but with all the blood, he guessed it looked worse than it was. Painful but not life threatening, and he'd had worse. "I was careless. I wasn't expecting an attack at that particular point. My supposed informant was long gone."

"This is the second time. What if it had nothing to do with the meeting itself? You said yourself it was a dangerous place to be, especially at night." Antonia dropped the bloody garment on the blanket.

"He didn't attempt to rob me."

"Because your reaction surprised him. Maybe he just wanted to kill you first so he could relieve you of your purse without trouble."

Outside in the garden a night bird called in a low, melodic sound, incongruous to the grim conversation. Michael shook his head. "No, I think the two events are connected. The attack last week was much the same. No

warning, just an ambush. I should have been expecting
this. Usually my intuition is a bit more accurate. It's telling me now to beware. I thought it had been inordinately
quiet and wondered if our quarry had left the country
again. Now I am not so sure."

"Bah, we have lost him. Again."

As she leaned forward and began to wipe the blood
away, ebony hair spilled over the shapely shoulders of the
woman inspecting his wound. She was Castilian by ances-
try and it showed in her olive skin and striking features.
Her cheekbones were aristocratic and high; her nose a
shade too long, but the defect lent an unusual character
to her face; and her mouth was generous and full lipped.
The lush curves of her figure would lure a saint.

God knew Michael didn't fit into that category.

Her robe gaped open a fraction and though he might
be wounded and bleeding he wasn't dead yet, so he
couldn't help but admire the firm, full curves of her naked breasts tipped with dusky nipples. Tempted? No,
they'd ended that association several years ago. But he
was still male and she was a very alluring woman. Without apology, he enjoyed looking.

"You'll live," she pronounced in a crisp tone, taking
the cloth and wringing it out over a basin of warm water.
She pressed it again to the spot where blood still welled
from the parted skin. "It's long but not horribly deep. I'll
have Lawrence go get a physician."

"No, thank you."

At the polite but firm refusal, she blew out an exas-
perated breath. "I knew you were going to balk. This
needs stitched. Have you seen my embroidery? Trust
me, you'd have yet another very interesting scar."

"Just bind it up."

The last thing he needed was word leaking out that
the Marquess of Longhaven had been stabbed by a
street thug. Attention was like poison. The less people
who knew, the better.

Antonia put her hands on her hips. "*Miguel*, I—"

"Please, it is rather late for an argument."

She hesitated a moment and then shook her head and theatrically threw up her hands. Her eyes were as dark as midnight and reflected surrender. "I would lose anyway. I've learned that from past experience. Fine. Have it your way, you stubborn man."

Michael watched her disappear into her dressing room. She emerged a few moments later with what appeared to be a chemise made of fine linen. She proceeded to cut it into strips with a pair of small scissors. The idea of being bandaged with female undergarments would normally have been amusing, but his current predicament made it hard to laugh.

"As you said, I'll live. I'd surmised that already, but this makes one devil of a problem for me." He sat in quiet acceptance of her ministrations as she pressed a pad of the cloth over the cut, his moody gaze fixed on the marble fireplace across the room. "I am supposed to get married in two days. This is going to take some inventive tale to explain."

Antonia glanced up, her mouth set in a thin line. She reached for a longer length of the fine white cloth. "You are really going to go through with it? I find it hard to believe."

"The wedding? Why should you? The engagement has been formal for months now."

"It isn't you, *Miguel*."

They'd had this conversation before. He sighed in resignation. "Whether it is or not, yes, I'm going through with it."

"You'll marry some insipid young chit right out of the schoolroom just because your father wishes it?"

"I would appreciate it if you did not refer to my future wife as insipid."

It might have been his imagination, but it seemed she pressed the wound with a little more force than necessary as she began to wrap it. He gave a small grunt of pain.

"She'll bore you to death."

He lazily arched a brow. "I don't think it's her job to entertain me. I have plenty enough excitement in my life as it is, which might just include the fact that someone out there seems to want me dead. Let's set aside my young bride for the moment, if you please, because we don't agree on the subject anyway. Do you think the source of the attack could be internal?"

She wrapped the bandage around his naked torso, leaning so close he could smell the delicious scent of woman and a hint of attar of roses. Ebony hair brushed his cheek and her skillful fingers moved against his skin. "I am not certain," she admitted in a quiet voice. "I think you are important to anyone who realizes what you are."

What you are. He wasn't even sure what he was, other than an expert at subterfuge and deceit.

He mused aloud. "It could be something specific set this off."

"Perhaps . . . the determination to catch Roget? Not that I disagree, as you know."

He knew. "Perhaps."

"Care to elaborate?"

"Not yet." He rubbed his jaw and narrowed his eyes. "In light of this evening's events, I'm contemplating the different variables before I settle on a theory."

"You already have one. Don't try to fool me." Antonia finished, tying off the bandage with a small flourish. "The last attempt takes on a chilling significance, doesn't it? If, as you theorize, they were both failed assassination attempts, there will probably be more until the job is done."

"I'd prefer my death not be referred to as a job, my dear."

She gave a small, inelegant snort. "Tell me how else to describe it."

Blithely, he ignored the comment and went on. "Unfortunately, the first assailant didn't survive the attack, or I might have had my answers right then and skipped this night's enchanting little encounter." It had been self-defense and Michael hadn't even been the one to kill the man; on that occasion his coachman had seen the attack and produced a pistol at just the right moment. Or the wrong one, depending on your opinion. The elderly man had proved to have a very accurate aim.

Inconvenient, though it was expedient at the time. A shame, really. Wounded men tended to talk very readily. Dead ones were very disappointing in that regard.

"But since it has happened . . . what are you going to do?" Raven brows arched in concerned inquiry.

"He *was* set to kill." Michael was grateful for that split-second glint of the moonlight on the steely blade that almost saved him. Had he not jumped the wrong way, he would be unscathed. The mistake was a problem, but better than a knife in the heart.

Still, how was he supposed to explain the injury on his wedding night? Even with the lights out and under the shroud of the blankets, she would feel the bandages. The wound might not be severe enough to disable him, thank God, but it could hardly be unwrapped in two short days without breaking open.

Well, hell. Life had a way of being complicated and this fit nicely in the slot. Bleeding all over his new wife would hardly be construed as romantic, and would, once again, require an excuse of some kind.

Damnation.

"I don't suppose you have brandy?" It wasn't so much for the pain as just to help clear his head. Michael moved restively in the chair.

Antonia smiled in a feline curve of her lips. "Of course. Contraband French brandy, though it goes against my principles to admit the bastards do anything well. I bought it from English smugglers, so that eases the pain a little." With graceful precision she rose and moved across the room to wash the blood off her hands. There was a crystal decanter and glasses on a small table, and she poured them each a measure and turned, barefoot in her pale robe, as feminine as always with her dramatic beauty and that ever-present dark fire in her eyes.

"Thank you." He accepted the glass. The heady fragrance filled his nose and he took a hearty sip. "I'll also need a new shirt. Maybe Lawrence can spare one? With everyone in residence at Southbrook in anticipation of my nuptials, I can't be assured of an anonymous arrival, no matter that it's late. I'll leave my jacket here, if you'll dispose of it."

"Whatever you need, I can take care of it."

The husky, sensual promise wasn't lost on him. Antonia was incredibly useful in some ways, but she wasn't subtle. He said in a neutral tone, "And your loyalty and resourcefulness are appreciated."

"But you still are intent on marrying your little ingenue?"

He looked at her over the rim of his glass. "Indeed."

"I delivered your precious package almost to his prestigious doorstep."

Antonia glanced up from where she sat by the fireplace. "Your jealousy ill becomes you."

Lawrence—if it was a surname or a given, she wasn't sure, but it was all he offered of his mysterious past—stood with one broad shoulder propped against the doorjamb. The jagged scar that bisected his left eyebrow had missed the eye but continued across his cheek to the taut jawline. Despite the disfigurement he was still attractive, if you liked your males a little raw and rough, with a shock of dark, unruly hair and impressively wide shoulders.

Nothing like the more refined, classic good looks of the Marquess of Longhaven, but yes, dangerously attractive in an earthy, sinful way.

"At least I *have* emotions. I can't say the same for him. He's always been a cool one. I was surprised to see all the blood. You'd think he'd bleed icy water."

"Not at all." She could argue the point easily. There was nothing cold about Michael. He was all banked fire without a hint of smoke. The flickering blaze was there, however, ready to singe whoever came into contact with him if necessary.

He *always* did what was necessary. Michael was brilliant as a cut diamond, but also every bit as hard. The facets too were many.

"I take it he declined to stay the night." Lawrence lifted his deformed brow.

"How do you know I asked?"

"There's a certain disappointment in your eyes, my lady. Besides, with him, you always ask."

"You are presumptuous."

"And you, my lady, are misguided when it comes to the marquess," he said softly.

"It isn't your business." She tried to sound haughty and indignant, but couldn't quite pull it off.

For that matter, maybe it was more accurate to say not when *Lawrence* was the one questioning her about Michael. Through the course of the war, their arrival in England, and their alliance, it had all become somehow tangled together.

"Isn't it?" He was unfazed by her curt, dismissive tone.

She laughed, but it had nothing to do with humor. "In case it escaped you, the man arrived with a knife wound in his side. Amorous bed play was not on his agenda."

"It didn't escape me. Who cleaned up the trail of blood to your bedroom, who gave him a clean shirt, and who drove him close enough to his grand home for a discreet arrival at this ungodly hour?"

"Your efficiency is always appreciated." It was true. Lawrence fulfilled many roles in her household, and in her life for that matter. Whether he was driving the carriage, playing footman and serving claret to guests, or various other not-so-mundane tasks, he was always competent and discreet.

"Shall I name how I'd like to be paid?" Lawrence shifted his powerful body, all hard muscle, in one athletic movement. The way he moved into her room was reminiscent of a stalking panther—slow, riveted, intent.

He'd dressed to drive Longhaven home, but changed back into his dressing gown. It gaped open and showed a well-defined chest, and his dark eyes held just a slight erotic glitter. In the feminine surroundings he always looked out of place. Too rugged against the trappings of silk bed hangings and fine Persian rugs, the vase of flowers by the side of her bed incongruous with his dominant masculinity.

Antonia felt her heart begin to beat faster. When he had that look in his eyes, he was very difficult to resist. The trouble was, she wasn't even sure she wished to resist. She protested, "It's late. I'm tired."

"You can sleep afterward." He corrected himself. "You'll sleep *better* afterward."

She should turn him away.

All too often, she didn't.

"You always do," he reminded her, the hoarse edge to his voice indicative of his need.

Yes, it was true, but she usually woke regretful. Using him for transient pleasure, for the comfort of strong arms around her, always stirred a conscience she wasn't even sure she possessed any longer. But still she tried to argue. "It isn't fair to you."

Lawrence reached for her and hauled her to her feet, the movement not precisely rough but still demanding. The heat from his body warmed her, and she felt the rigid length of his desire between them.

His hot mouth grazed her ear. "I can take care of myself, Antonia. Let me love you."

She surrendered.

Maybe it wasn't surprising she couldn't sleep, but it was annoying just the same.

Julianne Sutton wandered over to the window and

pulled the curtain aside, staring into the darkness. A thin moon illuminated the rooftops of the nearby houses and made blank eyes out of the windows.

Two days.

She was supposed to be married in *two* days.

A shiver of apprehension ran up her spine. It wasn't as if she could recall a time she didn't know she would one day marry the Marquess of Longhaven, but the phrase *day after tomorrow* took on an intimidating immediacy.

Maybe she'd always, for as long as she could remember, accepted the idea that the intended marriage was fait accompli, but what she hadn't expected was the change of identity of her bridegroom. If Harry had lived, she wouldn't be so nervous.

Harry. With his easygoing smile and teasing manner . . .

A soft knock startled her out of her reverie. "Yes?"

The door opened and a male voice drawled, "Still awake? I saw the light under the door. What on earth are you doing up at this hour?"

"I might ask you the same thing," she said dryly as her older brother strolled in. The strong odor of brandy and tobacco came with him, and he'd removed his cravat sometime during the evening. A little disheveled and coming in so late. It wasn't hard to guess what he'd been doing. As usual the discrepancies between how females were constantly chaperoned and how males could do as they pleased struck her. She said tartly, "At least I'm ready for bed and in my dressing gown, not just stumbling in."

"I didn't stumble."

"You've sobered up a little, then."

"Maybe," he agreed in rueful honesty, running his fingers through his hair, a slight frown on his handsome face. "I lost track of time playing cards, and yes, there were a few glasses of brandy involved. What's your excuse for not being sound asleep?"

"Just . . . thinking."

"Ah. Wedding jitters?" Malcolm selected a silk-covered chair and dropped into it, looking a little ridiculous in dark evening clothes superimposed over the feminine, peach upholstery. "I saw Longhaven earlier tonight at our club. He seemed perfectly calm, as usual. No nerves at all, or if he has them, he doesn't show it."

She wasn't sure *calm* was the right term to apply to her fiancé. *Calm* was too simple. *Controlled* might work better. Something about him spoke of leashed intensity and the smooth, almost neutral exterior somehow enhanced the impression.

"Good for him," she muttered with a small sigh. "I admit I wish we weren't virtual strangers. At least I *knew* Harry."

"He was a good sort." Regret colored the comment. "Damned shame."

Malcolm wasn't entirely sober or he wouldn't have sworn in front of her, but she agreed with her brother's sentiment, if not the language.

Yes, his death had been a shame. A fluke, an anomaly that at the age of twenty-seven an apparently otherwise healthy young man would complain of pains in his chest and be dead just hours later. His parents, the Duke and Duchess of Southbrook, had been devastated. Immediately they'd sent word to their youngest son, at the time on the Peninsula fighting the French, begging him to come home. It was difficult to say if he would have dutifully resigned his commission and returned to England or not, but the war decided it for him, finally coming to an end.

So Michael Hepburn had come home to take his older brother's place. To take his title, his position as heir to a dukedom, *and* his fiancée. Their parents still insisted on the match. The engagement between her and Harry hadn't yet been officially announced before he died, and the marriage contracted was between Julianne and the Marquess of Longhaven, so the official documents didn't even need to be changed.

Julianne had argued with her father that the five years the younger Hepburn son had spent in Spain meant they didn't know each other at all—she'd been all of thirteen when he left, so she'd barely known him anyway—but for whatever unfathomable reason, the new Lord Longhaven had agreed to an engagement when the proper mourning period had been observed.

She'd been thoroughly overruled.

Harry's death had been well over a year ago, and Michael had been back in England for some time now, but she really didn't know him any better than before his return. Polite but distant, charming but enigmatic, he was still a stranger.

"Yes, it was a shame," she agreed with genuine grief, remembering the genial young man she'd always thought she'd marry. The two brothers looked similar, with the same lean build, chestnut hair, and vivid hazel eyes. Their aristocratic features had the familial Hepburn handsomeness stamped on them, but right there all similarity ended. Harry and his younger brother weren't at all alike.

She wasn't an expert on the subject of men, but she had a feeling Michael Hepburn was . . . *complicated*. "I do miss Harry. He was always laughing."

Malcolm might be a little inebriated and it was very late—or early, depending on how one looked at the time—but he still caught the bleak inflection in her voice. "Life changes sometimes, Jule, and we can't do anything about it. Maybe this was really meant to be, you and the new marquess. Harry was a bit too tame for you, I always thought. Michael Hepburn isn't tame at all, I'd guess. It is a little difficult to tell what he's thinking."

She guessed the same thing, if the compelling, cool assessment of his gaze was any indication.

Another nervous shiver touched her.

Chapter Two

"This should have been stitched together." Fitzhugh tossed aside the crusty bandage and sent him a level glare of disapproval. "I say you should damn the questions and summon a physician to look at it, sir. It's a right nasty one."

Michael returned the look with a small smile, though the injury was sore as hell and the removal of the wrapping had caused a light sweat to sheen his skin. "I am uninterested in having a physician perhaps reveal to someone he treated the Marquess of Longhaven for a knife wound. I've been hurt worse and you've seen to it. Stop fussing and just get on with it."

The older man shook his head but obeyed, cleaning the wound and placing clean linen on it before wrapping strips of cloth to keep the pad in place. Stocky, weathered, and trustworthy, he played valet with as much efficiency as he'd performed his duties when they served together under Wellington's command. A few moments later Michael eased into his shirt and surveyed his appearance in the mirror. Clean-shaven and dressed, he looked perfectly normal, except maybe for the faint shadows under his eyes. He hadn't slept well, partly due to the wound itself, and partly due to its cause.

Two murder attempts, a volatile matter to handle for his superiors, and now a problematic wedding night.

No wonder he hadn't managed more than a half doze for a few hours.

His former sergeant had an uncanny ability to read his mind. "What are you going to tell her, if I might ask, my lord?" The form of address still came awkwardly. Fitzhugh was used to calling him *Colonel* and frequently lapsed out of sheer habit.

"I'm not sure." He finished tying his cravat and turned around. "I thought of saying I fell from my horse, but I fear even to an inexperienced eye, it looks like what it is—a knife wound. Eventually the bandage will come off and the scar would prove me a liar. Not an auspicious way to start a marriage."

There was small, inelegant snort. "The lovely young lady had better get used to half-truths, with the business you dabble your toes in."

He ignored the comment. "I have to come up with something else."

Fitzhugh picked up his discarded robe and bustled off to the dressing room to hang it up. It was a warm morning and brilliant sunshine lit the bedroom with golden light. Michael hadn't taken Harry's suite of rooms—it felt like the worst kind of betrayal to take anything more that once belonged to his brother. He'd already inherited his title, his fortune, and his fiancée, so moving into his apartments was out of the question. The furnishings in his suite were a bit austere, the same as before he'd left for Spain. Plain dark blue hangings on the carved bed, a simple cream rug on the polished floor, matching curtains at the long windows. He'd been twenty-one when he'd boarded the ship to sail away to war, and decorating was hardly a top priority in his life at that time. It still wasn't. Maybe Julianne would care to redo their portion of the Mayfair mansion, but then again, maybe she wouldn't. He knew very little about her, really.

Too little. And the distance was deliberate and entirely his fault.

It doesn't matter what she might be like, he reminded himself. He was going to marry her regardless, for his parents mourned his brother with acute grief.

He'd been startled and off guard when they had asked him to please honor the arranged marriage and take Harry's place. Though he wasn't at all sure that years of war and intrigue hadn't hardened him to a frightening degree, there still must be some vestige of sentiment left, for he hadn't been able to refuse. He'd come home, assumed his brother's position as the heir, and now was going to appropriate the young woman destined to be his wife.

It would make him feel much less guilty if Harry hadn't been so enamored of her and looking forward to the union.

The dutiful letters from home at first only hinted of it. His older brother had mentioned how beautiful she was becoming as she matured, how intelligent and good-humored, how charming and gracious. The final letter, which hadn't reached Michael until Harry was gone and in his grave, had explained how fortunate he was to be pledged to a woman who would not only grace his arm in public and his bed in private, but also enrich his life.

Did Michael feel undeserving?

A resounding affirmative to that question, he thought as he sighed and ran his hand through his neatly combed hair, ruffling the thick strands. He was nothing like Harry. There wasn't an easygoing bone in his body and his mind worked in circles, rather than straight lines. He'd seen enough horror that he'd come to understand it, and that was frightening in itself, and all the scars he bore were not just skin deep. He told his valet, "My marriage will be a matter of convenience."

"Yours or hers?" Fitzhugh was as blunt as always. "You conveniently go about your business and she conveniently doesn't notice stab wounds, long absences, and late-night comings and goings. Is that how it will work?"

"How the devil do I know how it will work? I have never been married before, but most aristocratic unions—especially those arranged by parents—involve a certain level of detachment. Besides, she's very young. Not even twenty."

"What does that have to do with it?" Fitzhugh furrowed his brow. "She's got eyes, doesn't she? A very pretty pair of them, at that. Now, I say you'd better come up with a good excuse for your current state of incapacitation, Colonel, or there will be all hell to pay from the beginning. I'm guessing, from the looks of that wicked gash, you're not going to be in top form tomorrow night to claim your husbandly rights. Young or not, that bonny lass will wonder why you didn't enjoy taking her, or worse yet, why *she* didn't enjoy it."

"I can't imagine she'd know the difference between a good performance or a poor one on a sexual level," he said dryly. "And thanks for your confidence in my masculine prowess."

A flicker of humor washed over the other man's broad face. "I imagine you'll get the job done."

"Thank you. Ah, at last, some flicker of faith."

"My faith is in her allure doing the trick, Colonel." Fitzhugh grinned. "There's no denying she's a beautiful girl. It wouldn't be like you not to notice."

"I've noticed." Michael turned and restlessly moved across the room.

Yes, he had. The unusual rich color of her glossy hair, like mahogany silk, warm and soft, framed a face that was fine-boned and elegant. Her figure was slender yet nicely shaped in the strategic places. And Fitzhugh was right: the long-lashed beauty of her dark blue eyes was striking. Julianne was a little quiet for his tastes, but then again, he hadn't really ever attempted much conversation with her either.

In his mind, she still belonged to Harry. Unfortunately, he got the sense he also held the same preconception.

It seemed like the worst treachery ever to contemplate bedding the woman his brother had wanted for himself. On the other side of the coin, his parents had set aside their acute grief in celebration of this marriage. His mother, especially, had thrown herself into the preparations for the wedding with almost frantic joy, and it was hardly a secret that in her opinion the sooner a grandchild arrived, the better.

Michael was in one devil of a dilemma because of the murderous assault, and that was discounting the mystery of just who had bloodthirsty designs on his person.

"I suppose I could just tell her the truth. That on my way home from an appointment, someone attacked me. I have no idea why, or who he was, but I managed to defend myself, and he ran off. I kept it secret so as not to put a damper on the celebration or worry my mother in her current state of happiness. What do you think?"

"The truth usually isn't your first choice." Fitzhugh looked both dubious and amused.

"It usually isn't an *option* at all," Michael pointed out cynically. "As for my mother, that is true enough. She has had little joy since my brother's death. Julianne might understand my motivation in keeping such an event to myself to protect my parents. I'm sure she still mourns Harry also and knows how important this wedding is to them."

"'Tis natural she would. So you do mourn him, sir, or you wouldn't be marrying the girl."

Did he? Maybe. He'd never given himself time to think about it. Sometimes Fitzhugh was too damned insightful for comfort.

Michael gave a philosophical shrug, and then grimaced as pain shot through his side. "I would have to marry someday, so why not her? It's expected."

"Not what *you* expected, sir. You usually go your own way."

That was true. He said neutrally, "She's lovely and seems even tempered and not as spoiled as some of the petulant young society ladies I've had the misfortune to meet. At least now I won't be besieged by eager mamas parading their daughters in front of me at every event. All my good friends have married."

For love. Both Alex St. James and Luke Daudet, his comrades and brothers in arms, had found the women who completed them—the women they had to have despite familial and social obstacles.

Not everyone was so lucky. So he would wed out of duty. As he'd just said, Julianne was perfectly acceptable.

He added succinctly, "It's time, and there's freedom in being a married man."

His valet chuckled, the sound rumbling out into the sunny room. "Freedom? Let me know if you still feel that way in a few months, Colonel."

The state of the pink orchids in regard to how open the blooms were in comparison to the white ones did not really interest her much. Julianne listened with only half an ear as her mother and the Duchess of Southbrook chatted on over the flowers for the next day. Her attention was more on the knot in the pit of her stomach.

The elegant room seemed too small and close even though the long windows were open to the pleasant breeze. A cerulean blue sky outside showed not a single cloud, and the scent of roses wafted by like an elusive ghost, sweet and unseen. One would think the gorgeous weather would buoy her spirits, but instead she felt a dismal sense of fate when she thought about tomorrow.

Tomorrow.

Heaven help me.

It wasn't precisely that Julianne didn't want to marry Michael Hepburn. After all, he was handsome, wealthy, titled, and all the other things a young woman was supposed to admire. It was just that she sensed his attitude toward the match was as ambiguous as hers.

And why wouldn't it be? He was as dragooned as she was, both of them pressured by their families and . . .

"Julianne?"

The sound of her name being said so firmly made her start. She looked up and saw two expectant faces. She stammered, "I'm . . . I'm sorry. What were we discussing?"

The duchess was a petite woman with thick chestnut hair much like her son's, and the same refined bone structure. She waved a hand in an airy gesture and smiled. "Your distraction is to be expected, I'm sure, my dear child, so do not apologize. I would wager Michael is just as distracted. He barely breezed in to breakfast and left without taking more than a few bites."

It defied her powers of imagination to picture the distant marquess as anything other than cool and self-possessed, but Julianne nodded politely. It was even harder to imagine him breezing anywhere, and that brought a small, involuntary inner grin.

The duchess rose, managing to somehow seem both regal and motherly at the same time. "The time between now and the ceremony will be a virtual whirlwind, so I'll take my leave. Let me know what you decide about the flowers."

What flowers?

Oh, yes, the orchids. Julianne flushed a little over so patently not paying attention. "Of course, Your Grace."

The older woman came over and patted her cheek, just a very light, affectionate touch. "This all makes me very happy. I cannot wait for the wedding."

It *did* make the duchess happy. There was no mistake when it came to that point. Her fiancé's mother beamed at her.

After the duchess left in a swirl of perfume and expensive silk, Julianne gave a rueful smile. "My attention didn't wander because I wasn't interested, but I do confess the color of the flowers really does not matter much to me."

"It is expected for you to have quite a lot on your mind." Her mother sipped her tea and then decisively set aside her cup. "I wonder . . . well, if since we are now alone and tomorrow will be here in the blink of an eye, if we shouldn't go ahead and take this opportunity to talk about the wedding."

It seemed like all they *did* was talk about the wedding and that had been happening for months. Julianne stifled an audible groan. "You've taken care of every detail, Mother. Other than the possible state of the flower buds tomorrow, I can't think of what else there is to discuss. Surely all is accounted for and in place. It's been planned to the most minute facet of what will happen."

Though her figure had gone from slim to a more matronly form and there was a faint hint of silver in her upswept auburn hair, her mother was both lovely and affectionate. They'd always been close in the sense that she was the only daughter, but they had also disparate personalities in many ways. Julianne tended to like books and music, and her mother was definitely a social creature, highly engaged in society. Julianne had known all her life that the match with a ducal heir was important in the eyes of her family. It pleased her mother, and, in turn, that pleased her father.

"We need to discuss your wedding *night*." The words were said with a certain prim resignation. "Now is as good a time as any, as we may not have the opportunity again before the event."

The event. That had an ominous ring to it.

The vague subject of husbandly rights, marriage beds, and procreating children had once been intriguing and off-limits, but lately Julianne tried not to think about it. It brought to mind a tall man with mesmerizing hazel eyes and chestnut hair with a glint of gold who supposedly was being granted the right to do with her whatever he wanted after tomorrow at four o'clock in the afternoon.

"If you wish." Julianne could hear the stiffness in her voice. She sat upright on a brocade settee, her palms a bit damp, so she surreptitiously wiped them on her skirts.

"What I wish is for you to be prepared, not a frightened, ignorant bride. The marquess is a worldly man. He'll expect a certain type of conduct."

It was irritating to think that everyone was concerned with how she pleased him, but no one seemed to worry over whether or not he pleased her.

Julianne stifled her annoyance. "Very well."

There was a palpable hesitation in which her mother fussily arranged her skirts. "You will be required to share Lord Longhaven's bed—you do realize this."

She probably realized a great deal more than her mother knew. Girls gossiped, which was just as well, because certainly no one else wished to tell her anything about the subject. That included her mother, for though she'd brought the subject up, there was a long pause.

The afternoon was very warm and a slight breeze ruffled the curtains by the open window. Julianne declined to comment, just looking at her mother with inquiring interest.

Finally, she said in a rush, "He will wish to touch you in certain places, maybe even remove your nightdress. It will please him, and you must allow it, and anything else he wants to do. Afterward, he will probably retire to his own room, but perhaps not. As in everything, it is his choice."

The lack of balance in power between men and women was one of Julianne's least favorite subjects. "It doesn't sound all that appealing if I have no say in the matter."

"You don't," her mother said bluntly. "It is how the world works. Keep in mind, you must give him the heir he needs. It really is not all that unpleasant. Just tolerate it without complaint and all will be fine."

High praise for the *event* indeed. *My wedding night becomes more appealing by the moment,* Julianne thought with ironic amusement. "I have never quite understood why, if it is a duty, some women willfully are unfaithful."

Apparently nonplussed, her mother took her time fussily pouring herself more tea. "It would be preferable for you not to listen to sordid whispers."

"What would be preferable would be a more candid explanation of the process. Some women must enjoy it if they risk public censure to take a lover. And how is it sordid to talk about the marriage bed?"

"Julianne."

The reproof wasn't a surprise. Julianne loved her mother but also knew she wasn't good at discussing deeper topics than the current fashions. This conversation certainly wasn't enlightening.

She explained, "I simply hope there is more to it all than the feeling of being a broodmare."

"Of course there is." Her mother raised the cup to her lips and took a genteel sip. "Just do as he says and allow him what he wishes and the two of you will get along in harmonious accord. When it comes down to it, the situation is simple enough."

Simple? Marriage to the Marquess of Longhaven? Somehow Julianne doubted it. With Harry it might have been, but everything had changed.

There was a time to acknowledge that a conversation was going no further, so she merely rose and went over to kiss her mother's cheek. "I appreciate the advice."

Her mother smiled, looking relieved. "You are going to make such a beautiful bride. He'll be enchanted."

Michael Hepburn enchanted? Julianne imagined it would take a great deal to stir the man in question to such a state. Much more than a beautiful gown and a ceremony that had been thrust down both their throats. Like her, he no doubt wasn't enchanted; he was *resigned*.

Not a promising start. Both of them resigned to their respective fates.

"I think I'll go upstairs and rest a bit," she lied, with a quick glance at the ormolu clock on the mantel, the steady tick a reminder that every minute that passed was important. Thank goodness the duchess hadn't lingered any longer over the orchid dilemma or she would be late.

Tomorrow I will be married, Julianne reminded herself.

Today, she had something even more pressing to address. She wasn't Lady Longhaven yet, and she had an assignation to keep.

His last night of unmarried life, and he was spending it in a cold, damp spot on a deserted wharf, soaked to the skin by a thin fog that had moved in like an avenging spirit, the moisture insidious and almost unseen, but nonetheless chilling him to the bones.

The figure materialized from the mist alongside a building that was given over to decay, the gaping doorway leering like a toothless smile, rotted timbers listing the entire structure to the side. Warily, Michael watched the quiet approach.

"Longhaven."

"Hello, Charles."

"Bloody inhospitable evening."

"I agree. Last night the weather was better, but the evening still a bit on the eventful side." Michael felt the throb of his wound, a small, ironic smile on his mouth. "As I was attacked after the meeting. Any ideas?"

"Attacked, you say?" The man in front of him frowned, his brows shooting together. "Again?"

"Again." It was a grim agreement.

"You don't look hurt."

"If that is praise for my fortitude, thank you."

His companion chuckled, but as the moonlight, hazy at best, shifted, gliding along the slick surface of the slippery pier, Charles Peyton's austere features held a troubled cast. "Because of this attack, you've come to the conclusion the first incident was not random, then?"

"I have the mark of a knife blade in my side to support my theory that someone seems to have some fairly bloodthirsty intentions."

"That's unfortunate. Did he escape?"

No solicitous concern over his health, but, after all, some danger was inevitable and Michael had obviously survived the ambush. "This one did, yes."

"Curious thing to crop up, don't you think?"

Yes, I do, Michael thought grimly, well aware of the ache of lacerated flesh under the tightly wrapped bandage. "It doesn't bode well for security within the organization. We can't ignore the probability someone is leaking information. Both times I was on my way from an exchange point. London isn't the safest city in the world, but two attacks in such close sequence make me wonder if whoever is responsible has prior knowledge of my whereabouts, which raises an entirely new set of questions. Let's start with who, how, and why."

"Hard to say." As always, Peyton showed very little emotion. "What are you going to do about it, and how soon can I know the results of your inquiry?"

"Damn all, Charles, I'm supposed to get married tomorrow. I'm contemplating my options, but I have to make a pretense of offering my new wife some of my attention. You're going to have to give me a few days at least. And can I mention I am asking you for information, not the other way around?"

"I admit I am intrigued by this particular development. If I find out anything pertinent, you will be contacted, as long as you promise a reciprocal agreement." A low laugh rang out. "And of course I realize your nuptials are impending. I'm invited, remember?"

As was most of London's exalted circles, if the guest list was any indication. Sir Charles certainly qualified. Even if he hadn't been knighted for his service to the

Crown, he was the brother-in-law of the infamous Duke of Rothay and had an aristocratic heritage as impressive as his own. Michael had to admit that the thought of the ceremony and the celebration following it made him want to grind his teeth. He was not one for ostentation, much less that kind of crush, and on top of it all he had to deal with his injury, along with being the center of attention.

And afterward, of course. The wedding night still loomed as somewhat of a problem. He hadn't yet decided how to explain away his wound.

A swirl of mist went by, the curling moisture brushing his face like tiny, wet claws. He gave a curt nod. "I look forward to seeing you there, Charles. But the wedding aside, I admit I am very fond of breathing and quite a few other things that go along with being alive. Any theories on how to approach this?"

"You're an inventive man. I'm sure you'll come up with something. What I can do is loan you help if you need it. Contact me the usual way."

It was the best Michael could hope for, and he nodded. The moment the real problem surfaced in the second vicious assault in less than a week, he'd known he was going to have to deal with it. Peyton rarely became involved directly. He was the girder under the bridge, holding it up but hidden from view.

They parted, going in different directions, the convoluted departure a time-consuming necessity. Though it was fine that he and Charles knew each other on a social basis, they made it a point to never be seen meeting. Questions would be asked, conclusions would be drawn, and the results could be disastrous.

He avoided going home and instead headed to his club. Southbrook House was crawling with relatives he didn't even know he had, and though he was prepared to be congenial and act the eager bridegroom tomorrow, he didn't have the fortitude to deal with elderly aunts and distant cousins at the moment.

A quiet meal and several stiff brandies in a secluded corner sounded like a more appealing idea.

As he handed his damp greatcoat to the steward, he couldn't help but think of how different Harry would be feeling at the moment. His older brother would have been happy, no doubt, and looking forward to the whole affair rather than dreading it, because at the end of the day, he would have his beautiful bride to warm not just his bed but also his heart.

Michael didn't in the least resemble his easygoing, idealistic sibling except in looks. He wondered if the lovely Lady Julianne realized the bargain fate had arranged for her. Instead of a man who was eager to wed her and dutiful in every way, and who would probably make an ideal husband and a splendid duke someday, she'd gotten nothing but a reluctant bridegroom with a legion of dark secrets and no desire for the pomp of his status in society.

Not much of a trade, in anyone's mind. She'd been cheated.

"Damp out there, isn't it, Longhaven? If you've a mind to, come join us. We were actually just discussing you, wondering if you might make an appearance. "

His attention jerked back to the moment and he saw Luke Daudet, Viscount Altea, sitting at a table, a glass of amber liquid in front of him and a faint smile on his mouth. Next to him, his face holding the same gloss of amusement, was Lord Alex St. James, his dark hair just a shade too long for fashion—not that he'd ever cared for convention—his gaze speculative.

If Michael could count anyone as his close friends, they both qualified. But this wasn't the night they should all see each other. Both had been recently married. St. James had taken as his wife the gloriously lovely daughter of an earl, and she was now expecting their first child, and Luke had recently wed a very beautiful young widow who was also embracing coming motherhood. Both men were, by their own admission, extremely contented in their newly wedded bliss and delighted at impending fatherhood. They might even want to talk about it, and it was a subject Michael wanted to avoid like the plague.

Bloody hell. If he wished to discuss marriage he could have just gone home and endured the well-meaning, enthusiastic aunts.

But it wasn't as if Luke and Alex were not comrades, after all. He took the proffered seat. "I thought you both were still out of town."

From across the table Luke, fair and classically handsome, gave him his infamous lazy smile, his silver eyes full of amusement. "Remember, we have a wedding to attend tomorrow. Madeline had a fitting for a new gown just this afternoon to wear to the nuptials. Her waistline has begun to disappear."

Michael made a noncommittal noise and glanced around for the waiter.

Alex remarked, "Amelia would never miss it, though her condition has become obvious. She made me swear we would sit near the back." He grinned. "I do not have the heart to tell her that will not make her less conspicuous, but if it reassures her, I will agree to anything. I think she is more beautiful than ever as she increases."

Where was that damned waiter? Michael nodded, enceinte ladies not his forte.

Luke reached out and offered his half-full glass of whiskey. "Though few people do, I know you. Both Alex and I do. Or as much as anyone does. You have *that* look. Here, take mine until your drink arrives. I just ordered it."

It was a decent gesture and Michael wasn't about to refuse. He accepted the glass and took a drink so large he almost ended up coughing. In a slightly hoarse voice, he asked, "What look?"

"Hunted." Alex nodded slowly. "I agree with Luke. Cornered. Trapped. Doomed. Condemned."

I knew they'd want to talk about it. Hell.

"Spare me more descriptions, please," he interrupted with a short laugh. The irony of the observation didn't escape him. He *was* being hunted and it had nothing to do with his upcoming wedding. "Damn all, I am not in the mood for sarcasm, but the whiskey is most welcome."

"Avoiding the well-wishing throng by hiding out here, eh?" Luke lounged back, his expression neutral. "I did the same thing the night before I married, and we had a small, private ceremony. Yours promises to be quite the event. I can honestly say I don't think I've seen you panicked before."

Michael admitted, "I concede, as someone who can make the comparison, I would rather face a French column than a bevy of nosy, well-wishing relatives, much less the pomp of the grandiose celebration my mother has planned."

"I understand the sentiment." Seated carelessly in his chair, Alex chuckled. "It is why I was married by special license. But ask my brother John; it passes eventually. Like a bad case of indigestion."

"Thanks." Michael gave him a wry look.

"Your intended bride is a beautiful girl. Madeline pointed her out to me one night at a function." Luke's silver eyes were reflective.

"Yes." Michael drank more whiskey. It banished the chill and eased the pain of his wound. If only it banished the image of Harry's smiling face and his own nagging sense of guilt over the current state of affairs. Logically, he knew it was irrational to feel that way, but he just did. He hadn't asked for the title, nor, as a younger son, had he ever expected to inherit, but it had happened and he accepted it, though reluctantly. Julianne was another matter. His brother had been in love with her.

"You'll survive." With a lifted brow, Alex watched him down his drink.

"I've certainly been through worse," Michael muttered. "The other evening comes to mind. Since you are here and I value your opinions, I'd like your advice. I have a certain delicate issue to address."

"Issue?" Luke raised a brow.

"I might have something to hide from my bride."

St. James choked on his drink. After a clearing cough, he said sardonically, "Just one something? I would more likely think you have hundreds of secrets she will never discover. For instance, that you were one Wellington's most celebrated spies and haven't completely retired the title either."

"That's part of it."

"Why am I not surprised?"

"I'm glad you find this amusing, but this is not a jest." Michael did his best to look bland. "I might have encountered a small problem."

"Small?"

"Perhaps not *so* small."

"Such as?"

"A knife wound."

That caught their full attention. In consternation, they stared across the table. "Maybe we should order a full bottle as you explain how that came to be," Luke finally murmured.

"The bottle sounds like a good idea, but I can't explain. I am not sure why, but I was unexpectedly attacked. It isn't the first time either, though in this instance, my assailant did some damage."

"How bad is it?"

"Bad enough I can't possibly conceal it."

"I see," Luke said after a quiet moment. "So in the service of the Crown, once again, you were wounded, and you—so used to devious practices—have no idea of a plausible excuse to give your new bride? Hmm. I may have to think for a moment on this one. More importantly, what steps are being taken to ensure your safety?"

Michael's smile was crooked. "You know full well the policy on intelligence agents. The war is supposedly over. We do not exist."

"In other words, it falls to you find out who wants your blood." Alex ran his fingertips down the side of his now-empty glass.

Thinking of Antonia and Lawrence, not to mention several other colleagues, Michael said neutrally, "I'm not entirely alone, and I'm on my guard."

"If we can do anything—"

"Oh, you can. You are both married men. Help me decide how to handle the question of why I'm currently wearing a swath of bandages. I have only until tomorrow before the ax falls."

The hum of conversation was low at this hour, and the subdued surroundings held a familiar hint of tobacco and the smoky essence of brandy. The waiter unobtrusively brought more whiskey and discreetly departed. Luke poured himself a glass, and when he glanced up his gaze was very direct. "I am not sure what to tell you except don't lie to her."

Almost instantly, Alex agreed. "He's right."

Michael's face tightened. It was probably so insignificant no one else would notice it, but he felt it. "I don't tell falsehoods as a rule."

"No, you don't. You are a master at redirecting the conversation instead, but in this case, she is going to be your wife. The mother of your children. Your lover and your partner. I know I am simplifying it, but surely if she shares your life she deserves to share your secrets as well."

Alex had never been good at equivocation. That was why he'd been a damned fine soldier, but not a spy.

This was, however, not a war, at least not in the sense most people knew it. Michael knew *his* secrets were a burden. He had never put them on someone else's shoulders and wasn't about to give them to a young woman he barely knew. He finished his whiskey. "Put that way, you were correct earlier. It does sound like a life sentence."

"You'll survive." Luke's mouth twitched. As a former aide-de-camp for Wellington, he understood compromise a bit better.

The wedding? Or the assassination someone seemed determined to execute? One loomed as ominous as the other. Michael set the glass on the table with a decisive *click*. He said, "I intend to."

Chapter Three

The scent of flowers filled the air and even the weather had cooperated and cleared, replaced by warm, benevolent sunshine. It made the church too warm, and everywhere fans moved in languid rhythm. It was packed with well-dressed guests, all of them craning their necks, impatient for the event of the season. The wedding of the handsome heir to the Duke of Southbrook was a coveted invitation. The tragedy that boosted a younger son into the spotlight seemed only to add a romantic edge to the situation that titillated the rapt crowd. His status as a war hero didn't detract from the attraction.

Antonia understood the romantic ideal of it all, even if she no longer believed in it. *If they all only knew the truth.* Oh, yes, Michael was a hero—more of a hero than any of them realized. That wasn't in doubt. But his status didn't conform to the conventional sense of flashing blades and bullets and defeated Frenchmen retreating in terror.

No. He was valiant in a different way. A man who used his mind besides his sword arm, and won with uncanny success. Had it not been for his keen intellect, she wouldn't even be alive.

Maybe that was incorrect. Her former life had been obliterated back in Spain, so that part of her was gone, but she wouldn't have been resurrected into a new form of woman . . . one who still fought against treacherous anarchy and ambitious invaders.

But today she'd lost this battle.

I'm a thrice-damned fool.

Antonia Taylor acknowledged it, accepted it, but hardly embraced the realization. Attending the wedding of the man you love when he's marrying someone else might even make you an imbecile. She was guilty of worse things, but this one might sting the most.

It was odd to think at one point in her life she'd despaired she would ever feel anything again, and when it happened, it had to be this. If she'd thought she was dead inside, she was mistaken. Apparently there was enough emotion left to form an unrequited passion for a man even more jaded, in some ways, than she was herself. A hopeless, unrealized desire for what she could never have.

Perhaps she'd thought it would be cathartic to see the finality of it. The book snapping closed before the last page, never to be reopened. The story was untold and lost.

Michael stood by the altar, composed and cool. Dressed with elegant, tailored formality in gray, offset by a dark waistcoat and pristine cravat, he looked strikingly self-possessed, not a sign anywhere that he'd been bleeding all over her bedroom just two nights before. Thick chestnut hair with glints of gold framed his face, and his eyes—that vivid hazel color she found so fascinating—were veiled and unreadable.

Everything about him, from the clean line of his jaw and nose to the sensual curve of his mouth and the width of his shoulders and lean height made her pulse throb in her wrist so fast she could feel the beat of her heart with acute awareness.

When he turned to watch his bride walk slowly down the aisle toward where he stood by the altar, it was all Antonia could do to not leap to her feet and try to stop the ceremony.

However, she wasn't a coward. She'd lost everything in her life once, and she could bear this also. It was a pity she wasn't still numb, and maybe she resented Michael Hepburn almost more for that than she did for choosing someone else. Love and hate could be such an odd mixture. She'd experienced both in her life, but not at the same time like at this moment.

"Dazzling." A large-bosomed woman next to her sighed. "Such a beautiful bride."

Antonia managed to wrest her gaze from the couple at the altar and summoned her most polite smile. "Yes, indeed. But aren't all brides lovely?"

The acerbic hint of criticism in the comment was lost. The woman beamed at her. "Lady Julianne more than most, I think. Don't you?"

Antonia didn't answer. She didn't trust herself.

Unfortunately, the irritating woman was right. The future Marchioness of Longhaven had creamy, pale skin, lustrous dark brown hair, and long-lashed blue eyes. The fragility of her features added to the aura of delicate femininity, and she was also slender yet had graceful curves. Her wedding gown was an ice blue, suiting the ethereal image.

That was just as well. It was easy to loathe perfection.

As she sat woodenly and watched the ceremony, Antonia had to wonder if this innocent young woman had any hint of who she was pledging herself to for life. No, she decided, the chit was too innocent, too sheltered, too spoiled by her wealthy, important family.

As she had been once. But life could change without

due notice. Antonia had learned it in the most difficult way possible. Was Michael's bride prepared?

Well, the sweet little kitten had married a tiger. A full-grown, predatory male who had instincts honed by years of war, with an affinity for danger and risk. He looked urbane and handsome as he stood there, but truthfully, he wasn't nearly as civilized as he appeared. Antonia had benefited from his expertise when he'd taught her how to move in enemy territory quietly and without detection, among other skills that were a bit more lethal. A skill valuable in war . . . But she doubted London society would see it that way.

He took the insipid girl's hand. The symbolic clasp held her gaze, her unwilling attention riveted on his long fingers entwined with another's.

The bishop began the ritual and said the inevitable words. Antonia watched, she listened, and a small part of her died.

But I've been dead before, she reminded herself, *and have risen from the ashes of that lost life.*

At last it was over.

"You may kiss your bride."

Antonia forced herself to watch Michael accept the invitation. It flayed her soul, but she would heal. She always had.

All she could do was pray this time wasn't different.

The world was surreal, blurred, as if the edges had been smeared by a careless brush of a hand across a not-yet-dried canvas. Julianne gazed up at the man standing next to her and was . . . paralyzed.

Among a thousand other things, none of which she could specifically define.

The current Marquess of Longhaven's face was unreadable, and his fingers grazed her chin and tipped it upward. For a moment he seemed to hesitate, and then with deliberate intent he lowered his head and kissed her.

Warm lips touched hers and settled there, his mouth firm but smooth, the pressure light and yet somehow insistent.

The contact might have lasted just a moment, but seemed longer, so long her breath fluttered in her throat. When he did break away, they simply stared at each other. His hazel eyes were a pure green flecked with gold, framed with thick lashes. It was the first time she'd been so close and also the first time she sensed she really had his full attention.

There was no doubt about it; she'd done it. She'd married Harry's enigmatic younger brother, for better or for worse, and the bargain was sealed with a kiss.

A very enlightening kiss. Rather pleasant, actually, though all the people watching them made her blush.

That moment, a voice inside her said, *Should have happened somewhere quiet and utterly private.* There should have been moonlight, and perhaps a fountain gently splashing in the background, and she certainly imagined she'd be wildly in love with the man who gave her that magical first kiss....

And, naturally, he would be even more passionately devoted to her.

Except this wasn't a romantic fantasy; this was life. He wasn't in the least devoted to her, but simply a dutiful son, as she was a dutiful daughter, and they had married to please their families.

Well, they had *that* in common anyway.

Michael Hepburn straightened, looked at her again for a moment with that singular intensity that always made her feel he was seeing much more than the outside woman, and offered her his arm.

That simple. One arm, extended politely, one moment when her life swung into the unknown. Automatically she responded, her fingers cold on his sleeve, clamped over the tense hardness of the bunched muscles under the clasp of her hand.

She flashed a quick glance at his face, noting the impassive outline of his classic profile, seemingly indifferent, but a muscle in his jaw twitched slightly.

Perhaps he wasn't quite as detached and imperturbable as he seemed. The notion both startled and relaxed her as they faced the assembled guests and he escorted her down the aisle. The sea of faces didn't register and the sensation was a little as if she floated rather than walked. Outside it was a lovely day, at least, and she took a shuddering, deep breath of fresh air as he guided her down the massive steps of the cathedral to the waiting carriage. The ducal crest shown on the side of the elegant equipage—a blazing image similar to the Stuart coat of arms, indicative of a connection to that royal family going back generations.

She was his *wife*. It would take a while to comprehend the reality of it.

Michael handed her inside the vehicle and clambered up after her, stretching out his long legs and saying something to the footman in formal livery who waited to close the door. The young man nodded, and a moment later the carriage began to roll away.

"You might wish to lean out the window and wave," her husband suggested, lifting one brow a fraction. "It's the glowing bride they've come to see, not the dull groom."

There *were* people crowded along the street, she realized, but in her relief to leave the formality of the church and the general sense of bemusement, it hadn't occurred to her to act the gracious bride.

"I didn't think of that," Julianne admitted, feeling gauche. She took his advice, forcing a smile she hoped looked at least half sincere and waving, listening to the spectators cheer in approval.

The ride was a blur and it set the tone for the rest of the day and evening.

Marrying a ducal heir involved a great deal of ceremony. She'd expected it would be intimidating, but the sheer number of guests pouring into the grand ballroom of Southbrook House was overwhelming. The duchess had outdone herself with the lavish decorations; urns of hothouse flowers everywhere; beribboned tables holding all sorts of delicacies from pink curls of shrimp in delicate seashell dishes to all manner of roasted fowl, suckling pig in a currant sauce, and a variety of pastries that must have taken a battalion of chefs to prepare; and dozens of other mouthwatering entrées. Hundreds of candles glittered, and the guests glittered even more with jewels and attire in the height of the latest fashion. The opulence of the celebration would no doubt be the talk of society for quite a while, and Julianne wished she could enjoy even a moment of it.

Just one moment. Was it too much to ask?

Unfortunately, she was just too overwhelmed.

Though she stood next to Michael throughout the ordeal of receiving the felicitations and goodwill of the crowd, they barely spoke to each other. There wasn't time, really, for much conversation, with the seeming endless stream of visitors and the necessary protocol, so perhaps everyone thought it was normal for the bride and groom to act like polite strangers. If it at all bothered Michael, she couldn't tell it. When she did manage to chance a quick look at the tall man at her side, he was usually in profile to her, his composure unruffled, strikingly male and attractive in his tailored clothing, and accepting felicitations with ease.

Only once did he touch her, and that was simply a very casual set of his hand at her waist as he introduced her to a dark-haired young woman wearing a stunning gown in a deep red that suited her flamboyant, exotic beauty. Julianne murmured an appropriate greeting, struck for a moment by what might have been a flicker of animosity in the other woman's eyes. It startled her and brought home afresh how little she knew about the man who had become her husband. Obviously the two were well acquainted, for Michael greeted this particular guest on a first-name basis. *Antonia.* Not an English name in any sense, and the woman's dramatic coloring and accent reflected her heritage.

"Lady Longhaven," she murmured with saccharine graciousness, "my congratulations."

As the woman walked away, the flicker of dismay over just how well acquainted they might be was unwanted, and did not help Julianne's hard-won and tenuous composure.

She certainly hoped *that* was not an indication of what their life would be like together.

When the room was packed to the point it seemed no one could move, the orchestra began to play. The venue moved from endless greetings to endless dancing, and as the bride, she was in high demand. *All the time spent with the dancing master was worth it,* she mused when she was swung into another waltz as the hours passed. Occasionally someone pressed a glass of champagne into her hand, though she managed to eat very little. Michael also danced often, but not with her.

Her feet began to hurt and her head to pound.

"You look lovely."

Julianne smiled up at her father—her current partner—but the attempt was rather tremulous. It seemed that as the bride she was not allowed a moment of rest. "Thank you, but I do not think you are unbiased. I am a bit tired, if you must know, but am hoping it doesn't show. I would hate to disappoint the duchess."

Once blond but now sporting a head of steel gray hair, his face showing the expected lines, her father still had eyes that were as blue as ever, and he fairly exuded satisfaction that things had gone so well. "I don't think there's anyone who would disagree with me you've done just fine. I've heard more than one gentleman tell your husband he's a lucky man."

She had to wonder if he *felt* lucky. It was very hard to tell. Michael Hepburn just didn't seem like the kind of man who would agree to an arranged marriage, but yet he had.

"Longhaven will treat you well, my dear."

She certainly hoped so, considering she'd just tied herself to him for life. A nod was her response as they swirled through the moving throng. There wasn't much question she was starting to become a little light-headed. The night before she'd barely slept, and all the exertion coupled with several glasses of champagne was taking its toll.

It meant she should retire, but that carried another implication aside from being fatigued from all the revelry. With neutral inflection, she commented, "I knew Harry much better, of course."

"We all did," her father admitted. He looked distinguished in his formal clothes, the fine lines next to his eyes deepening as he frowned. The music swirled around them, along with the babble of hundreds of conversations. "It seems wrong since this is a celebration, but I suppose it is natural to think of him at this time."

"I suppose." Her smile was probably strained.

"I am sure he would wish you and Michael all the happiness in the world. Harry was always such a congenial fellow." Her father paused. "The new marquess is not quite as easy to know."

That describes the situation perfectly, she thought as the music dwindled to the end. There was nothing *easy* about her new husband. Notice how her father called Harry by his first name, and Michael Hepburn by his title. Her searching gaze—for about the hundredth time that evening—swept the room and found a tall man moving with lithe grace among the dancers on the floor, his chestnut hair and clean-cut features striking. Even in the swirl of hundreds of guests he still stood out, and it wasn't simply his good looks. It was partly how he held himself, with a self-assurance she wasn't sure was conscious but very much there, and perhaps even more so the quality of intelligence you saw as he looked straight through you with those vivid gold-green eyes.

As if he sensed her regard, he turned then and their

gazes locked for a long, telling moment. A flush of heat touched her cheeks and a flicker of what could only be panic stirred in the pit of her stomach. To make matters worse, the music ended and he began to thread purposefully through the crowd toward her.

When Michael Hepburn moved with such determination, people scooted aside.

A cowardly impulse made her want to turn and run, but she didn't, though her fingers tightened momentarily on her father's arm.

Her husband reached them, nodded at his new father-in-law, and gently but firmly removed her hand from her father's sleeve. "It's getting quite late and you haven't had a chance to as much as sit down."

Such solicitude was nice, but the implication he had paid that much attention made her stomach do another very strange twist. If he had watched her, she hadn't noticed.

The statement—made in a very pragmatic, calm tone—was true, and the stuffy ballroom with the glittering guests had begun to overpower her, or maybe it was simply the persistent nervous tension. Either way, even though he hadn't said she should retire, it was definitely implied in the possessive grasp of his long, graceful fingers around her hand. As impossible as it was to do, she found she nodded in agreement.

"I'll escort you upstairs."

Oh, God.

"I shall see you soon, my dear." Her father kissed her cheek and left.

She was barely aware of his discreet departure. It was symbolic of her changed circumstances, of his abdication of responsibility. Julianne didn't resist as her new husband urged her through the milling guests, and she must have responded appropriately to the scattered well-wishes, but the actual words didn't really register.

Once they were out in the hall, she heard Michael take a deep breath. "What a crush. I'm not sure what my mother was thinking when she invited all of London proper."

The mutter wrung a nervous laugh from her. "I suppose we should be flattered so many attended the wedding."

"I suppose." He guided her along the polished hallway, nodding at a footman as they passed by.

"You needn't take me." Julianne was all too conscious of his hand, which now was firm at the small of her back.

A quixotic smile curved his mouth. "How would you even know where our apartments are? This house is definitely one of my ancestors' more ostentatious architectural displays. I think there are over thirty bedrooms. You would get lost. *I've* gotten lost. I don't spend much time here."

It was an inarguable point. But . . . *our?* It sounded so final.

Her mouth was dry. "A servant could—"

"Probably." He smoothly cut her off. "But I am as anxious to get out of the celebration as you are, if not more so. Let me escort you and we can both escape. I am afraid I'm not social by nature."

That she could believe. He had little of Harry's easygoing charm or gregarious tendencies.

The faint sound of music and laughter followed them, fading as they passed by the massive main hall and headed toward a graceful, curved staircase. Julianne hesitated at the bottom for a telling moment and Michael also stopped, doing nothing but gazing at her with inscrutable inquiry.

If she placed her foot on that first step, she'd acknowledge she was going to go upstairs with this man she barely knew.

Could she do it?

She just wasn't sure.

But yet she lifted her foot and began to climb.

*   *   *

If he wasn't ashen pale, he'd be surprised. Such bad timing. Michael conceded he had to deal with an uncertain young bride and her virginal fears and he hoped it was possible to manage it with some measure of patience and finesse. Though she'd acquitted herself well for one so young at the reception, *he'd* been a bit taken aback by the ungodly crush, and he was leagues more experienced at dealing with such functions. The tension in her slender form as they stood in the receiving line, and later, when she danced with just about every man in the room, was unmistakable to one paying close attention.

And he had been. It was a surprise, but *he had been*.

Between that preoccupation and the vicious gash in his side, he hadn't much enjoyed himself, but he had to acknowledge, now that it was done, that he'd watched his new wife.

The dancing had him breaking out in a light sweat that had nothing to do with the exertion required but the pain of his wound. When Malcolm Sutton had clapped him on the back earlier in congratulations, it was all he could do to not show a reaction to his new brother-in-law's enthusiasm, and he was fairly sure he was bleeding under all the layers of bandages and clothing.

Fitzhugh would tell him it served him right for refusing to see a physician. All he was concerned about at the moment was getting through the next few hours. A little bit of sleep would be nice, too. Though he could operate efficiently with very little rest, his injured state and the strain of the past few days had taken their toll. He wanted to fall into a bed for practical purposes other than attempting to seduce a nervous virgin.

Yet if it was his sense of family obligation that led to this marriage, he had to see it through.

Normally not such a hardship, not considering Julianne's beauty, but he was hurt, tired, and about to bed his brother's intended.

Next to him, her bosom lifting just a bit quickly under the sumptuous material of her gown, if his new wife was trying to hide her apprehension, she was not succeeding very well. Her fragile features were washed with a hint of pink, bringing the term *blushing bride* to the forefront of his thoughts, and she trembled a fraction as they gained the second floor.

Their suite of rooms was in the family wing at the end of the second hallway. Michael guided her through the formal sitting area, decorated elegantly with silk-covered chairs, rich Turkish rugs in patterns of pale green and cream, and his own recent contribution, an ornate carved table he'd had sent over from Spain. It had once belonged to a Spanish don who claimed it was a gift from Queen Isabella to his illustrious family. It was a beautiful piece, to be sure, so maybe the story was true, but even without the provenance of its royal history, Michael had purchased the piece because it appealed to him in an aesthetic sense. The relief of a spreading sunset on the top was done so cleverly he could believe it was a work of art commissioned by a monarch.

Maybe at some other time Julianne will notice it and make a comment, he thought in wry amusement, but he doubted she even saw their surroundings. He took her to the door of what was now her bedroom and relinquished her to the hovering maid, a plump girl who blushed just as deeply as his obviously uneasy bride, at the sight of him.

God help me.

"I'll give you half an hour."

Well, hell, that came out too clipped, too cool, too insensitive by half.

Nice effort, you buffoon. Try again.

He did so, tempering the tone of his voice. "I'll be in there." He gestured at the door that separated their bedrooms. "Please let me know when you are ready to retire."

Julianne just looked at him with her enormous dark blue eyes, her lush lashes lowered a fraction. "Yes, my lord. Whatever you wish."

The capitulation sounded all wrong, like he had just ordered her to sleep with him. Certainly he had conjugal rights, but he preferred eagerness in the bedroom, not resigned agreement. Still, it was a bit hard to concentrate on seduction when his injured body protested all the activity, and the glasses of champagne he'd consumed hadn't helped either. Normally he was very circumspect in his consumption of liquor. A man in his position couldn't afford to be impaired often.

"Please, call me Michael."

Breathtaking in pale blue, her dark, shining hair gathered in an intricate knot of some kind, pearls competing for luster with her flawless skin, she gave the barest nod. "Of course. If you wish."

The hushed tone of her voice spoke more than the words, and as the door closed behind her he stifled a curse that was definitely not meant for the ears of a young ingenue. She was apprehensive of what was to happen next, and, truthfully, so was he, though not in the same way, given his handicap.

He went to the adjoining room and started to shed his jacket. Sure enough, he saw the faint pink stain on his white shirt, indicating he'd opened the wound during the course of the evening and it had bled even through the swath of bandages. Fitzhugh hurried to help him.

"Nice ceremony, Colonel."

"Thanks." Michael gave his former sergeant a resigned look. "Let's hope the rest of the night works out as well. As you predicted, I am not at my best." He indicated his side. "This hurts like blazes."

"No worries, sir." Fitzhugh took the jacket and shook it out. "As I believe you mentioned, how would she know the difference? A young, sheltered woman like the marchioness will be very nervous. It is to your advantage."

Put that way, it sounded cold.

The marchioness.

It was so official. It *was* official. He had just gotten married. He was the bloody marquess and she was his wife. When he'd kissed her earlier, it had struck him with irrefutable immediacy, her lips cool under his and hundreds of people watching them.

Hell and blast. This was his wedding night. No, *their* wedding night.

On a growl, Michael muttered, "I'd certainly like it to be a memorable occasion, and I mean something to recall with fondness, not disappointment. Unfortunately, I'm bleeding."

"I see that." The Irishman helped him unbutton his shirt, giving the bandages a critical look. "Doesn't look too serious, sir. I'll rewrap it and you'll be right as rain."

"I happen to loathe rain," he muttered. "Remember Badajoz? That was one devil of a battle."

"Wet and cold, sir. I'll not deny it."

"Bodies piling up against the walls, cannon blasting . . . it was a nightmare." Michael tried to ignore the twinge as his valet pulled aside the bloody cloth. It was true. The citadel had finally fallen but it had been at an atrocious price, and Wellington had flung men at those walls with inhuman determination. It had worked, of course, because great generals knew how to win battles, but, oh, God, the cost.

Blood. Muddy ditches. Piles of bodies.

It was why he still risked his life for England.

That kind of carnage should never be for naught. Many men had died for a cause and he couldn't regard it lightly. Michael said in crisp irony, "I suppose Julianne will be apprehensive enough she might discount my less than debonair approach. I feel like my side is on fire and can't imagine effectively concealing it."

"A true dilemma, Colonel."

He shot Fitzhugh a sardonic look. "Your empathy is appreciated."

"I believe truthfulness to be the order of the day."

"I've noticed that about you a time or two in the years we've known each other. Not to mention Lord Altea and Alex St. James seem to have your same inclinations.

They think I should tell her the truth. Not just about the attempt on my life, but about what I am."

"You could." His valet got out a clean cravat and proceeded to tear the fine linen neatly in half. "But what would you do if she asks you to resign and instead groom yourself to be the duke, as you should? We both know that's exactly your place in life."

That was quite a question. Michael didn't mind risking his neck for England, but the burden of a dukedom hung over his head like a blacksmith's anvil.

"I don't know," he said grimly.

"As I thought." Fitzhugh chuckled and deftly finished his work with his usual precision, rewrapping the wound with the skill of someone who has performed the task far too many times. Then he handed Michael his silk dressing gown. "Will there be anything else?"

"No, thank you, Fitz. I have to manage the rest of this on my own, I believe."

His valet nodded, a small grin on his ruddy face. "As lovely as Lady Longhaven is, I doubt it will be much of a chore, sir. Good night, and please accept my congratulations."

Chore or not, his level of enthusiasm was a bit on the low side. Michael tied the belt of his robe in a loose knot and went over to pour himself a brandy. Instead of sitting down, he wandered to the window and stared out at the night. A sprinkling of stars were scattered like a handful of gleaming diamonds tossed on a swath of black velvet sky, and the moon was nothing but a thin wafer.

As he stood there, he couldn't help but think of his brother. Harry was gone and with him his quicksilver smile and expansive sense of humor, not an ounce of guile in his soul. On his wedding night Harry would never be sporting a wound inflicted in some dark, unsavory section of London and be forced to ponder just how he was going to handle explaining it.

Michael sipped his brandy and wondered if he would have to go to Julianne or if she would have the courage to open the connecting door. It was a bit hard for him to imagine how she viewed their marriage in general, mostly because he'd avoided talking to her as much as possible since his return to England. If he felt at a certain level she still belonged to Harry, Michael wondered if maybe she didn't have the same perception. After all, most of her life she'd known she was going to marry the Marquess of Longhaven, but *he* wasn't supposed to be the one with that title.

The more quickly she became pregnant, the better. Then he'd send her to the country estate for her confinement and they'd both be protected. He would be shielded from any questions that might arise in the natural course of things over his often unusual hours and curious absences, and she would be spared having to wonder and ask them.

One couldn't discount the reality that someone wanted him dead. He might not know her well, but he didn't want to put her in any danger either. It would hardly be remarked on if they had separate lives. Many *ton* couples did.

The click of the latch lifting made him turn around.

He'd underestimated his young bride, Michael realized as the door between their rooms opened and she stepped inside. She was either less nervous than he imagined or more courageous.

His fingers tightened around the bowl of his glass as he took in a mass of lustrous loose dark hair waving to her shapely hips, a pair of magnificent indigo eyes, and the almost defiant tilt of her chin. She wore something white under a pale pink silk robe, just a glimpse of lace visible at the neckline.

She was, he decided, breathtaking.

To his surprise, the reaction he experienced to seeing her standing there on the threshold of not just his bedchamber, but the beginning of their marriage, was not resignation and a sense of finality or duty. It was quite different, and it wasn't just about how he was struck with the beauty he'd done his best to ignore during their engagement.

Maybe it was the way she gazed at him, expectant, obviously not without trepidation, but . . . trusting.

His world was based on suspicion and deception.

Hers obviously was not.

Innocence was something he'd lost so long ago he could barely recall it. Maybe it was the novelty, but at this definitive moment in both their lives, somehow he found hers intriguing.

It could be his injury wasn't so much of a problem after all.

Chapter Four

It was natural to be apprehensive, and she knew this, but it didn't help matters much. Julianne hoped her nervousness wasn't too evident, but as composed as she wanted to look, the tall man across the room wasn't fooled a bit.

She had the impression he wasn't fooled often.

Under her robe she wore only a thin nightdress. It was something she was acutely aware of as she stood just inside her new husband's open bedroom door.

The ajar door had a particular symbolic impact on not just her emotional state but also her physical one. He affected her; there was no denying it. Whether it was the quiet, collective nature of his distance or his vivid eyes, she wasn't sure, but it was *there*.

She'd liked Harry very much, but she wasn't nearly as aware of him as a man.

There was no possibility she was going to be the one to speak first, and besides, she had no idea what to say, especially since Michael wore a dressing gown that was open enough she could see the strong column of his throat and an intriguing glimpse of his bare chest. He was a tall man, and that wasn't a secret, but never had he seemed so *inordinately* tall.

This was going to happen. He was going to make her his wife in all ways, and she was not only powerless to resist, she wasn't sure she wanted to in the first place. How very odd. Julianne hadn't anticipated this breathless . . . expectancy.

"I imagine the gaiety downstairs will go on for hours." The remark was said in a very offhand way, and her new husband took a sip of amber liquid from a glass balanced in his long fingers. "There is one advantage to being the bride and groom, and that's the excuse of being able to escape the crowd and relax a little."

If he thought she was relaxed, he was very much mistaken. "I suppose a person could look at it that way."

"You can come in. I promise I'm quite harmless."

Harmless? Why did she disagree? On the contrary, there was a certain dangerous air about him. Really, he should seem more ordinary—Harry had looked very much like him, and she'd been comfortable with him for as long as she could remember—but Michael was different.

Completely so. He was like an ordinary summer sky that could suddenly gather with clouds and turn volatile. The sunny blue was serene and attractive, and the impending storm dark and intimidating.

Yes, he was . . . *dangerous.* Why she knew it, she wasn't sure, but she did.

"I *wish* for you to come in. Does that make it easier?" He spoke in a very soft tone.

It was a little mortifying to realize she still hovered just inside the doorway. Julianne moved forward, cast around for a place to sit down as far away from him as possible, fastened her gaze on a chair near the marble fireplace, and headed toward it. The room was furnished with masculine simplicity, in simple blue and cream, dominated by a massive bed made out of some dark wood. Griffins and other mythical creatures were carved into the headboard and the posts were topped with small rampant lions. Otherwise there was no ornamentation anywhere, not even a portrait or painting giving a better indication of his personal tastes. Even his dressing gown was plain black silk, unadorned with any touches, not even the usual family crest embroidered on it. The stark color suited him, somehow emphasizing the classic masculine lines of his face and the width of his shoulders.

Is he wearing anything under that robe?

Quickly she sank into the seat in a self-conscious movement.

"Julianne."

She looked up, aware her cheeks were warm. Just the forbidden idea of being in her nightdress in front of a man—*this* man—was unsettling, not to mention she wasn't all that sure exactly what he was going to do to her. "Yes?"

There was visible amusement in his green-gold eyes and in the slight twitch of his well-shaped mouth. "Let me clarify a few things. I know you are skittish over what comes next. There's no need. I am not going to pounce on you. I am not going to seek to embarrass you either. I understand you're uncertain about tonight. However, please keep in mind that men and women have been sexually intimate with each other for as long as there have *been* men and women. Neither you nor I would be here if our parents didn't enjoy just such a relationship, so it really is nothing to worry over."

Easier said than done. She said with more tartness than she intended, "I don't know how to swim either, but telling me that if you toss me in a cold river I'll be able to splash about and save myself doesn't make me believe it. People *do* drown."

He laughed. It was spontaneous and made him look younger and more approachable. "Sharing a bed is hardly the same as drowning."

No, it wasn't, but both were frightening if a person was ignorant of the process. She muttered, "I'll be frank and tell you I'm not sure which one I'd prefer right now."

"Would you be so nervous if it were Harry standing here instead?"

For a moment she was nonplussed at the direct question. Then she simply told the truth. "No."

"Ah."

It was hard to tell what that meant exactly. His face was an impassive, good-looking mask of sculpted lines and defined hollows, his vivid eyes compelling. She waited a moment and then struggled to explain. "I knew him better."

"True."

"I was betrothed to him almost all my life."

"An irrefutable fact."

"You were gone."

"Vacationing in Spain. Yes, I remember." His mouth twisted just a fraction, but enough for her to catch the sardonic edge in the reply.

Risking his life and limb for England was hardly something to mock, and she knew she was more out of her depth than ever. Maybe it was an unforgivable thing to do on their wedding night, but she asked impulsively, "Do you miss him?"

Now, why did she ask that? Maybe because he looked so very much like his older brother. Maybe because she was nervous and stammering. Maybe because there was something about him that was dark and unapproachable and she wanted to know something—*anything*—about his feelings.

He went still, his glass arrested halfway to his mouth. Then he said with a rasp in his voice, "Yes."

For whatever reason, that was a relief. The sign of vulnerable human emotion eased some of her fears. So much so, tears stung her eyes.

Michael went on, his voice now cool and controlled. "If I could trade my life for his, I would. Yet with all of those bullets, all of the blood and disease and French columns marching at us, he dies and I live. Who would think it would work out this way?"

He was right. It was ironic that he had deliberately embraced danger and Harry had stayed in England, yet the duke and duchess hadn't lost their more reckless son but instead the more carefully protected heir. Julianne said slowly, "I believe fate toys with us. We tell ourselves our choices form the course of our lives, but it isn't true. From the moment we are born, chance is a variable we cannot control."

"Is that so?" A chestnut eyebrow edged upward. "You are a little young to have settled on that conclusion so quickly."

"Am I? I didn't know there was a limitation on how old one must be to have a certain perception on life."

A fleeting look crossed his face but she couldn't really interpret it. "Nor should a debate on the vagaries of chance be part of the evening after a marriage ceremony, at a guess. Forgive me, if you can, for asking the question that sparked it in the first place. Maybe we should start over. Let me say I think you are very lovely."

A nice effort from a man she sensed, even with her inexperience, did not use poetic language very often or bestow compliments. They were both on uncertain ground, it seemed, though in very different ways.

Julianne smiled, still nervous but not maybe as apprehensive as before she'd steeled herself to walk into the room. "Thank you."

"I've asked myself how to make this as easy for you as possible."

She wasn't sure what to say to that, so she said nothing.

"Perhaps you should come here." He set aside his glass on a small polished table of dark wood.

Go to him? Well, she'd promised to obey during their marriage ceremony, though just now his request didn't sound as much like a direct order as a suggestion. He stood there very casually by the window, his chestnut hair just slightly tousled, the width of his shoulders imposing under the dark silk of his robe.

I can do this. Slowly she rose and walked toward him.

When she was close enough for him to touch her, she stopped, trying to gauge his expression.

That was as futile as ever. She'd never known anyone so good at not *having* an expression at all.

"This is all new to me also." He touched her cheek, just a brush of the back of his fingers.

Julianne quivered as the caress slid down along her jaw and followed the curve of her throat. "Somehow I doubt you're inexperienced, my lord."

"I've never had a wife, I assure you." He began to ease her robe from her shoulders. "Nor would I touch a virgin."

An oblique way of saying there had been women, but she wasn't surprised. He was handsome, wealthy, and from an illustrious family, not to mention twenty-six years old. Harry hadn't been celibate either; she knew that very well.

"We'll have to learn together, then," she whispered as the material of her dressing gown glided down her arms to pool on the floor.

"I believe that is the idea of a marriage in the first place." His smile was nothing more than a faint, wry curve of his lips. "A mutual journey of discovery."

Those lips. She couldn't help but recall how he'd kissed her after their vows. Though there hadn't been anything passionate about it, it had been quite . . . well, nice. Since he'd just confessed he'd taken the time to consider how to approach what was about to happen between them, that in itself was reassuring.

Now, when she could tell he was about to kiss her again, she wanted moonlit passion and a pounding heart. This was her wedding night, and though he wasn't

Harry and it was all different, maybe Malcolm was right. Maybe it was possible she and Michael were better suited than she realized.

He gazed down into her eyes and one long finger followed the neckline of her nightdress, just barely touching her. She tried to suppress a shiver as the caress skimmed the curves of the tops of her breasts, an unaccountable sensation coiling in the pit of her stomach. The heat from his tall body warmed her she stood so close, and the faint tang of brandy had a heady effect.

One arm came around her waist and urged her even closer, up against him, nothing but the barrier of the delicate linen of her nightdress and the silk of his robe between them. His mouth lowered and touched hers, at first just like he'd kissed her in the church, with subtle, warm pressure. Julianne's lashes drifted downward and her pulse beat rapidly in her wrist.

Then everything changed.

"You even taste like innocence," he murmured against her lips.

She stood very still, trying to absorb the sensation of being held so closely . . . and kissed in an entirely different way than when they'd stood in front of witnesses. Like her dreams, this was . . . not what she'd expected. Not that she'd known exactly *what* to expect . . .

His hand crept up to her nape, cradling her head, and his tongue explored the seam of her lips, insistent upon entrance. When she realized what he wanted she was startled, and then a little panicked as he won the silent battle and her lips parted. The first brush of his tongue against hers made her stiffen, but after a moment she relaxed, the unique sensation causing her breathing to quicken.

It went on that way, his mouth possessing hers with increasing pressure, her now tingling breasts against his hard chest as she caught and learned the nuances of the dance of tongue and breath.

When he finally broke away, his mouth traveled with exquisite slowness across her cheek to finally brush her ear. "Let's move to the bed."

Bed. Yes. Of course, she knew that much. Whatever came next happened in bed.

Breathless, Julianne realized she now fully rested against him and he held her easily in the circle of his arms. She realized something else too. A hard length pressed against her stomach, rigid through the cloth that separated them.

It was alarming . . . but to her surprise she enjoyed the closeness of his lean body, and the kiss had caused an odd spiral of anticipation somewhere deep inside her.

She nodded.

Whatever he expected, it wasn't to become aroused so easily, so completely, by an innocent young woman he'd been forced by familial responsibility to marry.

Maybe it was the softness of her dark brown hair, the color a complement to its fragrance, like sweet honey warmed by the sun. Perhaps it was the feel of her against him, lush womanhood tempered by slender grace, the resilient firmness of her breasts tempting under the virginal white lawn of her night rail. Her eyes too, such a deep, dark indigo, reflected uncertainty, yet there was an acquiescence to his embrace he found unexpectedly moved him.

He wasn't at all what she deserved. The blood on his hands was because of necessity, but it stained him nonetheless, and in her sheltered world, the things he'd done and seen were incomprehensible. Julianne had no idea. For his bride there was no dark memory of Spain. The struggle had been won, the battles were over, and Bonaparte in his exile. She'd been a child when Michael had left England, and though she no longer was a child in any way, she couldn't comprehend the bloodshed and horror of war.

He found he liked that. How she was not connected to that part of his life that he couldn't quite seem to shed.

She was like the sunrise, he decided, tasting the tender hollow beneath her ear. All gold and warmth. All warm, entrancing promise.

He was bleak midnight. Pitch-black. No moon in sight. Dark, secretive, and dangerous.

A part of him was reluctant to touch her, to soil that compelling purity.

But that was not the part of him in charge at the moment.

He desired her. It was a bit of a revelation. Not because she wasn't beautiful—she was—but because he'd thought himself more removed.

She'd belonged all her life with Harry, who loved her. All Michael could do was offer what was left of himself to give. He was resigned to acknowledging it wasn't much. The war had taken its toll, but what godforsaken bloodbath didn't? If he wasn't hardened, if he wasn't cold, he would be of no use.

Only he didn't feel cold at the moment. Though he hadn't anticipated it, he was on fire for his new wife and it had nothing to do with the burn of his wound.

She'd agreed they should move to the four-poster bed set at a diagonal in the corner of the room. The barest inclination of her head registered and his heated body responded. Maybe he'd been too long without a woman. Maybe her shy enthusiasm to his kiss somehow touched his jaded soul. If he could have swept her up in his arms and taken her there in a grandiose romantic gesture, he would have, but the very last thing he needed was to reopen that damned injury, so instead he caught her hand.

"Come with me."

The unintentional innuendo almost made him laugh, but he knew she wouldn't understand so he bit back the urge.

Julianne didn't resist as he guided her across the room.

The capitulation was a lesson in trust, and he trusted so few people that he marveled at it. She went sweetly and didn't object even as he bent and lifted her slender body to deposit her on the bed linens, already turned back by the efficient Fitzhugh.

Now, how to explain the swath of bandages across his torso? Obviously her confidence in him was misplaced, since he was prepared to deflect her questions. The sharp twinge in his side as he laid her on the cool sheets was a reminder of his perfidy.

Full breasts lifted quickly under the fine fabric of her gown, and her eyes were dilated. The garment she wore was as demure as the rest of her, a simple nightdress in white that emphasized a fragile air of femininity. Superimposed on the spill of her silken hair, she was, he thought with an ingrained cynicism he couldn't seem to control, every bit the proverbial virgin sacrifice. He wondered what she was thinking. The loss of her sexual innocence was imminent and entirely due to the implacable insistence of their parents that a mingling of the bloodlines was necessary and desirable, but they weren't both culpable of being persuaded into this match. He could have refused, but she really didn't have much choice. Young women were left with little recourse except to submit to their fathers' wishes.

And that was that. He doubted Julianne ever even thought about refusing to follow the dictates of her family. The indoctrination had begun too young. Harry had been the same way, told at age ten the name of his future bride on the day of her birth, raised to a strict sense of honor and protocol and all the ducal ceremony that came with it.

There had been freedom in being a younger son, but the unexpected death of his brother had shaken Michael's firm belief that his destiny was the perilous path he'd chosen, however convoluted it had become.

The woman currently in his bed was not something he'd ever envisioned in his future.

"My lord, is something wrong?"

The softly spoken question brought him out of his reverie. Michael essayed what he hoped was a reassuring smile. "No, not precisely. Your comment about fate came back to haunt me for a moment. That's all."

A small flicker of alarm went across her face as he settled on the bed next to her and positioned himself on his good side. His dressing gown was open enough she could probably see the bandages now, but her gaze was riveted on his face as he leaned forward to kiss her again.

Beguile her, his mind whispered. *You've used sexual persuasion before to distract attention from questions better left unanswered.*

Her soft mouth trembled just a fraction as he took it, rose-petal lips parting this time with less reluctance for the sweep of his tongue. It was leisurely, an exploration, and the heated length of his erection stiffened even more. Michael inhaled her scent as he smoothed a hand over her hip, the enticing curves beneath the cloth utterly female.

Maybe that was the key to how to deal with this. His erotic expertise pitted against her naive inexperience, and she would have no chance. It might not be fair, but then again, life wasn't fair. Look at what happened to Harry.

Or maybe it was death that wasn't fair. Michael couldn't be sure. Death was a lot more familiar.

"Do not worry," he whispered, his lips still on hers, his hand traveling upward over the dip of her waist. "We will do this together."

"I believe that is the point, my lord. Can one consummate a marriage alone?"

He couldn't suppress the small chuckle at the tart reply, even though it was tempered by a slight breathless note to her voice.

"No." He agreed. "A most valid point. Which I am now about to prove to you." His fingers found her breast, fondling the nipple in teasing play, caressing the smooth flesh of the underside with gentle strokes.

An inarticulate sigh was the response, but that was a good sign. Sighs would lead to moans, and moans to cries of passion, if everything was done properly. He knew the pattern, and a sigh this early in the game was a promising development, even if it was from an untried, proper miss.

Or was she so proper? He smiled a few moments later as she didn't object when he pulled free the ribbon on her bodice. Instead she was yielding against him, long lashes pillowed on her smooth cheeks as her breath went in when he parted the confining cloth and exposed one perfect, firm breast. Not large, not small, just exquisite in every way. His mouth trailed along her collarbone, went lower, and traced the subtle rise of mounded flesh as he sought her nipple. His lips closed around the taut peak and his tongue gave a light, playful swirl.

"Oh."

What a sexually telling single syllable. He suckled her breast with persuasive adhesion, softly and then with more force, and her slim hips shifted in a restless motion. Small hands came up to tentatively rest on his shoulders, the touch light but arousing.

It wasn't what he'd expected, but he found her state of virtue intriguing. He was used to women who wanted to please and be pleased and knew exactly what to do. Julianne had obviously never even been kissed in an intimate way before. It didn't surprise him all that much that Harry hadn't touched her. She'd been barely eighteen when his brother died, and no doubt they were rigorously chaperoned when they saw each other.

At least she wouldn't be comparing them in the bedroom. In every other facet of life he wasn't sure how he'd measure up to Harry's ebullient and easy appeal, not to mention his more simple approach to life. To his older brother, he was certain marriage meant a home, wife, and the subsequent children produced from the match, but for Michael having a family was a more abstract concept. He wasn't sure how to be a husband and even less so about being a father.

However, a swift pregnancy to satisfy his mother and father's need for a surrogate for their lost beloved son was probably best, and then exile to the country for Julianne while she was in her confinement.

It was gratifying to know the mission to get her with child would be his undoubted pleasure.

"I'm going to undress you." He murmured the warning against the valley between her breasts, his hands beginning a leisurely exploration of her body as he eased her nightdress aside inch by delicious inch. "Don't be alarmed. I just want to look. And taste," he added.

Her brows drew together.

She had no idea what he meant, he realized with a wicked inner sense of amusement.

The removal of her sleeping gown was a matter of a bit of skin exposed here, an ease of the material downward in small increments there, of mouth and hands in persuasive investigation that brought small inhales and sexy sounds as he began a systematic assault on her senses and nerve endings. He slowly bared tantalizing breasts, a slender rib cage, slim hips, and, of course, the dainty triangle of dark hair between her legs.

Michael finally slipped the garment completely off his bride and tossed it by the side of the bed.

Now to really capture her attention. It was not his plan to shock her with something she might deem unnatural, but he truly wanted her to both enjoy their first intimacy and to be overwhelmed by the experience.

Always keep your opponent off balance.

Words to live by. While Julianne wasn't precisely the enemy, she wasn't going to be an ally either. If all went well, she'd never share the most important part of his life or even know it existed.

His mouth followed the smooth plane of her stomach in lingering perusal. "Uhm."

She shifted, obviously uncertain as his hands ran down the inside of her pale thighs, the skin like satin under his questing fingertips. At his gentle push she tensed in resistance, but once again that ingrained sense of obedience must have asserted itself, for she finally parted for him.

Since he was no more experienced in wedding nights than she was, this was unique. However, he was in charge, he had a vested interest in her participation and enjoyment, and *distraction* was the word of the day.

Always the master spy, he thought in mocking self-disapproval as he inhaled the fragrance of the beginning of arousal. Deviousness tended to be easier than a direct approach, or so he'd learned over the past years. If he had to be married—and he was, so there was no debate involved—it might as well be as pleasant as possible for both of them.

A wedding night was an initiation. It made sense to use the most persuasive way he knew to make sure she understood the pleasure possible and looked forward to his bed, because he doubted they would spend much time together otherwise. Keeping a distance between them was important for a myriad of reasons, not the least of which was how he intended to send her away as soon as she conceived.

As for the conception . . .

With that in mind, he gently parted the soft folds of her sex and ignored her sudden squirm of protest and outraged exhale of breath. The small bud hidden in the protective sheath looked pink and perfect and . . . delicious. His reprobate soul must be asserting itself, for he'd never entertained the thought that a virgin might be more delectable due to her untouched state.

Michael leaned forward and pressed his mouth to that most sensitive of all places and was rewarded by a shocked cry. He held her firmly by her hips as she tried to pull away, and after a moment she went very still.

Very still.

Good, he had her attention.

She tasted sweet and was satin soft under the pressure of his questing lips and tongue. With each lick and nibble she quivered, the reaction becoming more pronounced as he teased and tantalized, doing his best to bring her innocent body to sexual climax. An experienced man, the telltale signs of her growing need did not escape him, and when she spread her legs wider and lifted her hips against his mouth, he experienced an inner flicker of surprise at her swift, uninhibited response. Her fingers slid restlessly through his hair.

"Oh . . ."

That's it . . . come for me.

It happened faster than he'd expected, the telling cry of her climax ringing through the bedchamber, her slender body shuddering into a tense arch. Michael kept her there for as long as possible, taking in each gasp of pleasure and surprise with satisfaction. When she went limp he lifted his head and smiled at the sight of Julianne's flushed face, her eyes half closed under the lacy fringe of her lashes, her breasts quivering with each quick breath.

He was hard as hell, his own need a driving force despite the persistent ache in his side. At least now he knew she was as ready as a woman could be for the necessary deflowering, well lubricated from her release. He slid off the bed and discarded his robe with an impatient shrug.

Her eyes widened. At first it was in surprise as she took in the bandage wrapped around his torso, but then her gaze dropped lower to his erection, the rigid length of his cock upright against his stomach.

It hadn't occurred to him to use her ignorance of the workings of the male anatomy as a distraction from his wound. It was leagues out of his own experience to imagine how a sexually naive young woman who had probably gotten a very rudimentary lecture on wifely duty might feel about seeing a man in full arousal for the first time. To her credit, she didn't really seem afraid, just a bit taken aback.

"I . . ." she faltered and trailed off.

"You . . . what?" With care to not frighten her and because he didn't want to reopen the wound, Michael eased back onto the bed next to her. She was warm and luscious as he took her in his arms, the resilient pressure of her breasts against his bare chest as he cautiously adjusted position.

"You're bigger."

He stopped for a moment, not sure how to respond.

"Than I imagined," she amended hastily, her cheeks pink.

God only knew what her mother—who he thought was a somewhat frivolous woman—had told her. "We can fit together perfectly," he whispered against her mouth, hoping a kiss would be reassurance. He'd never bedded an innocent young lady of the upper class—no prudent young man who was anywhere close in succession to a dukedom took that sort of chance. How much pain there would be, he wasn't exactly sure, but at least she had experienced pleasure first. With his knees he spread her legs, the balance between pure need and the soreness of his injury an interesting sensation. To his relief she didn't resist, but her hands flew up to grasp his upper arms and she broke the kiss, turning her head to the side and closing her eyes, her lacy lashes dark against the rosy hue of her cheeks.

He hesitated, the tip of his rigid sex pressing against yielding flesh. The idea that she was bracing herself for what came next made him realize the finality of the moment. The minute he entered her they were tied together forever. Consummation meant there was no going back. Not that he intended to change his mind anyway, but the very act of bedding his bride irrevocably made her his wife in truth.

This was a crucial moment in both their lives and no matter his determination to stay detached, he found, inexplicably, he would rather they not share it with her turned away from him.

"Julianne," he said, his voice holding the husky rasp of sexual need, "look at me."

Chapter Five

The smoothness of the sheets felt cool against the heat in her face.

Look at me.

The words were ordinary enough, but there was nothing pedestrian about the moment. Julianne sensed the leashed restraint of the man poised over her, the nudge of his erect sex solid against her female cleft. Under the grasp of her hands, the muscles in his arms were rock hard.

Slowly she complied, turning her head and opening her eyes.

His were that unusual, brilliant gold-flecked green, at the moment holding a glitter that was not something she'd seen before, but then again, this night had brought to the forefront how little she knew him. Though she hadn't known quite what to expect in the bed of the Marquess of Longhaven, she certainly hadn't dreamed he would wickedly put his mouth between her legs. Or the sinful pleasure of it. Her heart still pounded, her brain registering the significance of his effort to please her while at the same time rejecting the outrageous method. She'd never imagined anyone doing such a scandalous thing.

But it *had* been wonderful.

"That's better." He didn't precisely smile, but the corner of his mouth—that skillful, tantalizing mouth—lifted a fraction in approval.

The declaration had an autocratic tone to it, and she wanted to point out to him that even her own mother had explained it was her responsibility to submit to his needs, but at that moment she felt the stretching pressure as he began to enter her.

"Don't tense." The words were murmured, warm and persuasive. "It will be over in a moment."

Since he'd said he didn't touch innocent young ladies, how can he be assured of that, Julianne wondered with a frantic sense of panic over the sheer size of the long length of swollen flesh that even now slowly possessed her body. It didn't hurt as her body adjusted to the hot, hard invasion, but was different from anything else she had ever experienced.

With Michael. The idea of it was still foreign, even after the engagement and her realization the marriage was going to happen.

Even with him naked and looming over her, his face set in an intense expression as he eased into her passage with what she, in her inexperience, could even recognize as exquisite care. A small bead of sweat ran along the edge of his lean jaw but he kept their gazes locked. Thick chestnut hair curled against his neck, gleaming in the soft lamplight.

He stopped, there was a stinging pressure, and then she cried out as he surged forward to bury himself completely.

"That's it." With one arm braced to support his weight, he lifted the other hand to touch her cheek in a surprisingly gentle gesture. "It's done."

Julianne swallowed hard, her senses overwhelmed by

the strangeness of having him so deep inside her, a little confused over whether or not she felt pain or pleasure. Something made her instinctively lift her hips, and while the discomfort of what had just happened hadn't passed, it eased a little. With a conscious effort, she relaxed her grip on his arms. If that was as bad as it was going to be, she was relieved. "I'm . . . fine."

"Fine?" One chestnut brow went upward in an arch. "I'd like to attempt for a bit more than that. Let me give it my best effort."

Though she wasn't sure exactly what he meant, Julianne had to stifle a small sound as he slid backward and then thrust forward, settling himself against her so his hips forced her thighs wide. Her husband moved with slow, contained power, easing out almost all the way and gliding the length of his cock back until the tip went to her womb.

At first it was endurable, then vaguely pleasant, and as he began to move a little faster, even enjoyable. Her body seemed to know more than her mind, for it responded to the rhythm in small, subtle ways, her pelvis undulating to his possession, her hands moving from his arms to his muscular shoulders, then sliding down his back, arrested by the cloth wrapped there.

Bandages? She wondered why—just as she had earlier when he'd disrobed and she'd gotten the first look at his hard, honed body—but her interest was fleeting, overcome by tumultuous sensation.

She'd ask him later.

After something miraculous happened.

His hand slid down her side, sensuously rubbed her hip, and then slipped between her legs. Julianne felt a moan escape when he touched her in a certain way, all her attention centered between her open thighs. A peculiar excitement she now recognized coiled in the pit of her stomach.

"Please," he said on a suffocated breath.

She wasn't sure what the request was for, exactly, or

even if it was directed at her, but she clutched at him, her hands now on the small of his back below the swatch of mysterious bandages, a shudder beginning to ripple through her.

"Yes." His fingers pressed with delicate precision, working subtle magic.

It blossomed then, like before, but different and more intense this time with him inside her. The world went blank; warmth and pleasure rolled over in shocking waves that carried her forward until she couldn't breathe. In a haze, she was aware of him stiffening and dropping his head. A hot liquid surge flooded her, each pulse echoed by her own inner spasms.

It was unsettling, but afterward her first traitorous thought was of Harry. Not traitorous because she was betraying Michael by thinking of someone else even as his hard chest heaved against her breasts and their damp skin was pressed together, but just the opposite. She knew deep down that her wedding night with his older brother would not have been the same.

Harry had many good qualities, but he hadn't been sensitive. She was sure he would have preferred she enjoy their physical union, but she doubted he would have spent much time thinking about *how* to make it enjoyable for her the first time.

She didn't even know Michael, and she'd always liked Harry so much. How was it she knew somehow her new husband had taken more care with her than how things would have been if tragedy had not stepped in and changed their lives?

Michael spoke first, his breath ruffling her hair. "Are you . . . well?"

It was an awkward question for a man she guessed rarely was awkward. Her response to each caress, to each touch and kiss, had hardly been in question and she knew he'd felt it. Since he still rested inside her, hard and long, shyness seemed incongruous, but she stumbled over her response. "I . . . I think I should ask you instead, my lord.

I am not the one with a swath of cloth wrapped around me. What happened, if I may inquire?"

"I wasn't paying full attention to my surroundings and had a small accident." The response was fluid and smooth. His mouth grazed her cheek. "It is of no consequence."

Judging from the thickness of pad that obviously covered the injury, she wasn't sure she believed him. "No one told me you'd had a mishap."

He distractingly nibbled on her earlobe. "Why should they?"

Why should they? What kind of question was that? She explained with more curtness than she intended, "I would think maybe your betrothed should be kept informed of your well-being."

"It didn't interfere with the wedding." He kissed her throat, making the spot tingle as his lips whispered against her skin. "Or fulfillment of my husbandly duty. Now, did it?"

"No . . . no." The evasiveness of his response bothered her, but she found it hard to concentrate with his mouth doing such delicious things to her neck. She was still a bit stunned over the enormity of what had just happened. He had not withdrawn from her body and she was all too aware of the stark intimacy of their position, with his lean hips balanced between her open thighs.

"I believe I'll fulfill it again if you'll give me a few moments."

Again? Her mother hadn't mentioned more than one time in one night, but then again, her mother's reluctant little talk hadn't been very informative anyway. Startled, Julianne murmured, "As you wish, my lord."

He lifted his head and those mesmerizing eyes held hers. "Spoken like a true obedient wife. What do *you* wish? I was under the impression you enjoyed it."

She had, which he knew full well, and she wondered if the involuntary sounds she'd made were considered unladylike. Maybe enjoying it in the first place was unladylike. The gossip she'd heard seemed divided into two camps: those women who made sly references to the pleasure of having a lover, and those whose distaste for the marriage bed conjured up words like *obligation* and *animal needs*.

Since it had to be part of her life, she was glad she seemed to be in the former bracket. To the devil with being a lady if it involved eschewing the incredible sensations she'd just experienced.

Julianne bit her lip and stared into her husband's eyes. He would find out soon enough she wasn't a meek milk-and-water miss. Had he paid any attention at all to her before now, he would know it already. "I enjoyed it very much," she admitted. "It was not the repulsive act I imagined."

"Repulsive?" Michael looked openly amused, his weight braced on his elbows so he was carefully balanced above her, but she could sense he did favor one side. The golden brown silk of his rumpled hair framed those aristocratic, masculine features, and the span of his muscular shoulders emphasized their disparate sizes. "Who told you it would be repulsive? No wonder you looked as if I were dragging you into Newgate Prison when I suggested we go upstairs."

"All brides are entitled to a bit of nervousness, are they not? After all, it is a new experience and no one wishes to explain it in satisfactory detail ahead of time." There was a defensive note in her voice. "Or at least no one did to me. My mother tried, but, from a more enlightened perspective, it wasn't a very good effort."

"Come, now. In her defense, do you think it is possible to really explain physical, sexual pleasure?"

He had a point. The spectacular pinnacle of rapturous sensation was beyond imagining.

"Maybe not." She gave a small, breathless laugh. "Demonstration is probably the only way. Please . . . kiss me again."

Something flickered in his striking eyes. Surprise at

her brazen, spontaneous suggestion? She wasn't sure. She'd just surprised herself. He lowered his head and said softly, "With pleasure, my lady."

And he kissed her.

Then he kissed her again.

"Is that what you wore?"

Antonia smiled in a deliberate feline curve of her mouth. She fingered the satin material of her claret-colored skirt before replying. "I wanted to make sure he noticed I was there."

"A scarlet woman at a wedding? You needn't have been so dramatic. I am sure he noticed. I am sure he would have noticed anyway. Few things escape Long-haven. It is how he's stayed alive so far."

She lifted her empty glass in a mock salute. "I needed to share the happy moment with the beautiful couple. Now I am toasting it. Pour me another, darling."

Lawrence reached over and moved the decanter of brandy a discreet distance, just far enough that it was out of reach. "That's quite enough. Do you wish to compound your current state of self-pity by having a heavy head in the morning?"

"Heavy head?" Offended and ready for battle anyway, she narrowed her eyes.

"You're foxed, my love. Or at least well on your way."

The reasonable tone of his voice annoyed her. Antonia sat back in her silk-covered chair, her lashes drifting down. He was wrong: she hadn't yet drunk *enough*. She wasn't inebriated; she was, unfortunately, dead sober.

Was it even possible to drink enough to ease this unremitting ache?

"I saw them leave the ballroom to go upstairs," she explained, suddenly very tired. She wasn't sure she even wanted to have this discussion. "I shouldn't have stayed that long, but I couldn't help myself, like tonguing a sore tooth. She is probably in his bed as we speak."

"Probably," her companion agreed in that irritating

sensible tone. "That is directly where I'd take my new wife."

The windows of her bedroom were open, the air humid from the recent rains, though the night was crystal clear and a smattering of stars shone as she turned her head to stare outside. The lamp flickered as the wash of a welcome breeze ruffled the curtains.

The elegant furnishings usually embraced her and reminded her of what she'd regained after all she had lost, but this current devastation might just be more than she could bear. Tonight she didn't see velvet draperies and Louis Quatorze furniture.

Tonight she saw nothing but emptiness.

It was unfortunate, but she knew just what the Marchioness of Longhaven was experiencing in her new husband's arms. A skillful tenderness, just the right touch, maybe the ghost of a compelling and all-too-rare smile, and, of course, incomparable, calculated pleasure. Even wounded, Michael would approach his wedding night like he did anything else—with a deliberate strategy designed to disarm, beguile, and conquer.

It was always planned, and usually oh so effective.

He rarely failed if he set his mind to something. Perhaps one could say he *never* failed. Women found Michael fascinating not just because of his refined good looks and fortune, but because he had an indescribable air of understated confidence.

There was something about him. She couldn't capture it with words, but she *recognized* it.

He was a hero, and in her life she had met so very, very few. . . .

"She doesn't love him. Michael barely knows the girl." She snapped out the words, shrewish even to her own ears. "When the ceremony was over, do you think either of them looked happy?" Antonia rested her head back against the chair. "To marry not by choice—what kind of a life is that?"

"Had it not been for the French, *you* would have been

wed to a Spanish nobleman of your father's choice. In
dynastic families like yours—and even more so that of
your precious marquess—it is how it is done." Lawrence,
looking tough, unreachable, and critical, wore a sardonic
smile. He lounged across from her in a wing chair by the
fireplace, all powerful male grace, his long legs extended,
his booted feet crossed at the ankles, a full-sleeved white
shirt open at the throat to show a V of bronzed skin.
"How much easier to be a peasant like myself. No one
cares if my bloodlines are carried on. I am not required
to breed so my family can continue to grasp with both
hands the position and fortune their name provides."

"How coarse it sounds when put that way."

"Yet how very accurate."

That was true enough about how her marriage would
have been just as arranged as Michael's, but she was in
no mood to admit it. Damn Lawrence for being correct,
and damn him even more for his infuriating understanding. There were times when she wasn't sure about his
motives, but she always knew he was there in the background, waiting.

He went on evenly. "You shouldn't have gone to his
wedding. You shouldn't have stayed, have danced, have
pretended to make merry when in truth you'd like to
garrote Longhaven's little bride—which I can attest
you could do with practiced ease—and take the groom
for yourself." Lawrence lifted his own beverage to his
mouth and looked reflective before he drank, the flickering light playing over his scarred face. "However, he
did what he said he was going to do and married the chit.
It's done, Antonia."

It's done. The finality of that truth hung between them
in the air.

Morosely she lowered her empty glass and studied it.
"I know. I was there, remember?"

"A self-inflicted wound if there ever was one, my
sweet."

She stirred a little, though she was both lethargic and

defeated. He was right. Inside, she bled. Hopelessly, she said, "He looked more handsome than ever."

"Is that so?" Lawrence's tone was dry as dust. "I suppose to a man, it is hard to see, but I'll take your word for it. God knows something about him obsesses you. I have wondered all along if it is just because you cannot have him."

She ignored the sarcastic observation. "His bride too—damn her to a burning hell full of cackling demons—was very pretty, if you favor bland brunettes with vapid faces and wide eyes. It would not surprise me if the protected little darling hadn't been kissed before that moment at the altar after their false vows of eternal love and fidelity."

"Why did you watch, you bloody fool?"

Antonia stared at the man across from her, trying to ignore the tightness in her throat and the stinging in her eyes. It amazed her that she was about to cry. She *never* cried. Not since the French had come, destroyed her home, killed her family, and she'd been left behind, traumatized, destitute, and alone in a war-ridden country that no longer had a king, a government, a . . . soul.

"I've watched worse," she said, but her voice broke and she hated the sign of weakness. "We both have."

Lawrence's expression softened. He knew—who better—of what she spoke. "Yes, we have. And survived and moved on. You'll forget Longhaven in time. You know it, my sweet. You are just doing what you do so well and fighting it."

She rose in a flurry of scarlet satin and loose dark hair to pace across the soft rug. She should be embarrassed about how she'd dressed to attend the wedding, and actually how she was dressed *now*. It was a harlot's costume and she was no harlot. What had possessed her? No wonder Julianne Hepburn had seemed startled. Now, in retrospect, with the bitterness of loss a reality, she was at least slightly ashamed of herself. "Forget him? I hope so. Or I'll die trying, at least."

"Don't say that." Lawrence was also on his feet in a moment, catching her arm to jerk her around so there was no choice but for her to look him in the eye. It wasn't a gentlemanly action, but then again, neither was he a gentleman. He didn't even try to be one, and as far as she could tell, he didn't believe in giving apologies, nor did he expect them. In some ways they were kindred souls. "The two attempts on his life now worry me. Not for his sake, but for yours. I want you away from the marquess. Away from the intrigue he has brought on his head. If he wants to play his games for England, let him, but there is no need for you to be involved."

"*You* are involved."

"We work for the same people. It's different. You have money and the security of being the widow of an important Englishman. I want you—"

She twisted free. "You *want*? Well, as one who can testify at this very moment we do not always get what we want, there's little you can do about it."

Sometimes, she wondered if she would one day push him too far and he would leave. It was there in the twitch of his mouth, the slight flare of his nostrils, the set of his jaw. In those burning midnight eyes. He loomed over her, dark and dangerous, his voice a rasp. "You condemn me for being jealous of him. I could throw that in your face as well. If his new wife is as uninteresting and innocent as you perceive, Longhaven may well seek your bed in the future. I wish joy of it. Unfortunately, a tumble is all you'll get from his exalted lordship because he cannot give more. In the meantime, I am more than happy to see to your needs."

Antonia had to admit she was tempted. Michael had been a skilled, considerate lover during their brief affair. Lawrence was something else altogether. Raw, uninhibited, wild, ravenous even.

He didn't just want her—he *needed* her. Michael did not. She often wondered if Michael needed anyone.

The answer, she suspected, was no. Especially not her.
But I love *him,* she thought in despair.

And tonight he lay with another woman. They were
together; he held his bride in his arms at this very
moment. . . . He'd given her his name, his protection,
and since his virility wasn't in question, there would no
doubt be children. . . .

Perhaps they were making love right *now.*

It hurt—terribly—and Antonia wasn't at all sure she
could bear it.

"Fine," she bit out. "Take me."

Maybe it was the fierceness in her tone; maybe it was
her expression. But for once, Lawrence stepped back,
releasing her suddenly as if she were on fire. His disfig-
ured face settled into a mask she could not read—and
she was good at reading men. After a moment, he said,
"I will take you, trust me, but not tonight. I won't be a
party to it."

Was he serious? After all the posturing over her hopeless romantic longings, he was going to deny her?

"What?" she demanded, outraged. Her clenched fist
hit her thigh.

He stepped back another few paces, as if putting distance between them would help. "You'll be thinking
about him. I have no interest in the comparison. I'm myself, not a surrogate."

Antonia wanted to shriek, and she'd felt the urge to
strike out at something—someone—all day. "You are
more than willing to climb between my legs at any other
time," she taunted, being deliberately crude.

It got through, for his face tightened. "But not tonight, Lady Taylor. It should tell you something."

It did, but there was no question she was not in the
mood to listen.

"No casual fuck? How disappointing." She essayed a
shrug. Maybe she was a little inebriated after all, for the
room spun.

She must have swayed, for suddenly Lawrence swept her up in his arms. It wasn't an impetuous lover's embrace, but rather a rescue.

I don't need to be rescued, she insisted to herself even as she rested her head against his chest. *Damn him.*

He whispered roughly, "Come on, love. I'll undress you. The only thing you need your bed for tonight is sleeping. Tomorrow will be brighter. I vow it."

Would it? She wasn't sure. But his words were oddly comforting. Dismally, she mumbled against his shirt, "I hope you are right."

"It happens now and again that I am." He deposited her on the bed and began to unfasten her gown. Not with his usual impatient, needy hands, but with gentle care, his long fingers slipping each fastening free until he could ease the garment from her shoulders. His gaze was concerned, not lustful. "Did you eat anything at the reception?"

How could she eat when she felt not only sick physically, but sick at heart? "Nothing," she confessed.

"I'll bring up a cold supper. You can't possibly go to sleep with a stomach full of brandy and nothing else." He deftly removed her slippers, garters, and stockings.

It's not like I'm a little girl, she thought, and a part of her resented his presumption.

But a part of her was glad he cared at all. That *someone* cared. She'd lost so very much. . . .

Michael cared too. She knew he did, but it wasn't in the way she wanted. Oh, yes, he would die for her—he'd proven that—but she'd never reached him in the way she craved. She'd never, ever touched his guarded soul.

The woman who could do *that* might not even exist.

Chapter Six

The dawn was as he liked it best: soft and gentle as a mother's embrace.

Michael nudged his horse with his heel, urging a canter from the sleek bay. The early-morning ride was part of his routine, but he took a different route than usual, mindful of recent events. His side hurt at the faster pace, but he'd discovered in the most difficult way possible by being wounded so often in Spain that he was a fast healer, and this injury seemed consistent with the ones he'd experienced on the field in that regard.

After all, he'd done fine the night before bedding his bride.

There was just the slightest fog hanging low, obscuring the riding paths in the park as it drifted in spectral wisps. He slowed Hector with a tug on the rein and walked him between the wooded areas, his mind preoccupied with this new and unanticipated side of a marriage he'd viewed with both dispassion and studied indifference.

It was all very . . . *interesting*. Julianne was beautiful, so he hadn't doubted he could become aroused and acquit himself adequately in bed, but her reaction hadn't been exactly what he'd anticipated.

Unrestrained enjoyment from a virginal, untried young woman was not at all how he'd pictured the evening's events. Yes, he'd done his best to pleasure her, but the sensual response to his lovemaking showed a side of her he hadn't anticipated. Despite obvious misgivings, she'd embraced physical passion. Because she'd always appeared so demure and ladylike in his presence, he had expected the same response in bed.

What else didn't he know about her?

He guided his horse through dew-laden grass, his thoughts abstracted. In retrospect, maybe he should have done more to get to know her before the wedding. Would it have tempered his decision to marry her?

No. Had she been plain and stout instead of beguilingly lovely, he still would have agreed. Michael remembered the grave look on his father's face when he'd petitioned for him to consider going ahead with the marriage agreement. The Duke of Southbrook would never plead, but there had been unspoken desperation in his eyes, a need to move forward rather than dwell on the death of his beloved son. He and Julianne's father were close friends, and when they'd both married months apart as young men, they had vowed to pledge their children to each other if fate allowed it. Harry had been born, and a good decade later Julianne had come into the world. The betrothal was done when Julianne was still in the cradle. She'd grown into womanhood knowing she would one day be the Marchioness of Longhaven and eventually Duchess of Southbrook, but no doubt she'd barely given Michael a thought except as her future brother-in-law.

There was little use in pondering how things might have been different had Harry lived. *Julianne is* my *wife,* Michael reminded himself—his surprisingly passionate, engaging wife—and that was what fate had decided for them both.

What troubled him now was that he had a feeling his concept of what he was getting in the match didn't coincide with the reality. Yes, she was young and still naive, but she was also intelligent and more adventurous than he'd guessed. Case in point: her unabashed sexual participation of the night before.

Heated sighs, soft-as-satin skin, eyes the color of a midnight sea under the moon . . .

To his surprise, he'd found her . . . enchanting. Deliciously memorable to a man who had made it a point to not hold on to past experiences if at all possible. He'd approached his marriage like he would any mission. It had to be done and he could perform the task needed with detachment and to the best of his ability. But Julianne had disarmed him and beguiled not just his senses but also his intellect with her innocent candor, both in bed and in conversation. Seducing her body was one matter; he'd counted on his ability to stay distant on all other levels. Now he wasn't quite as sure.

It bothered him that he'd been taken by surprise. His ability to read other people had kept him alive.

It didn't fit his plans very well to have Julianne distract him.

An hour later he turned for home, still unsettled. He needed to solve the dilemma of the two attacks, because he certainly didn't want to have to explain away any other mysterious injuries. Julianne hadn't pressed the matter, but she was understandably curious. Though using seduction to divert her questions had worked for the moment, he had the impression she was far too bright to be put off for long.

Damnation.

The neoclassic glory of Southbrook House roused the same unsettling feeling as did musing over his newly acquired wife. The mansion sprawled across an impressive expanse of Mayfair, palatial and ostentatious in every way possible. The rosy morning light gilded the brick facade with gold and red, and the graceful sweep of the drive was protected by not only a gatehouse, but also an ornate fence. Since Harry's death proved having wealth could not ensure good fortune, Michael wondered if he would be doing any child a favor by bringing him into this unsettled world. Even with prestige and a noble family, no one could be assured a happy life.

It was the first time he'd ever really contemplated the realities of being a parent, but then again, before last night, he'd always been a careful man. Now he was supposed to do his best to father a child, and the more quickly it happened, the better. What he hadn't anticipated was, since it was possible he had already gotten his wife with child—after all, often enough it took only one time—how he would feel about it.

This was all so different than he'd imagined.

As he dismounted and tossed the reins to a stable lad who scurried to take them and lead the stallion away, he guessed he had avoided much more than just contact with his prospective bride in the past months. It was uncharacteristic, but he hadn't really thought things through. He'd avoided *the situation*.

It might be something he shouldn't put off any longer.

"Good morning, my lord." Rutgers, the butler, swept the door open with a flourish. "I trust you had a pleasant ride."

An introspective one, yes, but he wasn't sure *pleasant* qualified. Michael said in a neutral tone, "The weather is very accommodating today."

Silver-haired and efficient, always the epitome of decorum, the older man inclined his head. "It is indeed."

"I take it most of the guests are abed?" Michael tugged off his gloves in the spacious foyer. Overhead on the mural in the high ceiling, cupids cavorted and playfully pointed bows. He hadn't really paid much attention to it before, but the symbolism didn't escape him now.

"The party went on until just a short while ago, my lord."

"I saw the line of carriages still in the drive. I am glad it was a success."

"A resounding one, if I may make the observation."

His wedding night had also been an unexpected success, but he was hardly going to disclose that piece of information. Michael merely said, "I'll take breakfast upstairs so as to avoid any more well-wishes. At the risk of sounding ungrateful, I think I have had my fill for a while."

"It seems understandable to me, my lord." Rutgers looked as impassive as usual, his severely tailored clothing immaculate.

Since the man had been with his family as long as he could remember, Michael queried on impulse, "My parents . . . they enjoyed the festivities?"

Had he really just asked that? Of a servant, no less? But then again, Rutgers was more than a servant; he was a permanent part of the household—the family, even, in some ways—and he could answer the implied question.

Rutgers let his solemn expression slip for a moment. Pale blue eyes blinked and he cleared his throat. "Your mother, my lord, is happier than I have seen her since . . . well, *since*."

Since Harry's death. Michael understood. After all, it was why he'd agreed to the marriage in the first place. He nodded and headed for the sweeping staircase at the end of the main hall. It was early yet and he wondered if Julianne was awake. He'd left her sleeping in his bed, all tangled dark hair and dewy, smooth skin, her long lashes resting on the delicate arch of her cheekbones, and each breath lifting her delectable breasts under the fine linen sheet.

Please . . . kiss me again.

No man with a drop of blood still flowing in his veins could have resisted that sweetly whispered—yet provocative—request. He hadn't, that was for certain, and his erection had surged with astonishing speed considering he'd just spent himself. The second time they'd made love he'd been just a little less restrained, and his young wife had responded to every touch, every caress, every thrust, with both willingness and obvious enjoyment.

It had been delightful.

Now, in the stark reality of morning light, he had to decide how to deal with her.

She was alone.

Julianne rolled over, coming slowly awake, at first a little confused over the unfamiliar room. Dark blue silk hangings on an ornately carved bed, tall windows with drawn drapes against the daylight, an armoire in the corner, the door to the dressing room discreetly closed . . .

Her husband's bedroom.

Memories of the night before floated back, at first a trickle, and then a torrent. Heat spiked into her cheeks and she made a mortified sound as she realized she was stark naked under the fine bed linens. Her nightdress was a pale heap of cloth by the side of the bed, and her robe was still by the window, where Michael had been standing when she'd entered the room.

She jabbed her elbows into the mattress to lever herself upward and sucked in a breath as a twinge of discomfort spiked through her. There was little doubt she was tender between her legs, and she could feel stickiness on her inner thighs. More cautiously she sat up and then rested her shoulders against the softness of the pillows, propped up against the headboard. There was a clock on the mantel of the fireplace and it ticked in a solemn rhythm, but otherwise it was completely quiet.

With one hand clutched in the sheet to keep it over her bare breasts, Julianne contemplated the strangeness of waking in the bed of a man she barely knew. It wasn't as if she didn't understand that the moment she walked down the aisle of the cathedral and her hand was placed in his, before all and sundry, her life had irrevocably changed in a monumental way, but knowing something was going to happen and experiencing it were two different things.

On the one hand, she mused, staring abstractedly at where the sun struggled to pierce the draperies, her wedding night hadn't been at all like she'd expected. Michael had touched her with care—very scandalously so—but she had to admit to herself it was a trifle embarrassing to recall her unmitigated acceptance of those wicked caresses. It brought up the very real problem of how little she knew him, for before he took her in his arms that first time and truly kissed her, she would not have judged him a considerate man.

Julianne frowned. Well, that wasn't accurate either. She hardly pictured him being *inconsiderate*, for he was polite always, formal without being stuffy, solicitous to his mother, even charming on occasion. But the formidable aura of control that surrounded him was undeniable.

Even in the moment when she'd felt him give in to sexual release, she sensed his reluctance to relinquish his power even over his own body.

She'd thought him complex before the wedding, and he'd added another facet to the picture she struggled to form of him now that he was her lover.

"I see you are awake. Would like for me to ring for your maid?"

Since she hadn't heard the door open, she was startled, her gaze flying to where the subject of her thoughts stood. Dressed for riding in a coat, white shirt but no cravat, tan breeches, and polished boots, his brows lifted just a fraction in inquiry, he looked once again remote and enigmatic. Strikingly attractive, yes, in his refined, aristocratic way, with his thick chestnut hair and remarkable eyes, but unapproachable too, as if a cool mask slid neatly into place sometime between when she'd drifted to sleep in his arms and woken to find he'd left.

Gone was the tender lover. She sensed the withdrawal. Julianne cleared her throat and blushed. It was impossible *not* to blush. "I'll go back to my room and ring for her myself, my lord."

"Very well. Please excuse me." He regarded her with cool detachment.

She gazed back, confused, her hand tightening on the sheet, as if covering her body was still an issue, when she'd lain naked underneath him and wantonly moaned with pleasure. He'd seen everything of her there was to see, yet she anchored the sheet against her chest with almost desperate modesty.

It wasn't like he didn't notice either, for his glance touched on her clenched fingers. However, if it amused him, it didn't show in his impassive expression.

He explained briefly, "I'm afraid I have a busy day. I believe my mother has a late luncheon planned since we have so many guests. If possible, I will join you."

If possible? Weren't they just wed?

That was it? She felt . . . dismissed.

This is what it will be like to be his wife?

It was a little difficult to interpret his swift, graceful bow and the way he turned and went into his dressing room. Julianne stared at the closed door in consternation over the obvious indifference with which he treated her, but perhaps she was wrong to be surprised. He would hardly show any affection since he really had none for her. How could he? He didn't know anything about her. In bed, he might desire the use of her body, but that was different.

She was young and probably naive in many ways, but she knew that much. Sexual desire and deeper feelings did not necessarily go hand in hand.

Still, it was disconcerting to think that all she garnered was remote courtesy, despite the intimate things that had happened between them the night before.

As quickly as possible, she scrambled out of the bed and grabbed her nightdress, slipping it back on with clumsy fingers. She practically fled to her room, stopping just long enough to scoop up her robe. *It is ridiculous to be disappointed,* she reminded herself.

Ridiculous.

She tugged on the bellpull by the bed and waited, her emotions a confusing mix of vague resentment and relief. If he wished for them to be one of those couples who led completely separate lives, it might make things simpler. Independence was something she'd always craved, and though her parents were kind, they had also been very mindful of proper behavior and she was closely chaperoned at all times.

She was now a married lady and no longer a sheltered ingenue. The idea held some appeal. Her allowance also was significantly increased, if what she remembered about her father's comments over the marriage settlement were accurate. That would be very convenient.

No, Julianne thought as Camille bustled in, all inquiring eyes, bobbing curls neat under the crisp mobcap she wore, her uniform starched and perfect for service in a ducal household. She was not going to dwell on the negatives of her marriage. There was little point in it, and she'd wondered ahead of time if Michael Hepburn's reserve wasn't a difficult wall to scale.

Did she even want to try? Marriages in the beau monde were often detached and more formalities than relationships. If the day after their wedding her husband already had no time for her, maybe that was how he viewed their future.

Why did it give her a sick feeling in the pit of her stomach? How could she expect more? It was probably true also that he was a busy man. Wealth and title were privileges, but a fortune had to be managed to sustain itself, and titles came with responsibilities.

"Would you like breakfast, your ladyship?

Distracted, Julianne looked up. The young woman had an anxious look on her face. Twin spots of color graced her plump cheeks, and the girl dipped into a curtsy.

The deference was a bit startling and pointed out
her changed status in the world. Her maid at home had
been more friend than servant, but she hadn't wanted to
switch employers. Julianne cleared her throat. "Tea and
toast would be fine. And hot water so I can bathe."

"Yes, my lady. Right away."

The night before she'd been too anxious to really appreciate her surroundings but while she waited, Julianne
studied the somewhat grandiose bedroom, decorated,
she guessed, by her mother-in-law when she married Michael's father before he was the duke. It was done in subtle shades of different yellows, from pale lemon to deep
gold, the canopied bed gilded with small filigree roses, the
carpet beneath her feet ivory and ochre. A set of French
doors opened to a balcony, and when she wandered over
to open them she discovered she shared it with the adjoining room, the balustrade stretching between their suites.
She also had a dressing room of impressive proportions,
her clothing already neatly unpacked and put away.

Of course. She was the Marchioness of Longhaven,
and a future duchess.

Since she'd always anticipated the marriage, that part
was not so unsettling. It was Michael who had her rattled.
She plopped down in a beautiful chair done in creamy
white with yellow stripes and felt again the betraying
discomfort as her bottom made contact with the seat.
With more care, she eased into place. The soreness between her legs was a vivid reminder of the night before.

Had she pleased him?

It was a little unfair, because she had absolutely nothing to compare the experience to and he undoubtedly
had many.

Plucking at the folds of her nightdress, Julianne stared
at the window and wondered if it was better to be a chosen paramour or an obligation like a wife. She had his
name and protection, but not his affection.

It would be nice to have both, but from his shuttered
expression earlier, she doubted if it was even possible.

*   *   *

Lawrence pushed a small bag of coin across the scarred table. "There will be more when you have something to tell me."

The thin young man scooped up the offering in a thrice and slipped it into his pocket. "Agreed."

The tavern room was noisy, the patrons ill smelling. A blousy barmaid whirled past, spilling ale from the mugs clutched in her hand. Considering his nefarious past, the setting was hardly unfamiliar. Lawrence raised his brows, feeling the pull of his puckered skin on the left side. "Once a week should suffice for a bulletin on how it goes. All I wish is for you to stay close to the marquess and report to me anything suspicious. There have been two attempts on his life already. I anticipate there will be a third."

"Aye, then, Captain. I'll watch 'im."

Johnson was capable despite his youth, and Lawrence had used him before upon occasion with great success, but he knew a warning was in order. "You'll have to be very careful. Longhaven is no one's fool and on his guard. All I'm asking of you is to observe and see if anyone else is trailing him."

The boy grinned, revealing crooked teeth. "He'll not notice me any more than his bloomin' highbrow shadow."

"Don't underestimate him," Lawrence said slowly, running one finger along the brim of his now-empty tankard in a thoughtful gesture. "His lineage and privileged life aside, Longhaven is no fop. I can say with authority he would be a tough bloke in a fight, be it fists, knives, or any other weapon. He has an edge as sharp as honed steel under those polished manners and fine clothes."

Not yet twenty, with foxlike features and thick, untidy hair the color of new straw, Johnson nodded. "I'll keep me distance."

"You know how to reach me if there is anything of note to report."

"Aye."

The young man finished his ale, wiped his mouth with his sleeve, and then slipped away. With approval Lawrence watched his quicksilver movements, confident he'd made the right choice. He ordered another drink, ignoring the red-haired barmaid's roguish appraisal, her overblown figure not at all to his tastes.

He preferred his women lush and raven haired, with soulful dark eyes and a haunted past.

When he'd left the house, Antonia had still been sleeping. He hadn't done quite so well for himself, settled in a chair by her bed in case she woke and needed him, all too aware of the level of her melancholy over Longhaven's dutiful marriage. Once, she and the marquess had been lovers. The affair was brief and long over, yet her attachment held fast. The trouble was, even while Lawrence resented the devil out of the handsome aristocrat, he understood all too well Antonia's feelings. To her, the man was a heroic, romantic figure, and to a certain extent, in a grim way, it was probably even true. Longhaven had rescued her from the French, seen to her protection, and in the end, given her a new life by encouraging her marriage to Lord Taylor. When her husband had been killed, she had come to England.

The war had changed Lawrence's circumstances as well.

In fact, the three of them were all tied together. The death of the Duke of Southbrook's oldest son had affected all their lives. Antonia had followed Longhaven to London, and because of Lawrence's ties to some mutual colleagues, their paths had crossed. They all still fought the war, but instead of operating behind the French lines, capturing confidential communications and confounding the enemy's intelligence forces, now they worked together in a more subtle way.

Apparently it was a deadly dance. The reason he wanted Longhaven followed was simple: he knew Antonia would enshrine the blasted man forever in her heart if something happened to him.

Lawrence lounged back in his chair, ignoring a burst of raucous laughter from the corner of the seedy tavern where three unshaven and definitely unsavory men indulged in a game of dice. *The marriage of the marquess has turned our interesting triangle into a quartet,* he mused, waving away a noxious waft of some particularly vile tobacco smoke. Antonia loved Michael Hepburn, Lawrence loved her, and, in the past, Longhaven had loved no one as far as he could tell. Yet somehow he had agreed to marry this sheltered young woman without so much as an argument.

Lawrence knew everything there was to know about her. After all, information was his business.

Julianne Sutton had been promised at birth to Harold Hepburn, Longhaven's older brother, though the betrothal had been more an agreement between their two fathers, and the young man had died before the official marriage settlement had been drawn up and signed or the engagement announced. She was educated, refined, accomplished in the usual things such as music and dancing, and her family's wealth and position in society would have ensured her a good marriage even without the early betrothal. Because of the duke's eldest son's death, her formal debut into society had been postponed as both families grieved, and from what Lawrence understood, she hadn't minded the delay and genuinely was distressed over the tragedy.

Interesting. How did Michael feel about his new wife's former attachment to his older brother? It was no doubt a waste of time to even speculate on it, but how did Lady Julianne react to the change in bridegrooms?

If he wanted, Lawrence suspected he could find out the young lady's favorite color, if it would be useful. Her former nurse had been loquacious, according to the man he assigned to investigate the woman Longhaven would marry, and one of the footmen in the duke's household was only there because Lawrence engineered his employment.

Knowledge was power. Always.

He had to admit he found the new marchioness interesting. She was young, but in reality Antonia was less than five years older, just legions more so in taxing experiences. Julianne Hepburn was now married to someone who had influence over Lawrence's life. That meant he was going to make sure he understood the dynamics of how the new situation would work.

As a rule, he left nothing to chance.

Chapter Seven

"I haven't seen you."

"Why would you? It has been unnaturally quiet, almost." Michael looked unperturbed. "I'm here now though. What is so urgent?"

Damn her wayward emotions. Antonia drank in the sight of him as he quietly let himself into the study and closed the door. He was dressed formally in a dark blue superfine coat, his cravat intricately tied, boots polished, a touch of lace at his sleeves. The quintessential gentleman, urbane and titled and—in his case—dangerous on many levels, one of which was to her peace of mind. He even moved that way, with a certain lethal grace.

I need to touch you. . . . Hold me . . .

She squelched the thought. "I have something. It involves Roget."

That got his attention. He paused, and then selected a velvet-covered chair and sank into it, his expression thoughtful. "How did you stumble across this information, if I may ask? I haven't heard a whisper in several months and we both know I have been looking."

Without being asked, she poured him a drink and rose to hand it to him. He accepted with a nod of thanks, his gaze fastened on her face.

If she could not hold his attention any other way, at least she had this common ground with him that his little wife did not. It was gratifying she could meet him as an equal in some measure. Respect might not be love, but it was something. She settled back into her own chair. "Smugglers. We intercepted, via a healthy bribe, a curious note. I cannot decipher the message, but his name is mentioned."

"Let me see it."

She'd expected the request and smiled at him. With deliberation, she withdrew the missive from the bodice of her evening gown. It was warm from her skin and scented with her perfume, and their fingers brushed as she leaned forward in an intentionally provocative movement meant to showcase her décolletage.

He noticed. There was an appreciative, amused flicker in his eyes, but he accepted the piece of vellum without comment. Quickly he scanned it, his brow furrowing, and then he looked up. "The symbol of the hawk is indisputably his, I agree. This is a good sign. I thought we'd lost him."

So had she. Without inflection, she said, "I want his blood."

"If possible, I'll spill it for you."

Antonia gazed at him. "I know you will."

Michael simply took a drink from his glass, abstractedly studying the communication. "The code is a new one, or at least I haven't seen it before."

"It's a puzzle," she agreed, relaxing in her chair. It was a nice night, the evening warm. Michael sat comfortably across from her, the strength of his presence filling the room. When he was with her, somehow, even in times of the gravest danger, she felt safe. Antonia pointed out, "I imagine he could be the reason for the attacks on you."

"It would explain a lot, except he would normally do it himself. The two inept assassins so far are not at all the caliber of Roget's skill." He stared at the paper spread on his knee. "I hope I am not dealing with two separate camps intent on my demise."

"You confounded Bonaparte's spies at every turn. There is probably a long list of people interested in your demise." Antonia affected nonchalance. She feared for him every single day, though she doubted he would appreciate her worry. It wasn't a discounting of her emotions as much as disinclination that anyone should waste their time in concern for his fate. Michael always seemed surprised when people cared about him.

She loved him desperately.

He tapped the paper with a finger. "Thank you for this. I'll see if I can't figure it out. It would be invaluable to know what Roget is up to right now. Charles has offered help, and if I can't make the missive out, then I'll turn it over to him to pass it into the right hands. This has a personal edge for me, as you well know."

"Me also."

"Yes," he agreed after a moment, his voice quiet, "for you also. Though we do not know how much of a hand Roget had in the killing of your family."

They sat for a moment, mutual memories holding them captive, and then Antonia forced a smile. "So, how is it?"

He didn't misunderstand, but then again, they knew each other well. Michael sank a little lower in his sprawl in the chair. "My marriage? It's going well enough."

Why did she perversely want to torture herself? She managed what she hoped was a cool tone. "Well enough. It sounds like heaven on earth. Can you not do better than that?"

"As I have never been married before, I am not exactly an expert on the subject. We are both adjusting to it."

"Adjusting? How unromantic you sound on the matter." Antonia knew her smile had turned as brittle as an icicle.

What would I do if he told me it was heaven and his bride an angel?

Luckily, she didn't have to find out, for he was typically Michael and gave a somewhat evasive answer.

"I don't think women look at things the same way as men. Naturally marriage is something anyone must get used to, my dear." His look at her was pointed. "*You* were married, so you should know what I mean."

"To a man three times my age who only offered me his name out of chivalry because *you* suggested it." She knew she sounded ungrateful, and that wasn't intentional. In her own way, in time she'd actually been very fond of her husband. He had been older, yes, but he had also been kind. His death had left her with yet another void in her life.

"The general enjoyed having the prestige of a pretty young wife." As always, Michael didn't rise to the bait enough to participate in a real argument. He was too restrained and detached for a heated debate over the past. "And it provided you with an entry into society and enough money to make you autonomous."

He was infuriatingly right. He often was. It did not improve her mood. With an effort at the same indifference, Antonia asked, "Your little innocent pleases you?"

"Pleases me?"

"In bed."

His hazel eyes were direct and his voice quiet. "You aren't really asking me for details, Antonia, are you? That is between me and her."

She *was* asking. She wanted to hear he found the new Marchioness of Longhaven a bore, a disappointment as a lover, an empty-headed doll with little more to recommend her than that glossy hair and pretty face. Antonia took a quick sip from her drink and then said with barely a wobble in her voice, "No. Why should I care?"

"You shouldn't." His agreement was soft but firm.

But she did. God help her, she did.

"She is going to fall in love with you." Antonia found a perverse pleasure in informing of him of that impending pitfall in his life. "And you will hate it, for you dislike anyone forming too strong an attachment. You will *hate* it, but it is going to happen."

He stood, the missive in his hand, and said with an offhand smile, "Thank you for bringing this communiqué to my attention. I will let you know what I find."

A week had once meant nothing. Seven days, usually passed with mundane activities, but this was different, Julianne thought, sitting at her dressing table, a hairbrush in her lax hand. One week into her marriage and she was acutely aware of the minutes that ticked by during the daylight hours. It was partly an adjustment to living in a new household, and Southbrook House was imposing in many ways. Both the duke and the duchess were warm and welcoming, but Michael didn't fit into the same category.

She very rarely saw her husband. If she was brutally honest, she might even speculate he avoided her company. Only twice had he been at luncheon. Dinner was a formal affair and there were usually guests of some kind, so it ended up being more polite small talk than anything else. Though several times he'd escorted her to a social function, it was fashionable for husbands and wives to go their separate ways, and he almost immediately excused himself and went into one of the gaming rooms.

When darkness fell, it was a bit different. He took her to bed each night so far without fail, and she *thought* she satisfied him, at least sexually, but for all she knew he was simply being diligent in his duty to beget an heir. It was unfair to not be able to know the difference, but she had no other experience.

Asking him was out of the question. He was *not* a man who invited intimate questions.

Julianne studied her reflection in the mirror. Loose, flowing hair framed her face and tumbled down her back. Her eyes looked large and dark, the candlelight enhancing the effect. The negligee she wore, designed by a French modiste, bared her shoulders and was little more than a shimmer of cloth, and so revealing there was high color in her cheeks despite her resolve to appear composed and sophisticated. The bodice was so low her breasts threatened to spill free, a single wisp of ribbon tied in a small bow holding it together. It was supposed to be the gown she wore on her wedding night, but she'd lacked the confidence to put it on and had instead worn a plain nightdress like her usual sleeping attire.

If it took a provocative gown to make him notice her more than as just an obligation to his title, then she was willing to give it a try.

She was starting to realize a few things even in her ignorance as a new bride. The first was that Michael's distance was deliberate. Oh, it wasn't that she expected him to fall at her feet. . . . She really didn't know what to expect from her marriage, actually, but a concentrated effort to keep her at arm's length wasn't it.

Michael Hepburn wanted nothing to do with her other than in the bedroom. So if he did enjoy exercising his conjugal rights, it seemed like the best place to start to see if she could break through his determined indifference.

As much as he would allow.

The extent of his control bothered her. No. It bothered her *immensely*.

There was still nothing she knew about him except the delicacy of his touch and how carefully he bedded her.

A sound in the next room made her go still, hairbrush suspended in hand. His voice, and then the response of his valet, carried through the thick wooden door, though she couldn't hear what they were saying. She sat there, an unwanted tingle flicking through her body at the thought of what was to come.

When the door clicked open she was still there at her dressing table, her hairbrush now set aside, her hands folded in her lap. In the mirror she watched as he moved up behind her. He wore his black robe loosely tied at his lean waist, and his lashes were lowered just a fraction over those vivid eyes.

"Coming to bed?" He touched her loose hair, just with a brush of his fingers.

"If you wish, my lord," she responded, wondering how he would react if she refused him. Surprised? Angry? Indifferent? It was so hard to judge just how to get his attention.

"I wish," he said with a slight smile playing on his lips. He grasped her waist and urged her to stand up. A certain heat flared in his eyes and his gaze dropped to her barely concealed breasts. "What are you wearing?"

In her opinion she wasn't wearing anything, the filmy material merely an ornament, not a garment. "This was made for our wedding night," she explained. "I'm afraid I didn't have the courage."

"I like it, I admit." His hands lingered at her waist as he examined her bosom in a leisurely perusal, the clasp light and undemanding. "Any man would."

It was that sort of comment that made her feel as if he constantly distanced himself. Now it wasn't just him admiring her body through the barely there lace, but any man. It annoyed her because she didn't understand him. What she wanted was for them to grow close, not just as lovers, but as two people who shared a life. "It's for you only," she said deliberately. "Who cares whether or not any other man would like it?"

Something flickered in those hazel depths, her irritation apparently not unnoticed. "It was a compliment, but perhaps ill phrased. Forgive me. I simply meant it showcases your undeniable beauty."

That was a little better, but not much. "If I please you, I'm glad. I . . . I wish to." Hesitantly, because she still was adjusting to the intimacy of physical closeness, she placed her hand on the hard plane of his chest through the opening in his robe. His skin was smooth like warm satin over granite. Under her palm his heart beat in a strong, regular rhythm.

"If you wish to please me, a demonstration is in order." He lifted her in his arms then and carried her to her bed, which was different, as he usually preferred his room. "It's closer," he said in explanation as he laid her down and followed, his body pinning her to the soft coverlet. "And I'm hungry for you."

He was, if the hard length of his erection between them was any indication. His mouth hovered over hers and then took possession, his tongue slipping past her lips to tangle with hers. Julianne was learning that he seemed to like it when she participated rather than passively accepting his touch, and she kissed him back, clasping his neck, the softness of his hair brushing her fingers. He licked the corners of her lips, skimmed her teeth, and then plunged his tongue deep again and again as his hands slid the whisper of silk and lace from her body. In turn, Julianne boldly worked her hand between them to pull loose the tie on his robe. Her hands explored his bare torso, the muscled strength of him impressive and a little overwhelming. With a small shock she realized the pad of bandages was gone, replaced with only a small strip of cloth.

"You smell like roses." He whispered the words as he nuzzled her neck.

The warm feeling of his breath and lips was beguiling. She said, "You gave me the perfume, my lord. Remember?"

"Did I?" He paused for just a small moment in his deliberate seduction, and she had at least one answer to a question. Each night since their wedding she had found a small gift, elaborately wrapped, on her bedside table when she went to dress for dinner. A pair of beautiful pearl earrings, a charming miniature on a small gold stand, a lovely Chinese painted fan, silk gloves . . .

This evening it had been perfume in an exquisite, small glass bottle, the fragrance opulent and seductive like a warm summer evening in a garden.

But she'd wondered all along if he had been the one selecting the gifts. The amount of thought that had gone into the selections made her doubt it. Though a card with his signature had been left with each one, there was a generic feel, as if he might have signed seven cards and handed them to his secretary, or maybe his valet, Fitzhugh, who seemed to be the height of efficiency, with a careless request from Michael to pick up something appropriate.

It was disappointing, but she wasn't precisely surprised.

He moved to stand up and let his robe fall to the floor. "A good choice, apparently. It suits you."

"Thank you for the thoughtful gesture," she said, wondering what he was really thinking. Though she was getting used to seeing him nude—and even more difficult, letting him see *her* without a stitch on—she still reacted with unwilling fascination.

His body was sleek, defined, all male, especially that part of him that was rigidly erect against the flat plane of his stomach. Julianne could see the pulse of the veins in his stiff cock, in tune with the beat of his heart, the flared tip beaded with liquid evidence of his desire. The candlelight played across the fine-boned features of his face, shadows hollowed under his cheekbones. It accented the gold glints in his rich brown hair. The combination of potent virility and the air of male power was exhilarating.

Her breasts were taut and a warm flush infused her skin under the scrutiny of his gaze as he examined her naked body, the filmy nightdress discarded at the foot of her bed. Julianne waited, watching from beneath her lashes, her breathing already altered into the faster respiration of arousal.

Was this all she could ever have of him? If so, she meant to embrace every moment.

*   *   *

There were some definite problems arising. Michael hadn't anticipated one of them, and it was the allure of the entrancing beauty on the bed before him, her indigo eyes dark, those glorious breasts he found himself thinking about at inappropriate times quivering with each lift of her chest.

Her rosy nipples were pointed and erect, the tight buds an indication that she was well on her way to arousal. And he would wager his very considerable fortune that when he touched her between those long, luscious legs he was going to find her wet and ready for him.

The innocent maiden he'd married out of duty and guilt was turning out to be a very passionate woman. Not only did she embrace sexual intercourse with enticing sensuality, but she unsettled him in other ways, too. The way she had looked at him when he mentioned the perfume held a vague hint of reproof, and he had a feeling she knew he wasn't responsible for the gifts, except for in the abstract sense that he'd paid for them. How extraordinarily discerning for someone so sheltered and young. What else might she guess?

Fitzhugh had done well at picking out items she would enjoy and appreciate, and it was Michael who had blundered with that awkward response to her reminder he'd been the one to give her the perfume. Part of it was the news of Roget's reappearance; part of it was how distracting his wife was in general.

Just take her as often as you wish. She wants it, you want it, and there needs to be a child, or you've bound yourself for life for nothing. . . .

He listened to the inner voice with the cynical knowledge that the advice was a bit self-indulgent. It wasn't for nothing, because it pleased his parents . . . and if he were honest, at the moment it pleased him very much as well.

Michael slid on top of her, kissed her again with ardent urgency, and began a systematic wooing of her responsive body. With lips and tongue he brought her already pointed nipples to full attention, caressing, stroking, his mouth taking deep the straining peaks. Julianne gasped, moved, arched, all the reactions satisfactory in his mind, his needy body having been primed by the sight of her sitting at her dressing table in that sheer gown, obviously designed to bring a man to his knees by someone who knew just what she was doing.

Perhaps I should give the canny seamstress a bonus, he thought, the depth of his arousal surprising him. He'd gotten hard almost instantly.

At the moment, he was so eager to be inside his wife it consumed his world. Michael ravished her mouth as he slipped his hand between her legs, gratified when she opened them for him without resistance. She was predictably warm, wet, and so tight that when he penetrated her with one finger, the clench of her inner muscles almost made him come then and there, like a randy adolescent.

Michael moved, adjusting himself between her open legs, settling against her and holding her bottom in his hands, lifting her for his entry. His hard shaft probed moist softness and tested the give of her yielding body, and he glided forward into paradise.

"Perfect," he muttered.

Julianne grasped his upper arms, her nails biting in, her inhale audible. Not until he was fully embedded did she exhale, and it was a long, very feminine sigh.

Of enjoyment.

How the devil someone so innocent and untried could make a sound like that and send heat spiking through his blood he wasn't sure, but she did. There was also the shadow of her long lashes on her cheeks, the tinting of arousal in her face, and the heave of her luscious breasts against his chest.

With long, slow strokes he started to move in and out, his cock withdrawing and plunging deep as he strove to take them both to the summit. She caught the motion easily, her hips undulating into every surge, a moan escaping her lips as her eyes drifted shut. Such unrestrained enjoyment fueled his own pleasure. In the past, his lovers had always been experienced women who knew what they wanted and understood the subtle games between the opposite sexes. This was different. Her sensuality was his alone and Michael found he was possessive of it.

The feeling was unique.

He watched her as her climax rose, responded to the shuddering in her body, saw the deepened color in her face. He leaned forward and brushed her mouth with his as she tightened her clasp on his biceps to a fevered degree. "Let it happen," he urged.

"I . . . I . . ."

Whatever she was going to say was lost as she uttered a low, keening cry and stiffened. It was like the floodgates opening for his straining body, and he went still a moment later, milked by her inner tremors, his seed spilling in a tempestuous release that tore the breath from his lungs.

It took conscious effort not to collapse on top of her, and he rolled, his face buried in the silken mass of her disheveled hair, his ragged respiration loud in the otherwise quiet room. Their limbs were entwined, the embrace still intimate, and as they both gradually relaxed, somehow it became *more* intimate.

How the hell is that possible? Michael pondered the question, unmoving, liking the warm, soft feel of her length against him, with him, part of him. How could pleasure take on a whole new meaning with a woman he'd never wanted in the first place, not to mention someone so untutored he was her only lover?

Julianne stirred. She turned her head enough to look at him and a tremulous smile curved that soft, sweet mouth. "I take it you are recovered?"

Was it a sexual innuendo? He doubted it and hoped not. A second performance was still at least a little while away. He couldn't help a muffled laugh. "I beg your pardon?"

"From your injury."

That damned inconvenient knife wound. Since she really hadn't asked about it except that first night, he'd hoped she wouldn't mention it again. Michael looked into her eyes and smiled. "I'm fine, if you couldn't tell."

"I can't ever tell anything about you."

A flicker of warning went through him despite his physical contentment. He levered up on one elbow and his hand lifted and brushed a stray silken curl off her smooth shoulder. "I am not sure how to respond to that," he answered truthfully. "I'm afraid I am a private man, Julianne. It is something you are just going to have to adjust to. Changing one's nature isn't an easy thing to do."

She gazed back, and he reflected that while she might find him guarded—and he was, deliberately so—she was quite the opposite. Her beautiful eyes held a wistful quality that told him a great deal. He supposed he shouldn't be surprised someone as young as Julianne would want a more romantic, attentive husband, but he neither had the time nor the inclination to become more involved than he had to be.

In truth, he was protecting her by keeping his distance.

"I am not asking you to change, my lord. I wouldn't presume. But I think it would be nice if we shared more than a bed each night."

Juggling the necessary obligations that came with his title, the estates he now owned, investments, *and* his duties to the Crown left very little time to dance attendance on his new wife. Michael said, "I am a busy man."

"If you knew me a little better, you might like me." Her smile trembled just a little. "I'm told I am tolerable company by my friends."

That was undoubtedly true. She was unspoiled for someone born to privilege and wealth, especially since she was also beautiful. For that he was grateful. But she was proving to be a little too perceptive despite her youth. "I'm your husband, not your friend."

At once he knew he'd made a mistake.

"I . . . see. I fear we have very different views on what a marriage should be, my lord. I admit I am surprised. Your parents obviously love each other very much."

Michael weighed his answer, for the flash of hurt that crossed her lovely face made him experience an unwanted pang of remorse. He murmured, "They are the exception and not the rule among aristocratic alliances, my dear. You surely know that."

"I think rules are merely guidelines and some are made to be broken." She lay there, framed in the mass of her shining hair, the gauntlet thrown, but it was one he could not pick up.

An unwilling smile rose at the defiant tilt of her chin, but he couldn't explain to her his motivations. His cynical thoughts on the subject of love would also disillusion her, so what choice did he have but to deflect the conversation to something else? Or maybe it was best to end it altogether. "Your hair is such an unusual color," he murmured, lifting a handful and rubbing it between his fingers. "I confess I am not poetic, but it reminds me of rich sable, not quite brown, not quite black, and with a subtle ruby hint." He let go and dropped his hand, lightly skimming down to circle one perfect, pink nipple with a questing fingertip. "At night, my time is yours. Shall we use it wisely?"

"In other words, the discussion is over?" She phrased it delicately, but there was an overtone of resentment in her voice.

Yes, Julianne was definitely too insightful for his peace of mind. He lowered his mouth and licked the luscious underside of one enchanting breast. "I'm afraid we are going to be otherwise occupied."

Chapter Eight

Lawrence tipped back in his chair and regarded Antonia with jaded contemplation. Today she played the demure widow in a simple green gown, her dark hair looped into a chignon at her slender nape, no jewelry or other ornamentation. The expression on her face was schooled to indifference, but he wasn't fooled. Slowly, he asked, "You are certain you wish to do this?"

"Of course I do. If I didn't, why would I suggest it?" There was an edge to her tone.

He recognized it. It usually meant she was restless and needed action of some kind. Too much time on her hands and she brooded over the past, so maybe it was for the best that she take on the task. "It's a rather bold move, my lady. He may not like it."

They sat in Lord Taylor's study, the room still redolent with the background aroma of aging tobacco smoke and brandy, the desktop holding documents and correspondence of the most banal quality: invitations to balls and dinners, the newspaper, cards from callers, personal letters. In the locked drawers, though, two of which had secret backs he had personally had installed, there were messages and contraband code guides that would be disastrous if they fell into the wrong hands.

The repercussions of war, he'd discovered, were never quite over.

Antonia practically jumped to her feet and prowled across the room. She paused by one of the bookcases, ran a finger along the spine of a leather-bound book, and then turned. In the afternoon light she looked lush and her olive skin held a glow despite her conservative mode of dress and hairstyle. "Michael is preoccupied, or he might have come up with this on his own."

It was impossible for Lawrence to cover his snort of derision. "I doubt somehow he wants you near his little bride, and though he's no saint, he would never ask it of his former mistress to protect his wife. I know him well enough to say that with certainty."

"I was his lover, not his mistress."

He inclined his head, uncertain why the difference was important to her, but when it came to Longhaven, she was touchy. "As you wish."

She went on stubbornly. "Two attempts have been made on his life. Now he has a weak spot in *her* to lure him into danger. Roget is no fool. Once he learns of the marriage—and I am sure he already knows with his far-reaching resources—it is a natural step to aim in that direction. A man trailing around behind her would be noticed and spark alarm. Someone like me, a social equal, a friend of her husband's, will seem natural enough. I will strike up more of an acquaintance. Besides, we go to many of the same functions already. I'll keep an eye out for any sign of a threat."

"Johnson has noticed nothing so far. No one following the marquess, no others watching that ostentatious pile of rock he lives in, no suspicious additions to the household. It could be the two attacks were really random attempts to rob him. After all, he was in dangerous places both times, and while he may think he can disguise his nobility, he carries himself a certain way." Lawrence watched her agitated pacing and added, "Born into a family such as his, what else can you expect?"

"*I* was born into such a family," Antonia said with audible, acid pain. "It is no guarantee of happiness and privilege. It did not help us when the French overran our home and slaughtered everyone they encountered. Don't preach to me about status and wealth. It can be snatched away at a moment's notice."

She reminded him always of a wounded bird. In Antonia's case, not some pretty songbird, but a bird of prey. Angry, dangerous, flapping her wings as she desperately tried to take flight again, her talons extended.

He wanted so much to be the one to set her free.

The idea to insinuate herself into the life of the Marchioness of Longhaven didn't come so much from protective instincts as it did from a desire to know everything possible about the woman who now shared the life of the man Antonia believed she loved. Lawrence knew this because he knew *her*. She needed to size up the competition, and yet she had already lost the battle.

It wouldn't do to reason with her and point out the cold, unpalatable truth. She needed to come to the conclusion—and accept it—herself.

"I wasn't preaching," Lawrence said as he crossed his booted feet in a deceptively lazy movement. "I don't believe in it, and you are too stubborn to listen, so what is the use? What makes you think Longhaven isn't having her guarded anyway?"

"He probably is. Fitzhugh is efficient and dangerous in his own right, but he can't be there at the society events like I can. He wouldn't fit in." Antonia gestured with her hand in a careless brush. "Roget is not as intelligent as Michael, but he is infinitely more ruthless. She probably can't be protected enough."

That might be true, if it *was* Roget targeting the marquess. If there was even a threat at all. Not that Longhaven didn't efficiently direct an intelligence ring for

King George, and was thus important enough the enemy no doubt wanted him dead, but he was far less vulnerable in London than he had been back in Spain. On his home soil Michael Hepburn wielded more power than ever. He could take care of his wife.

"Since you are determined to do this anyway, I won't argue, though I do debate the comment over Roget's intelligence. So far the usually competent Longhaven hasn't been able to find him, though he's done his damndest. What do you propose to do about the marchioness?"

"I'll start tonight. The Redmonds are giving a ball this evening. I am sure she will be there."

"So will he," Lawrence pointed out with unerring practicality. "How do you think Longhaven will feel about you cozying up to his bride when he didn't instruct you to do any such thing?"

"I don't know," she replied in a slow purr, "but we'll find out. Won't we?"

An amused part of him was sorry for Lord Longhaven. When Antonia made up her mind, she was relentless.

Like in her quest for the infamous spy, Roget, whom she hated with a depth that rivaled the deepest trough in the ocean. If only he, the man sitting with her now, could bring forth such volatile emotion.

"This isn't the way to capture his attention, my love," he told her. "The marquess wants you to follow orders, not intrude on his life."

Antonia stared at him, back to the paneled wall, her dark eyes suspiciously luminous. Under the bodice of her gown, her tempting breasts heaved as she took a deep breath. "When does it matter what *I* want, Lawrence? When?"

The bitter despair in the last word was like a knife in his heart.

He had no answer except that it mattered all the time—to him. Life had dealt her a very harsh hand, but then again, he hadn't gotten off lightly either. They were forged together in a unique way, if she would only allow herself to see it. Longhaven never had needed her like she yearned for a man to want her, like *he* wanted her. Lawrence acquiesced gently, "It seems like a sound plan, actually. With Johnson following the marquess and you watching over his marchioness, perhaps we will get a hint of danger if there is one."

"Roget hates him."

Lawrence sometimes hated him too, but then again, that was on a personal level and was based on jealousy more than anything. Longhaven himself he admired in many ways, but he naturally loathed what he represented to Antonia. "So he should hate him. They were archenemies, were they not? Fighting not just a war, but a battle of wits. No one likes to lose, especially a man like Roget. Longhaven did his best to eliminate him."

Antonia suddenly wrapped her arms around her stomach as if she were cold. "We were so sure he was dead."

"Maybe he is," Lawrence pointed out. To him, Roget *was* dead. The war in Spain was over. Why did this have to linger on? "Someone else could be using his signature. We know nothing for certain. Longhaven is no doubt using every resource now that you turned over the note. If it is Roget, the marquess will deal with it."

"He can no longer give matters like this his full attention." Antonia said stubbornly. "He has to play the role of heir to a dukedom, and now he has a wife to placate also. If he is spread too thin, he might trip up. I want to help."

"If he needs you, Antonia, he will ask. Every man has his limitations and he isn't so arrogant to believe he is an exception." Even as Lawrence murmured the assurance, he wondered if she wasn't right. Part of the reason Longhaven hadn't bowed out of his role was because at this stage of the aftermath of the war, transferring the power of his responsibilities would weaken a link that had become a very viable part of the British espionage system. Longhaven knew things no one else did, and though he no longer ran the operation on Spanish soil, he was invaluable to the war minister because he could interpret the information they received with the accuracy of one who understood the enemy and their tactics. Lawrence also suspected that because of who and what he had been—and still was—Longhaven was hesitant to be put in a position where he no longer had access to knowledge of what was happening as Europe struggled to recover from such a long conflict—Roget's resurrection being a prime example.

Michael Hepburn would remain a French target until the animosity between their countries was over, whether he was still serving his king, or simply playing the elegant aristocrat. To protect himself, he needed to be aware of the machinations of his enemies, and he had many. To be aware, he needed to continue to do his job.

It was one devil of a quandary.

Lawrence would do the same exact thing in his position. In fact, he had taken the same precautions. Never would he completely resign. It wasn't an option unless he left England. "I already told you I wanted you to stay out of this, but that was a futile hope, wasn't it? Part of the problem is one gets addicted to danger . . . used to it. I do not miss the physical hardships of war, but pitting myself against our foes . . . yes. I think you suffer from the same malaise, love."

"Yes," she admitted, her dark eyes shadowed. "I am not done with my battles."

He canted his head a little to the side and studied Antonia, letting a smile play across his lips. "So, I suppose, if you want to play nursemaid to the pretty marchioness, it can't hurt. Because we are the good little spies we are, things are getting nicely convoluted, aren't they? You will watch her, I'm having him watched, surely he's having her followed, and out there somewhere, someone is probably stalking him. All very satisfactory, if you like things complicated. Toss in Roget and his wily evasion of capture and perhaps the situation will get interesting."

This was a dratted nuisance and she had to tamp down a sense of chagrin over how to handle it. Julianne looked at her husband's valet and said with credible calm, "I have my maid to accompany me, Fitzhugh. I'll be fine."

"His lordship requested most specifically I see you safely anywhere you wish to go, my lady."

There was an implacable edge in his tone that said he wouldn't be put off. He was one of those men whose age she couldn't really gauge, his broad face eternally bronzed by the sun, his graying hair in wispy curls, and his very erect carriage like he was always at attention. The rich Irish brogue in his voice spoke volumes about his heritage, and her maid had mentioned Fitzhugh had served with Michael in Spain and elected to come back to England to take his present position.

"It isn't necessary," she insisted, having a sinking feeling that she was going to lose the battle.

"My orders were clear. Surely you do not wish for me to be reprimanded for dereliction of duty?" Dapper in smartly tailored clothes, Fitzhugh regarded her with unswerving observation as they stood in the circular drive in front of Southbrook House.

"Of course not."

"Then you will allow me to accompany you."

"I . . . I was thinking of visiting a friend," she said lamely, trying to calculate how to work this sudden problem. "It might be hours."

He opened the door to the carriage with a flourish. "I am a master at waiting. Shall we?"

So now she had the problem of both him and her maid. Julianne climbed into the carriage and thought furiously, *What should I do?* Being a married woman should bring more freedom, not less. She sat with her hands clasped tightly in her lap over her reticule. . . . Skipping her intended visit was an option, but not a good one. It upset the very delicate equilibrium of the situation and she was trying hard to not do that, plus it carried an inherent danger of exposure.

So, she would go with her original plan, which had always worked well in the past, and hope no one noticed anything. Camille would probably not have been a problem, but Fitzhugh was a different matter. She had a sense he was extremely observant.

They arrived at Melanie's right on time, and she was shown into the drawing room. Immediately her friend rose, her light brown hair caught up in ringlets around her face, a smile on her mouth. She crossed the room and caught Julianne in a quick hug. "I've been dying to see you. I'll ring for tea."

"I can't stay but a moment," Julianne confessed.

Melanie, pretty and sweet tempered, looked disappointed but resigned. "The worst part of all this is we now rarely get to really see each other. Everyone thinks we spend hours and hours in each other's company, but—"

"I know." Julianne felt the same loss. "But I really am not sure what else to do. Worse, it is getting more complicated rather than less. For whatever reason, my husband has decided his valet *and* my maid have to accompany me everywhere."

"Oh, dear." Melanie sank down in one of the chairs. Her fine brows knitted together. "Well, I suppose it isn't like the servants can really question you."

"My old maid didn't," Julianne observed wryly, "because she had a penchant for one of your father's footmen. It was to her advantage for me to stay here as long as I liked. I just hope Fitzhugh and the girl the duke hired to tend to me don't start to get suspicious. I am not as much worried about Camille as him. He and my husband don't seem to have an ordinary employer-servant relationship."

Melanie dimpled as a small smile curved her mouth and she adjusted her skirts, her eyes holding open curiosity. "I realize you have to rush off, but tell me, how is it being a married woman?"

Her friend was also engaged, and Julianne didn't blame her for the personal question, but Melanie's somewhat foppish, lighthearted fiancé was nothing like Michael. Lord Day was a good catch and had a respectable fortune, but marriage to him, she had a feeling, would be entirely different. Evasively she murmured, "It is . . . interesting."

"Please, Jule. What kind of an answer is that? Interesting in a good way or a bad one?"

Julianne blushed. "A good way, mostly, though I don't see a lot of him during the day. Most of our interaction is . . . later."

"Oh, yes. I see." Her friend looked embarrassed but intrigued. "The marquess is rather formidable. I did wonder how you got on."

Julianne couldn't help but think of all the intimate things he did to her naked body—and how much she liked it. Her cheeks grew hotter. She would have said they were getting to know each other, but that wasn't exactly true. Instead she substituted, "We seem to have found some common ground."

Or a common bed anyway.

Julianne still hated to think of it only in that way, but maybe over time . . . well, she wasn't sure, but all she could do was try. At the moment, a more pressing issue was foremost in her mind. "Is it safe to use the servant's entrance now? I don't think I should be gone as long as usual, so expect me back a little early."

"I'll go first, as always, to make sure no one sees you leave." Her friend rose and motioned her to follow.

Luckily it was done without mishap, and Julianne found the hired carriage in place, the driver waiting for her as arranged. She slipped inside the vehicle and they set off down the alley, rumbling out onto Curzon Street. The journey itself always took over an hour, which left her with maybe two for the visit itself, and as they rolled along, the neighborhoods becoming less and less fashionable, she wondered what would happen if she ended the subterfuge and simply told the truth. Though her motives were based on good intentions, she still wasn't sure everyone would see it that way.

How would her husband feel about what she had done? Much less the duke and duchess? Would the entire Hepburn family condemn her?

She had no idea.

When they pulled up in front of the correct address, she alighted and nodded at a woman who passed by on the street. The elderly lady was thin and stooped and she held a loaf of bread. Her eyes took in Julianne's fashionable gown with bright interest. While it wasn't a disreputable area and at least not as dangerous as many places, it wasn't a neighborhood where one found fine ladies in silk gowns either. Instructing the driver to please wait for her and promising a reward, Julianne climbed the small steps up to the discreet doorway and knocked.

Sharply. With purpose. The one time she'd panicked and worried that Leah had moved without telling her had been both shocking and horrible, leaving an indelible impression.

To her relief, the door was opened by the usual slatternly charwoman. The servant muttered, " 'Tis you, milady, is it? Good. She's been fair onto frantic awaitin'. They're in the parlor now."

The place smelled vaguely like boiled cabbage, but then again, Julianne already knew Leah didn't spend much of the income she gave her on the household. She followed the elderly servant to the small room furnished with fraying settees and faded draperies. The woman hadn't lied, for Leah was there, vibrant as ever in an emerald satin gown suited for a different time of day, a little stained and worn, but with her figure shown to advantage. She whirled as Julianne entered and sputtered, "Where the devil have you been?"

A long time ago she'd learned to not respond to

that particular snarl in the woman's voice. Julianne said calmly, "I'm here now."

"Did you bring the money?"

"Don't I always?" She flipped open her reticule and took out a small bag full of coins. "Here it is."

The young woman fairly lunged for it, snatching it out of her hand. "I'll take that."

"I had no doubt you would," Julianne murmured dryly, but she was uninterested in Leah's obsession with drink. Her gaze went instead to the small child sitting on the floor, a doll clutched in her arms. Brown silken curls framed a cherubic face, but the rest of her was too thin, and her eyes too solemn for a child of not quite three.

Julianne had gone to quite a bit of trouble to select that doll. The perfect porcelain face was a contrast to the little girl's grubby cheeks.

Leah muttered, "You'll be wantin' her alone, then?"

"For an hour or so. It is all I can spare."

"Right," the other woman spat. "You being the grand marchioness and all."

If she deigned to answer there would be more unpleasant words, so she didn't say a word. The other woman waited, her auburn hair piled up on her head, her lips tinted red by artifice, her eyes flashing dislike.

But Leah needed her, and they both knew it. After a moment she flounced out the door in a swirl of green, muttering a vulgar curse under her breath.

Julianne crossed to kneel in front of the child watching her with that so intent gaze. Julianne whispered, "Chloe."

No response. There rarely was. Surely the child should be talking by now, but she seldom made more than a few small noises.

As always, when Julianne held out her arms, there was a moment of hesitation before Harry's little daughter scrambled up and flung herself into the proffered embrace, doll and all.

Chapter Nine

The milling crowd swirled around them, the music vying for attention with the babble of hundreds of conversations. Michael shouldered his way through the crowd, the too-warm atmosphere of the ballroom stifling. He was never one to favor frivolous entertainments and this evening was no exception. The refusal of all invitations was not socially acceptable, so he settled for being very selective. Now that he was married, he should take Julianne's wishes into account also, though there was no rule that said husbands and wives had to attend the same functions.

He didn't know her thoughts on the matter, but maybe he should ask.

I fear we have very different views on marriage, my lord. . . .

It was his impression she'd meant that very sincerely.

Case in point: his pretty young bride wasn't like most of the superficial young ladies of fashionable society. The money and title she'd gained when they married didn't seem to hold her interest as much as the merging of their lives. She wanted more from him than his sexual interest; that was clear enough.

God save him from idealistic and romantic young women with entrancing indigo eyes and skin like warm, smooth silk, because he wasn't convinced he had more to give.

Julianne was more than stunning this evening in deep rose tulle embellished by small silver ribbons, the cut of the bodice showing the upper curves of her delicious breasts, her arms and shoulders bare. The dark silk of her hair was swept up into a simple style that suited her natural beauty, and the only other ornamentation, a pair of pearl earrings, drew attention to the graceful line of her neck. At least he'd had the sense to ask Fitzhugh for a description of the gifts and a record of what days they had been given so he wouldn't trip up again. Usually he was very good at details, but he did have other things on his mind besides bottles of perfume and jewelry.

He was being followed. The surveillance was covert and professional, but he had still noticed and was debating on how to handle it. He could wait and see if there was another attack. Now he was very much on his guard and he was armed at all times, so he wasn't going to be easy to kill. If he could capture his assailant, the odds of getting information were almost certain. Every man could be persuaded to divulge his motives if the interrogation was handled the right way.

The second problem was the usual one: locating Roget. Charles had sent a brief communiqué stating he had feelers out to see if there were whispers anywhere of his reappearance.

Michael stepped aside to let a matronly woman go by, and scanned the jammed room. It was huge, with arched Gothic ceilings and elaborate moldings, the chandeliers sending flickering light over the milling guests. It was almost impossible to find anyone, even with the advantage of his height.

"Longhaven." A hand clapped his shoulder. "Looking for someone?"

He turned, seeing the familiar face of Niles Beckham. They were actually first cousins on his mother's side, and Niles was both likeable and intelligent. They even looked alike in some ways, though Niles was a little shorter and his eyes were dark. At the moment they held an amused look.

"In this damned crush, how could anyone find another person?" Michael's mouth curved in a wry smile.

"If you're looking for your beauteous young wife, I just saw her over there by the terrace doors." Beckham gestured with his champagne flute toward the southeast corner of the ballroom. He grinned. "So, tell me, what's life like as a married man?"

That same question had been posed to him a multitude of times—mostly by bachelor acquaintances—and Michael was getting tired of it. He suggested dryly, "Try it and find out."

"That's no answer."

"It wasn't meant to be." Michael glanced in the direction his cousin had pointed. "As a matter of fact, I *was* looking for Julianne. Is she dancing?"

"No. Chatting with Taylor's widow, I think."

Michael stopped, arrested in the act of taking a drink from his own glass. *Chatting with Antonia?*

That was interesting. No, that was *alarming*. With studied casualness, Michael murmured, "I see. If you'll excuse me, then, perhaps I'll go claim her for the next waltz."

Niles inclined his head, waving him away. "By all means. Can't blame you. Your marchioness is a diamond of the first water. Everyone thinks so."

Why the statement annoyed him, Michael wasn't sure, but somehow it did. *Julianne is lovely and men are bound to notice,* he reminded himself as he found a passing footman, handed over his glass, and then shouldered his way toward the location Niles had indicated. The pressing issue right now was, *what the devil is Antonia up to?*

She was a creature of passion, and he knew she wasn't happy about his marriage, for she'd made it clear. Their past bound them together in some ways, but not the one she wished. He regretted her disappointment, but knew her feelings for him were a complicated mixture of emotions she probably didn't even understand, and he doubted any of them were truly love.

He wasn't even sure true love existed. What she deserved was a man who would give her back the same fierce fire and utter devotion, and he had known that from the very moment he'd met her, forsaken, alone, and devastated back in Spain. Her family had been slaughtered, their home commandeered by the French, and she had escaped only because two loyal servants had forced her to leave when the first soldiers arrived. They'd smuggled her out the back way and dragged her to the relative safety of the nearby hills, where they had hidden for three days.

When they finally did go back, there was nothing but rubble and carnage. Michael, in charge of a small British intelligence patrol behind French lines, had seen the wisps of smoke still rising from the fires and found her there, vacant-eyed and in shock, sitting in the littered courtyard of what had once been a beautiful villa. He decided to take her with them, for leaving her behind was as good as murder, and it had taken nearly a week to get her to speak. Her first words had revealed a clear glimpse of her fierce spirit.

I'll kill them. I'll kill them all.

She'd become one of his best operatives, and true to her word, she'd dispatched more than her share of the enemy. Vengeance was a powerful motivation, he'd found, and Antonia felt it in full measure still.

Having her attention focused on Julianne made him a little uneasy.

Michael finally spotted them by the open terrace

doors, half shielded by a potted plant, a contrast of dark and light, Julianne's fair beauty offset by Antonia's dramatic, sultry coloring. They *were* talking, he observed grimly, and Antonia seemed particularly animated, gesturing with her hands and smiling. When she was out to charm, she could be very skilled at it. As Michael approached he heard Julianne laugh.

"Good evening," he said pleasantly as he strolled up, making them both turn.

"My lord," Antonia murmured in a throaty tone, extending her hand in a graceful gesture.

He took it and bent over it, and the betraying quiver in her fingers told the story. She was definitely up to something. Releasing her, he straightened and tried to gauge her expression. This evening she wore lemon silk, the color a flattering contrast to her raven hair and olive skin, a jeweled comb holding her elaborate coiffure in place. She looked sophisticated and beautiful, but he didn't miss the calculating gleam in her dark eyes.

"It's always a pleasure to see you. I trust you are enjoying the party?" He looked at them both in neutral, polite inquiry.

Antonia waved a careless hand. "It's a terrible crush, so your darling wife and I took refuge in this corner. It was delightful to get a chance to talk for a few moments. I explained you and I are old friends."

"Did you?" Michael cursed inwardly, wondering just what the hell she'd said. Julianne looked more curious than anything, those long-lashed indigo eyes, he admired, thoughtful as she gazed at him.

His wife said, "Lady Taylor tells me you met in Spain."

"Indeed. She was married to a fellow officer." After all, half-truths were his specialty.

Antonia interjected, "Michael actually introduced me to my husband." The languid wave of her fan matched the heavy-lidded look in her eyes. Both were indicative of a motive he did not trust.

He said in a noncommittal tone, "As predicted, Lord Taylor was entranced immediately."

"You are too gallant." Antonia sent him a glimmering smile.

"Not at all." In a more proprietary gesture than he intended, he took Julianne's arm, uninterested in further intrigue. Luckily, the orchestra struck up the desired tune. "I realize husbands and wives are not supposed to be in each other's pockets, but if Lady Taylor will excuse us, would you grant me a dance?"

It was interesting, Antonia thought, a false smile plastered on her face, to watch a usually detached man like Michael come to the rescue of his pretty, naive little wife. What was he afraid of? That she might tell the truth? Confess they had once lain in each other's arms and she had tasted the passion of his kiss? That she knew the potent power of his desire? Recount how her hands had traced hard muscles and lines of sinew, and knew the texture of his hair?

That was not at all her plan.

She flicked her wrist, sending an unsatisfying gust of stale, warm air from the ballroom across her face from the lace fan in her hand. With a critical eye she watched from her vantage point in the little alcove. They waltzed well together and were a striking couple. Julianne Hepburn was graceful and feminine, and he was so irresistibly handsome and all male. She said something and he answered, a brief smile crossing his face.

Antonia recognized that smile. It was practiced, and usually meant he was thinking about something else.

Probably wondering what *she* might be up to. Good. Just what she wanted.

When Michael had approached them and looked at her with that usual inscrutable expression on his face, she'd still seen the unspoken question in those vivid hazel eyes.

Antonia turned toward the French doors onto the

terrace and practically stumbled outside across the flagstones, dragging in a breath of fresh air. For a moment she leaned against the balustrade, listening to the swell of the music, the faint chirp of the insects in the trees surrounding the garden, the tinkle of a nearby fountain.

She wondered if Michael had made any progress with the coded missive she'd handed over. Some things she wasn't privy to. In the past she used to ask the outcome of their missions, and she usually got an evasive answer, if she got one at all.

As long as they foiled the French, it was all she cared about.

And Michael. She cared about *him*, unfortunately.

Was it any wonder? She could still remember the first time they met. It had been dusk and the air cooling, but it hadn't accounted for her shivering. Antonia had heard the approach of the horses, but in her dazed state she hadn't cared any longer. She'd spent that afternoon burying her parents and sister, the brutal evidence of what they'd suffered before their deaths so horrifying, her mind had gone numb. The house had been sacked, all the food was gone, and the servants were dead or scattered. What wasn't burned was destroyed, the desecration so complete she suspected her soul had also been shattered into a million fragments.

So she just sat there and let them come. If it was the French, they could murder her also. She would not have cared.

But it wasn't the French. It was a tall man wearing a dark coat, nondescript fitted breeches, and dusty boots, with a hat pulled low. She watched, no longer afraid, no longer even really interested, as he dismounted in the ruins of the courtyard of what had once been a splendid hacienda, and came slowly toward her. When he reached the pile of rock she sat upon, he'd crouched down and looked into her eyes.

She'd seen something in those green-gold depths that

pierced through her shock. An intensity, a resolve, and a compassion that still glittered with anger.

Then he reached out and gently touched her cheek and she knew—she *knew*—the anger was on her behalf.

It flickered something to life within her cold apathy. In the following days he'd coaxed her to eat and finally to speak, and at night, when she screamed in her sleep, he'd held her quaking body. Never, not once, did he offer any platitudes that everything was going to be fine. Michael wasn't one to give meaningless sympathy. He knew her life had been altered forever and he was pragmatic in the extreme. She had no money, no family, no home. She had *nothing*.

But as the hatred stirred inside her, he offered something wonderful. With her sheltered background as a genteel Spanish lady, she hadn't considered that she had any power, much less this gift.

Revenge.

It had kept her alive.

"May I ask just what all *that* was about?"

The quiet voice made her turn, a slow smile curving her lips. It was *him*. How long had she stood there, recalling the past . . . their past? She didn't think much time had gone by since he'd hurried off with his little wife. Very sweetly she said, "I am not allowed to make the acquaintance of the marchioness? After all, you introduced us."

Michael glanced around in a quick, assessing sweep of the darkened gardens, his gaze flicking over the shadows, his vigilance evident. "You were in the receiving line at our wedding reception. Did I have a choice?"

"I thought you were dancing with her." Antonia leaned backward a little, the stone railing at her back. "It was rather touching to see your husbandly devotion."

He was apparently satisfied there was no threat, for he transferred his attention to her face. "The waltz ended. She is now dancing with Lord Pearson. Please answer my question, Antonia."

"I was merely being pleasant."

"Were you, now?" Elegant in tailored evening wear that suited his lean build, he sounded skeptical. "Please remember, I know you quite well. That's not even a convincing lie. You can do better."

"Perhaps. I learned from the best." Antonia's smile was brittle. "Tell me, how often do you offer her falsehoods? Or I suppose an easier question would be, how often do you tell her the truth?"

Something flickered across his face. Frustration, maybe. Regret? No, not Michael; he couldn't afford regret. "How I deal with my wife is none of your concern. Given our circumstances, I think you should keep your distance."

"Our circumstances? Do you mean because I work for you or because we once shared a bed?" She prodded him deliberately. "Both concepts would shock Miss Innocence, I suspect."

Antagonizing Michael was never a wise idea.

He glanced away for a moment, his profile remote and stern, and when he turned back, the set of his mouth implacable. "I envy her that innocence. I am sure you do also. I would give yours back to you if I could, but it is out of my hands. It was ripped from you before we even met."

Michael had the disturbing habit of being able to touch her conscience. Just when she was convinced she no longer had one, he dragged it from its slumber and nudged it awake. Antonia flicked open her fan, snapped it closed, and then let out a ragged sigh of surrender. "I'm merely watching out for her. I intend no harm. If I wanted to disenchant her over your nefarious past, I could have done so already. Don't be so suspicious."

He still was. It was there in his eyes. "Fitzhugh is watching her."

"A woman would be more effective," she argued.

To her surprise, he hesitated and then admitted, "You

are right, but I need someone I trust, and I assumed you weren't interested in the task."

"Because I'm jealous?" She said the words delicately. "Hmm. If I were any other woman, perhaps. Oh, I *am* jealous, it's true, but don't forget, I want Roget more than you do. I want to carve out his heart and hold it, still beating, before him in the palm of my hand. To that end, I would gladly guard your bride in case one of his men comes after her. If I capture an assailant, trust me, he will talk or lose his ballocks." She added, "One by one."

A look of horror crossed Michael's face and he gave a choked laugh. "You are, as always, very fierce, *senora*. I hope we always remain on the same side."

"I will guard her, then?" Antonia tried not to question her perverse need to get to know this young woman who had what she wanted so much.

Or *did* Julianne Hepburn have him?

Only in name. In duty. In obligation.

In truth, she thought neither of them had him. Maybe they were more sisters than adversaries.

"If you wish the duty, then yes. I would be grateful." Michael's expression was inscrutable.

Antonia stepped forward and asked in a husky tone, "How grateful?"

"I'd better go back inside," he said, his voice even as he ignored the insinuation. "Keep me informed."

With mixed feelings, Antonia watched him slip back into the ballroom. In a way she'd won, because she could now freely court the Marchioness of Longhaven with Michael's permission.

She'd lost too, because he'd walked away.

In her experience, he always did.

Chapter Ten

The carriage rattled along, and Julianne watched the man across from her from under the fringe of her lashes, trying to not seem as if she were studying him like one might analyze an exhibition in an art gallery.

What would the display be called? *Lessons in an Inscrutable Man?*

An apt analogy in many ways. His expression changed about as much as a painted facade on a canvas. Michael merely sat there, obviously deep in thought, his face averted just enough that she could see the clean line of his profile. As usual, he looked remote and it was also reflected in the way he sat against the squabs, his lean body seemingly relaxed, those long legs carelessly crossed at the ankle.

But it was a deception. There was nothing relaxed about him. Whether he wished it or not, and she had a feeling he didn't wish it at all, Julianne was beginning to know certain things about her handsome husband. One of them was the more detached he became, the more involved he really was in the situation.

At the moment, he seemed very, very distant.

Lady Taylor was the culprit. However good Michael might be at controlling his expression, Antonia Taylor was not. At the ball, the woman had looked at him in a singular way that really left little doubt as to her feelings.

And Julianne had no idea how to deal with it, or if she even had the right to say anything. Men of her class were largely able to do as they pleased. It was clear Michael didn't want to acknowledge anything but a passing acquaintance with the lovely Spaniard, but there was obviously something more there.

How much was the real question.

Was she jealous? Julianne wasn't sure. Their marriage was based on their parents' dictates, not personal choice, but for her anyway, it was impossible to separate the passion and intimacy they shared from her emotions. They were lovers in the physical sense, but he did his best to make sure that was the extent of it. Was Lady Taylor the reason?

On the other hand, he had come over and whisked her away, and she found that a small satisfaction. He cared a little what she thought anyway.

"Lady Taylor is quite charming," she said, testing the waters, adjusting her skirt in a casual manner as if the comment was offhand.

"Yes."

"It's clear the two of you are very well acquainted."

"Is it?" His response was noncommittal.

Of course it was. She was just disinclined to allow him to get away with it. It wasn't like she'd sought her out. Antonia Taylor had deliberately approached *her*.

"I suppose," she said as if just contemplating it in an abstract way, "the war would lend a certain commonality to even the most disparate of people, wouldn't it? Create friendships where normally perhaps there would be none?"

"Are we in a philosophical mood this evening?" His

smile didn't quite reach his eyes. Those hazel depths were instead . . . watchful? No. Perhaps *wary* was a better word. That was natural enough, she guessed. Any man might be wary when questioned by his wife about a former mistress.

He and the vibrant Lady Taylor were lovers once—and maybe even still enjoyed that relationship. Julianne knew it with a growing conviction and dismay. She had no desire to share her husband. Was it over between them?

"I am not so much philosophical as I am puzzled." She deliberately made a statement where he would have to ask a question in response.

Michael, of course, didn't cooperate. "We are all puzzled from time to time. It's an irritating fact of life."

What was irritating was his ability to be equivocal. Julianne battled the urge to simply ask him outright about his paramour, and won only with supreme self-control. She wasn't good at playing games. In her world, if she had a question, she just asked it. "I'm sure you're right," she murmured, turning to look at the very uninteresting view of the curtain drawn over the window of the carriage.

If he sensed her withdrawal and unease, he gave no sign of it. When they reached the ducal mansion, he escorted her inside with his usual detached courtesy. Once in her room she let her maid assist her out of her elegant gown and quickly dismissed the young woman, going about the business of brushing her hair and otherwise readying for bed, but in truth listening for the telltale sound of the door opening between her and Michael's room.

It didn't.

She sat and waited, watching the ormolu clock on the polished Italian marble mantel tick away the hour. Though she hardly relished the idea of being caught eavesdropping, she even tiptoed to the door eventually and listened for sounds of her husband speaking to Fitzhugh.

Silence.

Finally she got up the nerve to actually open the door on her own, only to find the bedroom quite empty. The impersonal, undecorated walls; the huge carved bed; the expanse of the expensive rug—all were familiar, but her groom seemed to be missing. Even his loyal valet was nowhere in sight. There was no sign of Fitzhugh anywhere.

Michael had changed out of his evening clothes. The neatly tied cravat he'd worn earlier was tossed carelessly over the back of a wing chair by the fireplace, his jacket on the bed. Emboldened by the absence of anyone who could see her, she walked in, leaving the door ajar.

It was possible he was downstairs in his father's study, or maybe had decided on a stroll in the gardens around the mansion, but she doubted it. Instinct told her he'd changed his evening clothes and gone out. Since the fastidious Fitzhugh wouldn't normally leave his master's clothes lying about, it seemed likely he might have gone along.

Michael had said nothing about having other plans. While he didn't have to explain himself to her, she still thought it odd he hadn't mentioned he was leaving again.

If she was puzzled before, she was even more so now. Julianne went over and picked up the tailored dark coat Michael had worn earlier. It carried his scent, masculine and spicy. With a guilty look over her shoulder, she dipped her hand into the front pocket. Nothing. Not even a pouch of tobacco or snuffbox or stray coin. Since she had already done the unthinkable and searched one pocket, she went through them all, with the same results. Even his handkerchief was pristine and untouched.

Could the man be *more difficult to know?* She wondered it with frustrated annoyance. She wasn't even privy to his bad habits. If he chewed his nails or tapped his fingers incessantly when he was bored, or even drank too much claret, she hadn't noticed it. Julianne sat down on the bed in her nightdress, the jacket still in her hands, and stared at the empty fireplace. What she needed was more information.

And a plan.

Michael was too guarded. He would never tell her anything. He didn't *want* to reveal anything about himself. It hurt to acknowledge it, but the conviction had grown that she was right. He claimed to be a private person, and from what little she knew so far, she agreed. But the real question was this: was it innate and unchangeable, or calculated?

She didn't know.

If it was the former, it put her in the depressing position of being married to a man who might keep himself from her for the rest of their lives. If it was the latter, it meant she had to find out why he had built such formidable defenses.

Generals won battles between great armies, but it took strategy. Having a larger force didn't necessarily mean victory. Surely one woman could breach the defenses of her husband if she approached it the right way?

Fatigue and frustration made her lie back for a moment against the luxurious pillows, discreetly monogrammed with the Hepburn family crest. She clutched her husband's velvet coat in her arms, her mind a blank when it came to the issue of how to handle her vexing—at least to her—situation, and tried to define her options.

On the positive side, he was polite to a fault, a considerate lover, and most definitely generous when it came to how he provided monetary support, such as her allowance.

On the negative side, he was purposely distant, secretive, and, for all she knew, at the moment in the bed of the exotic and unpredictable Lady Taylor. She'd seen him leave the ballroom and when he returned, Lady Taylor strolled back in not long after. They'd met out on the terrace. She had no doubt in her mind.

Where is he now? With her?

To her chagrin hot tears pricked Julianne's lids. The sensation startled her, for while she didn't think it was unnatural for her to resent the idea of her husband having a mistress, she didn't expect to cry over it.

It was unsettling to think her feelings might be engaged. It wasn't like she loved him.

Was it?

The only time Julianne felt like there was anything real in her marriage was when he held her close and she experienced the careful seduction of his kiss and touch. If it was an act, it was well orchestrated, but the real man was elusive. Falling in love with Michael Hepburn would be a foolish thing to do.

The bed was comfortable, the hour late, the lighting low.

She was immersed in a mystery. It was her last thought as she felt herself drift away.

Chapter Eleven

He hadn't expected success on his midnight quest, which was just as well, because he hadn't found it either. Someone was toying with him. Offering little tidbits of information that proved to be entirely too vague, leading him on. Michael opened the door to his bedroom, his thoughts still occupied by the perfidious Roget, and stopped dead on the threshold.

Though he had in the past been greeted by a variety of women who waited in his bed for a myriad of reasons, he couldn't recall ever being so surprised.

It was the nature of the picture, symbolic in a way that froze him to where he stood, and not so much what it represented, but maybe—God help him—what he *wished* for it to represent.

Julianne was on her side, so the enticing curve of her bottom was visible through a virginal nightdress of fine lawn, the gleaming cape of her hair spilling across her porcelain cheek and bared shoulders. She looked lovely and very young, his evening jacket nestled against her breasts in her clasped arms as she slept.

All he could comprehend, all he could think of, was that she slumbered with his coat in her grasp, as if it were something precious.

Arrested, riveted, he stood there, wondering if there was anything she could have said, anything she could have done, that would have made such a visual and emotional impact.

He—he who had literally saved his life in the past by his lightning reaction to difficult situations—was rendered impotent to know how to handle this. Disarmed by one innocent young woman who now happened to be his wife.

Eventually he moved into the room and sat down to pull off and discard his boots, glad he'd told Fitzhugh he wouldn't need him further that evening. The sight of his beautiful wife in his bed was his alone, and besides, the Irishman had already made more than one comment about Julianne's possible effect on his judgment. All in all, he thought he was doing a good job keeping a detached attitude toward his marriage, but at this moment he was off balance.

What he *should* do was pick her up and carry her back to her room and tuck her safely in her own bed. It would be dawn in just a few hours, and though he had learned throughout his time in Spain to function on almost no sleep at all, he had also learned that snatching the opportunity to rest if it was available was a good idea.

But, his hardening cock argued, waking his innocently alluring wife in the most pleasurable way possible was an even better option.

Indecisive, he sat there, restive, his shirt half buttoned, his moody gaze fastened on her slender form. Was this a seduction and he the quarry? If he made love to her, it was an affirmation she had some measure of control over his actions.

That was his one absolute rule: keep the upper hand always.

If I just sleep in the chair, I won't have to touch her,

he brooded, distrustful of his ability to resist temptation once she was in his arms. God knew he'd slept in less comfortable places.

Had she not stirred then, he might have even stayed where he was. But she sighed and turned over to face him, her soft lips parting, the material of her nightdress molded to the fullness of her breasts. Through the thin fabric he could see the faint pink of her nipples and a hint of tantalizing shadow at the apex of her thighs.

Suddenly he was on his feet, his half sprawl in the chair abandoned. *Why not,* he told himself as he jerked the hem of his shirt from his breeches and shrugged out of the garment. She was his *wife.* Moreover, one of the reasons he'd married was to continue the Hepburn family line, and there was only one way to accomplish that mission.

His breeches hit the floor. Naked and fully aroused now, Michael eased onto the bed. He began by running his fingers through her tumbled hair, the silky strands soft and warm. Long lashes fluttered as he skimmed the arch of a fine brow with a fingertip.

He'd already discovered that she looked entrancing when she woke. There was something remarkably intimate in the moment as a person passed from sleep to consciousness; the gentle gasp of breath, the languid movement of a hand, the subtle change in posture. When Julianne fully opened her eyes and recognition of his presence dawned in those blue depths, he deliberately took his jacket from the now lax circle of her arms and tossed it on the floor. Fitzhugh would have an apoplexy in the morning to find the expensive garment in a wrinkled heap, but Michael didn't care at the moment.

"My apologies for waking you. Let me see if I can persuade you to forgive me." He reached for the ribbon on the bodice of Julianne's nightdress. When the cloth parted, his hand slid inside, cradling a firm breast. The resilient, warm weight of it was perfect, beguiling, and his thumb lazily circled the crest.

She shivered and her body reacted, the nipple hardening into a tight bud under the light caress. "I . . . I didn't mean to . . . oh . . ."

He cut off what he imagined to be a stammered explanation for her uninvited presence in his room by brushing aside the material of her open nightdress and lowering his head to suckle the other nipple into a similar taut peak. Kneading, licking, he lavished attention on both her beautiful breasts until she arched against him and her hands urgently caught his shoulders.

"You like this," he murmured against her fragrant skin.

"Yes." There was still shyness in the whispered admission, but something else also—a womanly acknowledgment of receptive awareness that her enjoyment fueled his own.

In fact, he was on fire.

And from the look in her eyes, she knew it.

Though he usually had more finesse, the time spent sitting in the chair, musing over what he was going to do, had taken its toll on his control. Michael shifted, pushing up the skirt of her night rail to her waist, his hand trailing the inner side of her slim thigh until it found dampness and heat. He slipped a finger inside her, gratified to find her wet and ready so quickly.

"Michael." She breathed the word, her cheeks flushed. She trembled, and he wanted to tremble with her.

He didn't respond and instead withdrew his hand, nudged her legs apart, and entered her in one swift, hungry thrust.

That quickly. Without the usual preliminaries of soft kisses and prolonged foreplay. Without calculated seduction to make sure she was panting and eager and wanted him with equal fervor. He hadn't even fully undressed her, but as he sank deep into paradise, he didn't care. Neither did she, he discovered, if her response to such impetuous carnal possession was an indication of her feelings. Her hips lifted into each long stroke of his hard cock, her eyes heavy lidded and half closed, her bared breasts quivering as he drove into her body. Again and again.

Sublime, he thought with incoherent appreciation of the ecstasy flooding his senses. She was so tight, so liquid around his penetration, so gloriously female in her dishabille beneath him. Julianne's hand pressed the base of his spine, drawing him closer, and he gave her what she wanted—what they both wanted—chest to breast, their bodies moving in a feverish rhythm.

He hoped it would happen for her first but wasn't sure he could hold out until it did—a rarity in his experience. When Julianne gave a choked sob and her inner muscles clenched, he uttered a blasphemous prayer of gratitude and welcomed his own explosive release.

Barely sensible enough to keep his weight balanced so he wouldn't crush her, Michael let his forehead rest against the bedding as he struggled for breath. Her lustrous hair tickled his nose, soft and sweet smelling.

I've just fucked her, he realized with a small frisson of what could be chagrin. She was a refined lady, well-bred, new to passion, and he'd lifted her skirt and taken her without so much as a kiss. He was surprised she'd even climaxed, because he'd done little to urge her to that sexual peak.

There was nothing he hated more than apologies.

Well, that wasn't true. He intensely disliked unpredictable behavior, especially when it was his own.

For instance, like what just happened.

Julianne trailed her fingers along her husband's neck in a tentative caress. In contrast with the hard muscles, his thick hair brushed her skin in silky curls.

It had been startling to wake to him, naked and aroused, looming over her, but in a very, very pleasant way, she decided, the intoxicating sensation of his hard, long length still pulsing inside her.

Maybe she'd just won some sort of victory. A part of

her worried he might resent her foray into his bedroom without a specific invitation. In her defense, she hadn't meant to fall asleep on his bed, but from his reaction, he hadn't minded.

Or did he?

Michael hadn't moved or spoken in the aftermath of his uncharacteristically reckless lovemaking. The intimacy of their joined bodies didn't make her privy to his thoughts either—if, she thought, anyone ever was cognizant of what he was thinking.

He finally lifted his head, a rueful look on his face. "Tell me I wasn't too impatient."

She smiled. "I'm quite well, I assure you."

"I didn't hurt you?"

"No. Did I seem uncomfortable in any way?" Julianne lifted her brows a fraction, his muscled strength still something she found uniquely exciting. In his arms she felt dwarfed by his much larger frame, yet protected rather than afraid. The idea of him ever hurting her wasn't one she'd considered. He might be inscrutable in many ways, but she knew that much about him.

Michael smiled then, with a genuine flash of humor she saw far too rarely. "No, now that I think back on it, maybe my concern is for nothing."

She felt a twinge of loss when he moved, sliding free and rolling to his back. In the filtered moonlight coming through the window, his skin had a faint sheen of perspiration and one bicep bulged when he bent his arm and put his hand behind his head. The long, dark evidence of the wound she'd noticed on their wedding night was vivid, without any bandages now, a jagged line across his ribs.

He might be a titled gentleman from one of the wealthiest families in England, but when they were like this, with him naked and reclining next to her, it was evident he had the honed body of warrior and the scars to go along with it. Besides the recent injury, the most significant were a silvery puckered scar on his left thigh, at least seven or eight inches long, and a small, round reminder of a gunshot to his right shoulder.

Even more interesting were several puckered marks, red and shiny, that looked like burns on his abdomen.

"London must be tame after the rigors of war." She spoke the thought out loud before she really considered if she should say it.

Eyes half closed, Michael didn't move, but she sensed a slight, sudden tension in his muscles. "I take it some of my less than attractive souvenirs from Spain inspired that observation. I never really considered if the scars might repulse you. If so, my apologies. But take my word, I didn't acquire them gladly."

"They don't repulse me," she answered truthfully. She was in utter disarray, with her nightdress bunched above her thighs and her bodice unfastened, but too deliciously sated to care. "I think it is more that I am reminded how much I don't know about you."

"We will learn about each other as time passes."

He was an expert at making innocuous observations that were no indication of his emotions. "I hope so," she said softly, shifting a little so she could see his face better. The sculpted planes and angles gave little hint of what he was thinking.

"I know a few things." It was a reckless statement, but she was feeling adventurous after the way he'd awakened her. If she had stayed meekly in her room, she'd still be sleeping, alone and bereft.

Michael elevated a brow. "Do you?"

"You dislike most kinds of fish, with the exception of sole, I am going to guess, for you ate that the other evening at dinner. Neither do you have a great affection for sweets, but usually choose something plain instead or decline dessert. You never sleep past dawn, and the slightest sound wakes you instantly. If there is music playing you give the appearance of enjoying it, but I think most of it bores you, with the exception of Bach's more complicated pieces." Julianne paused, wondering if it was wise to venture further. "You didn't want to marry me, but sense of duty is one of the things that drives you, and, in truth, you are doing your best to recompense your brother's loss to your parents."

She had his attention. He hadn't moved, but she could tell she had it. After a moment, he said dryly, "You are very observant, apparently. Most of what you just said is accurate."

"Oh? Where did I go wrong?"

"I very much like Scottish salmon, if properly prepared." Her husband's hazel eyes glittered as he gave her a long, considering look.

"I will make a note of it," Julianne said lightly.

"I had no idea I was so interesting."

"Then perhaps you don't understand women, my lord. You are my husband. Of course I find you interesting." A small smile curved her mouth, and she was well aware of her exposed body and the glistening rivulets of his sexual discharge on her thighs. Whatever power she had in her marriage was in the bedroom. She wanted more— not *from* him so much as *with* him—but this seemed the only venue where she could capture it.

For now. If she could do it, she wanted to change that.

"I have never pretended to understand women." Michael said the words with amused sarcasm. "It is my opinion few men do, and furthermore, it wasn't ever meant to be that we should."

He hadn't denied that he didn't want to marry her. It stung a little, but why, she wasn't sure. She'd known it all along. Julianne hadn't really wanted to marry him either.

But now, for all of his distance, she was glad she had. Was it too much to want him to feel the same way?

"In turn," she said with slow, combative emphasis, "men also frustrate us. Part of it is your inability to discuss anything vaguely bordering on emotional attachment."

"If you want emotional, I admit I am hardly an expert." He moved suddenly enough that she gasped as he rolled on top of her again. "Guilty as charged, my lady. But if you want physical, I am more than willing. I think we'll go more slowly this time."

His kiss was deep, wickedly seductive, and robbed Julianne completely of coherent thought. This time he slowly stripped off her nightdress and wooed her body with practiced caresses and tender touches, and when he settled between her legs again, the sleek power of his penetration drew a long, quivering sigh from deep in her lungs.

She knew something else about him, she realized, drowning in rapturous sensation. He liked to cut short personal discussions in a very distracting, pleasurable way.

It had been three days since he'd seen the sun and it was still the most excruciating part of the rescue, when he'd been unable to open his eyes against the glare of a Spanish midday. Too weak to do more than barely manage to swallow, the cool water trickled against parched lips. He'd been nothing but a mass of bruises and broken bones, and pain had become a religion he worshipped with each breath he took because it meant he was alive.

Alex St. James had been the one to physically lift him and stagger out from the small fort where the French not only stored munitions, but also, apparently, incarcerated their more notorious captives. If it hadn't been for Alex, and also Luke Daudet, who had insisted Wellington spare the men to try to find and free him, he would have been dead.

The British had blown the place to bits after his rescue, so the horrible little cell where they'd held and tortured him was gone. But the memory of it lingered.

Julianne had lightly touched the scars on his abdomen where a particularly sadistic French colonel had tried to extract from him the name of which one of his officers had stolen a set of battle plans that had been found on Michael's person when he was captured.

Michael had politely refused. The rest of it he only barely remembered, and for that he was grateful. It wasn't so much the pilfered plans that had fallen into his hands, but that the French had been waiting to get a chance at him for most of the war.

Maybe he should have explained to Julianne what happened, but part of him valued her innocence too much to destroy it, so he had made love to her instead.

It had been deeply satisfying, but sleep had never been his friend, and this night was no different.

This morning, rather.

Michael registered the dim glow of the rising sun only in an abstract way, his thoughts completely centered on the woman curled next to him. Julianne slept sweetly, like always, with the peace of the guiltless, one hand under her cheek, her curvaceous body lax, lacy lashes like fans on her delicate cheekbones.

Not that she was completely unworldly.

His delectable little bride was intelligent, and, worse, observant. Earlier that evening he'd known she was curious about Antonia, which was probably his fault for overreacting to the sight of them together. He hadn't responded to Julianne's tentative queries about his relationship with the volatile Senora Taylor, though he'd known that was what she was getting at by her oblique statement that she was puzzled.

Though he wasn't accustomed to explaining himself, maybe he should assure her his relationship with Antonia was not an intimate one. It was the truth, and offering that information freely would be a sign of goodwill between them. He doubted any woman, whether the marriage was arranged or not, liked the idea of her husband being unfaithful, especially if just recently wed.

He certainly would never allow Julianne to take a lover.

Where the devil did that possessive thought come from?

Perhaps it was just that he was tired and physically sated, and her tempting person was currently soft and warm in his arms.

The mixed feelings he had about Antonia offering her protection to his wife were compounded by the lack of intelligence available about his old enemy. Had it not been for the two attempts on his life, he might discount the rumor of Roget's return. With Julianne as a factor, he couldn't afford to be less than meticulously careful until he had some solid information.

She was a weakness. A liability he'd never had in the past. In clear, rational thought he'd known that having a wife would be a disadvantage, for she was the easiest target for revenge or leverage in the dangerous games he played, but he hadn't really realized how much.

Julianne was no longer an abstract concept. Something foisted on him by guilt and a need to assuage his parents' grief.

The woman sleeping in his bed was symbolic of change in his life.

Whether he wanted it or not.

He brushed a stray curl from her cheek with one finger, marveling at the smoothness of her skin. It was a surprise to him, but maybe he did want it.

Chapter Twelve

"What you are telling me, then, monsieur, is that Roget has been active in his own nefarious way in the circles he used to frequent. You are, of course, sure it is him?" Antonia suggestively smiled and swirled the wine in her glass.

The operative nodded, his gaze now and then flicking to her bosom. "Yes, madam. He has the same distinctive voice. I heard it before he was rumored to be dead, and the other night, it was unmistakable."

"Tell me again."

"He suggested there were new plans." The young man licked his lips nervously. "The Marquess of Longhaven was mentioned. It caught my attention. When I started listening in earnest, I realized who was speaking."

So few people knew Michael's true role in the English government, it smacked of a lie. Antonia leaned forward just enough. "So," she purred, "you came to me. Why?"

"Your relationship with the marquess is well-known."

No, it wasn't. That is, unless you were in just the right circles. Roget knew, the bastard.

So his men knew. There was always the chance this youth was a double agent, sent by Roget himself to lead them into some sort of trap.

The hair lifted just slightly along the nape of her neck and she adjusted her elbow-length glove in a languid movement. "What is in this for you?"

"Let us just say my employer would prefer the marquess stay alive. He sent me."

"Who?"

"I am not at liberty to divulge his identity, madam."

Charles Peyton would be her guess, if this was a legitimate English agent. The man had a longer reach than the king himself and certainly he had used Michael's considerable skills to his advantage.

Her visitor leaned forward, wispy, fair hair framing a long, narrow face. His voice was low. "Roget is more than dangerous. If he is the one trying to kill the marquess, my superiors would like for Longhaven to deal with the situation as soon as possible."

"Why not visit the marquess yourself?" Antonia eyed him with cool suspicion.

"The French watch him. Forgive me, but you are not quite as important." The young man shrugged and rose to his feet, giving her a small polite bow. He was dressed like a member of one of the affluent lower classes, well but without ostentation. "The ducal household also is run in such a fashion that a lowly silk merchant wouldn't call and ask for the marquess himself and expect an audience. You live more simply and are more accessible."

There was just the slightest hint of innuendo in the last word, and she'd seen how he'd looked at her. In truth, he was attractive, young, and no doubt virile, but Lawrence would skewer the man if she as much as looked sideways at him, and she had no desire for a murder in her household. Instead, she rose and offered her hand with a composed smile. "I will pass on the information. What Longhaven does with it is up to him. He is very much his own man."

After he was gone, she sank back down in a brocade-covered chair and brooded at her half-empty glass. It was only a few moments before Lawrence joined her, uninvited but not unwelcome. She needed to think out loud. It was interesting, for while the two men were worlds apart in their place in society, Lawrence, in his own way, was every bit as confident and astute as Michael.

The mystery of his past intrigued her, but though she'd tried several times, he refused to speak of it with such cold withdrawal that she understood and let the subject drop at once. She knew all too well life could hand a person bitter experiences best not revisited.

"What the devil did your visitor want?" In midafternoon Lawrence wore a white, full-sleeved shirt, fawn breeches, and unpolished boots. Instead of taking a chair, he went and stood by the sideboard, pouring himself some claret. "Not to sell you cloth for new gowns, I'm going to guess. If he is a silk merchant, I'm a Catholic nun."

She eyed the width of his shoulders and his imposing height, plus the cynical gleam in his dark eyes, and laughed. "I think God might take issue with the depth of your devotion, and I'm not sure the uniform would suit you."

"He must take issue with my faith," Lawrence agreed, sipping from his glass. "He has tested it often enough. Now, then, what did our devious friend have to say?"

"Friend? Do you know him?" Antonia quirked a brow in inquiry.

"I know his kind. I am ever amazed any of us can fool each other. He had that careful way about him, and when he asked for you, I sensed it had nothing to do with textiles."

She laughed again, but it wasn't inspired by mirth. "Spies know spies, is that it? Let us all hope it isn't true, though I have never really considered myself in that category."

Lawrence lifted his glass to his mouth and asked casually over the rim, "What are you, then?"

But there was nothing casual in the intent look in his eyes.

"An instrument of justice in whatever form it might take," she answered smoothly, the memory of the atrocities visited on her family in Spain no longer fresh, but still half healed over, leaving a gnawing ache in the background that she feared would never go away. "As you know, I have been, when necessary, an assassin. Roget is certainly a black spot that needs to be obliterated. It will be my pleasure."

"Your pretend silk merchant came about Roget?" Lawrence halted in the act of lowering his glass from his mouth, his gaze riveted on her face.

"It seems more and more likely he is in London."

He swore under his breath, softly enough that she didn't catch the words, but the sentiment was clear enough from his expression. She didn't blame him. The bastard had been a thorn in their side the entirety of the war. To eliminate him would be a pleasure she had been looking forward to for years now.

"Let the marquess handle this matter, Antonia."

"Of course." She smiled and reclined against the back of the chair, aware that her low-cut gown showcased her breasts in a tantalizing manner. "But, if in the course of keeping an eye out for his naive little bride, should I stumble across Roget myself, well . . . that would be fate, would it not?"

"I still have a hard time believing Longhaven agreed to your plan to shadow his wife."

"He knows my *capabilities*."

The heavy innuendo irritated Lawrence, as she'd known it would. Antonia regarded him with a heavy-lidded gaze, aware she pricked his jealousy on purpose, but not sure of her motives. Lawrence made no secret of his desire for her, yet she tested him constantly. Part of it was probably her past, experience being a bitter pill to swallow. Through no fault of their own, her parents and then her kindly husband had left her by dying. Michael, whom she loved, had married someone else.

Lawrence might also walk away. It was frightening to realize how much she'd come to depend on him always being there, always being ready to defend her, and worrying over her welfare.

She simply was not comfortable with such weakness.

"I'll take the message." Lawrence's scarred face held the hint of a scowl, his glass looking absurdly delicate in the grip of his long, powerful fingers. "You barely slept last night. I think a nap this afternoon would help refresh you before the festivities this evening."

"How do you know how I slept?" It rankled that he hadn't come to her, but she was hardly going to admit it.

"I know everything about you," Lawrence said softly, "whether I occupy your bed or not. For instance, you are right now wondering why I didn't approach you last night."

Antonia started to disdainfully deny it, but he interrupted.

"And you were restless without me," he added, with irritating accuracy, before she could speak.

She had been, damn him, and though she'd all but ordered him to join her in her bedchamber, he had never made an appearance. "I slept quite well. Thank you."

"Liar. You've been sulking all morning." His mouth quirked at the corner. "It gives me hope. I rather wondered what you'd do if I declined your charming offer."

She flushed, and that was a rare thing indeed. Maidenly blushes were for other women and she hadn't been a maiden in quite some time. It was true, maybe she had been a little brash upon her return from the ball. It was partly too much champagne, partly a sense of triumph—mixed with an equal measure of despair—over her discussion with Michael.

He'd danced with his pretty wife, and Julianne Hepburn had gazed at her husband with a particular expression that Antonia recognized all too well. She was already under his spell, but that probably wasn't all that surprising. Did men realize that the trust needed for a woman to give herself to a lover was as great a gift as the lovemaking itself? Where women trust, love often follows. Who knew what romantic notions Lady Longhaven might have held about marriage in the first place. She was young and sheltered, and Michael was a very attractive man. Yes, it was inevitable that she would fall in love with him.

It was irksome to realize it had happened already, but Antonia could hardly blame the chit. After all, it had happened to her as well.

"I was in the mood for a little dalliance." Antonia shrugged. "You were conveniently available."

"I'm convenient? How flattering."

Under his dry, amused tone, she sensed she'd hurt him. But his rejection had also affected her, as much as she hated to admit it. "Apparently not too convenient," she said coolly. "I slept alone."

"I am always available, in case it has escaped your notice." Lawrence's tone was modulated and even. "But never to ease your desire for Longhaven. Last night was much like the evening after his wedding. You were thinking of him, not me. I am not just a surrogate cock, ready to service you when you mourn the loss of what you never had in the first place."

Because his words stung, Antonia said hotly, "I've had him, believe me."

"No, my love," Lawrence corrected, "never. Not in the way you desire."

Fury rose at the observation, but just as quickly, it subsided. *He is right,* Antonia realized with morose introspection. Michael had never been hers in the way a man should be bound to a woman.

And Lawrence was right about something else too. She was suddenly quite listless. If she was to pit herself against someone like Roget, she needed to be alert and ready.

Antonia wearily inclined her head. "I agree. You should take the warning to the marquess."

Lawrence murmured, "Very well. I'll give him your regards."

His rival sat in stoic challenge across from the desk, his face impassive. The puckered scar from a previous injury was stark in the slanting afternoon sunlight.

Michael watched Lawrence as he negligently tossed a piece of paper on the desk, but he wasn't fooled. There was nothing nonchalant about his visitor.

"So Roget is truly in England," Michael said with no inflection. "It is nice to know his whereabouts, though I do admit I wish it were elsewhere."

"Preferably interred somewhere in the rocky Spanish soil." Lawrence smiled with a brief flash of white teeth. "We both know the world will be better without his presence. I thought we'd taken care of it."

"Apparently not."

"Apparently."

This was all his responsibility. He'd never had any illusions over it. Michael sat back. "I assume Antonia is intent on finding him."

"Isn't she always?"

"Yes." The emotional Lady Taylor tended to do nothing halfway. "She does realize Roget might be the one who orchestrated the information? We have no idea if it is accurate."

"I agree. If it is a trap, better you or I fall into it." Lawrence didn't dissemble.

"True."

"Then how shall we deal with this?"

"I'll find out from Charles if that was his man who came to see her. Tell me," Michael asked, "has the man you hired to watch me seen anyone else performing the same task?"

There was a brief silence, and then Lawrence laughed. His expression was resigned. "I suppose it was naive of me to think you wouldn't spot him."

There was nothing naive about Lawrence. Michael lifted a brow. "I wondered if it was friendly surveillance or inspired by an enemy, so I did a little investigation of my own. I was relieved to find out he was in your employ. Has he reported anything interesting?"

"Johnson will be crushed to know he failed."

"Forgive me, but his feelings were not uppermost in my thoughts when I realized I was being shadowed. Naturally I took steps. However, I have noticed no one else. Yet the man who visited Antonia says the opposition is watching my house, correct?"

"You cannot be sure Roget has anything to do with it. Pardon my frankness, but as you just pointed out, you have other enemies in this world, my lord. In our line of work, it is inevitable."

That was true enough, but this situation bothered him. "Others do not worry me as much as Roget."

"He is a canny foe, I admit."

Julianne had gone out earlier. Michael picked up a paperweight and twirled it idly in his fingers, glad he'd sent Fitzhugh with her, though he could tell she disliked the restriction of being escorted everywhere by both his valet and her maid. There was safety in numbers, most certainly, besides the fact that Fitzhugh was both capable and a crack shot.

"He has seen only one suspicious thing, my lord." Lawrence looked bland. "It has more to do with Lady Longhaven than yourself, but Johnson reported it just the same, in case it was significant."

The paperweight went still in his fingers. Michael asked sharply, "What?"

"When he lost you one day—and I assume now since you admit you knew someone was tailing you that you purposely foiled his surveillance—he followed her instead to see if maybe your schedules included a mutual destination. Do you know when she goes to meet her friend Lady Melanie, it is a ruse?"

Michael hoped his expression didn't show consternation, but every muscle in his body had tensed. "A ruse in what way?"

"She goes in, briefly greets her friend, and departs in a hired carriage out the back. Her return involves the reverse ploy."

That admittedly gave him pause. "It isn't possible. My valet accompanies her."

"I am telling you only what my man's notations of her activities indicated."

Julianne, deceptive? It didn't follow what he knew of his young wife. Michael sat there, hoping he didn't look as disconcerted as he felt.

Why would she do such a thing? He didn't ask about her schedule, nor dictate her activities, so the subversion was even more disturbing because it wasn't necessary.

Or, the cold logic of his profession pointed out, he just didn't see *why* it would be necessary.

Yet. There always was a reason.

Michael steadied himself, aware of Lawrence's scrutiny. "You and I both know all people have secrets. Since we are discussing Julianne, I am certain hers is innocent enough. But thank you for bringing it to my attention."

"I found it rather interesting." His visitor hesitated, then he stated bluntly, "I am very surprised you agreed to Antonia's plan regarding your wife."

"Do you honestly believe I could stop her?" Michael asked mildly. "When Antonia is intent upon a course of action, it is much better to manage the flood than try to hastily construct a dam to stem the tidal wave."

"True enough." Lawrence sat very still, his heavy-lidded eyes direct. "You understand her better than I gave you credit for, my lord."

Though they worked together and therefore interacted, they had never discussed man-to-man Michael's previous relationship with Lady Taylor, or Lawrence's current one.

Maybe it was time they should.

"I represent to her a tie between now and the past," Michael said slowly, navigating how to begin this conversation with care. "She will realize it in time. She hasn't healed yet. If she lets go of me, she has to let go of her hate and acknowledge the war is over."

"I agree. Do you think she ever will relinquish the battle? After all, you know her well, and I am curious of your opinion."

By nature, Lawrence wasn't humble, so asking the question revealed the answer was valuable to him.

"I don't know." Michael well remembered that shattered woman sitting amid the debris of what had once been her home. "She has a lot to forget, and this is not her country. For Antonia, that is a great deal of compromise and she is not a woman who compromises easily."

"I have noticed that." The other man's smile was thin. "I have run afoul of her Spanish temper more than once. She is hot-blooded, but she is also one of the most courageous women I have ever known."

"We agree there, at least."

"Let me know what you discover about Roget." Lawrence rose, gave a small, mocking bow, and left.

Michael sat thoughtfully, ordering his priorities. Roget first, of course. He'd been after the infamous spy for years. But Roget worked for the French, and Michael was convinced more and more his rival was English, and apparently within his reach.

He should be elated, ready to move, to strike, to end this deadly game at once.

Instead he found himself pondering why his lovely wife would go through such subterfuge as to pretend to visit a friend. It was a distraction he didn't need.

But his specialty was solving little mysteries, after all, and he would solve this one.

Chapter Thirteen

She was getting rather good at evading the vigilant Fitzhugh. This time Julianne went with her mother to tea at the house of a friend, claimed an appointment later at the dressmaker's, and once dropped off, promptly flagged down a cabbie.

Even her husband's valet could not insist on accompanying her when Julianne was out with her mother.

That satisfaction was diminished, as always, by the arrival of the hired hack at the familiar address. It wasn't that she didn't wish to see Chloe. It was more that she always dreaded the inevitable confrontation with Leah.

As she approached the door, she squared her shoulders. For months she'd been dealing with this woman and she could do it again.

Her knock was answered at once, which told her Leah had been watching for her arrival. No surprise there, as the money was the only reason Julianne was allowed to visit in the first place. "It's about time," the other woman said with a husky note of resentment in her voice. "I've been waiting."

"May I come in?" Julianne had the money in her reticule, but she'd already learned to at least hold on to it until she was in Chloe's presence. Once before she'd paid, only to be told Chloe was out with an "aunt." Since Leah claimed to be all alone in this world, the aunt was an unlikely story, but it had taught Julianne to make sure she had at least one foot in the door before she handed over what Leah wanted so desperately. Their relationship could be at best described as symbiotic.

"If your ladyship insists." Leah, attired today in a shabby brown gown with flounces of lace at the bodice, stepped back with deliberate insolence. "As you can see, my butler is on holiday."

So was her maid, if the untidy appearance of the hallway was any indication, though Julianne didn't say so. The dust and general aura of neglect were hardly encouraging. Nor was it a fit environment for a child, in her opinion. Her slippers made noise on the gritty floor, and the air was stale and dank. "Where is Chloe?"

"How's the new marchioness? His lordship givin' you a good time?"

The crudity might have made Julianne blush at one time, but she was used to Leah's resentful barbs. "Where is Chloe?"

"In there," the other woman admitted grudgingly, pointing.

At least after all the months she'd been coming to visit, they finally understood one another. Julianne tentatively went through the door of the parlor and saw the child sitting on the floor, absorbed in a pile of brightly colored painted blocks. Chloe glanced up and didn't smile, but that was too much to expect. But she looked at Julianne with wistful steadiness, her hazel eyes wide with recognition.

The blocks had been from her last visit. This time Julianne had brought a small paper bag of treats, the confections carefully chosen from one of London's finest sweet shops. Not that she trusted Leah to not confiscate the gift immediately, so she would wait until she was alone with the child to give them to her. Julianne said briefly, "I can only stay an hour. Who will care for her after I am gone?"

Leah propped a hip against the doorway, and her smile was unpleasant. "Have to get home to dress up for a fancy ball, do we?"

"Please just answer the question." There was a reason she hadn't handed over the money yet.

"The old woman next door." Leah straightened and jerked her head to the left. "Give me my money and take her there when you have to be off. She knows Mrs. Hopkins well enough."

She. Like the child didn't have a name. Julianne knelt, at the same time taking from her reticule the payment and setting it on the floor. She ignored the other woman as she swooped down and grabbed the money.

How much longer can I do this? Julianne asked herself that question as she looked into Chloe's eyes. Walking away became more difficult with every visit, and now . . . somehow, as a married woman who could imagine having a child of her own soon, the poignancy of the situation was more acute than ever.

It is like any other lie, Julianne thought with a mixture of guilt and sadness. *The longer you keep up the pretense, the more difficult it is to tell the truth.* In this case, the lie wasn't entirely hers, but she wasn't sure others would see it that way.

"Good afternoon, Chloe," she said softly, reaching out to gently touch the toddler's grubby cheek. With disregard for the dirty floor and her muslin skirts, Julianne sat down. "Shall we build a castle like the last time?"

And was rewarded with the smallest nod and a hint of a shy smile.

It was difficult to know if he should be flattered or ashamed of himself that the conversation came to an abrupt halt when he walked into the room. Late-afternoon autumn sunshine poured through the mullioned windows of the informal drawing room, giving warmth to the scattered groupings of chairs and small tables, the setting perfect for an afternoon tea *en famille*. In the act of pouring, his mother stopped, a look of surprise crossing her face. His father also was startled, and Julianne set down a plate with a half-eaten éclair, and reached for her napkin to dab at her mouth, her beautiful eyes questioning.

It was true, he supposed, he did not often join his family for meals, and never—not once since his return from Spain—for tea.

He didn't have time to leisurely sit and sip from a china cup and exchange pleasantries. It was a luxury, and one he couldn't afford.

As a matter of fact, he wasn't quite sure why he had decided to join them now, but he had to admit his wife looked charming in a blue day gown with a spill of cream lace at the elbow-length sleeves and her hair twisted up into a simple knot, with loose strands of silky dark brown hair brushing her graceful neck.

"Rutgers informed me you all were in here. I hope I am not too late," he said pleasantly.

"Of course not," his mother said, a telltale flutter in her voice that made him experience an extreme twinge of guilt for not doing this before. "Michael, we are *delighted*. I was just telling Julianne we don't see enough of you. Please sit down and I will pour."

See enough of him? More likely his mother was apologizing for his usual conspicuous absences to his beautiful bride. He was well aware his parents both wished he would acquire some of Harry's enthusiasm for running the various family holdings. For that matter, he wished he could summon some interest too, but though he met with bankers and solicitors, went through ledgers, and attended to other financial matters, he found it all dry as dust. And, truthfully, since he still had his other duties, he had very little time for it.

Yet this afternoon he found that he didn't wish to wait until later to see his wife, and he wasn't sure whether he found that intriguing or disturbing.

He chose the chair next to Julianne's, his booted feet brushing her skirts as he stretched out his legs, amused to see his arrival had, for whatever reason, brought a becoming blush to her cheeks. Or perhaps he knew exactly the reason, for he guessed she was remembering his reaction to finding her in his bed and their resulting impetuous lovemaking. "I like you in that shade," he murmured spontaneously. "Blue suits you."

Julianne's color deepened, but she also gazed at him as if he were a complete stranger. "Thank you."

Maybe he *was* a complete stranger. He'd certainly tried to be. Oh, he knew her exquisite body, but he'd kept his distance from *her*. Michael leaned forward and accepted a cup from his mother with a polite murmur of thanks.

"I understand from Fitzhugh you met with Liverpool yesterday. What did the prime minister have to say?" His father took a scone from the tea trolley, but he merely set it on his plate.

That was rather incongruous—a duke asking a valet about his son's activities. Maybe Michael's deliberate avoidance of his family was a mistake. The problem was, he still felt Harry's presence, and he was sure they all did. It was odd to think that he, who had seen so much death in war and had lost close comrades, was so haunted by a single ghost.

He'd *married* to please his parents, he quickly excused himself.

And that was not quite working out as planned. Michael watched Julianne take a dainty sip from the porcelain cup in her slender fingers. She moved gracefully, entirely feminine, her lush lashes lowered a little over the deep blue of her eyes. The neckline of her gown was hardly revealing, but it did emphasize the perfect curves of her shapely breasts. Later he would undress her and . . .

"Michael?"

All three of them were looking at him expectantly. "Liverpool," his father prompted, but there might have been a hint of a smile on his mouth.

"The war is over," he offered neutrally. "But there are lingering details to tidy up."

The elusive Roget, a detail? That was an understatement of epic proportions.

"I see." The Duke of Southbrook endured a frown from his wife as he took another scone for himself. "Suitably vague, but true, no doubt. Have I told you yet about Southbrook Manor's new estate manager? I just hired him last week, but he comes highly recommended. You'll want to be there when we go over plans for the spring, of course. I was thinking we'd all go to Kent in a few weeks. Will you be free?"

Not if Roget remained at large, but Michael could hardly delve into that topic. "I hope to be," he murmured, because that was the perfect truth, though he was not personally interested in the planting issues, tenants, and repairs to the enormous country house that had been the seat of the Dukes of Southbrook for centuries.

The conversation then fell to general subjects they could all discuss: the current lists of social events and a few tidbits of gossip. When a footman came in to discreetly remove the tea cart, Michael found himself covertly studying Julianne again.

She looked so artlessly beautiful, in such a simple gown with no jewelry and her hair just caught up in careless curls. "It's a lovely day. Shall we walk in the garden?" he asked, not sure where the suggestion came from, his mood unfamiliar, because, quite frankly, he'd always thought he did not *have* moods. He was calm, even calculating at times, but he lived his life without the undue influence of ungovernable emotion.

In his profession, he couldn't afford to let his personal feelings affect his actions. It was unwise to let the knife blade of vulnerability slide under his skin.

Except maybe that was all changing. It was still unwise—that wasn't different, but his resistance to it wasn't quite as effective as usual.

"I would love to." Julianne rose, her smile brilliant as the sunset. He extended his arm as a measure of courtesy and found the clasp of her fingers on his sleeve did something interesting to his respiration.

Moreover, he was all too aware of his mother watching them exit the room with a certain misty smile on her face.

If his wife hadn't been so tempting and distracting, he would have been more likely to resent his role as surrogate husband, but it vindicated his actions, it gave his parents that joy they'd lost, and . . . Julianne was so temptingly close.

"I am surprised," she murmured as he escorted her down the hallway toward where the main hall opened to the conservatory.

"How so?" he asked, though he knew quite well what she meant.

"What made you decide to have tea with us?"

I wanted to see you.

He didn't say it.

"I enjoy tea." He shrugged and lifted the latch on one of the glass doors and stood back so she could precede him. "Why drink it by myself when I could join you?"

"You never have before." She walked past in a whisper of sweet perfume, the fleeting glance at his face both questioning and tentative.

The nape of her neck fascinated him. He wished it didn't, but as she went through the doorway he followed as if that certain spot on her body was a beacon.

He wanted to press his lips there. To hear the resulting sigh and feel her shiver in response. To have all of the rest that would follow when she was beneath him and he made love to her with slow, wicked persuasion. . . .

And it wasn't even dark yet. *Damnation.*

The air was warm and mellow for autumn, and the sun had begun its inevitable descent, lending the formal gardens a burnished glow. Michael walked with his hands clasped behind him, choosing at random a path to his right.

He needed to ask her about the subterfuge he'd learned of, even though he wasn't positive it was the approach he should take. Why the devil would she pretend to visit a friend or fake a trip to the seamstress?

Where did she go?

Will she lie to me? He would guess her too ingenuous to fool him in any way, because he'd been lied to in almost every way possible and by some truly amoral and convincing adversaries. It was a questionable talent to have, but his skill at detecting untruths was honed to a fine point. "I understand you were out earlier with your mother. Tell me, did you have a pleasant time?"

"Pleasant?" She frowned. "I'm not sure it qualified to be described in that way. Let's say it wasn't a particularly eventful outing, but necessary."

"And the dressmaker? Shall I brace my steward for a bill for a bevy of new gowns?" His smile was deliberately charming to take any edge off the question.

Something flickered in her eyes.

Regret?

Guilt?

"No, my lord. My pin money is more than generous, I assure you."

He had to give her credit for a truthful evasion. He was rather good at those himself, but only when necessary. The question was—why was it necessary? Fitzhugh had reported that Julianne had gone only briefly into the shop after alighting from her mother's carriage, but almost immediately had flagged a passing hack. Unfortunately, due to some sort of accident between an overzealous man driving a phaeton and a hay cart blocking the street, Fitzhugh had lost the vehicle in the melee. When Julianne returned, it had been hours later, and she came on foot, obviously dropped off somewhere nearby.

Michael wasn't necessarily suspicious, just intensely curious.

Well, perhaps he was *a little* suspicious. Surely most nineteen-year-old newly married ladies did not have nefarious secrets, but she was taking pains to make sure Fitzhugh did not accompany her on these little excursions.

Why?

The slanting sun lit her rich hair and lent a golden tone to her creamy skin. Michael weighed his response, wondering if it was just simpler to ask her outright what she was hiding. But even though he was her husband, he wasn't entirely sure he had the right. Legally, yes, she answered to him, but in an ethical sense, it seemed wrong. After all, she had never questioned him about his frequent absences and distance.

It was more sensible—and fair—to let it go, he decided, especially since it was merely through chance that Fitzhugh had lost her earlier. Michael would know soon enough where she was going, and while he was puzzled at her deception, at the moment he was more enchanted with her presence at his side.

How odd to think an activity as simple as walking along a garden path with a woman could be so . . . diverting. He changed the subject. "As a child I loved this garden. When we were in London, I spent hours out here, among the paths."

When Julianne glanced over in unconcealed surprise at such a personal revelation, he added dryly, "Yes, I was once a child."

"Though I am younger, I remember," she said after a moment. "You were . . . quiet. Harry was the laughing one. You kept to yourself."

"You are thinking I still do."

"Now you read minds, my lord?"

He slanted a glance toward her. "Since it is true and you are an intelligent woman, it is not such a clever deduction, my dear."

"I suppose not." In turn her smile held a slight mischievous quality. "May I say I am glad you chose to join us, or will it remind you of those endless duties that keep you away and send you directly back into seclusion?"

He wouldn't mind a little seclusion at the moment, but not alone. As he'd just said, he knew every inch of these gardens. His secret spot would be private enough.

Chapter Fourteen

"This way."

Julianne hadn't explored the gardens to any great extent, but then again, she hadn't been a resident at the mansion for a month yet. The English autumn, too, had been wet this year, though this afternoon was gloriously warm and comfortable.

Or was the warmth an inner glow of hope, foolish perhaps, over the fact that Michael had bestirred himself to join them?

And then he'd invited her to walk with him. Surely progress of a sort, wasn't it?

Bemused and compliant, she simply allowed herself to be escorted to what she discovered was a secluded corner, with thick shrubberies around the perimeter. It appeared to be a dead end, but when Michael swept back some low-hanging branches and motioned her through, she stepped into a small walled garden, the square of grass literally cut off from the rest of the path and flower beds by the verdant foliage.

It was lovely, if somewhat overgrown, and on one wall

a spray of cascading white flowers covered the mossy
stones, the delicate petals turning pink from the reflection of the sunset. In the middle of the tiny space a tarnished sundial was half covered in moss, and there was a
stone bench. "What is this?" Julianne turned, delighted
but also astonished.

"Forgotten." Michael seemed taller than ever in the
confined space as he straightened. "Poor planning, I believe, on the part of Gerald, my grandfather's master
gardener, years ago when the gardens were redone. The
shrubberies cut it off from the rest of the path and beds.
I found it one day. It was like my . . . secret. I kept it carefully to myself and dubbed it my own kingdom."

Was there really a whimsical side to him? Julianne
would have never thought so, but his eyes held a glimmer of amusement . . . and maybe even nostalgia. It was
like getting a fascinating glimpse at the boy he'd once
been.

"So you hid here?"

Her husband's mouth quirked wryly. "I rather imagined I was being very mysterious, disappearing for hours,
but I am going to guess our governess eventually must
have followed me, for she stopped scolding and let me
be. Harry, though, never did find this spot, and he was
forever badgering me to tell him where I went."

Even as a child, then, he could keep his secrets.

"I wouldn't have had a notion this was here." Julianne walked toward the beautiful white flowers and
touched a velvety petal. "I don't recognize these. What
are they?"

"I haven't the slightest inclination toward botany, I'm
afraid. The way everything has gone wild, I am going to
guess it is a weed of some kind."

"It's beautiful."

"Beautiful," he agreed.

But his voice had definitely changed. Grown deeper,
with a hint of huskiness, and when she turned, he was
definitely not looking at the flower but gazing at her.

He took a slow step forward. "No one ever comes here. We are quite alone, and, yes, I find you very beautiful, Julianne."

Long fingers touched her chin, tipping her face upward, and he brought his mouth down on hers, effectively stifling her small gasp. The sudden contact of their bodies stirred a treacherous fire inside her even as the rational part of her brain stated emphatically they were *outside*, and the sun might be lowering in the sky, but it was still *light*.

The delicate play of tongue on tongue, the softness of his hair against the back of her hand as she clasped his neck, the strength of his arm as he slid it around her waist and brought her more firmly against him: all of it was made somehow more magical by the gentle whisper of the fluttering leaves above and around them, the silent, peaceful little garden, and the intoxicating scent of blooming flowers. Michael's breath was warm across her cheek as he broke the kiss and whispered in her ear, "I want you."

Held so closely in his embrace, she could tell he was being truthful, but his scandalous suggestion was shocking. "Here?"

"Now." He kissed her again, slow and long, and his fingers were already deftly unfastening her gown. When the garment slid from her shoulders, he stepped back, his smile a wicked gleam, and shed his jacket with impressive speed, spreading it on the overgrown grass as a makeshift blanket before going to work on his shirt. "Take off your shift. I want to watch while I undress."

He really meant it. He wanted to make love to her in this secluded, forgotten little garden.

Though the idea took some getting used to, she found she wasn't adverse to a little adventure, and it was gratifying to know he wanted her. From the bulge in the front of his fitted breeches, he wanted her with a great deal of enthusiasm.

Very well. It fired a wanton side of her she didn't know existed.

First Julianne pulled the pins from her simple chignon. Not only did it let her hair cascade downward in a deliberately seductive movement, but as she raised her arms, it also lifted her breasts under the thin cloth and border of lace of her chemise.

Michael most definitely noticed, his gaze riveted as she delicately tugged at the ribbon on her bodice.

Am I really doing this?

Yes, it appeared she really was. It took some fortitude, but she let the material of her shift drift down her arms, leaving her almost naked.

Her husband also shed his shirt, tossing it aside. He sat down on the small bench to yank off his boots. "Leave your stockings on," he instructed, even as she bent to unfasten her garters. "Do not ask me why, but I like the idea of the stockings and nothing else."

"I'd never ask you why," she said with more candor than usual, because she was empowered by the desire in his remarkable eyes. "It's futile. You keep to yourself quite well, my lord."

"Michael," he said with quiet intensity, and when he stood and caught her in his arms, his kiss betrayed an urgency his words never did. His hands roamed over her body and ignited not just passion, but her soul. Julianne melted into every caress, every touch, and when he lowered her to the blanket of his coat, she watched through half-closed eyes as he peeled off his fitted breeches. In the soft light of day, his arousal seemed somehow more primal, rigid, the erect length swollen and slick, a pearly bead of his discharge already visible.

He lay down beside her and took her hand, and to her surprise, lifted it to his lips in a courtly gesture that was somehow also erotic, his mouth feathering over her fingers in a languorous caress. The sun lent golden highlights to his thick chestnut hair and gilded the muscled contours of his lean body.

"I don't think my schoolboy imagination conjured delectable ladies wearing only these when I hid away in this spot all those years ago." He touched the top of one silk stocking, his finger sliding to her inner thigh. "May I?"

She had no defense for the power of his suggestive smile. Julianne nodded and watched him untie her garter and very slowly, as if he relished the task, slip the silk of her stocking down her leg. He did the same with the other stocking, and after he was done, his hand journeyed back upward in a lazy voyage of exploration and tantalizing discovery. When he stroked between her legs, she closed her eyes and arched at the deft manipulation, a flush tingling her skin. Then he shifted in a fluid movement, settling between her parted thighs, and entered her in one gliding, deep movement.

The breath left her lungs at the possessive penetration, pleasure obliterating the sunlit garden, the softness of his jacket beneath her bare back, the deepening blue of the sky . . .

The response was so powerful, so moving, she wondered at her complete submission even when she sensed it was unwise. It wasn't that he only took—he gave in full measure—but like the young boy years ago, he still hid, keeping some of himself sheltered and separate, and he wasn't going to relinquish it easily.

But he will, she decided, dying in rapture in his arms as he took her body until she shuddered in exquisite pleasure. There amid the fragrance of the crushed grass and blooming flowers and autumn sunset, when they lay panting together, she *knew* he would eventually.

Why the confidence? She wasn't sure. Perhaps the intuition of women was not overrated, because she sensed that even bringing her to this spot was an oblique surrender of sorts. He'd denied Harry this clandestine place, and he'd denied his family, but he had included her.

A poignant triumph.

Hopefully this was just the beginning.

*   *   *

Magic. The setting sun. A glorious nymph in his arms . . .

It seemed a bit surreal.

As a boy he'd used this place to spin dreams. Now as he lay on top of his wife, slightly out of breath, his weight barely balanced, awash in the flux of orgasmic release, Michael reflected that he had certainly found some sort of mystical connection to fate, or whatever it might be labeled.

Something had to have tempted him to lure her into the gardens with the sole purpose of a late-afternoon seduction. It had happened—gloriously so—and Julianne had responded with sweet acquiescence and diverting passion.

The scent of crushed grass mingled with the fragrance of her hair, and his face pressed to where it lay in silky disarray. *This is,* he thought, *where I inevitably fail her.* Tender words should follow the physical union when they were both naked and replete in each other's arms. Before Julianne, he hadn't thought much about it, for his previous lovers had been no more committed than he was, except on the basis of transient pleasure.

He was skilled in some areas, but romantic gestures were not one of them.

With effort, he lifted his head. Her face was rosy, her eyes half shadowed. Speaking first, she said on a breathless laugh, "May I say I find your little secret most . . . delightful?"

"Do you?" He lazily kissed her throat and wondered if she knew she had disconcerted him. Often enough he used physical diversion to keep from deep discussion. "I confess I didn't set out to ravish you when I suggested we walk, but I agree the outcome was delightful indeed."

That was the truth. And this was the second time he'd been so overcome with desire for her that he'd yielded to carnal impulse.

He was never impulsive.

She was . . . so very different.

"I admit that if you'd told me I would find myself naked in broad daylight out of doors, I would not have believed it." She lightly ran her fingers down his spine.

And even though he'd just climaxed, he found the light touch arousing.

Moreover, he actually wished to know what she was thinking. Perhaps it was the sybaritic setting and languid satisfaction of the moment, but he was not only a lover but a *husband*. Having tea with his parents, who had always had a very easy sort of relationship, might have given him a startling insight to married life. . . . Or had it happened when he saw the surprise on Julianne's face when he joined them?

"Tell me what pleased you," he urged, drawing his hand over her breast. It wasn't a subversive caress, though, just a gentle touch as he watched her expression. "You say I keep to myself and I won't argue the point, but compromise is the basis of any treaty, and if you were to consult me, I'd say a marriage is a treaty in the most defined sense of the word. Two very opposite parties coming to terms and forming an alliance."

"You make it sound like we are at war."

He had. Was he so used to thinking in those terms that he even applied it to his marriage? "Maybe it was ill phrased," he equivocated. "All I meant was, men and women often look at the same situation differently."

"I'd guess that's true." She hesitated, but then said, "While this place is lovely, I find it delightful because *you* are here." Her smile was shy and charming, her eyes ingenuous as they met his with complete candor.

Well, almost complete. Like this, with her soft and willing in his arms, he nearly forgot her earlier deception over her whereabouts.

. . . because you are here . . .

What the devil did that mean?

Antonia's words came floating back. *She will fall in love with you. . . .*

"Now, fair is fair," she said quickly, as if to divert his

attention from what she'd just said. "Tell me something I wish to know about you."

"Such as?"

"What is your favorite color?"

The simple request was amusing and yet also endearing. "My favorite color?" he repeated. "I think I expected a much more probing inquiry."

"Did you?" There was a provocative lift in her voice, and her fingers skimmed his back again. "I think you will find wives—or at least yours—might not be very predictable, my lord."

He agreed, especially with the magic of her laugh and his current state of contentment. "Blue," he said, looking into her eyes. "Not the color of a sunny sky on a summer day, but a deeper hue, dark and rich and velvet."

"Very poetic." She didn't miss the reference to the unusual beauty of her eyes. "I suppose that fulfills your promise because it does reveal something of you I didn't know existed."

"I'm intrigued. What does it reveal, my lady?" He traced the line of her collarbone with his finger in a casual movement, but he was acutely tuned in to her response.

"You are confounded by me."

His hand halted, his brows lifting slightly in surprise. He was starting to believe that was true, but he had no idea she realized it.

Lush, disheveled, and more tempting than he guessed she knew, she went on. "You married me for reasons we both understand, because I had no choice but to do the same. Has it ended up being quite as you imagined?"

No. It hadn't. But if he agreed, what would that do to his life? She had a valid point. For one thing, he was naked in the back garden in the late afternoon after coaxing her into an indiscretion. *Out of character* didn't even begin to describe his actions.

"It hasn't for me," she confessed in a small voice.

"Though I admit I worried because Harry was so *easy*, and you are . . . not."

He cleared his throat, still sprawled on top of her luscious body. "It's true. I'm nothing like him."

"And though I would never have thought I'd feel this way, I am glad," Julianne said simply, reaching up to touch his cheek. "You are . . . *you*."

Inexplicably, he was undone, then and there.

He was nothing like his carefree, easygoing, likeable brother, and for the first time in his life, someone was glad.

Chapter Fifteen

The woman seemed to be everywhere. Julianne smiled graciously at the footman who refilled her glass, wondering if it was coincidence or design that Lady Taylor was seated across from her at the dinner table. This evening, her husband's former paramour was stunning in emerald green silk, her dark hair upswept and held in place with a Spanish mantilla that emphasized her exotic beauty.

How can I possibly compete, Julianne wondered, unsettled and undeniably jealous. Michael was conspicuous by his absence, making his excuses at the last minute in a brief note and letting her accompany his parents instead. The sight of the stunning Lady Taylor brought to the forefront a disquieting sense of his pronounced absences.

Was he with *her* when he was gone?

Actually, Julianne tried to remind herself in wry honesty, he couldn't be, because it seemed in the past weeks that if he *didn't* escort her to a social function, Lady Taylor was there instead. If they were trying to make a point about not having an affair, it was well-done, but she had the sense something else might be going on.

First Fitzhugh practically dogging her every step, and now this woman.

It almost felt as if Michael was having her watched.

Why would he? If he knew about her visits to Chloe, surely he would just ask. . . .

"Are you not enjoying the roast lamb, Lady Long-haven?"

The cool question, asked in accented English, jerked Julianne out of her reverie and she glanced up at Antonia Taylor. "It's quite delicious," she answered, though she'd taken only one bite.

"You aren't eating."

"How vigilant of you to notice," Julianne replied, picking up her wine.

The other woman flushed, which was telling. It wasn't much, just a hint of red in her cheeks, but the glint in her eyes said more than anything. "I just wondered if something might be amiss, the way you are picking at your food."

"Not at all." Julianne forced her most gracious smile.

Luckily, the man next to the beauteous Lady Taylor engaged her in conversation then, his avid gaze fastened on her bosom, and Julianne was able to eat—or not. Lady Taylor was right: she was just picking at her meal—until the dessert course was served. The ladies then retired so the gentlemen could enjoy their port.

This time she paid close attention as seats were chosen, their gracious hostess a contemporary of Michael's mother who chattered with animation as they all settled into the drawing room.

Yes, Lady Taylor deliberately maneuvered to a spot next to her, Julianne realized. That was interesting, to say the least. Because of the seating arrangements and the fact that almost all the women were older, she and Lady Taylor ended up relatively alone in one corner of the room, next to each other on a small settee. Julianne endeavored as pleasant an expression as possible. "I understand you and Michael knew each other well in Spain."

"Is that what he said?" The other woman smiled in a way that didn't reach her eyes.

"He didn't say," Julianne answered, taking in the splendor of the Spaniard's glorious coloring and voluptuous form. "If you do know him well, you will agree he rarely expounds on anything, much less his past."

"What makes you think I know him well?" Lady Taylor reclined, graceful and overtly female, against the green-and-cream-striped silk of the settee, her smile genial but her eyes . . . watchful.

Julianne was learning to interpret that look. Michael had it often.

Bluntly, she said, "Because of the way the two of you look at each other." She paused and shook her head. "No, not so. Because of the way you *don't* look at each other."

"Whatever does that mean, Lady Longhaven?"

"You disappoint me," Julianne said after a moment, keeping her voice modulated. "I thought you'd be more honest."

"Como?"

She sat politely, not understanding the word.

"I'm sorry." Lady Taylor sighed. "At times I lapse. I meant I do not understand what you might be insinuating."

"And see, yet I think you do."

Antonia narrowed her eyes. "You are not as innocent as he thinks, are you? You have my admiration. He isn't easy to fool."

"I have no idea what he thinks of me." Julianne wasn't sure if this conversation was wise, but she had, after all, started it. "But perhaps you can tell me. How innocent does he think I am?"

"Speaking for Miguel is never wise." The shrug of Lady Taylor's shoulders was negligent.

Yet the implication was there that her husband had discussed her with his ex-lover, and Julianne found it irritated her, because the implied intimacy of it caused another twinge of unwanted jealousy. That unproductive emotion was no doubt doubly useless in regard to Michael. As coolly as possible, Julianne said, "I am sure you are right."

The ensuing pause was awkward, and Julianne wondered how rude it would be to simply rise and leave the room. Very, she decided. But truly, how polite was she required to be to a woman who clearly either once had, or worse, still did have, a relationship with her husband? It wasn't that she had any solid evidence other than Michael's admission they'd known each other during the war, but that evening when Lady Taylor had approached her at the ball, he had certainly done his best to cut their conversation short.

"I sense I have upset you in some way." Antonia Taylor reached out and lightly touched her arm. "It was not my intention. We are not so far apart in age, and I am still a stranger here in England in many ways. I live in my husband's house, but never with him, for he was killed at Quatre Bras. So close to the end of the war." She shook her head. "A shame. He was a *caballero* . . . a gentleman. But it is so, and I accept it. Yet I could use a friend."

Put that way, it would be churlish to refuse, but Julianne was still a bit skeptical of the other woman's motives. "Of course," she murmured.

"Miguel saved my life." The words fell quietly amid the chatter at the other corners of the room. Dark eyes regarded Julianne with intense directness. "The details are not . . . important, but he and I will always have that between us. Otherwise, we are merely friends."

It was enlightening, but Julianne wasn't sure how to respond. Michael had played knight errant for this beautiful woman.

Lady Taylor went on, "Here in this big city, with your

parties and balls and oh so proper manners, you cannot imagine the atrocities visited upon my country. We were allies, England and Spain, and yet your homeland was not ravaged and overrun." She turned away, and her expression was fierce for a moment. "I do not blame you for not understanding, because I wish *I* did not."

She didn't, Julianne acknowledged silently, because she knew nothing of invading armies or bloody battles or wanton destruction. English history was steeped in the fight to keep the tenuous hold of sovereign rule, but not in her lifetime—at least not on English soil. She was widely read, but not able to directly empathize. "At least it is over," she said inadequately, because how *could* one adequately address the loss of a nation, even if it had been, in the end, regained?

"Spain as I knew it is no more. Do not fool yourself, Lady Longhaven. It *isn't* over."

Taken aback, their conversation so far removed from whatever had the other ladies laughing and whispering, Julianne stared at her companion. "Bonaparte is disposed."

"A war is fought along many fronts. In this case, there is a clear loser, but the cursed Corsican is only one man. He did not take half the world alone. Not all of them have paid for their soulless crimes."

The vehemence of the speech was not lost on Julianne. She sat back, not precisely stunned, but certainly shaken. Was Michael still involved in this ongoing "war"? He certainly seemed to have duties that occupied him almost constantly.

If so, why hadn't he simply told her?

"What, precisely, does my husband do for the Crown?" she asked sharply enough that a few heads turned.

"I have said too much." Antonia Taylor grimaced, and even in that unladylike action she was still compellingly lovely. "Ignore me. When I speak of my native country, I become quite passionate. Now, then, perhaps we should change the subject. Tell me, Lady Longhaven, what do you think of the new display of Italian paintings at the National Gallery?"

Charles Peyton pushed a piece of paper across the desk with a forefinger. His expression was regretful but not apologetic. "I have six names and a possible seventh, taking into consideration many factors, not the least of which is your assumption that Roget is English."

Michael scanned the list. "One of them is yours," he pointed out with wry humor.

"Based on your criteria . . . yes. I fit." Charles sat back behind the table and folded his hands. "Loyal servant of the Crown, privy to the most confidential information. Note I didn't omit Lord Liverpool either. Not sporting of me to leave out such an obvious suspect, is it?"

"The prime minister?"

"Your outrage is unflattering. I would think *my* name would give you more pause."

A muffled laugh escaped Michael's lips, though his only other response was to scan the list again. Then he murmured, "I am surprised at two of them. Only two. What does that say of our profession, Charles? I could believe easily enough any of the other five could be Roget's source of information."

"I won't ask if I am one of the two or one of the five. Anyway, what it says of our profession is that we keep our secrets and do it well, especially if one of us is guilty. How would the rest of us not suspect?"

"Ah, see. There's the trouble." Michael tapped the document. "What am I to do if Roget's accomplice is on this list?"

"Apprehend him. The proof had better be irrefutable, I warn you."

"In theory, that sounds possible. In actuality, I am not so sure."

"My lord, it is your only recourse if you wish this matter settled, and we both know you do."

The little room was in a deserted part of Whitehall,

musty and dark, with a single burning lamp and the chill of fall air giving a dank feel to the square, unappealing space. This wasn't Charles's normal office—Michael had never been to that part of the official building. And maybe it was years of subterfuge, or maybe it was his responsibilities as a marquess, or even his status as a married man, but the intrigue of it all didn't appeal as it once had.

Perhaps he was just tired.

Perhaps it was Julianne. Never before had he entertained the notion of settling into a more sedate life. Not—God help him—the life of a gentleman farmer that his father wished, but a more conventional existence actually held a glimmer of appeal. He would no longer have to worry over her safety, and he couldn't deny the idyllic interlude in the garden the other afternoon could certainly stand a repeat performance. The huge ducal estate in the countryside had a lovely secluded park around it. . . .

"It is possible I will retire after we corner Roget."

"You'll be bored." The chair Charles sat in creaked loudly as he shifted his weight. "And you are quite good at your job. England needs you."

"I didn't want it, but I am now the heir to a dukedom. My *family* needs me."

"I see your lovely young wife is having a predictable effect on your priorities."

The drab room was suddenly oppressive. "Julianne has nothing to do with this decision."

What a lie.

Charles knew it too, and usually Michael could deceive so well.

"I'm a married man," his colleague informed him softly. "Happily so. I have three children, and my wife is the love of my life. I adore her. But, unfortunately, the world is not a perfect place. Were it not for me— and men like you—England might not be a safe place to raise my family. I serve a very distinct purpose and I recognize it. Once, just after I married, like you now, I realized I was no longer risking only my life by choosing my line of work, but the well-being of my family. I respect your reservations, believe me."

"If I wanted a lecture, my father would be most willing to deliver it." Though Michael did his best to interject dry humor into his voice, he didn't quite accomplish it.

"But I'm not your father. Nor am I lecturing. I am pointing out the salient facts as one who knows the challenge you now face."

It wasn't particularly the advice he wanted to hear. "My job is not involved with my personal life."

A soft chuckle followed that declaration. "I think you need to come to terms, my friend, with the realization that your personal situation is going to affect everything you do. You now have a wife, and soon children will follow, and as much as you would like to detach yourself from it, take my word: it contains you. The man who once routinely performed missions hundreds of miles behind enemy lines does not exist any longer."

Perhaps that was true. He considered a moment. "My priority is to handle this as discreetly as possible. How much latitude do I have?"

There was a small clock on a dusty shelf and it ticked loudly as Charles frowned in contemplation. His pale eyes were somber. "A trial would be messy and embarrassing for the British government."

"I'm not an assassin, Charles."

"No, but you know a few. I trust you to, as always, take the appropriate action. I give you carte blanche."

It was about what he expected. Michael nodded and rose to his feet, his smile cynical. "Which essentially means nothing, for if matters were to go awry, you would deny any knowledge of it anyway. Am I correct?"

"Of course." Charles reached for his pipe and tapped it on the table before he dipped into the small tobacco jar. "How perfectly we understand each other."

Chapter Sixteen

It was raining, coming down in cold, thin sheets, the turn in the weather abrupt and making Julianne shiver, even while wrapped in her cloak, as they slogged along muddy roads.

This particular evasion had been more difficult than most. First she'd had to invent a reason to keep Fitzhugh from going with her, which was becoming increasingly difficult. Since telling falsehoods did not come easily, she'd had to resort to having her maid distract her husband's valet. To say she felt guilty was putting it in a mild slant, but she had no idea what else to do.

The situation was becoming more and more of a problem.

The house looked dismal as she pulled up, the gray sides of the structure streaked with moisture, the street a mess of sodden pedestrians and puddles. Julianne alighted, pulling the hood of her cloak up over her head, and ran up the steps.

The first unanswered knocks made her irritated as she

shivered on the stoop. The second sharp series of raps were more urgent, and yet still there was no response.

Leah always wanted her money.

A sense of panic caused her to pound on the door, her heart beginning to thump in her chest.

Nothing. No sound of movement in the house. The windows also, even on this dreary afternoon, were dark.

This had been her fear all along. That Leah would one day take Chloe, disappear, and just leave her . . . bereft. Julianne slammed her fist against the door with even more force until she realized that no one was going to respond.

It couldn't be. Leah needed her. *Needs my money,* her mind corrected at once, and she'd paid so faithfully ever since she had found out about the child . . . .

Through the wet, her hood down, she ran down the sidewalk and around the front of the hired hack. The driver was elderly, sitting patiently, and if he was surprised at a well-dressed lady visiting such an address, he didn't show it.

She didn't care about the clandestine nature of her visits at this crucial point. She was too worried about Chloe. "Please," she said, trying to catch her breath, she was so agitated, "I need your help to get into that house. I'm the Marchioness of Longhaven. My husband will reward you."

Was she allowed to make promises in Michael's name? In this case, she'd have to concern herself with that issue later. She was beginning to truly panic at the moment.

The small man clambered down and dubiously looked at the run-down house, but then assessed her expensive gown and cloak and nodded. "I'll do my best to help ye, madam."

True to his word, he ambled up to the door, tried the knob, and squinted for a moment before he used his fist to make an impressive noise. When that didn't work, he shouted and rattled the knob.

The lack of an answer was frightening.

Perhaps, she told herself, taking in a deep breath, her cloak growing more sodden by the moment, *I am overreacting.* Maybe Leah had simply forgotten their appointment and was out. *Only,* a coldly reasonable voice pointed out with compelling logic, *Leah* never *forgets.* She wanted the money so badly, usually Julianne barely got in the door before she demanded it.

No, something was wrong. She *felt* it.

"I have to get in." If Leah had really moved without a word, her belongings, such as they were, would also be gone. "Do you think you can force it open?"

The old man set his shoulder against the cheap door, but it didn't move. Just her luck.

When he stepped back, she tried, throwing her weight against the panel, but it held. She let out a sob of frustration.

"Can I be of assistance?"

She whirled at the sound of the soft Irish brogue. Fitzhugh stood there, the dripping brim of his hat shadowing familiar features.

Later, Julianne decided, *I will demand to know why he appeared so promptly.* For the moment, she was glad of his solid bulk and familiar, competent air.

"I need to get inside this building."

"Allow me, Lady Longhaven."

Her husband's valet—whom she'd always had a sense might be a great deal more than just someone who pressed his clothes and saw to other small needs—proved to be most helpful. The door creaked, the lock snapped, and Julianne rushed in, brushing past the driver. "Leah?"

There was no answer and the place was cold, just a ghostly drift of old chimney smoke and the hint of stale, long-past meals in the air. With a sinking heart, she bypassed the foyer and checked the shabby drawing room, and then, because it was the last place she'd seen Chloe, the small room off the kitchen.

The house was deserted. It was so obvious, and not because of the empty rooms and the cold, but the utter silence. Not even the rude old charwoman who normally answered the door was in sight. Since Leah was not known for her reliability, maybe Julianne shouldn't be so surprised.

So devastated.

But she was. She'd tried to do good. . . .

"She's not here." Julianne tried to stem the tide of flushed distress, but it was impossible. "I have made such a mistake. Oh, God help me. . . ."

"Who, my lady?" Fitzhugh asked the question somberly as he saw the twin trails of tears now streaming down her face.

"A small child . . . she's this tall." She held her hand near her midthigh. "There's a woman next door . . . perhaps she has her . . ."

Then she heard the sound. It was faint, not even qualifying as a whimper, but it was there. Julianne swung around. "Chloe?"

"It came from there." Fitzhugh was already moving purposefully toward the kitchen.

"I was in there already . . ." Julianne lifted her damp skirts and ran after him, stopping in the dark space, casting around. She said louder, "Chloe?"

Another sound. Tiny, almost inaudible. Julianne followed it, a fateful sense of horror mingled with relief when she pushed open the door to the dank little pantry and saw the small form huddled in the corner. She knelt by the child, unable to believe that even someone as resentful and irresponsible as Leah could possibly leave a child alone in what seemed to be an abandoned house.

"It's Julianne," she whispered, hesitant to gather the little girl into her arms.

"Who left this wee one here?" Fitzhugh asked in a

raspy voice. "Of all the sights I dislike in London, it's the abandoned children I hate the most. But this tiny one, locked in this cold place . . ." He stopped speaking and shook his head.

Huge eyes regarded her with their usual solemn scrutiny, but this time, when Julianne leaned forward, Chloe came to her without a pause, allowing her chilled, trembling body to be lifted, held close. Julianne said clearly, "We're going back to Southbrook. Right now."

"Yes, my lady."

She looked him in the eye. "I suppose we will address later how you appeared so fortuitously."

"Is she injured?" Fitzhugh eyed the child in her arms and ignored her comment. Just as well. She was cold, wet, and in no mood to argue.

"I don't think so." Julianne gazed down at Chloe's wan face. "Hungry, I'd guess, and frightened, but from the way her arms cling to me, she's not been alone for too long. She's still strong."

Was it only a few hours? From how cold it was in the house, Julianne was afraid it might have been longer. Overnight? One terrifying night alone in a deserted building was too much for any child.

Julianne wanted to weep, but she was also joyous, in a curious way. It was over. She was going to have to tell the truth.

What a relief.

The damned attack took him unawares. The bullet caught his sleeve and forearm, tearing through his cloak. Michael instinctively fell—an old soldier's trick—and weighed his options as he rolled into the shadow of a clipped hedge. Already people were shouting, because while many of his acquaintances were sporting men, Mayfair didn't normally echo with the resounding retort of gunfire.

Regardless of the damage to his expensive coat and breeches, he opted to crawl through the shrubbery and try and get a glimpse of his assailant in the driving rain. He was armed, but not with a rifle or pistol.

The assailant was hidden. This was not a casual attack on a well-dressed man for his purse.

Still . . . very careless to attempt the shot in this weather. Not at all like Roget. Michael slid into the shadows and crouched behind a dripping bush, waiting to see a dark figure emerge from the alley across the street. It was almost dusk, and the light was indistinct.

Once you located the enemy, then the game became more even.

This was not the time to sprint across the street in obvious pursuit. In the steady downpour, perhaps his attacker thought he'd hit his target. Michael edged sideways and watched for any movement.

There. A silhouette appeared in the streaming rain, the glint of a pale face showed, and then the figure turned, went still as he obviously realized there was no body on the ground where it should be. Then he ran toward a nearby alley, to be lost in the rain.

Missed, you bastard, Michael thought grimly. Though he was tempted to follow, and normally would have, he wasn't carrying a sidearm.

Curious, that. Usually, he would have followed, wounded or not. But he had a feeling that his days of risking his neck, as he'd told Charles, might be over. In the meantime, he was bleeding, which seemed to be a common occurrence lately. He jerked back his sleeve, cursed, and then got out his handkerchief and did his best to stem the flow of blood. The number of shirts and jackets he was replacing these days would make his tailor a rich man.

A third clumsy attempt . . . this wasn't Roget.

That conclusion was both reassuring—he was still alive because it wasn't Roget—and disappointing. As it all stood, he had no idea who was trying to kill him, and his old enemy was still at large.

"You all right, my lord?" A young footman from a

nearby house dashed up, rain dampening his fitted jacket and hair. His gaze dropped to the bloody handkerchief pressed against Michael's sleeve. He looked almost comically horrified. "You're shot."

"Just a graze," he assured him, muttering an inner curse that it had happened so close to home. Obviously the servant recognized him, and in very little time word would spread that Lord Longhaven was attacked on the street.

"Shall I summon a physician?"

"No need, but thank you," he assured the helpful young man. To stave off any other offers of assistance from the other staring pedestrians, he set off briskly down the street. He could go to Antonia again, or Luke, for that matter, who lived perhaps five houses away. However, he pictured himself arriving, bleedin~ en Viscount Altea's doorstep, and it would just inflame the gossip. Luke wouldn't blink an eye, but servants talked.

No, it was best to just go home and try to go up to his rooms as unobtrusively as possible so he could assess the damage. Fitzhugh was off shadowing Julianne, but he could take care of the wound later, if need be. It burned, but didn't feel serious.

A much more serious matter was explaining it to his wife. A wicked knife wound was out of the ordinary and he hadn't ever offered any kind of reasonable explanation, but not long afterward having a graze from a ball on his arm would require more frankness. They were getting to know each other in ways besides the communion they had in bed, and he knew she'd have—and ask—questions.

Were our positions reversed, he told himself as he walked up the wet grandiose steps of Southbrook House, *I would certainly ask* her *what had happened. And moreover, I would expect the truth.*

The very idea of Julianne being injured was . . .

Unacceptable.

No, that word was cold, inadequate to his powerful reaction to the idea of anything marring her perfect skin, causing her pain, endangering her life. He trusted Fitzhugh, but she'd evaded his valet more than once. With this third attempt on his life, maybe he should assign an operative to watch Julianne. With two vigilant men plus Antonia, surely she'd be safe.

Unless, of course, a sharpshooter decided to target her from a distance. Safe was an illusion. What he needed to do was find whoever wanted him dead and end this.

"Good afternoon, my lord." Rutgers stood in the foyer, moving to take his cloak. Michael shook his head, keeping the concealing cloth pulled around him. "I'm soaked through. I'll have Fitzhugh take care of this upstairs. Perhaps dry it by the fire."

"Very good." The elderly butler stepped back.

"Is Lady Longhaven home?"

"Not as of yet, my lord."

It was getting dark. What the devil was that about?

A drop of blood splashed on Michael's boot. "I would like to be informed of her return immediately," he said with as much aplomb as possible before he turned away and headed down the hallway toward the huge double staircase that led to the private family apartments. He hoped he didn't leave a trail of scarlet spots behind him.

An hour later, after bathing in hot water to ease the autumn chill, a makeshift bandage over what proved to be, as he suspected, just a flesh wound, and dressed in dry clothes, Michael joined his father in his study.

"You wished to see me, sir?" He selected a chair and dropped into it, the throb in his forearm not quite a crescendo but certainly a melody in the background.

The sixth Duke of Southbrook splashed expensive French brandy into a glass and passed it over. "I assume you'll be joining us this evening."

Michael quirked a brow. "Put that way, it doesn't

sound quite like a ducal decree, but I am guessing it is one."

"I know it sounds dull as unbuttered toast, but your mother's dinner party is important to her."

"For Lady Hampton's niece, correct?" It did sound dull. The young woman was a debutante, and if memory served, inclined to giggle. They were cousins in some remote way, and of course, being sponsored by the Duchess of Southbrook was always a coup.

"Lady Felicity happens also to be a friend of your wife." His father smiled genially over the rim of his glass.

The inference was that Michael would please both his mother and his wife by attending. "Please tell me you'll dip into some of your more rare vintages as recompense for my cooperation."

A chuckle. "Of course. I am not looking forward to it all that much either, but marriage is a compromise."

Or a treaty, as Michael had whispered to Julianne when they'd lain together in the garden. Perhaps she was right: he'd had too much war in his life. Compromise sounded better, but, truthfully, they were the same.

Michael glanced at the case clock in the corner of the room. "Speaking of my wife, she seems to be running late."

Damnation. Fitzhugh, I hope you are taking care of her. . . .

"Dinner isn't for several hours," his father pointed out.

True. Michael forced himself to relax as best as possible since his recent experience with a bullet whizzing out of the dreary afternoon was so fresh in his mind. His sore arm made the event difficult to set aside.

Can I confine Julianne to the house until this was settled, he wondered, moodily settling lower in his chair, only half listening to his father's description of the stallion he was considering purchasing to put to stud to improve their bloodstock.

No, he couldn't forbid her to go out without explaining that he was afraid she might be in danger.

Not without revealing more than he cared to about who and what he was.

Restively, he drank more brandy and wondered where she might be.

Chapter Seventeen

The wheel had broken, stranding them.

It was an old hackney cab, so maybe not so surprising, but the sideways lurch of the vehicle into the mud hadn't been welcome, and the incessant rain had rendered the roads a quagmire. As if poor little Chloe hadn't been through enough.

The stalwart Fitzhugh had come to the rescue yet again, putting Julianne and her small charge up on his horse and leading it, but that took forever, and at the end of the journey all of them were soaked to the skin, shivering. And now it was well past dark.

Well past dark.

How late was it, precisely? She wasn't sure. They had stopped at a tavern to make sure Chloe had something to eat, and both Julianne and Fitzhugh had sat in silent consternation to watch such a small child devour an entire meat pie and down several glasses of water as if parched. As usual, she'd said nothing. Once, Julianne's husband's valet had given her a questioning look over the child's silence, to which she'd just shaken her head.

They were all miserable when they reached the rarified streets of Mayfair, and none of them looked as if they belonged there. Julianne's silk gown was ruined, her slippers unrecognizable and certainly not functional, and her cloak so wet it did nothing to stave off the cold. The only amusing part of it was that Julianne couldn't tell which of them—she or her husband's valet—was more chagrined as they alighted, muddy and disreputable, from his weary horse.

The lights of the mansion were brilliant, and belatedly she realized there was a dinner going on and perhaps the festivities had started. Her heart sank. It wasn't at all how she wished to do this.

Not exactly an ideal arrival.

"There is always the servant's entrance, madam."

Fitzhugh's tone was so pained, she almost laughed, but she was hardly in a mirthful mood. The thought of even going around the house was too much. She wanted to get inside to warmth as soon as possible, not for her sake so much but for Chloe's. "No," she said with finality. "I know there are guests, but I refuse to drag her in through the back door, Fitzhugh. She's been hidden enough."

For a moment it looked like he would argue, but then he gazed at the wet, bedraggled child in her arms and nodded. "It could be you are right, Lady Longhaven."

"I am not anxious to tell everyone what I've done," she confessed. "You know Michael better than most. Will he forgive me?"

"The colonel is most fair. You will have to walk through that door to find out." Even wet and muddy, the former sergeant held himself with formidable dignity.

She gazed at the formal portico with the elaborate carved door and reminded herself Chloe had every right to be there. It would be preferable if she weren't bedraggled and tired herself, and the situation certainly not how she ever wanted to reveal this secret, but it had to be done, and perhaps it was best to have it over quickly.

Actually, she didn't see any other way. Sneaking in the back might be fine otherwise, but not to hide Chloe. She was a human being and though the circumstances of her birth were less than perfect, none of it was her fault.

Still, in front of a bevy of guests . . .

Hopefully they were all in the dining room, so Julianne could at least enter discreetly and bathe and change before she had to begin the explanations.

Even now, she wasn't at all positive how the duke and duchess were going to react. "Come on, darling." She brushed back several sodden curls from Chloe's forehead. The little girl was obviously exhausted, her eyes half closed. "You'll like it here. I promise."

Squaring her shoulders, Julianne went up the steps. To her surprise, the door was yanked open before she even got there. Michael himself stood outlined by the welcome light that spilled into the chilly night. In contrast to her current state, he was beautifully dressed in tailored evening clothes, his cravat snowy white, his boots polished to a high sheen.

"Where the devil have you been?" he demanded, his gaze traveling over her soaked, disheveled appearance, and then shooting in accusation to his valet. "What's happened?"

"I'll explain it all, Colonel." Fitzhugh responded in his usual stoic, calm tone, standing beside her.

Julianne was shivering. "No, *I* will explain. But may we discuss this inside?"

Her husband seemed to realize he was blocking the doorway, for he stepped back. She gratefully entered the warmth of the house, her skirts leaving a muddy trail across the polished floor. She was dripping everywhere, she knew with resignation, even droplets from her eyelashes. Julianne blinked and wished for a dry handkerchief to blow her nose.

"May I take your cloak, my lady?" Rutgers stood

there politely, as if she hadn't arrived in a sodden mess, carrying a small child.

Ruefully, she said, "I think it is possibly past salvaging."

"Throw it out," Michael said in clipped tones, slipping the wet garment from her shoulders.

The austere butler seemed to agree, for though it wasn't obvious, he held it away from his impeccable clothing and nodded at one of the footmen, who hastened forward to take it from him. Her slippers were even worse, but she was hardly going to take off her shoes in the grand foyer of the ducal mansion. "I'm sorry for the mess, Rutgers," she apologized. "There was a bit of an accident."

"No need to worry over it, my lady. Shall I have hot water sent up?"

"That would be wonderful."

"What kind of accident?" Michael demanded. "Are you injured?"

"No."

"Julianne."

Though she'd avoided meeting his eye so far, she was forced to look at him, the tone of his voice soft yet implacable. In turn, he was staring at the child nestled in her arms. Chloe, incredibly, had fallen sound asleep.

"Could we possibly discuss this upstairs?" To her dismay, there was the faintest wobble in her voice, and, unexpectedly, the prick of tears stung her eyes. "I'm . . . I'm quite cold and wet, and I truly had the most awful day."

No, she refused to start sobbing in front of everyone, but despite her resolve, a tear rolled down her cheek.

"Fitz, get into dry clothes before you catch your death," she heard Michael say decisively. "Rutgers, we'll need a maid for the child and that hot water as soon as possible. Please discreetly make our excuses to my mother."

"Of course, my lord."

Julianne let out a small gasp as she was suddenly swept, sleeping child and all, into a pair of strong arms. The sound of booted feet rang on the marble floor as Michael carried her down the hallway.

"You'll ruin your clothes," she protested, but, quite frankly, he was warm, solid, and smelled wonderful, which, she suspected, with wet filth clinging to her skirts, she did not.

"It seems to be happening quite a lot lately," he muttered.

What does that mean?

"Besides," he went on, "this seems expedient, and I must confess I am more than a little curious to hear exactly what course of events led to you arriving home dripping wet and carrying a street urchin."

"She isn't a street urchin," Julianne said defensively, though, to be fair, with Chloe's ragged clothes and less than clean appearance, she could see how he'd come to that conclusion.

"No?" He started up the staircase, carrying them both with seemingly little effort. "Who is she, then?"

A rather difficult question to answer. In the end, Julianne said simply, "Ours. She's ours."

Pouring another glass of claret, Michael watched his lovely wife pick at the savory chicken glazed beautifully with a reduction of honey and port. They were in her bedroom, a small table had been carried in and dinner delivered discreetly by Julianne's maid. In a light blue satin dressing gown that draped her slender body, his wife had been extraordinarily quiet during their informal meal. But then again, he'd stopped the rush of her initial explanation by saying he didn't need to hear it until she'd had something to eat and time to reflect on what she was going to say.

A strategic delay. A good idea? He wasn't sure. It was an undeniable fact that he often dealt with those accustomed to deception, not delectable young ladies with moving, midnight blue eyes. Dealing with his wife was quite different from dealing with his usual adversaries.

But he *was* used to interrogation. He was exceptionally good at it. That he would get the truth, especially from someone like Julianne, was not in question.

Waiting was one of the most effective ways of rendering the suspect nervous enough to reveal her deepest secrets. For instance: the child.

It wasn't hers. It had been his initial, gut-wrenching reaction that maybe, just maybe, she'd not been the trembling virgin on their wedding night. Certainly she had enjoyed their lovemaking and not been nearly as shy as he'd expected, but then again, there had been physical evidence of her loss of innocence, and he had also experienced the moment when he'd breached her maidenhead.

No. Not hers.

So, what in God's name was she doing showing up with a waif in her arms, and as defensive as a lioness with a cub?

"You should at least make an effort to eat," he said with as much neutrality as possible. "Whatever you have to tell me can't be so catastrophic that you need to make yourself ill."

"It might be." Julianne reached for her glass of wine and took a swift, convulsive sip. Her eyes shimmered, and he fervently hoped she wasn't going to cry again.

He'd endured two days of relentless torture by the French in a filthy little cell and held fast, but that one glistening tear streaking down her cheek earlier had undone him.

"Julianne," he began to say.

"You haven't eaten much either," she pointed out, her hand visibly trembling as she set down her glass.

To be honest, his arm hurt, he'd been so damn worried about her that he'd nearly worn a path in the hallway waiting, and now . . . well, he was just too confounded to eat.

"*And* you are studying me as if I am an exhibit at a

museum. Some sort of curiosity you are trying to understand," she added in a small voice.

He might just be guilty of said crime. Michael shifted
slightly in his chair. "I understandably have questions,
but at the same time, I hope not heartless enough to put
you through an inquisition when you are tired and hungry. Finish eating."

"I can't. It would be easier to just tell you." Glossy
strands of her hair, still damp from her recent bath,
framing her face, his wife delicately set aside her fork.
"Chloe is Harry's."

What did she just say?

His brother—the perfect paragon of a ducal heir—
had fathered an illegitimate child?

"I don't know the exact date of her birth, but I'm told
she's almost three."

Michael had to admit the disclosure took him off
guard. And he prided himself for not being off guard
often. His brother hadn't been a rake particularly, and
though his older sibling had enjoyed life, Michael had
never had the impression that Harry was promiscuous
or careless. He sent a swift glance at the bed, where
the small form slumbered under the tumbled blankets.
"How the devil did that happen?"

For the first time that evening, Julianne showed a
hint of amusement. "I can testify firsthand, my lord, you
know exactly how it happens."

He smiled wryly. "Not quite what I meant, my dear.
Start from the beginning, if you please."

All humor vanished. "The beginning? I wasn't there
at the beginning. I had no idea about Chloe until he
died. I didn't know what to do." Julianne's voice was
hushed and barely audible. "Your parents were in such
grief. Leah sent me a note and asked for us to meet. She
knew I was Harry's intended. She told me she'd had his
child . . . that he'd been paying her for Chloe's care and
to keep it all quiet. If I didn't do the same, she would

contact the duke and duchess. I wasn't sure they could bear it at the time, so I agreed."

It took a moment to assimilate that information. "This woman blackmailed you?"

"I suppose that is one way to look at it." Julianne's delicate features blanched. "I prefer to think of it as helping to care for Chloe."

"How in the name of Hades do you even know the child is my brother's?"

"Have you really looked at her?" Slender shoulders straightened, and her gaze was defiantly direct at his blunt question. "She is unmistakably a Hepburn. She looks nothing like her mother. Besides, he must have known Chloe was his, for he was the one paying for her support. She showed me notes in his hand, outlining the arrangement."

All Michael had seen was tousled chestnut curls and a small, wan face. His experience with children was nonexistent, but notes sounded a bit more convincing. "You've been paying ever since his death? How?"

"My father, naturally, gave me a small allowance . . . and I sold a few bits of my grandmother's jewelry."

Michael had no idea what to say. A young, unattached woman her age had little recourse, and no matter how generous her father might have been, her spending stipend could not have been much, with her family providing for her every other need. Whereas *his* father—the child's grandfather—was a rich man. She needn't have made the sacrifice.

"Since we married," she went on in a soft voice, "it has been much easier. The generosity of the pin money you gave me was enough to pay her and not have to worry over it."

There wasn't much question that he was at a loss. Michael carefully set aside his wine. "A part of me wants to thank you," he said with raw honesty. "But a part of me wants to also demand to know why you didn't tell me about my brother's child before now. I am your husband, Julianne."

"I didn't know you well enough to judge how you might react."

And more than once she'd mentioned how he held himself aloof.

Damnation, he *did* hold himself aloof.

Her reticence could be entirely his fault. No, not so—it *was* his fault.

Julianne said evenly, "I wasn't trying to deceive you, but you know better than anyone how devastated your parents were by Harry's death. I assumed he didn't want them to know or he would have told them already about Chloe, and so I didn't do it just for them, but also for him."

For Harry. The man she'd envisioned would be her husband almost her entire life. Michael was the substitute. The substitute marquess, the substitute heir, and, yes, the substitute husband.

Damn all.

She went on haltingly, "I vow to you I tried to help, not particularly to keep her hidden. I hated that part of it." Julianne's expression was poignant and vulnerable. "I've discovered that once you embark on such a journey, secrets hold you prisoner."

Secrets. He was well versed in that arena. She spoke the absolute truth. But her secret was born from good intentions, and the only sin was of omission. The vow was unnecessary.

"Did you love him?" Michael didn't even know he was going to ask the question. It was spontaneous, and he found the answer was important to him.

Julianne looked bewildered. "Love him?"

"Harry."

"Oh." Her gaze dropped to her virtually untouched food. There was a pause, and she said softly, "No. Not in the way you mean."

How selfish of him to experience a rush of relief. God, would he take that from his brother too?

None of what he had inherited had he wanted. Not even Julianne. But that had changed. The title didn't matter, the legacy of the dukedom was more a burden than a prize, but his lovely wife was different. He definitely wanted her.

"I might have loved him eventually. I think I would have in time." She sat there, beautifully disconcerted, gazing at him with those glorious eyes. "Still," she went on, her voice taking on a peculiar husky tone, though also curiously full of dignity, "I don't know how I am so sure of it, but strange as it is, I know—*I know*—it would never be like it is with you."

She is going to fall in love with you. . . .

Was Antonia correct? Suddenly this was important. So very important.

"How is it with me?" Michael was usually more adroit at controlling his tone, but in this case he failed miserably. To his dismay, he *wanted* her to say she was in love with him. That passion had translated into a deeper feeling. That though he'd done his best to keep her at arm's length, he'd failed.

How odd. He wanted to know he'd failed.

Because he'd certainly not been able to keep himself from getting involved.

Suddenly the bedroom seemed small despite its palatial size, and Julianne was too close, with her dark blue eyes and rose-tinted lips. Her tempting figure, so lushly curved in the right places and slender in others, was covered only by a thin dressing gown. He wanted her, he knew, his fingers tightening on the stem of his glass, but he also wanted her answer more.

A lot more. The emotional over the physical.

Unprecedented in his life when it came to a woman.

Chapter Eighteen

How is it with me?

   A certain part of her took issue that he could even think to pose the question.

   The trouble in answering was the nature of the man asking it. Had he been someone else—anyone else—she could have sworn there was a hint of vulnerability in his voice, but this was Michael.

   Vulnerable? No. Before this moment she would have sworn it impossible. Yet the way he was looking at her, unmoving in his chair, his brilliant hazel eyes so focused . . . maybe he did want to know.

   Would he even welcome a declaration of deeper feeling?

   In indecision, Julianne took a shuddering breath. *Or,* the voice of reason pointed out, *maybe it would merely make him take a step backward, which would ruin the hard-won closeness I've sensed growing between us.* Was he testing the waters, or was he trying to decide if he should head for dry land as soon as possible?

   She wished she were a bit better at this sort of game.

He had unquestionably more experience. For that matter, Antonia Taylor would no doubt know exactly what to say in response. It would be witty, they would both laugh, and the personal moment would be avoided.

"Not like I thought it would be." It was an answer worthy of one of his evasions.

He didn't accept the equivocation, but there was a flicker of acknowledgment in his eyes. "Fair enough. How did you think it would be?"

"I have already told you I didn't know you as well as I knew Harry."

"And I have already conceded that is true." He lounged there, imposingly tall, informal now that he had discarded his cravat and coat and unbuttoned his shirt, and drinking wine with seeming unconcern. But she'd already learned he was never casual.

It was always there in his dangerously beautiful eyes. He could hide almost everything, but not that intensity.

"I think eventually I would have loved Harry," Julianne said carefully. "But I doubt I would have ever fallen *in* love with him. I do not have much experience, but I think the concept is different."

"Loving a person and falling in love is not the same?"

"I don't think so."

"What are you saying?"

"My lord, precisely what are you asking?" She folded her hands in her lap and looked steadily back. Why should she confess her feelings? What possible good would it do either of them? It was one matter to be a besotted fool and another to admit it.

"Julianne, I have the impression you are being deliberately obtuse."

"I have the same impression of you."

A smile tilted his lips. "May I say, madam, you can be slightly vexing?"

Her laugh broke the slight tension. Though she wore only a robe, and despite how cold she'd been earlier and the rain still pecking at the window, the room was suddenly overly warm. "Only if I am allowed to mention your habitual reticence again."

"You are allowed to mention whatever you wish."

"What will happen to Chloe?" This was important to her ... so important their interesting discussion was temporarily dismissed. "I hold your parents with affection, but I have never been certain they will accept her. Many aristocratic families ignore illegitimate offspring."

"Where is her mother?"

Leah. It had been difficult all along to think of her with any kindness, and at the moment, Julianne genuinely detested her. "She's not a lady, and I am not alluding to her social standing in any way. She is addicted to drink, as far as I can tell, and I suspect spends the money I give her in taverns, for she certainly does not use it to care for Chloe other than in the most basic of ways. When I arrived this afternoon, the house was shuttered and locked up. I am glad Fitzhugh was following me, for he was able to break in the door. We found Chloe hiding in the pantry. Otherwise, the house was deserted."

"A child that young left all alone?" Michael's expression took on a grim cast.

He did not, Julianne noticed, address the issue of why Fitzhugh was following her in the first place.

At the moment, she was so glad he wasn't angry with her that she wasn't going to press the matter. Apparently her ruse of escaping out the back had been detected.

"I was horrified." She looked away for a moment, swallowing hard. "It's my fault. I left her in Leah's care when I knew ... or I suspected what she was like. Chloe doesn't speak, and as I said, she must be at least three years old. I shudder to think what Leah is like when I am not there. It is clear she considers the child a burden, and yet since Chloe's existence provides her with a good income, she has never abandoned her before that I know of. Whenever I come, she is waiting eagerly for her money. I swear to you I never thought she would forsake her own child. She's ill-mannered and brash, but I always assumed it was directed at me, and though it might seem odd, I understand it. She had Harry's child and yet he wouldn't wed her, but intended to marry me. In her place, I'd harbor resentment too."

"From your description of her, I can imagine the exalted past Dukes of Southbrook spinning in their regal graves should he have contemplated doing so," Michael said dryly. "It sounds to me like he made a careless mistake he regretted, and there is not one of us who walk this earth who cannot say he hasn't done the same. Harry's resulted in a child, though, and he should have told my father of her existence so she could be cared for if something happened to him."

Julianne agreed. Telling his parents would not have been easy, and if they'd ever met Leah they would be appalled, and so Harry had avoided both. "In his defense, he was young and seemed in good health. I am sure he didn't imagine anything would happen to him."

"There's no need to defend him, but cease taking blame in this situation. It isn't your fault." Michael's voice was even and his gaze steady. "It is my brother's fault for impregnating this woman in the first place. Besides, I hardly think a young, unmarried lady could be expected to take a child from its mother and raise it, even if she was affianced to the father. This isn't your scandal, my dear, nor was it your responsibility to step into the breach when Harry died."

"I should have told your father." It haunted her still whether she had made the right decision.

"It's hard to say if you should have or not. My parents at least have some distance from their grief now. I'll explain everything. However they feel about the child, you needn't worry. Obviously she is attached to you. It seems logical enough for us to care for her."

The offer, so easily said, left Julianne in a state of semishock.

"It's my brother's child," he offered with a brief, now humorless smile. "I am unlikely to forsake her. Wouldn't she be better off with our children?"

Our children. Of course he wanted an heir—all men in his position did—but the words were somehow so intimate. "Thank you."

"Please explain why you should thank me." Michael got to his feet, dropping his napkin, and with lethal grace came around the table.

He tugged her to her feet. Julianne rose willingly, and when his arms came around her, she melted into his embrace. To her surprise, Michael didn't kiss her, but simply held her against him for a moment, before he said in a husky tone, "You are no doubt exhausted. I assume, considering we have a guest who might awake in the middle of night, confused and frightened over her new surroundings, you will wish to sleep in here with her. I would suggest having one of the maids stay with her instead, but that would be selfish of me. She might need you. Tomorrow we will go about selecting a nursemaid."

If she wasn't head over heels in love with her sometimes-enigmatic husband already, she would have fallen then and there.

So *she* kissed *him*. Her palms slid upward over his chest to his shoulders, and Julianne saw in his eyes a brief flare of heated understanding of what she wanted before he obligingly lowered his head and touched his mouth to hers.

It wasn't an explosive kiss, nor a seductive one, but tender and soft enough to weaken her knees.

"I think," he murmured against her lips, "I should retreat to my room now, or my noble intentions will be quickly abandoned."

Julianne nodded and stepped back. He was right, of course; Chloe had endured enough, and at least Julianne was a familiar face in a strange place. But Julianne would miss sleeping in his bed.

She would miss *him*. His arms around her, his respiration in the dark, the warm, solid feel of him next to her.

*   *   *

"At least he missed, Colonel." Fitzhugh gave Michael's haphazard bandaging a disparaging scrutiny as he unwound and tossed away the bloodied material. "Apparently your would-be assassin needs lessons on the pitfalls of attempting murder on a windy afternoon in the pouring rain."

"I'd appreciate it if you didn't give him any."

"A less dramatic display of gallantry might have been better, too. I doubt carrying the marchioness up the stairs helped matters."

"It's a scratch," Michael muttered, shirtless, sitting on a carved chair and well aware of Julianne asleep on the other side of the door separating their bedrooms. "I should have chased the bastard, but the chance of an ambush was too great. I couldn't see him any more than he could see me for a clear shot."

"Getting cautious, are we?"

"Do I have a choice? My parents aside, now I have a wife and apparently have inherited a child. Julianne expressed her gratitude for your timely intervention. I do as well."

His valet merely shrugged and deftly wound a bit of cloth along the gouged flesh from the bullet. "I wasn't sure if I should reveal I was nearby, but Lady Longhaven was clearly distressed. It seemed best to step forward and offer my assistance."

"I am going to have some explaining to do, both for this"—Michael gestured at his arm—"and for why you were shadowing her in the first place. She was too tired and distracted tonight to address it, but I am coming to know her, and she won't let it be for long."

"She is a plucky little lass."

It wasn't particularly easy to win Fitzhugh's regard, and that was definitely a compliment. Michael raised his brows. "I sense Julianne has an admirer."

"Her ladyship told me the story in bits and pieces as we sat in a somewhat questionable inn and that little girl ate what looked to be the first good meal she'd had in some time. I don't think rightly Lady Longhaven would normally divulge such confidences, but she was tired and muddy and frightened for her reception when we arrived here." Fitz drew his graying brows together. "I like compassion in a woman. It makes her beautiful."

"My wife is already beautiful."

"Ah, there, sirrah. I thought you'd noticed the lass a time or two. But beautiful inside isn't the same as beauty on the outside, in me opinion."

"Don't produce that rolling Irish brogue." Michael's smile was cynical. "You only do that when you want to irritate me."

His valet didn't dignify the accusation with an answer, but instead tied up the wound neatly.

"She was protecting my mother and father."

"That's the impression I received also, Col . . . my lord."

"Tell me what happened."

The older man complied, his short recital of the events of the day tallying directly with what Julianne had told him earlier. As Michael slipped on his shirt, he said, "The woman . . . the child's mother—I think you need to find her. I don't want later for her to upset my wife by trying to claim the child was kidnapped. I'd like to make the situation clear. The child stays with us. I'll arrange a settlement of some kind."

"I am sure that can be accomplished." Fitzhugh handed him his jacket. "I understand the marchioness's happiness is paramount."

There was a short, profound silence. When Michael had agreed to the marriage, it hadn't ever occurred to him he would so swiftly become involved. It hadn't occurred to him he would *ever* become involved.

Michael turned around and adjusted his lapels. He spoke softly. "I'm in trouble, am I not?"

"Indeed." Fitzhugh offered his watch and chain. "The marchioness is most charming."

"Most women are a confounded nuisance."

"If only we could exist without them, sir."

"Are you possibly laughing at me, Sergeant?"

"I no longer hold that rank, my lord." Fitzhugh grinned.

Blast it, Michael didn't want to go out this evening, but he must, as the game had changed. "Stay here and watch over her."

"I think I should go with you."

He shook his head. "I am fine alone. No one is eternally lucky when it comes to a determined assassin, but, truthfully, I prefer you here, Fitz."

"Then here I will stay."

He sat down to pull on his boots. "If she should ask where I am—"

"Come back before she awakens and does. It shouldn't be so difficult."

Michael shot a sardonic sidelong glance at his friend and rose. "I will do my best."

Chapter Nineteen

His growing arousal was an unneeded distraction. It wouldn't have happened if Antonia's very tempting backside wasn't pressed against him as she leaned forward to peer around the edge of the building.

It might have been on purpose. Lawrence wouldn't put it past her. That was why they were so well suited. He didn't put *anything* past her. Like him, she was a survivor.

It also could be his recent abstinence. Lawrence had wondered more than once, and particularly at his moment, if he wasn't being a damned fool to refuse to bed her in the weeks since Longhaven's marriage. Part of it was pride, and Lawrence was fairly sure he'd dismissed useless pride more than a decade ago when he'd found himself a beggar and a thief. Once you'd compromised your principles for survival the first time, scruples became more of a flexible ideal.

But at the moment, business was the order of the day.

Antonia was convinced this was their chance to catch

Roget. Johnson had traced the man who had shot at Lord Longhaven back to this very address.

The marquess would be in his debt if Lawrence was the source of discovering the person behind the attempts on his lordship's life, and it was a payment he fully intended to collect. He slipped his arm around Antonia's waist and pulled her back, even closer. Nuzzling her ear, he whispered, "I'll go in first. No argument."

"Masculine privilege annoys me," she whispered back fiercely. "You know that."

"Many things annoy you," he responded in amusement, "but your safety matters to me. It's a selfish decision, not a heroic one. If something happens to you, I will be most upset. For instance, who would I have left to annoy?"

"Do not try to be amusing."

"Ah, but I wasn't. I was simply telling the truth for a change. Without you my life would be devoid of all interest."

He knew how to silence her. When would she learn he knew *her*?

Never gracious when forced into a compromise, Antonia scowled, but she did allow him to draw her back into the shadows. She was dressed all in black like a slender boy, her dark hair drawn back and tucked under a hat, and her mouth was sulky. "I'll give you two minutes."

"Five," he argued, drawing out his pistol and checking it.

"This alley isn't particularly safe either," she pointed out. "Would you leave me here alone?"

"No, it isn't safe with you in it," he agreed with a flashing grin. "Don't terrify any footpads while I am gone."

He slid down the damp wall of the building and made his way, light-footed and quiet, to the entrance door. The building wasn't familiar but he'd been in places like this before, he decided as he entered the dirty foyer and noted the sweating walls and rat droppings on the filthy floor.

It was unlikely a master spy like Roget would be in such surroundings, but it also was exactly where Johnson had tracked the man who had made an attempt on Longhaven's life. The mystery of why this was all happening was still unclear, and Lawrence carefully counted the doors until he found the right one. It was best to start this interview without Antonia, he knew, if their quarry proved to be home. She was too passionate about Roget, too vengeful. His name having been linked to the murder of her family gave her very little perspective.

To knock or not to knock? He opted to go ahead and rap sharply on the warped wooden surface. Already he'd made some assessments of the enemy. Truly dangerous men usually had better accommodations. Special skills gave you a value most governments—or other potential employers—noted, and you could afford more.

There was movement inside the room. He could hear the scrape of boots on the floor, and a woman's sleepy murmur.

Johnson had better not be wrong. . . .

Lawrence put his hand in his pocket and grasped the handle of his pistol. He timed it perfectly, so that when the door opened a crack a single forceful kick did the trick. The man answering was caught off guard and staggered backward, tripping over a small rug. He landed on his arse, and it gave Lawrence the opportunity to step forward and plainly show his weapon. "I just need a few words."

The man was built with whippy leanness, his face slightly pockmarked, and Lawrence saw he was not well dressed. Nor was the flat, at a swift, assessing glance, prepossessing. It contained a few sagging chairs and a disheveled bed with a half-naked woman sitting up, her mouth agape, and there was a distinct odor of spoiled food in the air.

If Roget wanted Longhaven killed, Lawrence thought

with sardonic amusement, *he wouldn't go about it by hiring such an obvious amateur.*

Who *had* hired him?

As expected, he heard a noise behind him, and knew it was Antonia. She wasn't patient in bed either.

"Is he armed?" she asked, not waiting for an answer as she shouldered past Lawrence with a long, wicked knife in her hand. In her black clothing, her hair caught up under the concealing hat, she resembled an avenging angel, if, albeit, a fallen one.

"No," the man squeaked, holding out his hands. "I've no weapon on me."

The woman on the bed whimpered and pulled the blankets over her head.

Lawrence had to actually stifle a laugh, because the sight of Antonia brandishing a knife was not for the faint of heart and their suspect was clearly petrified. He moved forward, grabbed the man's shirt, and hauled him to his feet. "As I said, we just need a word."

As soon as the quivering suspect was shoved into a chair, Antonia said, "Earlier this evening you tried to kill the Marquess of Longhaven. Tell me why."

"I . . . n-never did." It was an unconvincing squeak.

The light still gleamed off Antonia's knife as she tilted it and touched the blade with the pad of her thumb. The dim illumination cast shadows on her aquiline features. "Truly? For I have a friend who followed you here, and I trust him far more than I trust you. If I slit your throat, I suspect I will never know the truth, but I also think no one will care about your unexpected demise."

The response was silence, as if the man was afraid to speak. Lawrence said calmly, "I can keep her at bay if you will just tell us the truth."

"*Perhaps* he can keep me at bay." Antonia purred the words with definite menace, her gaze intently fixed on the man shivering in the chair. "But he is right. The sooner you tell us everything, the better your chances are of surviving this interview."

As always, her evident sincerity was enough to break any man. Especially the way she pointed the tip of the knife downward toward the man's crotch.

"Jest doing a favor for a friend," he blurted out, shivering in Lawrence's grasp, still trying to twist away. "I missed him anyway. Couldn't get a clear shot. No harm done. When I looked, he was gone."

"Who hired you?" Antonia demanded, her lethal expression enough to frighten even a grown man—including Lawrence, and he didn't think he frightened easily after what he'd endured in his life. He'd be squirming too, with her bent over him and that particular look on her face. The blade was inches from the culprit's most vulnerable area.

"I was sent a note . . . I swear." His pasty face held a hint of sweat. "Giving me the direction to his lordship's grand lodgings. I was to wait, and if the opportunity was there, to take a shot. I wasn't close enough, and whoever hired me didn't want me to take a chance on being seen or caught. That's all I know."

"A friend would have told you more." The knife edged closer and her smile was chilling. She did that very well.

It reminded Lawrence very much of when he'd first met her.

They'd been drawn together by Longhaven . . . of course. He was the recurring theme in their relationship. After the marquess—who was not a marquess then and not first in line for a ducal title either, but just Lord Michael Hepburn—had introduced them, Lawrence had immediately fallen for the raven-haired beauty. It wasn't a consideration at the time Longhaven and Antonia were lovers. It was war. That was different.

Lawrence wasn't quite as willing *now* to be passed over. The marquess had moved on and married. Antonia needed to move forward too.

"Tell her." He gave his prisoner a small shake. With his scarred face and size, he knew he was intimidating.

"I'm a fair shot," the man blabbered. "I know a bloke who spreads it around, and occasionally I get asked."

"Asked for what?"

"You know."

Such the wrong phrase to use with Antonia. She leaned in. "No, I don't. I want it all perfectly clear, you little toad."

The man sent Lawrence such a terrified look that he almost felt sorry for him. "You said—"

"I said I only *thought* I could keep her at bay." Lawrence kept his smile cheerful. "I've been wrong before. Were I in your position, I'd tell her."

"I get asked to do a little favor here or there." The would-be assassin's face was a peculiar shade of green.

"Specify."

The tone of her voice made Lawrence stifle a flinch, and he wasn't even the target. Bonaparte and Wellington would have backed away from that battle line.

It had the same effect on their prisoner. "Of the deadly sort."

"To not put too fine a point on it, you are admitting you are a hired killer, correct?" Antonia's voice was silky smooth.

Under that direct inquiry, the small man paled. "Please—"

"Just answer." The knife moved a fraction, ripping cloth.

"I've done a favor or two," he admitted, his voice quavering. "Now and then. For those who could pay."

"Who could pay this time?" Antonia lifted the knife and inspected it, the blade catching the flicker of the one meager lamp. "Don't lie to me."

Their prisoner was visibly sweating, his face like soapstone. "A woman. I don't care to die for her, so I'll tell you. Bright red hair . . . I don't know nothing else, I swear it. She wore a cloak. . . . All she gave me was instructions on how to find him and what she wanted.

She gave me half up front, half to come when the job was finished."

A woman? Whatever he expected, Lawrence hadn't expected that. "What woman?"

"I'm telling you I don't know. I never asked her name. You don't, not on a job like this."

"If you are lying . . ."

"I'm not!"

"What do you think? I am not sure I believe this one." Antonia asked Lawrence silkily. "Shall I kill him or just maim him?"

Lawrence dropped the frightened man, who collapsed to the dirty floor, and drew his companion back, his arm around her slender waist. "No, my love, I think he will be better punished to live the rest of his life with the shadow of your vengeance hanging over his worthless head. Our time would be best served to look for whoever wants your marquess dead."

"He isn't mine."

Now, that was progress. She'd never admitted it before.

If he pointed it out, he would only lose ground, so he said quietly, "Perhaps we should pay Longhaven a visit in the morning and apprise him of this new development."

So, a *woman* wanted Michael dead.

Interesting.

As she pondered this new development, Antonia tossed her hat on the bed and tugged free the piece of ribbon securing her long braid. It still could be Roget, of course, for he might have hired this unknown female to seek out the inept assassin, but there were other possibilities. It was sloppy. She hated him with every fiber of her being, but Roget would have been dead a thousand times over if he were sloppy.

A lover? Another woman who might resent his marriage, besides Antonia? Surely Michael hadn't been celibate since his return to England, and certainly he hadn't been sleeping with her, no matter that she'd offered the privilege freely, so that was possible.

Damn him. He was too honorable to use her body when he couldn't give her more.

She was not nearly as noble. Dropping the ribbon on her dressing table, she began to unfasten her shirt.

Lawrence had kept his distance lately and it had bothered her more than she cared to admit. She wanted him, wanted to taste the fierce passion of his kiss, the rough, almost wild way he took her, and then the solid feel of him next to her in the bed afterward while they lay amid the chaos of rumpled sheets. There was nothing tame about him as a lover. While Michael had been controlled and skillful, Lawrence held nothing back.

Tonight she needed him. Strangely enough, she was starting to wonder if it had anything at all to do with Michael. It was simply between her and Lawrence.

How to seduce him was an interesting dilemma. In the past it had never been a problem, but he had developed a resistance since Michael's marriage, as if before he didn't care that she was in love with another man, but now that Michael was unavailable and the matter settled, Lawrence was not open to being the alternative prize. When the Marquess of Longhaven had been competition, he was willing to play the game. Now, when the option didn't exist for her, he had withdrawn.

How to convince him to change his mind was a challenge she never thought she'd face. He'd always been so hungry for her.

Still was, if the way his aroused body had pressed up against hers earlier was any indication.

A good place to start.

She undressed, dropping her clothes haphazardly, and then sat nude at her dressing table, picking up a small vial of perfume, the scent of attar of roses drifting out as she lifted the crystal stopper. In the flickering lamplight, she brushed out her hair first, the long dark tresses soft against her bare back. She touched perfume to the delicate dip under her ear, the pulse point at her throat, and the valley between her bare breasts. Antonia smiled into the gilt-framed mirror and picked up a small pot of rouge she rarely used, and scandalously touched a hint of deeper color not to her cheeks, but to her nipples.

In her armoire there was a thin, lacy dressing gown she'd never worn, for it revealed more than it covered. On impulse she donned it, slipping her arms into the wide sleeves and tying the sash, wondering with uncharacteristic uncertainty if she could actually do this. Lawrence wasn't governable. If he'd come to a true conviction he wasn't going to bed her, he might still refuse.

For a man without principles, he had a great many rules, all of his own making. In his own way, he was as complicated as Michael.

Shaking back her hair and giving her appearance one last glance, she surveyed the courtesan's image of flowing hair, a provocative gown, and flushed cheeks with a critical eye. The outcome of this evening—no, it was already morning—would depend a great deal on the level of his resistance compared to his desire.

She intended, of course, to win.

Instead of using the bellpull, she slipped out the doorway and padded down the hall to his room. Though no doubt it caused gossip, he didn't sleep near the servant's quarters but in the family apartments, though his small suite was suitably far removed from hers. Antonia liked her privacy anyway, and her staff was limited. The polished wooden door was firmly shut, but Lawrence was still awake despite the late hour, judging from the line of light visible beneath it.

Her knock was at first met with silence, as if all activity in the room was suspended.

There was no doubt he'd know it was her. *Or he'd better,* she decided possessively as she waited for him to answer the door.

It swung open and he stood there, curly dark hair rumpled, still half dressed, shirtless but in his breeches, barefoot, his smile sardonic. The muscled contours of his chest gleamed in the light of the small lamp she carried, and his facial scar, as always, gave him a certain rakish air, as if he were a pirate escaped from the azure seas of the Caribbean, or maybe a highway brigand set to rob a coach in the midnight depths of a summer evening. In that way he was different from Michael, who outwardly did not bear the signs of his injuries, but when he removed his clothing, the reminders of what he'd endured were all too evident.

Lawrence had a very beautiful body in an entirely rugged sense of the word. Heavily muscled, almost overpoweringly masculine, and he used that dominance in bed in a way that made her shiver inside. . . .

"Well?" His gaze skimmed over her scandalous half attire with lazy, salacious interest.

But the sudden tension in his body belied that casual pose.

"May I come in?" she asked, her voice carefully modulated.

"It depends, my love, on your motivation." He lounged against the doorjamb, imposing and large, thick lashes lowered over his eyes.

"Your new scruples—"

"Annoy you?" he supplied, smiling with ironic amusement. "I think we established earlier this evening that is not difficult to do. Why are you here, Antonia?"

"Lawrence." She attempted her best throaty voice. "Why do you think?"

"That's an answer that cheats us both."

This wasn't much of a seduction. More like an interrogation. "Guess."

"No. You tell me."

"Because I want you." It took something to say it.

"Just . . . want?" He didn't move out of the doorway, his sultry gaze roving over her scantily draped body. "Surely, Lady Taylor, since you have come this far, you can improve on that sentiment."

He wished more from her, and if she were honest, he deserved it.

Honesty was for those who could afford it. Antonia summoned her most wicked, enticing smile. She moved into the room, brushing past him, with a gentle, provocative sway of her hips. She'd never been in there before; he'd always come to her room. To her surprise, she saw a collection of nautical maps framed on the wall, a miniature of a ship on the mantel, and a small tarnished brass compass in a glass case sitting on an unusual table made from some dark, exotic wood. It made her pause, desire tempered now by curiosity. She knew so little about him. Not even his full name.

"You were a sailor?" The closest print was a diagram of the South Seas, dotted with islands and trade routes.

"In a manner of speaking." He hadn't moved except to turn around to watch her, his eyes wary.

"Ship's captain." It wasn't hard to deduce and explained quite a lot. His deference to anyone, not just her, was always tinged with a hint of ironic amusement, as if he granted it rather than felt compelled by his position in society. It made sense now. He was used to complete command.

Why had she never guessed?

"In another life."

An interesting answer. She doubted he was even thirty yet. Antonia moved to another map. This one was of the Americas, lines drawn along the vast coast, along with arrows giving the direction of the currents. "Do you miss the sea?"

"Yes." No hesitation. "I've salt water in my blood."

She swung around. "What happened?"

"I am sure you didn't come here to discuss my past." He crossed his arms over his muscular chest. "Just what you *did* come here for you have yet to divulge."

It was odd—and somewhat disconcerting—to realize she was so obsessed with her own past, her own pain, that she hadn't been concerned with his. Maybe it was the war, where strange fellowships were formed, like hers and Lord Longhaven's. Though they were both aristocrats, with ancient lineages that entitled them to privilege, they were disparate personalities, certainly. She was the blazing Spanish sun and Michael was a cold English winter.

Well, maybe not as cold as he seemed. Besides, it didn't matter what Michael might or might not be any longer. He wasn't her mystery to unravel. Lawrence, on the other hand . . .

"That particular expression on your face never fails to give me pause." He straightened, his features portraying mock alarm. "I suppose I am safe enough because I can tell quite clearly you are not armed. May I offer my compliments on whoever designed your current attire? Though I am not sure just what it might be. It looks like a dressing gown, but certainly doesn't function as one."

The intensity of his bold stare made her breasts tighten and warmth pool between her legs.

Oh, yes, he wanted her.

"I'm glad you like it," she said softly. "Can I interest you in removing it?"

"When you tell me precisely what you came for, my love."

The implacable request was frustrating. She made an impatient gesture with her hand. "What is it you want from me?"

"More than what I sense you are offering. Your delectable body is delightful, do not mistake me, but I am arrogant enough to ask for some measure of your feelings. If all you wish is a stiff cock, I am sure you'd have men lining up for the opportunity to bed the sultry Lady Taylor, and you know that. Explain to me why you want to lie with *me*."

Confounded and intractable, she considered leaving. "Stop being so difficult," she muttered.

"Stop being so stubborn." He finally took a step toward her. "You know you can trust me. Say so."

"I trust no one." She lifted her chin defiantly.

"Not even Longhaven?"

"It depends on the venue in question. I trust his instincts, his intuition, his sense of honor, his ability to think on his feet, his courage, his intelligence . . . all of those things I trust."

"Yes, the man is a veritable paragon, I know. But what don't you trust?" He took another step. She could smell the slight tang of his cologne.

"He married another," she explained, which was ridiculous, because Lawrence already knew this. "But he didn't love her. In doing so, he betrayed me."

"He didn't love you either." Lawrence reached out and touched her chin, tilting her face up so she had to meet his eyes. "Come, now, Antonia. We've discussed this. It wasn't a betrayal. There was no understanding to betray."

"He was my lover."

"But it was long over. Give me a better argument." His fingers, warm and caressing, moved to trace the line of her jaw and skim her mouth.

"This isn't about him," she said almost desperately, involuntarily turning her face into the cup of his palm, like a child seeking solace. "This is about us."

"At last we are getting somewhere. Go on."

"I don't believe in love."

"Yet you think you love Longhaven. So I think it is more accurate to say you don't believe love is wise. Am I correct?"

Was he right? She didn't know. All she could concentrate on was how near he was, how the dark hair curled crisply against his neck, how if he would just cooperate and take her in his arms she would feel safe and cherished.

"Love me," she whispered, though it cost her. "I am here because I want you to love me."

"That," he said, lowering his head to kiss her, "is what I wanted to hear."

She leaned in, relishing the possession of his mouth, nothing subtle in the thrust of his tongue, in the way he hauled her suddenly up against his hardened body. And when he stripped off her lacy robe, the filmy material ripped but she didn't care, glorying in how he picked her up and practically tossed her on the bed before he stripped off his breeches. They came together in a tangle of limbs and heated flesh, and when he entered her she gasped and called his name, moving hungrily into each thrust until the imminent rise of her orgasm clenched her inner muscles and she dug her nails into his shoulders hard enough to draw blood.

The glorious physical burst came and ebbed, and when he pressed into her again, peaked once more. He tensed and let the wave sweep him away with her, the hot flood of his seed accompanied by a low, telling groan.

When there was breath in her lungs again, Antonia whispered in a complacent purr, her body still pulsing, "*That* was what I came for."

Lawrence lifted his head and held her gaze, a small smile on his mouth. "I agree it was a moving experience. But let's keep in mind, my sweet, the game has changed, shall we?"

"How so?" She lazily traced a finger down his chest.

He caught her hand and took it to his mouth. "Because you finally admitted you *want* me to love you."

Chapter Twenty

He just might be losing his touch. Michael had been so anxious to get back to Julianne he hadn't noticed anyone watching him the day before. Careless. . . . careless.

Never good for a spy.

Except he didn't feel so much like one any longer. It was like he'd gravitated slowly toward the sun after embracing the shadows for so long. Warmth instead of darkness. Light instead of gloom . . . and surprisingly, he didn't object to the change.

Because of his wife.

"Why would you bother to still have me followed? I thought Johnson understood I had spotted him weeks ago."

But not lately, he had to admit. Either the young man had set out to prove a point and was quite a bit more careful, or Michael had been preoccupied with his personal life.

Probably a combination of both, he told himself in rueful honesty.

"We care," Antonia said calmly, walking forward, her gaze taking in the ducal library where he'd decided to receive them. "Or I do. I can't speak for Lawrence, but you must admit his surveillance was fortuitous."

"Yes, Longhaven, feel free to admit it." The other man's smile was insolent. "And as we are discussing the subject, I do care to keep you alive, but my motives are somewhat different than Lady Taylor's."

Michael was sure Lawrence cared only as it suited his purposes, at least to the extent that it mattered to Antonia. He could hardly blame him.

She was worth fighting for, and had it all been different . . .

But it wasn't. As close as their tie was, he and Antonia hadn't ever shared what was needed between a man and a woman. Julianne was his main concern. Not to mention the child, Chloe. He still had a difficult time assigning a name to a niece he never knew he had. "What is so important you chose to call at ten o'clock in the morning?" He moved into the room and quietly closed the door. The civilized surroundings of book-lined walls and sedate furniture were echoed in the quiet garden view from the tall windows.

"Your special friend who shot at you yesterday was hired by a woman." Antonia moved closer, alluring and, for whatever reason, looking younger and less haunted. She was dressed in striped muslin with a lace overskirt, her shining dark hair drawn into a neat chignon. "He was less than adequate . . . not a proper assassin, *Miguel*."

"He still grazed me," he commented dryly. "His aim wasn't that poor."

"Years ago *I* shot you." She smiled with no humor.

"I know. I still have the scar. But you have always sworn it was an accident."

"And you will never know the truth. My point is there is no particular honor in it."

Someday she would come to terms with her jealousy . . . she would have to, and it would be best for both of

them. Deep down, he understood she wasn't holding on
to him as much as she was that wounded woman sitting
in the courtyard of her family's villa. The feelings she had
were based on an illusion, not the real man. He knew it
now more than ever since he'd married. Julianne looked
at him differently. There was no fierce, glittering possession in his wife's eyes, but rather a glorious softness and
something else . . . something he couldn't quite define.

Love, perhaps?

It astonished him that he'd pushed her the other evening to admit it.

Michael laughed shortly. "I agree. I will go so far as
to say I'd appreciate it if people stopped trying to do me
bodily harm. Tell me more about this man your agent
trailed and found."

"He said the woman who hired him had bright red
hair."

It meant nothing to him, which was interesting. Even
more interesting, he supposed, was that all those years
in Spain left him unsurprised that someone he didn't
even know was trying to kill him. Michael gestured at an
intimate gathering of chairs. "Please, sit down. Was there
more of a description?"

Both he and Lawrence stood politely until Antonia
chose a brocade-covered chair and settled in a flutter
of long skirts. Lawrence remained standing, moving behind her chair to rest his hand on the back in a gesture of
male possession Michael didn't fail to notice.

So be it. He'd be happy for them both, and if there
was a budding romance buried beneath the sexual tension, he wasn't exactly the person to judge what the outcome might be. His own life was in flux. He sat down on
a dark blue velvet sofa, crossed his booted legs at the
ankle, and broodingly pondered this new information.

"No more to it," Lawrence said. "And trust me, he
would have told us. There was nothing professional
about him. He was petrified when we found him."

The rain had cleared off, leaving the day soft and gray.

Thinking hard, Michael shifted his gaze to the French doors, still closed against the inclement weather of the previous day. "I can't imagine who it would be. Roget, I suppose, could have an associate. He usually has many, but London isn't Spain and his allies have dwindled. *Usual* no longer applies."

"Perhaps it has nothing to do with Roget. What if it is a spurned lover?" Antonia suggested, her eyes direct and more than a little accusing.

"I'm partial to brunettes." His smile was noncommittal. "Besides, I cannot think of anyone who would be so devastated when we went our separate ways they would resort to murder."

"No? Think harder." Antonia's voice was brittle.

"Ah, but you would kill me yourself."

"I considered it," she said silkily.

He didn't entirely disbelieve her. However, from the amused look on Lawrence's face at the moment, he might just be able to handle such a volatile creature. Michael said dryly, "I appreciate your mercy, but someone else out there is apparently not so compassionate."

"Your inept killer met her at the Hare and the Bottle in Camden Town." Lawrence produced a slip of vellum from his pocket and extended it with two fingers. "I take it you won't mind if Johnson continues to trail after you."

Michael supposed the other man was entitled to the hint of smugness in his tone. "I'm unclear why you bestirred yourself to the trouble and expense of assigning me a shadow, but as my objections would make no difference in what you decide to do anyway, the point is moot. Tell him I am grateful he had the insight to chase after my assailant."

"I have my reasons." Lawrence clearly didn't intend to offer them. "Besides, you've proven you can evade him if need be, so you can keep your deep secrets, my lord. But perhaps you should always consider he might be useful."

The door opened with a soft creak.

Had Julianne been paying attention she might have noticed the library was occupied, but she was looking downward at the small child she held by the hand. His study was a bit too informal to receive a lady, and Michael hardly wanted his mother to join him and his guests in the drawing room, so the library had been a safe and logical choice. Apparently luck was not on his side at this moment.

He rose to his feet. "Good morning."

Julianne looked up at once, taking in Antonia's presence and that of a strange man. "Oh." She was obviously flustered and said hastily, "I am sorry to interrupt. I didn't realize anyone would be using the library. . . . I was hoping there would be some picture books in here. I couldn't find any in the nursery."

"You are not interrupting," he said smoothly, noticing Antonia's gaze first fixed on the child and then slid to him, and back. He didn't blame her. He was a bit taken aback himself.

Now he understood exactly why Julianne was convinced this was Harry's child. Bathed and dry, her soft chestnut curls were exactly the same color as his own hair, and her eyes the vivid hazel color that was a Hepburn trait. Moreover, her facial features held a most distinctive familial stamp.

It took a moment to realize that Julianne was looking at him expectantly. He cleared his throat. "My dear, you know Lady Taylor, of course, and this is Lawrence. Lawrence, my wife, Lady Longhaven."

"Captain Lawrence," the man in question corrected him, and bent over Julianne's hand with beautiful courtesy. "A pleasure, madam."

Captain? Interesting. Michael had never been able to find out anything about Lawrence's past.

Julianne, sweetly pretty this morning in a white gown with small roses embroidered on the fabric and her hair loosely gathered in a simple style that allowed tendrils to frame her delicate face, murmured, "The pleasure is mine, sir."

Michael was aware that Antonia was staring at him with fixed accusation for the second time since her arrival. However, it seemed wrong to inform anyone else before his parents were told about his niece. He knew his two colleagues wouldn't gossip over it—in their profession, gossip was ill-advised—but he still had an ethical dilemma over revealing the truth to anyone else until he found out how his father and mother wished to deal with the unexpected existence of an illegitimate grandchild. Not that Michael had any intention of going back on his promise to Julianne over raising the child themselves, but he did want to take into consideration his parents' feelings over how to present her to the world. Had his father not had an early meeting, the discussion would already have taken place. After an evening of guests, his mother was still in bed, so hopefully she hadn't yet heard about Julianne's dramatic arrival the night before.

"What a beautiful child," Antonia murmured with icy intonation, still gazing at him.

Julianne caught the slant of inference, for she glanced down at the little girl standing so solemnly next to her and a faint pink appeared in her cheeks as she looked back up at Michael in clear uncertainty.

As if it wasn't bad enough to have some unknown woman out there hiring ruffians to kill him, and Roget possibly at large, and now this delicate family issue, it seemed his ill luck held with this new awkward-as-hell situation.

Lady Taylor obviously had come to the conclusion that Chloe was Michael's daughter. Julianne's initial reaction to that assumption was mixed. He was a grown man and didn't need her to defend him, but the question arose why the beautiful Spaniard was so outraged in the first place.

If they were just friends, as Lady Taylor had told her outright, why the fierce stare?

If their involvement was truly over, why was the woman even calling at this unfashionable hour? Julianne had expected to find the library deserted—and she certainly had not expected *this*.

Lawrence, the man with the interesting scar, said decisively, "Antonia, simple mathematics will deny what you are thinking. Come, now. We've given his lordship the information he needs. Let us go."

After a brief hesitation Lady Taylor rose in a sweep of graceful skirts, and though she doubted it happened often, Julianne thought she looked chagrined at the gentle rebuke, her olive skin slightly flushed. "Of course." She inclined her head. "Lady Longhaven, it is nice to see you."

Within a moment, Julianne was alone with Michael except for Chloe, who still clung to her hand, silent as always. "I intruded," she said as neutrally as possible. "In my defense, I thought no one would be in here. She woke early."

"There's no need to apologize. They were ready to depart anyway."

Julianne didn't really want to have an argument—was it even possible to have an argument with Michael?—but she especially didn't want to do it in front of little Chloe, who still stared with wide eyes up at the man standing a few feet away.

To a certain extent, Julianne didn't blame her for being intimidated. He looked very tall in the muted confines of the elegant library, dressed in conservative gray and black, his light brown hair waving back from his fine-boned face, his eyes unreadable.

He could do unreadable so well, and she couldn't do it at all.

They were very unevenly matched and it wasn't fair.

But while she had questions—she had considerable questions, actually—this was not the time to ask them, not with Chloe's small hand in hers. Though she had no experience with children, Julianne had the sense the little girl understood more than one might imagine at her young age.

The events of the day before hadn't been auspicious, and Julianne didn't blame Chloe for falling asleep out of sheer exhaustion. Her own night had been restless and she'd seen the faint circles under her eyes this morning in the mirror and resigned herself to the fact that this was not going to be an easy day either. She knelt and said in a conspiratorial whisper, "Darling, this is your uncle Michael."

How odd it was for such a simple phrase to undo such a normally daunting and self-possessed man. This time she *could* see a reaction. That he was nonplussed was not in question.

It took a few seconds, but he said quietly, "Good morning, Chloe." Then he addressed Julianne again. "You found something decent for her to wear."

"My maid told me Cook has a granddaughter the same age. She was only too happy to help."

"If that many of the servants already know, I'm glad I told my mother's maid to inform me the moment she wakes so I explain before the staff's speculation reaches her ears." The corner of his mouth lifted in a cynical quirk. "I wonder how rife the whispers are already with the assumption she is mine."

"I saw how Lady Taylor reacted. That part of it hadn't occurred to me." Julianne straightened and kept her voice carefully neutral.

"My reputation is somewhat less pristine than Harry's. Even I am surprised at his indiscretion." His agreement was resigned. "But I now see how you accepted the woman's allegations that Harry was responsible."

"The likeness is rather extraordinary, isn't it?"

"It is indeed."

"And Captain Lawrence is correct. You were in Spain when she was conceived."

"Believe it or not, my dear Julianne, soldiers frequently enough father illegitimate children; however, that is neither here nor there. I do not care what people think, but I do care about how my parents will react." He hesitated before he added, "Last night, while I contemplated how to handle this, I considered taking the responsibility for her existence, but decided it was too much to ask of you. The gossipmongers would delightedly pounce on the idea that I asked you to take in my illegitimate child."

"Whereas they aren't going to say a word that I am now raising the child of the man I was supposed to be affianced to?" Julianne couldn't quite hide her cynicism. She hadn't been out in society long, but long enough to understand the talons were sharp and the grip fierce. "Thank you for the consideration, but I think the truth will do quite well anyway. You've been self-sacrificing enough."

She'd startled him. It gave her joy to realize she knew him well enough to see it, for though his expression didn't visibly change, it was there in his eyes in a certain sharpening inquiry. "You married me," she expounded softly, "when you didn't wish to. You juggle the responsibilities you enjoy with the ones you consider to be drudgery without complaint, serving your country and your family at the same time. When you become duke, you will take on that mantle and deal with it to the best of your ability, which means with great competence and duty. I do not get the impression your personal happiness is something to which you give much thought, but it *does* concern me."

"Does it, now?" The question was murmured, but his gaze held hers with a sudden, palpable, searing intensity.

"Yes," she said firmly, an irrational joy invading her because of his reaction. He could conceal so much, but she *saw* it. "And I will not let you risk your parents' censure where you don't deserve it. Besides, Chloe is not a mistake, but a blessing. Though Harry might not appear as much the perfect son as before—he obviously wasn't perfect—that is no reason to love him less, and they won't."

"For someone so young and innocent, you are rather insightful. I don't think of myself as self-sacrificing, but then again, I don't analyze myself often." His lashes lowered a fraction. "I think it would be more apt to say I try not to look too deep. And no doubt you are right about my parents. I hadn't thought of it that way. Their love for Harry won't be changed."

"No," she agreed, her throat a little tight. It was how he was looking at her, as if it weren't ten in the morning, if the door to the library weren't still ajar, if Chloe weren't right there, he would take her in his arms as he'd done the night before and kiss her with the same lingering tenderness.

This was no longer just about passion for either of them, or at least she hoped so.

"I think about your happiness also." He took a slow step closer, but froze as Chloe pressed against her skirts. His smile was rueful. "She's afraid of me."

Julianne placed a comforting hand on Chloe's shoulder. It was no wonder the child was timid. Her life so far had no doubt been a difficult one. "She doesn't know you and you are rather tall, my lord. She will learn to trust you."

"Lord Longhaven?"

One of the maids peered in apologetically through the open door. "I am supposed to tell you Her Grace has just breakfasted in her room and suggests you join her in her sitting room for the audience you requested."

Michael said calmly, "Thank you. Has the duke returned yet?"

"Yes, my lord. Only just."

"Could you please ask him to join us?"

The girl curtsied and hastily departed, but not before Julianne caught a quick, furtive glance at Chloe. What did she expect? Her arrival in the midst of an elaborate dinner party, in a welter of mud with a small child that had slept in her bedroom was not going to be missed.

Michael might be his usual impervious self, but Julianne wasn't calm at all. Butterflies stirred in her stomach. "They may not love Harry less," she muttered, "but it is all too possible they will *not* be delighted with me."

"*I* am delighted with you and that is what matters most," her husband said. "Just trust me. Shall we go make the requisite clarification of why we suddenly are the guardians of a small child?"

I am delighted with you. . . .

It wasn't a declaration of love, but it was progress.

Julianne nodded, bending over to adjust the collar of the simple little dress that was slightly too big on Chloe's petite frame. The sooner it was over, the better. Though Michael's confidence was comforting, she knew full well that someone of the exalted rank of the Duke of Southbrook did not invite illegitimate children into his home. Provided for them, yes, but usually they were sent somewhere out of sight—and thus out of mind. Many aristocrats didn't participate much in the raising of their legitimate children, much less a by-blow. Now that they would know of Chloe's existence, Julianne would be powerless against their decision of what to do with her.

Well, perhaps not entirely powerless, she thought as Michael waited politely for her to precede him out the door.

Her handsome husband was no doubt a formidable ally.

Chapter Twenty-one

"That went better than expected."

"What *did* you expect?" His father poured him a measure of whiskey and gently pushed it across the desk with his fingers.

"I was braced for tears and protestations." Michael took the drink, swallowed a solid gulp, and then set it aside. "You aren't surprised?"

"What, specifically, is the question?" The Duke of Southbrook sat back, looking older, with lines around his mouth that Michael hadn't noticed before.

"I'm speaking of Mother's reaction."

His father wearily ran his fingers through his graying hair. "Surprised? No, not really. I am surprised Harry wasn't as careful as he should be . . . but he isn't the first young gentleman to make such a blunder, nor will he be the last, I'm sure."

"Julianne tells me the woman is an actress."

"Good God," his father muttered.

"For now, it appears she has disappeared. I feel confident, though, we shall hear from her again."

"No doubt." The two words were clipped. "I wish Harry had confided in me, but he didn't. As for your mother's reaction to finding herself a grandmother . . . she'd probably not have been happy to find out her son had fathered a child with a common actress a few years ago, but catastrophic loss has a way of adjusting perceptions. That child is part of our son. I think for her, as it is for me, it is enough no matter the circumstances of her birth."

It was true, apparently, for after the first shock had passed, there had been tentative joy, and if the sudden choked sound of his father's voice was an indication, both his parents were accepting of the little girl.

They were in the ducal study, the thickening afternoon clouds obscuring the light, but there was a warm fire and the rich scent of fine liquor hung in the air. "Then you agree Julianne handled the matter correctly?"

Michael watched his father contemplate the question. After a moment he sighed heavily. "It is incredible that a nineteen-year-old woman should be forced into a position where she is blackmailed for the support of her fiancée's bastard child. I agree that compassion for us ruled her actions, and I am still astounded she used her own funds to pay this woman to keep my dead son's secret, at some significant personal sacrifice. I commend her selflessness."

Michael smiled. He couldn't help it. "She's remarkable in many ways."

"I forced the marriage on you, but I admit you don't seem displeased." There was keen-eyed assessment in his father's gaze.

"I'm a grown man. You didn't force anything on me."

"On the contrary, emotional extortion is as viable as monetary pressure." His father shook his head and sipped from his crystal glass before continuing. "I owe you a deep apology. When I approached you about marrying Julianne, I knew what I was doing. I am just grateful it has not worked out in such a way that you are unhappy."

Discussing his emotions was not his forte. Michael deflected having to make a comment by returning to the subject at hand. "How do you wish to handle this?"

"I personally think the country is the place for a child. It is certainly more wholesome than London."

"Julianne will want to accompany her."

"That is, of course, up to you."

At one time Michael would have embraced being able to send his wife off to Southbrook Manor, but now he found himself resistant to the idea of a prolonged separation. Still, in light of the attempts on his life, he probably should get her out of London.

With resignation, he sighed. "Julianne will want to keep her close. It's clear through all of this she has grown extremely attached to Chloe, and it is obvious the child needs her." Michael paused and then said frankly, "I told her we could raise her as our own."

"You indulge your wife. A good sign." A chuckle followed the words.

"The smugness is unappreciated. I believe you just apologized for coercing me into marrying her." Michael dangled his glass from his fingers, his smile wry.

"It meant so much to your mother, and to me also. I apologize for my methods, not my motives."

"And you would give her anything." It wasn't a question, but a statement. He'd seen other *ton* marriages. His parents had a unique, deep relationship.

"I would."

"No conditions?" Michael didn't often ask for advice; it just wasn't in his nature. He approached problems in an analytical way based on his own experiences, and made snap decisions that had at times risked his life. But then again, he was used to danger.

Julianne and his marriage—not to mention unexpected surrogate fatherhood—was a bit different. His father knew about lifetime commitment . . . and love.

Was Michael in love? It was becoming clearer by the moment that in some way he was out of his depth with his young, beguiling wife. She'd said earlier she cared about his happiness. He found he also cared about hers.

His father transferred his gaze to the crackling fire, the leaping flames welcome in the chill of the gloomy afternoon. He gently smoothed his fingers down the side of his glass in a contemplative gesture. "There are some conditions. Life is always a compromise. I would never tolerate infidelity, though many men I know care very little about the personal lives of their wives once they have produced the heir needed for their titles and fortune. Those same men are promiscuous themselves, so they view the lack of hypocrisy as being indulgent, but I can't—and never could—see marriage that way."

"Though I am hardly beyond reproach, the lack of morality among the privileged class has always given me pause."

"I'm glad to hear your sensibilities match mine in that regard."

Michael cocked a brow. "So there is no objection to my wife and me taking charge of Chloe?"

"None, as long as your mother agrees, and she will. The role of grandparent is different from that of a mother and father, and this child in particular has been deprived of both of the latter."

Indeed she had. "I will ask Rutgers, then, if he has any recommendations for a temporary nursemaid among the staff and to contact an agency to begin a search for a permanent one."

"He's most efficient."

Michael was pleased the issue was settled in a way that would make Julianne happy, the lighthearted emotion incongruous to the lurking threat of his mysterious, murderous opponent out there. "I'll approach Julianne about going to Kent." Fitzhugh could continue to do his duty guarding her, but it would hardly do to tell his father that Michael's service to the Crown had put his wife in danger.

"Your mother will like that. She's been talking about returning to the country."

Michael finished his drink and rose. "I've an appointment that can't wait."

"That seems to be a constant excuse."

He must be slipping. He'd thought he'd balanced his life more effectively. "I'm not quite done with my duties to Wellington and the War Office."

"What happened to your arm?"

Now he knew he definitely *was* slipping.

"A minor injury," he said with a negligent shrug. Truth was, with all the distraction, he'd all but forgotten about the graze, but he must be visibly favoring it. "It's nothing."

"If you say so, I must take your word on it. But perhaps a little more caution is in order, son."

It was easier to choose to not address the speculation in that statement. Michael left his father's study to find Fitzhugh hovering out in the hallway. "What is it?" he asked sharply as his valet handed him his greatcoat.

"The devil's own business, sir."

"What particular devil are we discussing?" Michael slipped on the garment.

"You," Fitzhugh said serenely.

At least it all had gone well and the maid Rutgers had selected as Chloe's temporary nurse was a young, fresh-faced woman named Bryn from Wales with a soft accent and gentle manner. Considering the dramatic change in her circumstances, the huge house, the multitude of people when Chloe was used to much more meager contact with strange adults, Julianne thought the little girl did quite well. She didn't leave her until after luncheon, the shared meal with the maid at her insistence, for she cared very little about rank and title anyway, and, quite frankly, all she wanted was for Chloe to get used to the young woman.

When an assortment of blocks that made the ones she'd given the little girl seem quite humble were discovered in the nursery, the child's attention was absorbed. Julianne was finally able to sneak away as the smiling maid provided supervision. Someone—she suspected it was Michael, for he never failed to surprise her—had ordered it cleaned and opened. With the dust cloths removed and the shutters pulled back from the windows, it was a much more welcoming place, and a cheerful fire burned in the grate. Also, the picture books she'd wanted sat on the low table in the middle of the room.

The thoughtfulness of it all moved her.

Once downstairs, she found that her husband was not at home, but she had a caller who had been waiting. The woman had not left a calling card or given her name but insisted, Rutgers informed her in his genteel delivery, that she would wait as long as necessary for her ladyship to receive her.

It admittedly made her curious. Very few of her friends would refuse to identify themselves, nor would many be willing to wait indefinitely either. "Very well," she said, smoothing her gown. "Thank you."

"She is in the informal salon, my lady."

That surprised her, and evidently it showed. His expression said he knew exactly where to put each caliber of visitor, and had for decades before she was born, but he was infinitely too well-bred to mention it.

Informal was telling. This was not a typical social visit, then. Nor was it a typical visitor.

Julianne walked down the marble hallway and found the room in question, the more comfortable surroundings of scattered chairs and tables a contrast to the silk-covered walls and priceless paintings of the public rooms where the Duke of Southbrook received his visitors. When she saw the woman seated on one of the settees, there was no sense of recognition.

But she did recognize, with a small shock, that the

visitor had flamboyant red hair that clashed with her somewhat shabby pink gown.

"Good afternoon," she murmured, advancing into the room in a state of confusion. "I'm Lady Longhaven. I understand you wish to see me."

"So you're her." The woman stood, her eyes narrowed. "I expected something just like you. Pretty as a porcelain doll. Well, I suppose Harry wouldn't want to marry a hag, now, would he?"

Whatever does that mean and who is this woman?

"And you are?" Julianne said pointedly, not sure she wanted to sit down and entertain this particular guest.

"Leah McDermont."

"No," Julianne argued, shaking her head, wondering what was going on. She'd met with Chloe's mother every week over the better part of the past six months. This was not the same woman.

"You think I don't know my own name?"

It was difficult to answer when the world seemed to have spun off its axis. Yet, oddly enough, the sneering attitude was familiar. "I know Miss McDermont."

"The hell you do, my fine lady. You just think as you know her."

"What does that mean?" Julianne demanded, still only a few feet in the door, reluctant to go in any farther in the face of such blatant hostility.

"It means I'm tired of waiting on someone else to get me what I deserve. Tell me where your Harry's precious daughter is, or I'll go to a magistrate."

That didn't exactly clarify anything, and she blinked, at a loss. "She was left alone in a deserted house. Naturally, I brought her here."

"I didn't leave her alone; *she* did." The other woman sniffed. "I knew all along you wanted her. Always bringing presents . . . pretty things . . . Well, if you don't want me takin' her away right now, you'll pay up like she always said you would."

"Who is *she*?"

Julianne needn't have worried about not understanding. Her visitor had sufficient purpose to make sure her objectives were crystalline. In a mannerism she'd seen before—or at least had been mimicked very well by the woman she'd thought was Leah—she tossed her head and declared, "I want money. If you don't give me what's due I'll go to the bloody *Times* and give them every detail of how the Marquess of Longhaven tupped a barmaid and gave her a full belly."

"Go ahead."

The contained voice made them both swivel toward the doorway. The duke stood there, his usual affable manner absent, his normally pleasant expression taking on some of his son's inscrutable purpose. "I do not know precisely who you are," he said, strolling in and coming to Julianne's rescue with such ducal aplomb that she was sure the prince regent couldn't have had more presence. "But rest assured, I do not appreciate you threatening my daughter-in-law. You do realize a timely word from me would prevent any damaging gossip from being printed about my dead son by any publication on English soil. But even if you stood on the rooftop of every house in London and shouted your story far and wide, the Hepburn family is far above caring for such a minor scandal."

This Leah—Julianne did not know now who to believe was really Chloe's mother—had her mouth hanging half open unattractively at the arrival of the duke himself.

A barmaid? Leah—the other Leah—had told her she was an actress.

Bewilderment didn't even describe her reaction.

The duke then turned to Julianne with a small, humorless smile. "You have done more than enough for our family already, my dear. I will deal with this unpleasant situation."

As a dismissal, it was neatly done and with regal confidence. Truthfully, she was so confounded that she was only too happy to comply with the inferred order.

What motive would someone have, she wondered as she left the room, *to impersonate a young, impoverished barmaid who'd given birth to an illegitimate child?*

Chapter Twenty-two

The Hare and Bottle was hardly reputable, but it wasn't one of the blacker establishments either. Clad in a worn coat, his oldest boots splashed with mud from the street and his cravat removed, Michael alighted from the hired hack and entered the building. He found it half full of patrons, and the proprietor himself served ale to the modest crowd. A low cloud of tobacco smoke mingled with an ill-lit fireplace gave the interior of the taproom the look of a foggy morning.

He rather doubted he'd find out anything helpful, but one never knew. Parts of his job were actually tedious. He'd been meeting with informants ever since the second attack and learned nothing.

Of course, he'd been looking for Roget, but he now suspected he'd been asking the wrong questions about the wrong opponent.

Michael chose a chair in a corner, and when the man came over, he said succinctly, "I'll take a tankard, but I came for a bit of advice."

The owner was a burly man in middle age, with a bristling black beard and deep-set, sharp eyes. He scowled. "The ale I can provide, but as for the advice—"

"I've heard if I need someone to do me certain favors, this is the place to come," Michael interrupted smoothly. "You know to what I am referring, I'm sure."

"Don't be too sure of anything," the man said bluntly. "I'll get yer drink."

The game was a familiar one. So he sat back, cast the assembled customers a casual perusal, and waited. Trust was a hard commodity to come by, and he certainly didn't extend it easily himself.

When the tavern owner returned, he hovered a moment after plunking down the drink on the scarred table. "What is it you want?"

"We have a mutual friend. The name is Everett."

"I know 'im." The surly acknowledgment was accompanied by wary assessment.

"And I know what service he provides." Michael took a sip of his ale, postponing the moment. "I want to know if you saw him meet here with a woman recently. Flame-red hair, I'm told."

"Now, why would I remember that?" One beefy fist rested on the table.

"Because this is your establishment," Michael murmured, "and I wager you notice almost everything."

That won him a grudging nod.

"Everett?"

"More wind than worth."

"What do you know about the woman? I've coin, but it will only end up in your pocket if it is good." In his career, Michael had dealt with a great deal of different types of interrogations, and this seemed the straightforward kind.

The owner of the Hare and Bottle looked for a moment like he would protest, but then jerked his head to the side. "I've a private sitting room empty."

I don't wish to concede it, but I have a lot to thank Lawrence for, Michael thought as he rose, brought his somewhat less than appealing ale with him, and followed the man through a door that led into a back parlor.

A quarter of an hour later he emerged with at least a few tidbits of information that might be helpful. Everett's rooms had been empty when he had gone there to question him, and really, he'd seen hardened soldiers cringe before Antonia's particular brand of interrogation before, so he wasn't sure he blamed the man for decamping. Luckily the tavern keeper had been able to supply a list of suggestions of where the would-be killer might have gone. Finding him again shouldn't be too difficult.

And now he had a better description of the mysterious woman who wanted him dead. Slender, medium height, and, most interesting of all, a lady. There had been no doubt in the tavern keeper's voice when he said she was as out of place at the Hare and Bottle as a Whitechapel whore in a nunnery. He'd noticed it when she first inquired about finding someone to employ in a matter of some delicacy. It was in her voice, he'd said, and the fancy words she chose. Once Michael had produced a handful of coins to jog the man's memory, he had been quite frank in admitting he'd recommended Everett to her, as Everett had done similar tasks effectively in the past. The woman had arranged an appointment.

Michael had learned something else interesting also. The red hair was a wig. The tavern owner said he'd swear to it, but what business was it of his if she didn't want to be recognized? Michael wasn't surprised, considering she wanted to hire someone to kill a man.

God bless observant tavern owners, Michael thought as he walked back to where he'd paid the hackney driver to wait.

Three attempts on his life, all failed. Surely she must be getting frustrated, if she even knew yet that the last effort had not been successful. As he methodically re-tied his cravat and replaced his disreputable coat with a tailored one, he pondered again her identity, and a glimmer of a suspicion came to him.

He *could* think of a woman who might hold a grudge against him.

No, like Antonia speculated, there was no ex-lover he imagined cared enough to go to the trouble to try to have him killed, but upon contemplation of the information that she'd used a disguise, Michael thought of one female who might seek revenge of the deadliest sort.

Not his lover, but Roget's former paramour. The trouble was, he'd arranged for her to board a ship months ago. As far as he knew, and despite his failure to locate Roget, his sources were usually excellent and she wasn't even in England.

When the hackney stopped in front of his club he alighted, paid the driver, and went up the steps, all the time his mind working on this current puzzle. Casting back over the possible list of suspects for the three aborted attempts on his life, the evidence did point to someone who was used to intrigue, who would bother to conceal her identity, who would want him irrevocably eliminated just for revenge, because he'd thwarted and banished her.

Maybe he should have taken Alice Stewart more seriously. He was fairly sure she had murdered at least two people, and most certainly she was guilty of kidnapping. But he was much more used to dealing with threats in as quiet a manner as possible, and once she'd given him all the information he wanted, he had let her flee England. His superiors tended to want to keep intelligence matters quiet, and putting a woman on trial—especially a female spy—was a tricky matter.

So he'd let her go.

And now he wondered if he'd made a grave error.

"Good afternoon, my lord." The steward took his greatcoat with a flourish. "It is always nice to see you again."

"Thank you, Phillip. Is Lord Altea here, by any chance?"

"It happens he is. The usual table."

Good. It wasn't often, but now and then Michael needed to verbally muse over an idea, and Luke happened to know this particular story in a personal way. He'd hoped he might find the viscount having a quiet afternoon moment. Sure enough, Luke glanced up from reading the paper as he approached. Luke's smile was welcoming, but there was also curiosity in his eyes. By way of greeting, he said, "Were you really shot yesterday?"

Hell and damnation. Michael had forgotten entirely about the solicitous footman that had dashed from Lady Armington's house. A marquess being shot in a street in Mayfair wouldn't go unnoticed. He dropped into a chair and said, "Do I look like I was wounded?"

"Actually, no." Luke folded the paper and pushed it across the table, but his gaze still held a hint of skepticism. "But that doesn't mean much with you. Not too long ago you were stabbed and I couldn't tell that either."

THE MARKED MARQUESS? Word has it a certain Lord L— was the victim of gunshot injury while walking in one of London's finest neighborhoods yesterday. The question must be asked if the incident was an accident or if his lordship was the intended victim.

It appeared the sooner he told Julianne what happened, the better. Michael didn't comment, but instead asked, "What do you think about Alice Stewart?"

Luke's attention sharpened. He leaned back and nodded, his gray eyes narrowed a fraction. "My wife's cousin? That's an interesting question. She did her best to use my stepson as a bargaining tool to escape England after trying to publicly humiliate my wife. Quite naturally, I dislike the spiteful lady."

The question had been purely rhetorical, as they both recalled the incident all too well. "I always believed she had an association with a certain old friend of mine."

"Roget?"

"The very one."

"Care to tell me more?"

"Not about him, but I *am* wondering about Mrs. Stewart." Michael kept his tone neutral. "I take it your wife hasn't heard from her."

"No. Madeline despises her. If she'd contacted her, I would know it immediately."

"I'm starting to wonder if she might not be behind the attacks I've experienced lately."

The waiter arriving with their drinks precluded any response from Luke. When the claret was poured and they were alone again, his friend said without preamble, "How? I thought she'd left England."

"Oh, she did. One of my colleagues watched her ship weigh anchor, bound for India. The crossing takes months." Michael moodily contemplated his glass. "Yet the man who, thankfully, missed his mark yesterday was hired by a woman. I've tried to come up with a list of females who might seek revenge upon me, and when I contemplate it she is certainly at the top."

"But presumably an ocean away."

"I tend to find presumptions are dangerous."

Luke rested his forearms on the table. "Alice has no love for Madeline either, so your theory alarms me. How can I help?"

Michael had been shot?

As if the day hadn't been bewildering enough, this was hardly welcome news, nor did it help her already disordered mood. Julianne shook her head and looked at her mother. "It isn't possible. He carried . . ."

Oh, dear, had she just almost said he'd carried her up the stairs the evening before? That would raise more questions she certainly didn't want to answer, so she hastily amended, "He seemed perfectly fine last evening. Maybe the paper is incorrect, or they mean someone else."

Unfortunately, the duchess was an even worse actress than Julianne was herself, though to excuse her, she hadn't exactly had an uneventful day either. Resplendent in pale blue satin, her chestnut hair piled high, she took a gulp of tea and nodded. "Yes, that's it. Someone else."

With open skepticism, her mother looked from one of them to the other. "What other Lord L is a marquess? Besides, apparently Lady Armington's footman was a witness."

"Well, then, it certainly *has* to be true," Julianne said dryly, but inside there was a traitorous doubt as she remembered the swathe of bandages Michael had on their wedding night. He certainly hadn't shown any sign of being injured during their wedding or the celebration afterward. Yet the scar indicated the wound must have been painful.

With Michael, she was growing to learn, just about any secret was possible.

At least her mother knew when to gracefully retreat. She inclined her head. "I'm just glad it isn't the truth. You can only imagine my horror when I read this. I had to come over and make sure he wasn't seriously injured."

"Not at all. Everything is quite fine." Julianne's mother-in-law did not even come close to pulling off a serene smile, though she did try. Aristocratic fortitude, apparently, was compromised by the arrival of a grandchild she never knew she had, a woman impersonating the child's mother, and then the news that her only son had been shot the day before and failed to mention it.

Julianne really could not blame her for being so rattled. She was fairly rattled herself.

When her mother departed a good half hour later, she and the duchess just looked at each other. "Perhaps," Julianne's mother-in-law said as her shoulders sagged and her cup rattled on the saucer, "I should just commit myself to Bedlam and be done with it. What in heaven's name is going on in this house? For that matter, where is Michael?"

The formal drawing room was suddenly stifling despite the graciousness of the space and the cool afternoon. Julianne admitted, "I don't know."

"*Was* he injured yesterday?"

"I don't think so." She made a helpless gesture with her hand, and without thinking explained, "Chloe slept with me, so we didn't . . . that is . . . well, she needed me and . . ."

Her vivid blush at least brought forth a chuckle. Michael's mother said, "I see. And yes, I agree the child needs you. She needs us all and certainly not that appalling woman who claims to be her mother."

Julianne wanted desperately to tell Michael of that new development, but once again, he was still out and had been for most of the day. However, in light of her mother's visit, she now put new significance on the early-morning arrival of Lady Taylor and Captain Lawrence. "I am as confused as you are."

"The duke is also confounded, and trust me, my dear, that does not happen all that often. He is used to being able to order his world."

No doubt the Duke of Southbrook could normally command whatever he wished. However, Julianne was learning, life was a little less predictable than she had originally thought. "I admit *my* optimism of the world has been compromised by recent events."

"Maybe, but mine has been confirmed." The duchess looked at her intently. "I haven't yet thanked you for what you did for Harry and his child."

She didn't want to be thanked. What Julianne wanted was for Michael to be home, safe and sound. "There's no need to thank me. I was more afraid you'd be angry with me, one way or the other."

"I might have been," the duchess said, resting her arm on the settee, her face thoughtful, "right after my son died so suddenly. It was such a shock. At first I wondered how you could keep my granddaughter's existence from us, but after some contemplation, I see why you did."

"As I told Michael, I assumed if Harry didn't want you to know, I shouldn't tell you."

"And what did Michael say to that?"

Were this any other day, she wouldn't have said it, but Julianne smiled wistfully and answered, "He asked me if I'd loved his brother."

"Now, that," the duchess said emphatically, "is a good sign. What was your answer?"

"Am I interrupting?"

At the sound of the masculine voice, Julianne's head jerked up. Michael walked into the room, looking for all the world like the usual gentleman of the *haut ton*, complete with his perfect cravat and tailored clothing. But she thought he also looked tired, and there was a hint of mud on his boots, and his hair was windblown.

"Michael."

"Were you expecting someone else?"

To her surprise Julianne had to resist the impulse to get to her feet and run into his arms. Instead she blurted out, "My mother just left."

"I'm sorry I missed her." It was a polite answer. He didn't choose a chair, but remained near the doorway. "I hope all is well."

How could he look so . . . so blasted normal and banal? "Not precisely," Julianne said with as much calm as she could muster. "She seemed to think a reference in the paper might be to an accident you had yesterday and yet failed to mention."

"No."

"There was no accident?"

His smile was just a small, ironic curve of his lips. "No. I meant it wasn't an accident. Someone shot at me deliberately."

Not sure how to respond, Julianne just stared at him. The duchess made an inarticulate sound of dismay.

With exquisite politesse, he said, "Mother, can you please excuse us? I would very much like to speak with my wife alone. Julianne, shall we go upstairs?"

"You are leaving London."

He knew he hadn't delivered that edict well and quietly shut the door behind them. "Let me rephrase. I think you should take the child and leave for the ducal estate in Kent. Fitzhugh will go with you."

Julianne walked slowly over to the bed and sat down on the edge, her dark blue eyes luminous. "I will consider it if you will explain to me exactly what is happening. I am not unintelligent, my lord, and I have already gathered that you still serve the British government in some capacity that is, apparently, dangerous. The night of our wedding you were evasive when I asked about your injury, and you have not been more forthcoming since. I am not going to claim you owe me the truth." Her smile was tremulous. "I too kept a secret from you, and I am not that hypocritical, but I love you and want to share all of your life, not just the small part you have given me so far."

None of the moments of danger he'd faced in his life so far had ever paralyzed him. He'd been captured by the French— twice, no less—tortured for information, fought in bloody battles, and, after Talavera, once left for dead on the field, he'd pragmatically accepted that he might well lose his life if not found soon. So he'd crawled, bleeding and weakened, past fallen comrades until he heard the sound of voices before he collapsed.

That had been much, much easier.

At this moment, he couldn't move. The breath seemed caught in his chest and he just stood there, speechless and frozen.

He'd wanted to hear it, and he just had that wish fulfilled. What should he do now?

Julianne waited, her expression poignant, her hands folded demurely in her lap.

Finally, he cleared his throat. "I . . ."

"You?" she said when he trailed off after that ineffectual one syllable.

Damn her, he thought after another moment in which he groped for words. While she might be young and inexperienced, she still had easily gained the upper hand with her artless declaration, and from the very slight hint of a tentative smile touching her soft lips, she realized it too.

Michael took in a steadying breath and said quietly, "I will be as honest as I can. Some secrets are not mine to reveal."

Was she disappointed he hadn't fallen to his knees and sworn his undying devotion? She didn't seem to be.

Maybe she knew him better than he thought she did, and that realization didn't help his discomfort. She hadn't expected anything in return.

Frowning, Julianne said, "This afternoon a woman claiming to be Chloe's mother came to visit me. I have no idea how the visit ended, for your father came in and at his request I left them there to deal with each other. But it certainly was not the woman I have been paying these past months. She told me quite shamelessly they had some sort of collaboration to extort money."

A frisson of warning shot through him. That was strange indeed. "What else did she say?" he asked tersely. "Go over it for me carefully."

She did, explaining how the woman who had claimed to be Chloe's mother had declared she was tired of waiting for someone else to get her money for her, and various other sordid details that did nothing to clarify the situation but just further muddied it.

Two mysterious women and sudden chaos in his life . . . Michael mentally shook his head. Not only did his instincts tell him it was all related, but the coincidence of the timing was also telling.

The first failed attack on him had been right after his engagement was publicly announced. That was also about the same time Julianne had been contacted with the blackmail ultimatum.

Finally, enough evidence was piling up for him to sink his teeth into. This part of the game he knew. This was his forte. To assemble a puzzle, one needed pieces.

He walked over to the bed, pulled his wife to her feet, and kissed her with hard, lingering pressure, one arm around her slim waist, the other hand at her nape so their bodies were pressed tightly together. Arousal flared through him, but along with it came a deeper sensation, an indescribable sense of belonging. She belonged in his embrace, and he belonged there, holding her, kissing her, his fingers tangled in her hair.

When he finally lifted his mouth from hers and her lashes slowly rose, the light in her eyes humbled him. When he cleared up this nasty little mess, he'd join her in Kent, he decided. By necessity he spent most of his time in London, but England could do without his services for a while. Autumn was a beautiful time in the country, and he could suddenly see himself taking his wife for long morning rides down the winding lanes, going for picnics near the river, and watching the moonlight gilding her glossy hair as they drifted to sleep each night in each other's arms. . . .

When was the last time he'd simply enjoyed life? His marriage was making him reconsider his priorities, and while it had been acceptable to risk his neck for the Crown, it was different now that he had a family of his own. His first responsibility was to Julianne, and now there was a child to care for also.

"Call your maid and start packing." He touched her cheek and reluctantly let her go. "You'll depart tomorrow morning. Don't worry, love. I will take care of everything."

The endearment, said in a low tone, stopped him even as he turned to decisively walk away. He shouldn't linger; he needed to talk to his father and then possibly to send a message to Charles.

"You've never called me that before," Julianne said, her voice hushed. She gazed at him with tentative . . . what? Triumph? Hope?

She is young, he reminded himself. *Idealistic. She believes in love. She thinks she loves* me . . .

With all he'd seen and done in his life, he wasn't sure he could regain an idyllic view of the world. But for her, he found, he was willing to try.

"I will take care of everything," he repeated, and walked in long strides toward the doorway.

She didn't know it, but he'd never called *any* woman that before.

Chapter Twenty-three

It had started to rain. Again. England truly had a terrible climate, if you asked him, though Lawrence was from Manchester and a native. Once you'd sailed the Mediterranean, or, even better, the Caribbean, you became a devotee of sun-drenched beaches and azure skies. He'd discovered gems of small islands and palm trees in luscious coves and pristine white sands that stretched for miles.

Until, of course, he ran afoul of a French navy vessel, was thrown in chains, and impressed into Bonaparte's service on pain of death.

For a man who had scraped his way out of the gutter, that was not an acceptable existence. Cheating fate had become one of his special skills, and as an Englishman, however jaded, he wasn't about to advance the cause of the ambitious little Corsican.

So he had subverted it instead.

Would he have repeated every choice he'd made in his life? No, he acknowledged, turning his collar up against the driving precipitation, but neither did he believe in regrets. Too many choices had been made for him as it was, and he was owed enough apologies that he had none to give others.

Yes, he and Antonia were very, very much alike.

For now, he needed to discover if he had made a grave mistake.

Perhaps he had, for once inside the house, after hanging up his greatcoat, he found the housekeeper, Mrs. Purser, hovering in the hallway. "I'm glad you are back, Mr. Lawrence. My lady has a visitor and left instructions for you to join them upon your return."

He was well aware the small staff Antonia employed thought his relationship with their mistress an interesting one, to say the least, and weren't sure how much deference to pay him. Most of the maids called him sir, but Mrs. Purser, who was somewhat of a puritan, amused him constantly by giving a disapproving sniff whenever their paths crossed, which was inevitably quite often in such a small household. She obviously suspected he shared Lady Taylor's bed, and she certainly knew he came and went at strange hours.

"In the drawing room?" he asked, taking out his handkerchief to wipe his damp face. He was hardly dressed to receive visitors, but then again, he hadn't expected he needed to be.

"His lordship's study."

Antonia wouldn't entertain the average visitor in Lord Taylor's study.

Longhaven.

He'd wondered, actually, how long it would be before he saw the marquess again.

As usual, his archrival was handsome and urbane, even dressed as casually as Lawrence in fawn breeches, white shirt, and dark coat. He sat in Lord Taylor's chair behind the desk, which was somehow irritating, perhaps because of the implied proprietorship of the room. Antonia was dressed to go out for the evening, the material of her gown a telling deep ruby, complementing her olive skin and raven hair. She was every inch the flamboyant Spanish beauty, and Lawrence could have stood there for a lifetime just admiring the view.

Except for the open suspicion in her eyes.

Not good, a small voice whispered in his brain. *Something has happened.* Out loud, he said, "Good evening. You wished to see me?"

"I'm wondering now," the Marquess of Longhaven said in his best negligent drawl, "if Mrs. Stewart ever departed on that ship months ago. It is possible, of course, she did, and I am mistaken in my assumptions, but having had some time to think over the options, I cannot come up with a better candidate for a woman who so violently wants me dead."

As always, the man was no fool.

Lawrence strolled into the room, stripping off his gloves.

Antonia said stiffly, "Michael's theory is quite interesting."

The fire in the hearth made it a bit stuffy, but that was the least of his worries. With careful deliberation he chose a chair and sat down. "I'm apparently considered to be culpable in some way. Explain to me this 'theory.'"

"That's quite easy. Did Alice Stewart, a reputed close friend of Roget, sail on that ship months ago? You were supposed to see her board and watch it leave the harbor. If she didn't leave England, I think I have a fair idea of who is so determined to kill me."

"Oh, yes, the nefarious Mrs. Stewart. I remember the incident quite well." Lawrence wasn't even sure why he was stalling.

Michael Hepburn's gaze was steady. "Then you will have no trouble answering the question."

Lawrence could lie, of course. God knew he'd done so before and would probably do it again in his lifetime, and of his myriad sins, it was a minor one. But lying in general and lying effectively to Longhaven were two

different matters, and, besides, he found he didn't wish
to perjure himself in front of Antonia.

But neither did he want to explain.

A devil's own dilemma, to be sure.

So he equivocated. "She boarded a ship and I watched
it sail."

"Was it bound for India?"

"You truly think Alice Stewart is behind the recent
attempts on your life? Why?"

In the chair behind the oak desk, Longhaven stirred in
a singularly uncharacteristic restive movement. "I have
reason to believe she has made an effort to have access to
my family with a somewhat inventive impersonation."

"How so?" Lawrence was well aware he hadn't yet
answered the pertinent question.

"The details aren't necessary."

"Every bit of information is necessary," he countered.
As usual, Longhaven had secrets of his own. Lawrence
might not be aristocratic or privileged, but in many ways,
they were well matched.

"In this case, I am unwilling to reveal the details."

It must be nice to be born and bred to that uncom-
promising tone. That luxury was unknown to Lawrence,
and he smiled thinly. "Spoken like the exalted marquess.
Now, if you really wish to ask me questions, shall we regain our equal footing? Answer my question and I will
answer yours."

To Longhaven's credit, he didn't point out they had
never been equals. At least not socially. He merely
looked bland, though his eyes were watchful. "Fair
enough. I've always trusted you . . . at least as much as I
trust anyone. My wife was approached by a woman who
claimed she'd borne my brother's babe out of wedlock.
Needless to say, she wanted money. Julianne went to see
the child every week. However, as matters started to
complicate, it seems the mother of the child is not whom
my wife visited. The deviousness of it hardly speaks of
a simple arrangement of blackmail. There's a purpose,

and in light of recent events I am beginning to worry it involves more than simple avarice."

In light of this information, Lawrence worried about the same thing. "Why is Mrs. Stewart a suspect?"

"Should she be?"

Antonia rose to her feet then, her face flushed, her eyes flashing. "I am so tired of games! Speak plainly to each other for once. He told *you* what you wanted to know. Lawrence, simply answer his question. Did that woman sail for India or is she causing all this trouble?"

Of course, gentleman that he was, Longhaven immediately rose also, since she was standing.

Lawrence was not so refined. Perhaps it was time she remembered it. He stayed seated and said coolly, "Your impassioned demands are usually my pleasure, my love, but in this instance, it sounds too much like an accusation. I have no idea if Mrs. Stewart is our culprit. But no, she did not sail off to India."

Lord Longhaven did not look surprised. "Where was the ship bound?"

"France."

"Ah."

"Who would ever want to go there?" Antonia spat out the question, magnificent as ever in her disdain. She muttered something in Spanish that was obviously not flattering to that country. The majority of the French people, of course, were not responsible for the atrocities committed by Bonaparte's troops, but trying to tell her that was a lesson in futility. When she hated, she hated passionately.

When she loved, it was with the same intensity.

Lawrence wanted her to love *him*.

"I can tell you who might wish to sail to France instead of India. Someone who wanted to come back to England easily," Longhaven said thoughtfully. "It isn't a long passage. How did she convince you?"

The question was asked in a conversational tone, but

Lawrence understood that was not the sentiment behind it.

This next bit would be tricky.

"How did she convince you to not have her imprisoned?" Lawrence countered, steadily meeting Longhaven's appraisal.

The marquess answered readily. "You were there. She gave me information on Roget."

"Not very much. Just that he was in England—in London, in fact—but otherwise she told you nothing."

"On the contrary, she told me Roget was an Englishman."

Yes, she had. But she'd outright refused to give them the man's identity, under pain of imprisonment and probably the gibbet if they could prove she was a traitor spying for Bonaparte. Lawrence said evenly, "His name would have been more helpful. In reality, I don't think she helped you much, my lord."

"I doubt she ever knew his real name anyway." Longhaven rubbed his lean jaw. "And that is part of the reason I let her go."

"I could have gotten more information out of her," Antonia said with conviction. "You men are soft when it comes to females. A few moments alone with me, and take my word, she would have talked."

"Perhaps." The marquess's voice held a hint of amusement. "But I saw no need to be so bloodthirsty and torture is not my usual method. Besides, she was trapped and at least claimed she wished to leave England quite badly. So, Lawrence, may I reiterate the question? Why did you let her choose the ship to France instead of following the agreed-upon plan?"

"A woman's tears can move mountains." Evasive—and yet so true. Not that it was why he'd let Alice Stewart board a different ship. "She had already booked the passage to France and wept at the thought of India. It terrified her, she claimed, and I believed her. After all, she had spent a good deal of the war in France, and if she stayed in England, she would most probably hang. Why would I ever think she'd come back?"

"I never cry," Antonia declared derisively, reaching for the claret decanter and pouring a glass. The ruby liquid exactly matched her gown, and she lifted the goblet to her lips, taking a dainty sip.

"Why should you? You can move mountains without tears," Lawrence told her, his smile wry.

But she lied. He'd heard her crying once or twice in the middle of the night. No sobs—she wouldn't allow that—but small, subtle, shuddering breaths that held such sorrow it was all he could do to not reach for her and tuck her close into a protective embrace.

He would die to protect her. If it was possible, he'd die gladly to obliterate her memories. But it wasn't, and the past was what it was, and all he could offer was a future.

If she would consider it after he had put her precious Longhaven in danger, even if it was inadvertent. He was telling the truth. He never thought Alice Stewart would set foot on English soil again.

"Do you know how to find her?" the marquess asked him, his gaze speculative. "Operating, of course, under the hypothesis that Alice Stewart might have slipped back into England."

"No," Lawrence said with as little inflection as possible, "but from previous experience with the lady I know where to start."

"As in?"

"Where is your wife?"

In all of his experience, he'd never seen Longhaven react with other than perfect composure to any situation, but he could have sworn the man paled slightly. "She accepted an invitation for the Marstons' traditional autumn ball. My parents are also going, and Fitzhugh is going to drive them. I promised I'd join them later. Tomorrow I am sending her to the family estate in Kent, where she will be safe until we clear this up."

Lawrence spoke the truth when he said with hard-earned practicality, "There is no such concept as safe, my lord."

Little Chloe was sweetly asleep before they departed, but Julianne couldn't resist tiptoeing across the room to gently touch her tousled curls. The nursemaid, already dressed for bed and wearing a simple wrapper over her nightdress, and doing some sewing by the fire, smiled encouragingly. There were several bedrooms to choose from off the nursery, and Julianne had picked one for Chloe with a garden view that would be sunny in the mornings and had charming pictures of framed woodland scenes, completed with fuzzy flop-eared bunnies and cavorting lambs in green meadows. Chloe had stared at them in rapt concentration, her precious doll clutched in her arms, and then she had smiled.

It was a beginning.

The duchess had already expressed concern over the child possibly being a mute, but Julianne didn't think so. She was hardly a physician, but she suspected the silence was more an innate sense of self-preservation, and she hoped that once love, warmth, acceptance, and safety became a reality in the little girl's life, she would start to speak.

For the moment, she'd been so happy to see that unself-conscious smile of childish delight, she had felt a hot tightening in her throat.

"If you think she needs me," she whispered to the nursemaid, "you may bring her to my room. We won't be out terribly late."

"The little one will be fine, my lady," Bryn said in her soft accent. "I'm going to sleep right here, and we are getting along right well. Do not worry, and enjoy your evening."

"I will."

As ever, Julianne thought as she left the room and went toward the stairs, Rutgers was beautifully efficient in his selection, and she would have no objection at all if the girl was put in the position permanently. Bryn had acted as if she were pleased they'd be going to the country for at least a short stay. Julianne was still not sure of Michael's plans, but she wasn't resistant to getting away from London until all had been settled with Leah. The odd events of the past few days still had her off balance.

Especially that kiss after she'd told him she loved him.

It hadn't been skillful seduction or simply physical passion. She'd felt the emotion in that impetuous embrace.

"You look stunning, my dear." The duke smiled at her as she gained the foyer, rather impressive himself in his dark evening wear. The duchess was resplendent in emerald green satin, her hair upswept and a glittering diadem worth at least a small fortune accenting her perfect coiffure.

"Thank you." She wished Michael was there to accompany them, but saw with wry humor that the ever-faithful Fitzhugh would be also attending the event in the guise of driver, his livery perfect and his face expressionless as he opened the door of the conveyance with a small flourish. Her personal watchdog on duty yet again, and banished off to the countryside in the morning with her. Just how dangerous was all this?

A ridiculous question to ask, of course. Michael had been attacked twice.

"You have many talents, I see, Fitzhugh," Julianne murmured as he handed her into the carriage.

"Absolutely, my lady."

She paused on the step, her skirts gathered in her hands, her voice low. "I hear you will be coming with us to Kent."

"I hope that doesn't displease you."

"I think," she said with a faint smile, "I am getting very used to your company."

Chapter Twenty-four

It was just as well he'd enlisted help, for Luke was able to give him the address of Mrs. Stewart's last residence in London. It was for let, Luke informed him, and when he'd inquired—in the most influential way possible: for a bit of coin—the agent had confessed he did have the address where to send the remittance for the rent.

Nicely done, Michael thought. Now he had a destination, but he also had an uneasy premonition. It happened now and then . . . and usually was accurate. He swore steadily under his breath as the carriage clattered down the wet street in the cold rain.

It was the same address that Fitz had given him after following Julianne. Where little Chloe had been left alone.

At least he had a connection, but it wasn't a particularly welcome one. More than ever he was convinced Alice had stumbled upon his brother's secret and used it to get to Julianne.

Why the devil hadn't he forbidden his wife to leave the house this evening? In his defense, while he'd been distracted by the attempts on his life, he hadn't known about the blackmail until so recently that it required a great leap of assumption to connect the two.

At least he knew they *were* connected, and Mrs. Stewart was the common thread. The convoluted thought process that had hatched the plan was not easily followed, as far as he was concerned.

"Why can't I be dealing with a man?" he muttered.

Across from him, Lawrence grunted in agreement. "It isn't at all the same, is it? They think differently. This woman who is your enemy has cleverly found a way to gain access to your wife. I imagine every time Lady Longhaven visited that child, her life was in danger. No one knew where she was, and Stewart could, at her leisure, select the time to do what she wished. Perhaps she was waiting for your marchioness to become pregnant before she killed her. That would be revenge indeed."

Michael briefly closed his eyes. That possibility chilled him through and through.

Lawrence went on grimly, "Roget is not behind this. All along it has been done too clumsily, probably because Mrs. Stewart dared not let anyone suspect she is back in England, so her resources were limited. She had to disguise herself, hire others to do what she could not get close enough to try herself, and I am going to guess the blackmail was an indication she might need funds. To put it plainly, she is hiding from two dangerous men: not just you, but also Roget. She is as much a liability to him as she is to you, for she knows the man and could betray his identity, if not his true name. I would wager he didn't realize she was back in London any more than you did."

Michael removed his pistol from his jacket, checked it, and replaced it in the special pocket sewn in the lining. "I've wondered from the beginning what I was dealing with. It has all been too . . . unprofessional."

"True." Lawrence's gaze held ironic amusement.

"You are good, Longhaven, but if Roget truly wanted you dead, I think there is every chance you would be."

"We have to find her." Michael wasn't too concerned over that difficulty now that he knew what—and who—he was dealing with. London was a big city, but after tracking the enemy through foreign countryside, locating Alice Stewart was not such a daunting task with a trail to follow. "If you are right, and I suspect you are, she won't be able to tell us Roget's location."

"He is more ghost than man," Lawrence murmured, relaxed in his seat, his long legs extended, his damp greatcoat carelessly fastened. "Forget him."

"Should he meet Antonia, he truly will be a ghost."

"I agree. She isn't reasonable on the subject."

"No."

Michael could try to point out gently to her once again that there was no proof Roget had anything to do with the massacre of her family, but he'd done so before and knew it was useless. There was no doubt that the infamous French spy had provided the intelligence that allowed a small French force to slip past British lines, but what the soldiers had done in the name of conquering Spain could not be directly laid at his doorstep. God knew Michael was also indirectly responsible for the deaths of many by obtaining information and passing it along. It was his job, and it had been war. Yes, Roget was a thorn in his side, but he did not hate the elusive man like Antonia did.

He found he was much more interested in a quite different emotion.

... I love you and want to share all of your life, not just the small part you have given me so far ...

Had he handled such a sincere declaration of love well? Perhaps not. A passionate kiss was not the same as a verbal response, but it was the best he could do under the circumstances. And, oddly enough, he thought Julianne understood full well.

Maybe that was what a man truly desired in his life.

He'd known scores of beautiful women—Antonia was beautiful, for that matter—but though they'd shared a brief passion, all of them were very different from his wife.

Julianne brought a unique serenity to his life. He was adjusting to the new concept. He could manage chaos. Contentment was different.

"The house is dark," he noted as they rolled to a halt. "It's all too possible she isn't here, but let us be prepared. The lady has killed before."

"So have I," Lawrence said with equanimity as he alighted from the vehicle.

It was a formidable crush, but at least the weather was cooler so she didn't have to swelter. And the Viennese orchestra, enticed by a no doubt very generous incentive, was the same one that had played at the palace the week before. The lilt of the beautiful music vied with hundreds of whispered conversations and the rustle of silk skirts against dark trousers as the dancers moved through the huge ballroom in the rhythm of the waltz.

Michael, Julianne observed, her hand on the shoulder of a young man whose admiring stare was disconcerting, had not made an appearance yet. As avidly as she watched the doorway, she would have noticed his arrival, though the affair was quite the crush and it felt like everyone else in the *haut ton* was in attendance. The sophisticated and vibrant Lady Taylor *was* there, to be sure. She'd seen the lady an hour or so before, twirling in the arms of an obviously smitten blond young man, their disparate coloring making them a striking couple.

Well, whatever was detaining Michael, at least she knew it wasn't his former paramour.

It made no sense that she wasn't more jealous. Julianne wasn't worldly, but she knew, even without direct confirmation, Michael and Antonia Taylor had once been lovers. Moreover, she understood that Lady Taylor wasn't detached about the affair, but Michael . . .

She wasn't sure how Michael felt, but she was also intelligent enough to realize that the lady wouldn't be so jealous if he was willing to continue their relationship. It might be innocence, but, quite frankly, Julianne didn't think he was a man who would be unfaithful to his wife. An anomaly in their social circles, to be sure, but ...

"Lady Longhaven?" A maid dressed in a dark uniform with a crisply starched apron gave a small, reverent curtsy as the music stopped and Julianne and her partner exited the floor. "I'm sorry to interrupt, but your husband is here and wishes to speak with you. Will you follow me?"

Thank heavens. He was safe.

She turned, smiled graciously at her dance partner, and excused herself, slipping into the milling crowd.

At that moment she understood how worried she'd been, the cascade of relief like a cool ocean wave. She was entitled, she reminded herself, because, after all, someone had tried to kill him. Twice that she knew of, and considering his propensity for mystery, maybe more.

It frightened her, for he exuded an aura of invincibility, but no one was completely immune to such a threat or he wouldn't have been wounded.

The marble-floored corridor was much quieter than the crowded ballroom, and she followed the servant, grateful to be away from the noise and confines of the sheer number of guests. The more shadowed environment, away from the brilliance of the chandeliers, was welcome and a waft of air brushed her bared shoulders.

After they turned a corner and went down a long hallway to turn another, Julianne frowned, asking, "Where, precisely, is my husband?"

"He wasn't dressed for the festivities, so he asked you meet him in Sir Benedict's private library."

That explained the journey from the public rooms to the private sector of the house, and it was true, Michael hadn't been in evening wear when he'd left the house earlier. She wasn't aware her husband and Sir Benedict Marston were well enough acquainted that Michael could use his private library, but there were undoubtedly a lot of aspects of his life she hadn't discovered yet.

She hurried along behind the dark-haired maid and when the woman opened a carved door with a deferential bow, she went inside, trying to calm the twinges of anxiety. "Michael?"

To her consternation, the room appeared empty, lit by only one dim lamp. The outline of comfortable chairs, bookcases, and windows shuttered against the rainy weather showed no sign of her husband. She turned at the same time the door clicked shut.

The maid held a pistol solidly pointed at her chest. Just as Julianne registered the shock of the moment, the woman smiled, tossed her head in a familiar movement, and said in a completely different voice than the demure deference of earlier, "Remember me?"

Unfortunately she did. Though the red hair was gone, the features were familiar. It was the same woman who had impersonated Chloe's mother.

Michael had better appreciate this.

Antonia slipped up to the closed door, listened for a moment, and contemplated her next move.

It took a woman to understand a woman.

The voices on the other side were muted, but she could hear well enough despite the heavy panel. Cautiously she turned the handle, grateful the well-oiled hinges didn't creak as she opened the door a strategic crack. Sir Benedict had money and it showed.

Ah, Mrs. Stewart had a pistol. Resourceful of her.

That was fine. Antonia was also armed.

At least she assumed it was the devious woman who had evaded both Michael and Lawrence, which was not a particularly easy thing to do, so perhaps it would be prudent not to underestimate her capabilities.

This was also the woman who might be the one

who could finally give her information on how to find Roget.

". . . was a rather unfortunate turn of events. The weather was most uncooperative and I was stranded in Reading overnight due to impassable roads."

Lady Longhaven said stiffly, "Unfortunate for you and your plans, or unfortunate for a terrified young child left all alone?"

"How was I to know her mother wouldn't return as promised?"

Through the crack in the door, Antonia could see Michael's wife's trembling slender form. Her hands were clenched into fists at her sides, but her chin was lifted. "Maybe her reliability should have been in question, because you'd already been able to convince her to use her child in a blackmail scheme. She's hardly an ideal parent."

It didn't happen often, but Antonia had a certain reluctant admiration. Julianne Hepburn had surely never looked at possible death before.

Like taking a lover, there was always a first time.

The stark darkness of the marchioness's midnight blue gown contrasted with her alabaster skin, bleached pale by fear, but she didn't flinch even when the woman disguised as a maid raised her weapon and leveled it in a deliberate way. "Your husband is proving hard to kill. Difficult tasks need different types of leverage. I think with you dead, he will understand the game a little more fully. I had hoped to keep my anonymity, but I trust he has already come to certain conclusions." The woman— whose back was to Antonia—shrugged. "I intended at some point to kill you anyway."

"Go ahead." Julianne Hepburn stood resolute. "I won't beg so you can use it against my husband."

Que? The fool. What was this? Annoyed, Antonia realized she was going to have to do something right now . . . what an inconvenience. Her goal was Roget, and if she killed Alice Stewart . . . she might never get what she needed.

The click as the gun was cocked was loud, and so was the thud as Antonia shoved open the door and flung her knife with a deadly accuracy she had learned in the most difficult school possible.

The flying missile embedded itself between Mrs. Stewart's shoulder blades just before the gun went off, the bullet going wild. The woman stiffened and turned around, but it had been a good throw. One arm curled around her back, as if she could dislodge the knife, and she staggered a few paces before she slumped to the floor, the gun falling from her hand. Antonia stalked into the room and knelt by the fallen woman, ignoring the snow-white and shaking Lady Longhaven only a few feet away.

"Tell me who he is," she urged, but there was a froth of blood on Mrs. Stewart's lips, and her breathing was uneven. Dilated eyes stared into hers, but they were glazed, already showing death. "I want Roget . . . surely you owe him nothing, no allegiance. If you were allies he would have helped you kill Longhaven. What is his name?"

The infernal woman didn't answer, but instead went limp, her head rolling back.

After a moment in which she cursed in colorful Spanish phrases Michael's little wife would thankfully never know a lady shouldn't utter, Antonia became aware that blood was seeping onto the hem of her gown. She rose to her feet, with some effort tugged the knife free of the wound, wiped it clean on the white maid's apron, raised her skirt, and slipped it back into the sheath she kept fastened to her thigh. In exasperation, she said, "That did not work out at all as planned."

To her credit, Lady Longhaven responded to that with a choked, weak sound, but thankfully did not swoon. Antonia could not abide fainting females.

Chapter Twenty-five

How did one apologize for a debacle of this magnitude?

Michael hesitated by the door adjoining their bedrooms and wondered if his wife was already in bed. Perhaps she was. Certainly she'd had an eventful evening. He winced to think of how while he'd been off chasing shadows, she'd been face-to-face with a drawn pistol in the hands of a known murderess.

Very sloppy work.

With some hesitation, he put his hand on the latch and lifted it.

Julianne was not in bed, he discovered, but stood by the hearth, wrapped in her dressing gown, her slender form licked by the firelight. She turned at his entrance, her smile wavering. "For whatever reason I cannot get warm."

"You've been through an ordeal." He moved into the room, quietly shutting the door behind him. "I am sure you are exhausted. Shall I leave?"

"Don't you dare," she said with surprising strength. "If you had not come in just now, I had resolved to go find you, even if it meant roaming the house in my dressing gown. I think we need to discuss a few matters."

He liked the flare of her spirited answer and the way she faced him, even if she still shivered. Too many times he'd felt cold and alone after a battle or a mission. He understood. "So we should."

"You are sometimes infuriatingly reasonable."

Michael fought a smile. "I shall try to be more unreasonable in the future. What are we discussing, specifically?"

"Why did it all come about?" Julianne crossed her arms under her breasts. "Why did that woman pretend to be Leah? What purpose could there be? Why was Lady Taylor following me earlier? Is this very event what you anticipated, so you assigned Fitzhugh to watch me? Why—?"

Michael raised his hand. "I will answer all of it, but you are cold. Can we discuss this in bed?"

"I don't want you to seduce me as a way to deflect my questions."

He almost started to protest, but he was guilty of using that tactic in the past and he knew it. Instead, Michael said simply, "I just want to hold you while we talk."

After a moment, she nodded and whispered, "I *want* you to hold me."

Given permission, he stepped cautiously closer, judicious in his movements because he hadn't lied; he was sure she was tired, and someone had faced her down with a brandished pistol earlier, and a great deal of what had happened was entirely his fault.

But when he offered his hand, she hesitated only a moment before clasping his fingers and letting him draw her to the bed. She wore only a lacy nightdress under the robe and he didn't remove it, but simply turned back the coverlet, urged her onto the mattress, and then drew up the blankets around them as he reclined next to her. For a few moments she still shivered, but then her body began to relax.

"Tell me why that woman wanted you dead."

He supposed it was only fair he tell her the whole story. Michael touched the silk of her hair and said briefly, "She was an Englishwoman in the employ of Bonaparte at one time. I exposed her. I was under the impression she welcomed exile to death. I was wrong."

Julianne murmured, "I've been thinking about nothing else, naturally, trying to work out as much as possible myself. I assume the ruse about Chloe was to use me if she needed to get to you. It never even crossed my mind, though I did find it all strange. She said she was an actress when the real Leah was a barmaid. I think that was arrogance. She did play her part quite well."

"Why should it occur to you she was acting?" Michael drew her just a fraction closer, blessing inclement weather forever. If Alice hadn't gotten trapped the other evening, Chloe wouldn't have been left alone, and Julianne would probably still be clandestinely making those perilous visits.

He could have lost her. Not just this night, but on other occasions. When he thought of the danger she'd been in . . . His throat tightened. "I am happy to acknowledge you don't think in crooked lines. My advice is to avoid it forever. It overcomplicates just about everything."

Her laugh was a soft exhale. "An interesting way to put it. Now, who is Roget?"

Maybe, just maybe, if she hadn't nestled her head on his shoulder, he might have dodged around that one. Old habits were difficult to shake, but this was not the time for evasiveness. "A French agent. Or," he corrected himself, "another agent for the French who we think is English. I have been trying to catch him for years."

"So, apparently, has Lady Taylor. I think it was a definite conflict of interest for her to save my life in lieu of losing the opportunity to question that woman."

"It probably was," he answered dryly. "But in an odd way, I am glad it happened. In my mind there never was an obligation, but I think for Antonia, this settles the debt between us. She believes Roget is responsible for the deaths of her family. For her to miss the chance to find out his identity is a sacrifice indeed."

On an afterthought he added, "I believe it might just set her free." How much, he'd wondered more than once, was her determined affection for him due to that ingrained sense that she *owed* him? He hadn't ever looked at their relationship in that light, but then again, he and Antonia didn't think much alike and never had.

She had saved Julianne's life. She owed him nothing. He was now in *her* debt.

"What of Roget? Did what happened ruin your chances of ever finding him?" Julianne touched his cheek, bringing him back into the moment.

Michael inhaled the soft fragrance of flowers from his wife's hair and resisted, with considerable effort, the urge to run his hands down her body and draw her closer. The luscious weight of one breast rested against his encircling arm.

"He is more ghost than man." He repeated Lawrence's earlier words, struck by his wife's loveliness, by how much he had lost interest in the driving urge to settle an old score, to fight a war that was over and done in the eyes of the rest of the world. "At first I was sure he was behind the attempts on my life, but I know now, of course, it was Alice Stewart. I think my old enemy and I have come to terms with each other."

"If he is an Englishman, isn't he a traitor?"

"Take my word when I say war shapes people in ways they never would imagine. Look at Antonia. She can defend herself better than most men I know, but she was born a lady, sheltered her whole life by her wealthy family. Tragedy is regrettable, but in her case, it made her stronger. I think that is what happens to all of us. If we are not destroyed by it, adversity can turn to strength."

Julianne shifted in his arms, closer, her breath a whisper. "I owe her my life."

"No, *I* owe her your life. Now, if I have sufficiently answered your immediate questions, perhaps we could change the subject?"

"What do you wish to discuss?" Her fingertips drifted into the parted cloth of his robe and touched his bare chest.

Despite his resolve to simply hold her until she fell asleep, he lit on fire. Michael caught her chin and brushed his mouth against hers. "Us."

"Hmm. An interesting topic." Julianne's hand trailed downward, over the taut muscles of his stomach in a slow, tantalizing journey. A few more inches and she would encounter his growing erection.

Michael sucked in a breath, the heat of arousal spreading over his skin. "This marriage has not turned out as I anticipated."

"How so?" Her fingers skimmed the tip of his hardening cock.

This was difficult enough without the distraction of her touch. Michael caught her wrist to still that teasing touch and looked into her eyes—those beautiful eyes with the thick fringe of sable lashes and the delicate, arched brows above—and what he saw there was not just the physical beauty of the deep blue color and the shape and size . . . no, what he saw was compassion, intelligence, and, yes, he believed it, love. "I never imagined I could share my life with another person," he admitted. "In name, yes, but that is just a ceremony in a cathedral and a piece of paper. Pledging my name and protection is one matter, but my heart another."

Had he really just spoken of pledging his heart?

Just when she'd imagined the evening could not become more memorable, apparently Julianne was wrong. Michael Hepburn was not romantic. At least not the distant, aloof, complicated man she'd married. Physically, yes, and from the state of his arousal, she imagined he was going to be extremely romantic in that sense very soon, but he didn't ever whisper endearments or soft, poetic phrases, or give lavish compliments.

Much less mention his heart. Next to her, his tall body offering solid warmth and comfort, he cradled her close, the searing intensity of his gaze holding her prisoner.

"I know nothing of falling in love," he went on, the honesty evident in the halting struggle to find the words. In the light of just the fire, his fine features were thrown to angles, emphasizing the structure of bone, the line of his mouth, the shape of his nose and brow. "I've been a lover, but only in one sense of the word. But with you it is different. It has been since that first night. I desire you, but that is obvious." His smile was rueful and there was also a hint of roguish male as well. "But I have come to the conclusion that is not the extent of it."

"What *is* the extent of it?" Julianne knew she was taking a chance asking, but this seemed the night for it.

"The other evening, when you were so late, I was frantic. It was enlightening."

That was roundabout enough for the Marquess of Longhaven, but she wasn't willing to accept evasion.

Not at what could be the most important moment of her life.

"Care to define how it enlightened you?" She gently freed her wrist from his grasp and tugged the sash on his dressing gown loose, pushing the material from his shoulders. "I promise you it isn't so difficult to say." Julianne kissed his throat. "I have said it to *you*. Here, let me demonstrate again: I love you."

"You are far more idealistic," he said on a growl, and abruptly rolled her over to her back. "Not to mention you are wearing far too much."

She didn't protest as he tugged the ribbon on the bodice of her night rail free and slid the garment down her body to toss it away. His robe was discarded with equal speed. He covered her then, deliciously so, and a swell of both desire and exuberant joy possessed her as she wound her arms around his neck and lifted her mouth for a ravishing kiss. Flames shot through her body, inundating her senses, and Julianne arched against him, skin to skin. When he bent his head to suckle her breasts, she moaned freely as he lavished attention on one and then the other. Perhaps he would never say it, she reconciled herself, the brush of his hair erotic on her sensitized skin, as was the abrasion of the faint stubble on his clean-shaven jaw.

When he shifted, lifted, moved with smooth, muscular strength to adjust position, she opened her thighs in willing welcome, inhaling swiftly as he fused their bodies in one sure thrust.

"I love you," Michael whispered, his breath warm against her ear. "This seems the appropriate time to say it, and you are right—it wasn't so difficult after all."

Pleasure was enhanced by joy, she found, clinging to him as they moved faster and faster, rushing toward a common goal, breathless in their communion. Ecstasy peaked, hung suspended, and then Julianne fell, but Michael was there to plummet with her until they lay panting and entwined.

They didn't speak, and Julianne gave in to the drowsiness, the firelight now just a glow, her exhaustion pleasant despite her climatic day.

"Would you like to know a secret?" Michael asked her, his fingers tangled in her hair, his shoulder solid under her cheek.

The offer brought her out of her descent toward sleep. Her lashes lifted and Julianne looked at her husband's face. A small smile curved his lips. She said, "Tell me."

"Before you I didn't realize it, but happiness was an abstract concept to me."

That was no secret at all. He might be capable of many deceptions, might have changed the course of history with his service to his country, might command the respect of some of the highest officials in England, but he hadn't been able to keep that hidden from her.

Julianne didn't tell him. Instead she drifted into a contented sleep in his arms.

Epilogue

The park was cold, fallen leaves rolling under a crisp wind. Michael strolled toward a solitary figure standing on one of the paths, the normal riders and pedestrians forgoing an afternoon outing in favor of a warm fire and hot cup of tea.

Charles had the collar of his coat turned up, his hat shielding his eyes. "Good afternoon, my lord."

"Charles." Michael was bareheaded, his hair ruffled. "Thank you for meeting with me on such short notice. We are departing tomorrow morning for Kent."

"Hence the urgency. I see." There was a hint of cynical amusement in the other man's voice. "Off to bury yourself in the country. I don't picture it."

Only a few months ago, Michael would not have either. With Julianne, however, it took on a whole new light.

But there were a few details to be tidied up before he left.

"When, if ever," he said with neutral inflection, "were you going to tell me Lawrence is, in fact, Roget?"

For a moment, they just faced each other in silence.

"Shall we walk?" Charles indicated the path. "Keeps the blood flowing. Bloody cold out today."

"Fine." Michael fell into step next to him.

"So, you figured it out." His old friend sent him a sidelong glance. "I never doubted you would eventually."

Eventually. It had taken him too damn long, Michael knew, but then again, he'd been fed false information at every turn by his own government. No wonder he hadn't been able to put the pieces of the puzzle together earlier. "Why?" he asked simply.

"He was valuable. We needed to protect him. A double agent is a risky commodity at any time, for we all know that their loyalties could be to the other side. It is a game, Michael, and we couldn't have you catching him. So you were . . . deflected a time or two."

A time or two. That was putting it mildly. The chill breeze brushed his face, carrying with it the smell of decaying leaves and chimney smoke. "I couldn't be trusted with the truth?"

"I knew." Charles spoke with no apology. "And the war secretary. No one else. Not even the prime minister. It was integral that it be kept extraordinarily quiet."

"I chased him all over Spain."

"And in the course of doing so, sent back a lot of valuable intelligence."

"Damn you, Charles. Do not try to justify the means by the end."

"I never try to justify anything—you know that. Besides, it was rather amusing to put him to work with you once the war was over."

No doubt, Michael thought wryly. Once he'd begun to suspect, he found some ironic humor in it also. "He's persuaded Antonia to sell the town house and leave with him for the tropical islands off the coast of the Americas. If she ever finds out . . ."

"He didn't have a direct hand in the killing of her

family. His sole crime was providing a safe route for the French troops to avoid British lines, which was part of his duty."

"Trust me, she wouldn't see it that way."

"It is his choice if he ever tells her. As I understand it, he is rather devoted to your fierce Senora Taylor. Since she is willing to go away with him, the devotion doesn't seem to be one-sided. They will work it out together. It isn't your concern."

True enough. His concern was Julianne, his little niece, and any future children, if they should be so blessed. Antonia belonged under the sultry sun, and she needed adventure. He had his family.

Odd, how life took its twists and turns.

"But if you wish to discuss it with him, please be my guest. Keep in touch, and if you begin to tire of the bucolic countryside, fresh air, and all that rubbish, send me a message. I am sure I'll find something interesting for you to do." Charles swung on his heel, and just as he turned to go back the way they'd come, Michael spotted a man walking toward him on the path.

He recognized the broad build, the dark hair tugged at by the wind, and, of course, the signature scar.

He stopped and waited, the raw day suitable to this meeting. The first thing he said when Lawrence joined him was, "Charles thinks he's so damn clever."

"The trouble is he *is* damn clever." Lawrence agreed, his eyes wary. His face was ruddy from the cold.

"I hadn't told him until just now I had figured out who you were, yet he planned this meeting."

"When I explained to him our conversation over Mrs. Stewart last evening, he simply gave me a time to meet him here. I assume he knows you well enough to guess you'd finally have the information to put the pieces into one cohesive conclusion."

So like Charles to arrange the confrontation ahead of time. Michael said sardonically, "I was manipulated. But then, with Charles, I tend to feel that way at all times, my quest for Roget aside."

"If it is any consolation, it was somewhat of a blow to my pride to realize they were so confident you would catch me that they deliberately misled you whenever you were close."

"How did you come to work for the French?"

"Impressed into service . . . and I so resented it, I began at once a plan to insinuate myself at the highest levels, taking the most dangerous of jobs." Lawrence shrugged. "Truthfully, if I was killed, what did it matter? Eventually I was trusted enough to be a courier and then an operative. I had to do a good job for the French, you understand, to aid the English. I think you now understand both why Alice Stewart so adamantly refused to reveal my identity and why I let her board the ship for France instead of banishing her to India. I was standing right there during the interrogation and she didn't betray me. I might have killed her to protect myself, but maybe not. She evidently didn't want to take the chance, and besides, once you let her go, I felt I owed her for the loyalty. I had no idea she would seek revenge on you with such tenacity."

"Had Mrs. Stewart not pushed me with her desire for my demise, I might never have known you and Roget were one and the same." Michael turned his collar up against the stinging breeze.

"That," Lawrence said, as if he understood the concept very well, "is how fate works. Tell me, at what precise moment did you draw the correct conclusion?"

"I would say that your explanation about letting her board a different ship didn't exactly convince me, but it might have been possible. You certainly have a decided weakness for dangerous females, if your involvement with Antonia is any indication. But, quite frankly, it wasn't the definitive moment I knew."

Lawrence looked at him with studied inquiry.

"It was when we were in the carriage on our quest to find Alice Stewart last evening and you informed me if Roget truly wanted me dead, I would be." Michael's smile was full of irony. "I sensed you were telling the truth from a unique personal perspective."

"I have been pointing out all along, while trying to be as understated as possible, that whoever wanted your blood was not Roget."

He had, and Michael now knew why. "You also told me Roget was a ghost, yet rumors of him still being in England are filtering through."

"Yes, I've noticed." The Serpentine lay ahead, gray under the fall sky, brilliant leaves floating on the surface here and there. "That is because the French would like nothing better than to find me. I thought I had escaped cleanly, but apparently not. I think that Mrs. Stewart, in the end, also did me for a favor, for leaving England as soon as possible is no doubt for the best. When you started actively seeking Roget again, I realized there were others looking as well. I assume Charles told you Antonia agreed to go with me?"

"He did." Michael glanced at him. "Will you tell her the truth?"

"I haven't decided. What would you do, Longhaven?"

"Make sure I was well-armed, for one. And it might be best done at sea, when she can't escape you, though there still is the nasty prospect of being devoured by sharks when she tosses you overboard. I wish you luck, whatever you decide."

Lawrence gave a rueful chuckle. "My thoughts exactly."

"I'm resigning, too." Michael skirted a pile of wet leaves, his hands deep in his pockets.

"Conditionally? Charles will not let you go easily. You are too valuable."

"Unconditionally."

"It must be love, then," Lawrence observed, "for you to be so certain."

Michael thought about the warmth of Julianne's smile waiting for him when he returned. "It must be," he said softly, swung on his heel, and walked away from all the secrets.

Read on for a preview of Emma Wildes's
enthralling historical romance

My Lord Scandal

First in the Notorious Bachelors series

Available now from Signet Eclipse.

The alley below was filthy and smelled rank, and if he fell off the ledge, Lord Alexander St. James was fairly certain he would land on a good-sized rat. Since squashing scurrying rodents was not on his list of favorite pastimes, he tightened his grip and gauged the distance to the next roof. It looked to be roughly the distance between London and Edinburgh, but in reality was probably only a few feet.

"What the devil is the matter with you?" a voice hissed out of the darkness. "Hop on over here. This was your idea."

"I do not *hop*," he shot back, unwilling to confess that heights bothered him. They had since the night he'd breached the towering wall of the citadel at Badajoz with forlorn hope. He still remembered the pounding rain, the ladders swarming with men, and that great black drop below. . . .

"I know perfectly well this was my idea," he muttered.

"Then I'm sure, unless you have an inclination for a

personal tour of Newgate Prison, which, by the by, I do not, you'll agree we need to proceed. It gets closer to dawn by the minute."

Newgate Prison. Alex didn't like confined spaces any more than he liked heights. The story his grandmother had told him just a few days ago made him wish his imagination was a little less vivid. Incarceration in a squalid cell was the last thing he wanted. But for the ones you love, he thought philosophically as he eyed the gap, and he had to admit that he adored his grandmother, risks have to be taken.

That thought proved inspiration enough for him to leap the distance, landing with a dull thud but, thankfully, keeping his balance on the sooty shingles. His companion beckoned with a wave of his hand and in a crouched position began to make a slow pilgrimage toward the next house.

The moon was a wafer obscured by clouds. Good for stealth, but not quite so wonderful for visibility. Two more alleys and harrowing jumps and they were there, easing down onto a balcony that overlooked a small walled garden.

Michael Hepburn, Marquess of Longhaven, dropped down first, light on his feet, balanced like a dancer. Alex wondered, not for the first time, just what his friend did for the War Office. He landed next to him, and said, "What did your operative tell you about the layout of the town house?"

Michael peered through the glass of the French doors into the darkened room. "I could be at our club at this very moment, enjoying a stiff brandy."

"Stop grumbling," Alex muttered. "You live for this kind of intrigue. Lucky for us, the lock is simple. I'll have this open in no time."

True to his word, a moment later one of the doors creaked open, the sound loud to Alex's ears. He led the way, slipping into the darkened bedroom, taking in with a quick glance the shrouded forms of a large canopied bed and armoire. Something white was laid out on the bed, and on closer inspection he saw that it was a nightdress edged with delicate lace, and that the coverlet was already turned back. The virginal gown made him feel very much an interloper—which, bloody hell, he was. But all for a good cause, he told himself firmly.

Michael spoke succinctly. "This is Lord Hathaway's daughter's bedroom. We'll need to search his study and his suite across the hall. Since his lordship's rooms face the street and his study is downstairs, this is a much more discreet method of entry. It is likely enough they'll be gone for several more hours, giving us time to search for your precious item. At this hour, the servants should all be abed."

"I'll take the study. It's more likely to be there."

"Alex, you do realize you are going to have to finally tell me just what we are looking for if I am going to ransack his lordship's bedroom on your behalf."

"I hope you plan on being more subtle than that."

"He'll never know I was there," Michael said with convincing confidence. "But what the devil am I looking for?"

"A key. Ornate, made of silver, so it'll be tarnished to black, I suspect. About so long." Alex spread open his hand, indicating the distance between the tip of his smallest finger and his thumb. "It'll be in a small case, also silver. There should be an engraved *S* on the cover."

"A key to *what*, dare I ask, since I am risking my neck to find it?"

Alex paused, reluctant to reveal more. But Michael had a point, and moreover, could keep a secret better than anyone of Alex's acquaintance. "I'm not sure," he admitted, quietly.

Michael's hazel eyes gleamed with interest even in the dim light. "Yet here we are, breaking into a man's house."

"It's . . . complicated."

"Things with you usually are."

"I'm not at liberty to explain to anyone, even you, my reasons for being here. Therefore my request for your assistance. In the past you have proven not only to think fast on your feet and stay cool under fire, but you also have the unique ability to keep your mouth firmly shut, which is a very valuable trait in a friend. In short, I trust you."

Michael gave a noncommittal grunt. "All right, fine."

"If it makes you feel better, I'm not going to steal anything," Alex informed him in a whisper, as he cracked open the bedroom door and peered down the hall. "What I want doesn't belong to Lord Hathaway, if he has it. Where's his study?"

"Second hallway past the bottom of the stairs. Third door on the right."

The house smelled vaguely of beeswax and smoke from the fires that kept the place warm in the late-spring weather. Alex crept—there was no other word for it—down the hall, sending a silent prayer upward to enlist heavenly aid for their little adventure to be both successful and undetected. Though he wasn't sure, with his somewhat dissolute past—or Michael's, for that matter—if he was at all in a position to ask for benevolence.

The hallway was deserted but damned dark. Michael clearly knew the exact location of Hathaway's personal set of rooms, for he went directly to the left door and cracked it open, and disappeared inside.

Alex stood at a vantage point where he could see the top of the staircase rising from the main floor, feeling an amused disbelief that he was a deliberate intruder in someone else's house, and had enlisted Michael's aid to help him with the infiltration. He'd known Michael since Eton, and when it came down to it, no one was more reliable or loyal. He'd go with him to hell and back, and quite frankly, they *had* accompanied each other to hell in Spain.

They'd survived the fires of Hades, but had not come back to England unscathed.

Time passed in silence, and Alex relaxed a little as he made his way down the stairs into the darkened hallway, barking his shin only once on a piece of furniture that seemed to materialize out of nowhere. He stifled a very colorful curse and moved on, making a mental note not to take up burglary as a profession.

The study was redolent of old tobacco and the ghosts of a thousand glasses of brandy. Alex moved slowly, pulling the borrowed set of picklocks again from his pocket, rummaging through the drawers he could open first, and then setting to work on the two locked ones.

Nothing. No silver case. No blasted key.

Damn.

The first sound of trouble was a low, sharp, excited bark. Then he heard a woman speaking in modulated tones—audible in the silent house—and alarm flooded through him. The voice sounded close, but that might have been a trick of the acoustics of the town house. At least it didn't sound like a big dog, he told himself, feeling in a drawer for a false back before replacing the contents and quietly sliding it shut.

A servant? Perhaps, but it was unlikely, for it was truly the dead of night, with dawn a few good hours away. As early as most of the staff rose, he doubted one of them would be up and about unless summoned by her employer.

The voice spoke again, a low murmur, and the lack of a reply probably meant she was talking to the dog. He eased into the hallway to peer out and saw that at the foot of the stairs a female figure was bent over, scratching the ears of what appeared to be a small bundle of active fur, just a puppy, hence the lack of alarm over their presence in the house.

She was blond, slender, and, more significantly, clad in a fashionable gown of a light color. . . .

Several more hours, my arse. One of Lord Hathaway's family had returned early.

It was a stroke of luck when she set down her lamp and lifted the squirming bundle of fur in her arms, and instead of heading upstairs, carried her delighted burden through a door on the opposite side of the main hall, probably back toward the kitchen.

Alex stole across the room, and went quickly up the stairs to where Michael had disappeared, trying to be as light-footed as possible. He opened the door a crack and whispered, "Someone just came home. A young woman, though I couldn't see her clearly."

"Damnation." Michael could move quietly as a cat, and he was there instantly. "I'm only half done. We might need to leave and come back a second time."

Alex pictured launching himself again across more questionable, stinking, yawning crevasses of London's rooftop landscape. "I'd rather we finished it now."

"If Lady Amelia has returned alone, it should be fine," Michael murmured. "She's unlikely to come into her father's bedroom, and I just need a few more minutes. I'd ask you to help me, but you don't know where I've already searched, and the two of us whispering to each other and moving about is more of a risk. Go out the way we came in. Wait for her to go to bed, and keep an eye on her. If she looks to leave her room because she might have heard something, you're going to have to come up with a distraction. Otherwise, I'll take my chances going out this way and meet you on the roof."

With that, he was gone again and the door closed softly.

Alex uttered a stifled curse. He'd fought battles, crawled through ditches, endured soaking rains and freezing nights, marched for miles on end with his battalion, but he wasn't a damned spy. But a moment of indecision could be disastrous with Miss Patton no doubt heading for her bedroom. And what if she also woke her maid?

As a soldier, he'd learned to make swift judgments, and in this case, he trusted Michael knew what the hell he was doing and quickly slipped back into the lady's bedroom and headed for the balcony. They'd chosen that entry into the house for the discreet venue of the quiet private garden, and the assurance that no one on the street would see them and possibly recognize them in this fashionable neighborhood.

No sooner had Alex managed to close the French doors behind him than the door to the bedroom opened. He froze, hoping the shadows hid his presence, worried movement might attract the attention of the young woman who had entered the room. If she raised an alarm, Michael could be in a bad spot, even if Alex got away. She carried the small lamp, which she set on the polished table by the bed. He assumed his presence on the dark balcony would be hard to detect.

It was at that moment he realized how very beautiful she was.

Lord Hathaway's daughter. Had he met her? No, he hadn't, but when he thought about it, he'd heard her name mentioned quite often lately. Now he knew why.

Hair a shimmering gold caught the light as she reached up and loosened the pins, dropping them one by one by the lamp and letting the cascade of curls tumble down her back. In profile her face was defined and feminine, with a dainty nose and delicate chin. And though he couldn't see the color of her eyes, they were framed by lashes long enough they cast slight shadows across her elegant cheekbones as she bent over to lift her skirts, kick off her slippers, and begin to unfasten her garters. He caught the pale gleam of slender calves and smooth thighs, and the graceful curve of her bottom.

There was something innately sensual about watching a woman undress, though usually when it was done in his presence, it was as a prelude to one of his favorite pastimes. Slim fingers worked the fastenings of her gown, and in a whisper of silk, it slid off her pale shoulders. She stepped free of the pooled fabric, wearing only a thin, lacy chemise, all gold and ivory in the flickering illumination.

As a gentleman, he reminded himself, *I should look away.*

The ball had been more nightmare than entertainment, and Lady Amelia Patton had ducked out as soon as possible, using her usual—and not deceptive—excuse. She picked up her silk gown, shook it out, and draped it over a carved chair by the fireplace. When her carriage had dropped her home, she'd declined to wake her maid, instead enjoying a few rare moments of privacy before bed. No one would think it amiss, as she had done the same before.

It was a crime, was it not, to kill one's father?

Not that she *really* wanted to strangle him in any way but a metaphorical one, but this evening, when he had thrust her almost literally into the arms of the Earl of Westhope, she had nearly done the unthinkable and refused to dance with his lordship in public, thereby humiliating the man and defying her father in front of all of society.

Instead, she had gritted her teeth and waltzed with the most handsome, rich, incredibly *boring* eligible bachelor of the *haut ton*.

It had encouraged him, and that was the last thing she had wanted to happen.

The earl had even had the nerve—or maybe it was just stupidity—to misquote Rabelais when he brought her a glass of champagne, saying with a flourish as he handed over the flute, "Thirst comes with eating ... but the appetite goes away with drinking."

It had really been all she could do not to correct him, since he'd got it completely backward. She had a sinking feeling that he didn't mean to be boorish; he just wasn't very bright. Still, there was nothing on earth that could have prevented her from asking him, in her most proper voice, if that meant he was bringing her champagne because he felt, perhaps, she was too plump. Her response had so flustered him that he'd excused himself hurriedly—so perhaps the entire evening hadn't been a loss after all.

Clad only in her chemise, she went to the balcony doors and opened them, glad of the fresh air, even if it was a bit cool. Loosening the ribbon on her shift, she let the material drift partway down her shoulders, her nipples tightening against the chill. The ballroom had been unbearably close and she'd had some problems breathing, an affliction that had plagued her since childhood. Being able to fill her lungs felt like heaven, and she stood there, letting her eyes close. The light wheezing had stopped, and the anxiety that came with it had lessened, as well, but she was still a little dizzy. Her father was insistent that she kept this particular flaw a secret. He seemed convinced no man would wish to marry a female who might now and again become inexplicably out of breath.

Slowly she inhaled and then let it out. Yes, it was passing. . . .

It wasn't a movement or noise that sent a flicker of unease through her, but a sudden instinctive sense of being watched. Then a strong masculine hand cupped her elbow. "Are you quite all right?"

Her eyes flew open and she saw a tall figure looming over her. With a gasp she jerked her chemise back up to cover her partially bared breasts. To her surprise, the shadowy figure spoke again in a cultured, modulated voice. "I'm sorry to startle you, my lady. I beg a thousand pardons, but I thought you might faint."

Amelia stared upward, as taken aback by his polite speech and appearance as she was by finding a man lurking on her balcony. The stranger had ebony hair, glossy even in the inadequate moonlight, and his face was shadowed into hollows and fine planes, eyes dark as midnight staring down at her. "I . . . I . . ." she stammered. *You should scream*, an inner voice suggested, but she was so paralyzed by alarm and surprise, she wasn't sure she was capable of it.

"You swayed," her mysterious visitor pointed out, as if that explained everything, a small frown drawing dark arched brows together. "Are you ill?"

Finally, she found her voice, albeit not at all her regular one, but a high, thin whisper. "No, just a bit dizzy. Sir, what are you doing here?"

"Maybe you should lie down."

To her utter shock, he lifted her into his arms as easily as if she were a child, and actually carried her inside to deposit her carefully on the bed.

Perhaps this is a bizarre dream. . . .

"What are you doing here? Who are you?" she demanded. It wasn't very effective, since she still couldn't manage more than a half mumble, though fright was rapidly being replaced by outraged curiosity. Even in the insubstantial light she could tell he was well dressed, and before he straightened, she caught the subtle drift of expensive cologne. Though he wore no cravat, his dark coat was fashionably cut, and his fitted breeches and Hessians not something she imagined an ordinary footpad would wear. His face was classically handsome, with a nice, straight nose and lean jaw, and she'd never seen eyes so dark.

Was he really that tall, or did he just seem so because she was sprawled on the bed and he was standing?

"I mean you no harm. Do not worry."

Easy for him to say. For heaven's sake, he was in her bedroom, no less. "You are trespassing."

"Indeed," he agreed, inclining his head.

Was he a thief? He didn't look like one. Confused, Amelia sat up, feeling very vulnerable lying there in dishabille with her tumbled hair. "My father keeps very little money in his strongbox here in the house."

"A wise man. I follow that same rule myself. If it puts your mind at ease, I do not need his money." The stranger's teeth flashed white in a quick smile.

She recognized him, she realized suddenly, the situation taking on an even greater sense of the surreal. Not a close acquaintance, no. Not one of the many gentlemen she'd danced with since the beginning of her season, but she'd seen him, nevertheless.

And he certainly had seen *her*. She was sitting there gawping at him in only her thin, lacy chemise with the bodice held together in her trembling hand. The flush of embarrassment swept upward, making her neck and cheeks hot. She could feel the rush of blood warm her knuckles when they pressed against her chest. "I . . . I'm undressed," she said unnecessarily.

"Most delightfully so," he responded with an unmistakable note of sophisticated amusement in his soft tone. "But I am not here to ravish you any more than to rob you. Though," he added with a truly wicked smile, "perhaps, in the spirit of being an effective burglar, I should steal *something*. A kiss comes to mind, for at least then I would not leave empty-handed."

A kiss? Was the man insane?

"You . . . wouldn't," she managed to object in disbelief. He still stood by the side of the bed, so close that if she reached out a hand, she could touch him.

"I might." His dark brows lifted a fraction, and his gaze flickered over her inadequately clad body before returning to her face. He added softly, "I have a weakness for lovely, half-dressed ladies, I'm afraid."

And no doubt they had the same weakness for him, for he exuded a flagrant masculinity and confidence that was even more compelling than his good looks.

Her breath fluttered in her throat and it had nothing to do with her affliction. She might have been an ingenue, but she understood in an instant the power of that devastating, entirely masculine, husky tone. Like a bird stunned by smoke, she didn't move, even when he leaned down and his long fingers caught her chin, tipping her face up just a fraction. He lowered his head, brushed his mouth against hers for a moment, a mere tantalizing touch of his lips. Then, instead of kissing her, his hand slid into her hair and he gently licked the hollow of her throat. Through her dazed astonishment at his audacity, the feel of his warm lips and the teasing caress caused an odd sensation in the pit of her stomach.

This was where she should have imperiously ordered him to stop, or at least pushed him away.

But she didn't. She'd never been kissed, and though, admittedly, her girlish fantasies about this moment in her life hadn't included a mysterious stranger stealing uninvited into her bedroom, she *was* curious.

The trail of his breath made her quiver, moving upward along her jaw, the curve of her cheek, until he finally claimed her mouth, shocking her to her very core as he brushed his tongue against hers in small sinful strokes.

She trembled, and though it wasn't a conscious act, somehow one of her hands settled on his shoulder.

It was intimate.

It was beguiling.

Then it was over.

God help her, to her *disappointment* it was over.

He straightened and looked more amused than ever at whatever expression had appeared on her face. "A virgin kiss. A coup indeed."

He obviously knew that had been her first. It wasn't so surprising, for like most unmarried young ladies, she was constantly chaperoned. She summoned some affront, though, strangely, she really wasn't affronted. "You, sir, are no gentleman."

"Oh, I am, if a somewhat jaded one. If I wasn't, I wouldn't be taking my leave lest your reputation be tarnished by our meeting, because it would be, believe me. My advice is to keep my presence here this evening to yourself."

True to his word, in a moment he was through the balcony doors, climbing up on the balustrade, and bracing himself for balance on the side of the house. Then he caught the edge of the roof, swung up in one graceful athletic motion, and was gone into the darkness.

Read on for a preview of Emma Wildes's
enthralling historical romance

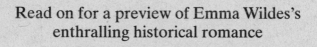

Second in the Notorious Bachelors series

Available now from Signet Eclipse.

He wasn't often rendered speechless, but Luke had to admit, as he gazed across the elegant, civilized drawing room at the beautiful woman he thought about far too often, he couldn't think of a single thing to say.

Madeline sat, ghostly pale, her slender shoulders visibly trembling, only a few paces away. No simpering ingenue, at twenty-six she was a mature widow with her own fortune, a reputation for wit and impeccable taste, and a darling of society, much sought after by any hostess of consequence.

Sought after by quite a few gentlemen also, himself included. As far as he knew, he was the only one who had ever succeeded in coaxing the delectable Lady Brewer into his bed, that one night indelibly preserved in his memory.

For her to be shaken out of her serene self-possession told him even more than her words had. Normally she was all poise and sophistication.

Except, an errant voice in his head reminded him, *when she is trembling and breathless in my arms.*

Luke finally found his voice. "I'd stake my life you aren't capable of deliberate malice, so maybe you'd better just start at the beginning and explain what happened. Please include where the incident happened. Who, why, and how might also be useful."

Midnight blue eyes, with a shimmer of hovering tears, gazed at him. "I am not even sure why I sent you that note."

"You know perfectly well why you sent it." It wasn't the easiest task on earth to keep his tone even and reasonable. "Because you realize, despite our differences, that I will help you. So just tell me."

"It was Lord Fitch."

This just got worse. Fitch was a prominent figure in British politics, with influence and money, and he was an earl in the bargain. Luke had never liked the swaggering bastard, but that was neither here nor there. His lordship's demise was unlikely to go unnoticed. If the man was dead, there would be inquiries. "He's annoyed me once or twice, but never enough for me to murder him. What happened?"

"I didn't *murder* him," Madeline shot back, and he was happy to see her square her shaking shoulders and some color come back into her face, even if it was due to outrage. "I accidentally killed him and it is quite different, thank you."

"I stand corrected." He felt a flash of amusement over her reaction despite the grim revelation she'd just made. "But keep in mind you have yet to tell me the sequence of events."

Her knuckles whitened as her hands clasped together tighter in her lap. "He's been making improper suggestions for quite some time. It has gone well beyond the stage where it is an annoyance and into downright harassment. I loathe the very sight of him."

The blackguard. Luke wished with savage intensity the man weren't dead so he could strangle him himself. "I am not a female and have never been subject to that sort of persecution, but I don't blame you for your aversion to his lordship. In fact, I wish you'd come to me sooner."

"I didn't want to ask for *your* help even in my current circumstances."

The trembling of her shapely body made him want to rise, go to her, and take her in his arms, cradle her close and promise all would be well. But he knew she wouldn't appreciate it, so he stayed where he was, though it took some effort. "Very well, perhaps I deserve that, but let's get back to the matter at hand. Fitch was lascivious and inappropriate. Go on."

"I've tried to avoid him." Her lower lip, so lush and full, quivered. "At every function, in public venues . . . *everywhere*."

"Madge, I am sure you have."

"It didn't work. He deliberately put himself in my path as often as possible."

Luke silently waited for her to continue, stifling futile fury at a man who was already dead.

"He . . ." She trailed off, looking forlorn and very young suddenly, with her pure, averted profile and tendrils of hair escaping from her chignon and caressing her neck. "He has something of Colin's."

Of her deceased husband's? Luke wasn't sure how that was possible, when Lord Brewer had died at least five years ago . . . perhaps even six.

With a tremor in her voice, she went on. "I very much want it back and endeavored to bargain with his lordship, but there is one price I am not willing to pay."

Price? His jaw locked. The use of her luscious body. She didn't even have to say it out loud. Luke felt the angry beat of his pulse in his temple and actually flexed his hands to keep from reaching for her when the crystalline line of a tear streaked down her smooth cheek. Even his jaded sophistication was no match for her genuine distress. "He's been blackmailing you?"

"No." She stared at the patterned rug. "Not precisely."

Not precisely. What in the hell did that mean? The gravity of the moment precluded him from muttering, *Women*, but he had to acknowledge a rising sense of frustration over the lack of a clear explanation. "I don't understand. It seems to me a person is being blackmailed or they are not."

She made a small hopeless gesture with her hand. "He . . . he knew things. And would mention them at inappropriate times. I began to suspect . . ."

By nature he wasn't a patient man anyway, and when she trailed off again, Luke prompted curtly, "Suspect what? Devil take it, my dear. Perhaps I am obtuse, but right now I have little more idea what has happened than when I walked in the door. Just explain it to me so we can deal with this."

"It's mortifying."

"Good God, woman, you just told me you killed a man. If it is mortifying, so be it, but get to the point. With my reputation, I am unlikely to judge you."

For a moment, she just stared at him, as if seeing him for the first time, her beautiful eyes wide. Then she nodded, just the barest tilt of her head.

"Colin kept a journal." She took a deep, shuddering breath but went on. "He was always scribbling something in it. Apparently, he wrote down everything, even details about our . . . our married life. Lord Fitch got ahold of it, though I can't really imagine how. After enough lewd but accurate comments and suggestions, I began to realize the odious man *must* have the journal. They weren't friends, and Colin would never tell him anything so private. I can't imagine he'd tell *anyone*. It was the only explanation. *I* hadn't even read it because it seemed like too much of an invasion of Colin's privacy, so I'd locked it away. Sure enough, it is missing."

And, it went without saying, it was certainly an invasion of Madeline's privacy as well. Luke knew she'd loved her husband with all the depth of a woman's first passion, and his death had been a devastating blow to her. He could only imagine the sense of violation she felt over his personal notes and thoughts being read by a stranger.

"I almost had him buried with it." Her voice was choked. "But I suppose I thought one day I might want to read it for comfort."

Instead a heartless toad like Fitch had made a travesty of the intimate writings of the man she loved. If the earl hadn't already met his untimely end, Luke could have killed the worthless scoundrel himself. He said with forced coolness, "Whatever happened to his lordship, it sounds to me like he quite deserved it. Where is he now?"

"In Colin's study."

The answer was said in such a low whisper he almost didn't catch it. Madeline looked blindly at the wall, her expression so remote it worried him. One slender hand plucked restively at her skirt. "Here?" Luke asked.

She nodded, the movement jerky. "I requested a meeting to discuss the journal. It seemed prudent and more to my advantage to conduct business in a way a man would do so, and Colin's study was a logical location. I had Lord Fitch escorted there when he called in response to my note."

At least they were getting somewhere. Luke rose. "Take me there and we'll sort this out."

As if one could sort out having a dead lord in a man's study. But he was willing to do his best. For her. Because, though he didn't wish to admit it even to himself, Luke had an admiration for Lady Brewer that extended quite beyond her matchless passion and undeniable beauty. Since defining it meant examining his own feelings, he'd avoided too much introspection on the matter, but he certainly had come running when she asked.

That was telling. Knight in shining armor was normally a role he disdained.

Woodenly, with the movements of a person who had

suffered quite a shock, she got up and without speaking walked out of the drawing room and led the way down the hall.

Her hope that it had all been some sort of bizarre dream was dashed when, unfortunately, Lord Fitch still lay in the same lax sprawl on the floor by the fireplace in a pool of his own blood. It was a pity, Madeline thought, because she'd always rather liked that rug, even if it was faded on one side from the sunlight that streamed in through the window in the late afternoon. Since Colin's death she had often come in and sat at his desk, the aroma of his tobacco in the jar on the desk familiar and poignant, his pipe just where he had left it the day he'd first complained about the headache that eventually blossomed into a fever, aches, chills, and, within two days, death. The room, with its paneled walls and worn books, was a comfort. Or it had been until now.

"I take it the fireplace poker was the method of dispatching his lordship to where, even now, I imagine he is shaking Satan's hand." Luke gazed dispassionately at the dead man, his tone cool and calm. "Not an original choice, but perhaps it is so popular because it is so effective."

"Yes." Lord Fitch had been taunting her . . . enjoying it. She could still hear his oily voice. *So, Lady Brewer, is it true you once, at the opera, behind a curtain, let your husband lift your skirts and . . .*

It had been impossible to reason with the gloating old goat, and certainly appealing to his nonexistent sense of honor hadn't been effective.

"When a request for him to return the journal didn't work, I offered him money for it. He merely laughed at me and said it was far too entertaining and wasn't for sale." Her voice was low and dull, but the awfulness of the evening had begun to take its toll. "I pointed out that it was mine in the first place, and returning it was the least any gentleman would do. He refused and continued to make the most disgusting, insulting suggestions you can think of."

"My imagination is excellent," Luke said in a tone that was pleasant, yet it sent a shiver up her spine. "For instance, I would have chosen a much more painful manner of execution for this piece of refuse right now soiling a perfectly good rug. Finish the story."

"He threatened to publish it."

Damn it all. Another tear ran down her cheek and she swiped it away with the back of her hand, like a child might. While the last thing she wanted to do was weep in front of Luke Daudet, of all people, in the light of this current disaster, she didn't care all that much.

"So you conked him with a poker. Excellent decision."

"I didn't conk him with a poker, as you put it," Madeline said defensively, "just because of that, though I was appalled. Men settle things with violence. Women are more civilized."

With irritating logic, he pointed out, "Ah, perhaps, but I am not the one with a dead man in my study."

Ignoring that comment, she explained haltingly, "I—I had by then realized any further discussion was useless and disliked the way he looked at me, so I got up to go fetch Hubert to escort the man out. When I came around the desk, Lord Fitch . . . He, well, grabbed me and whispered an extremely repulsive suggestion. He'd obviously been drinking, for his breath reeked. I was close to the fireplace, and as I struggled to get away, I must have grabbed the poker, for next I knew he was lying on the floor."

"Clearly self-defense." Luke reached into the pocket of his perfectly tailored jacket and took out a snowy handkerchief embroidered with his initials in one corner and handed it to her.

"Thank you." She wiped away another wayward tear.

Luke knelt by the body and took up one limp arm.

"He's still warm, so I take it you sent for me immediately. Where's his carriage?"

"That's the one blessing in all this. He must have walked, as he lives only a block or so away."

"What did you tell your staff? Obviously everyone is in bed."

"That his lordship dropped off due to too much drink and that I sent for you to see him home."

"Good thinking." He frowned, his handsome face in profile showing the first true expression of chagrin of the evening. "Only we have one enormous problem, my dear."

One? She'd just killed an earl in her husband's study. She had countless troubles ahead, as far as she could tell.

"The bastard is still alive."

"What? There's so much blood!" Madeline stared, not sure if she even believed him, crumpling the fine piece of linen in her hand. "He wasn't breathing—I'd swear it. I checked."

"You were understandably distraught, I am going to suspect, but I can feel a pulse. I'm no physician, but as irksome as it might be, it seems quite strong and steady. Head wounds, also, bleed with notorious profusion. I saw my fair share during the war."

She experienced a wash of relief so acute her knees nearly buckled. "Thank God. While I am not an admirer of Lord Fitch, I did not wish to be the cause of his death."

"You are kinder than I am, obviously. I'd gladly meet him on the field, and if he survives, I just might call him out. However, I can't countenance killing an unconscious man, no matter how much he deserves it, so I suppose our first order of business is getting him home and some medical attention. If you'll just open the door for me, we'll be on our way."

Call him out? Madeline was startled by the lethal vehemence of Luke's tone, not to mention the grim expression on his fine-boned face, but too distraught to address it.

Though Fitch was portly, he was much shorter, and Luke heaved his lordship's body over his shoulder with what seemed like little exertion.

"He's bleeding on your jacket," Madeline whispered, leaning limply against the desk.

"I have more clothing."

"I . . ."

Lifting Lord Fitch's plump posterior in the air, Luke looked at her, his brows elevated in sardonic question. "Just help me get this horse's arse out of here. Then have a glass of wine and forget it all happened."

How easy he made it all sound.

"Luke," she started in protest, for truly, though she wanted his help, she hadn't counted on him shouldering the entire problem.

"Open the door. I'm going to take care of everything. You needn't give it another thought." His voice was full of quiet, purposeful promise and completely unlike his usual flippant tone.

She moved to comply, preceding him through the quiet town house, helping with opening doors. When he slipped out the servant's exit, she watched his shrouded figure disappear into the darkened alley, only to hear the rattle of wheels a few moments later.

If locking the door was effective, she didn't know—not as effortlessly as Viscount Altea had accessed her house—but she did it anyway. Then she wandered back to Colin's study. The ghastly stain on the rug wasn't going to be dealt with easily, and she supposed the whole thing would have to be discarded.

And how to explain it . . .

Nosebleed, she pondered, wandering over to stare at the horrible spot, wishing she'd wake up and find it all a nightmare. Could she claim Lord Fitch had had a dreadful nosebleed and ruined the carpet?

Maybe. Until the selfsame lord told the true story. While she was glad she hadn't actually killed him, she wasn't all that delighted he was still going to be able to torment her. Madeline stood there, trying to imagine the rumors that would surface if Fitch spread the word that she'd invited him to come to her home, and twisted the reason why. He'd been smart enough to not actually blackmail her, so no real crime had been committed except some repugnant comments. All he had to do was deny he had the journal and accuse her of attacking him without cause.

The facts were the facts. If he'd been spiteful and sly before, he'd be tenfold worse now if he recovered.

If.

She took in a shuddering breath, clenching her hands into fists at her sides. Luke had sworn he'd take care of it.

That was another matter entirely.

Of all people, she'd called on Luke Daudet, the notorious and sinful Viscount Altea, sending her footman haring first to his club, and then apparently to one of the most shameful gaming halls in England.

Which was worse? Held captive by Lord Fitch's malicious amusement, or being beholden to Luke?

She wasn't sure, but certainly counted *this* as one of the worst evenings of her life.

ALSO AVAILABLE IN THE
NOTORIOUS BACHELORS SERIES

FROM

Emma Wildes

MY LORD SCANDAL

Alexander St. James may be a thief of hearts, but he is no burglar.
Nevertheless, he must recover an item belonging to his family to
avoid a scandal, and so he has stolen into the home of Lord
Hathaway, only to come upon the beguiling and chaste Lady
Amelia in her bedroom, wearing little but a look of surprise.
Alexander leaves Amelia breathless—but is it from fear or
excitement? Captivated by her beauty and charmed by her
intellect, he ignores the scandalous whispers as he sets out to
seduce the woman of his dreams...

OUR WICKED MISTAKE

Madeline May, the widowed Lady Brewer, is in a quandary. When
blackmail turns to murder, she knows that only one man can help
her—the Viscount Altea, a man used to dealing with men of ill
repute, and a man she despises with every fiber of her being.

As a connoisseur of beautiful women, Luke Daudet recognizes
Madeline's physical allure and the danger she represents. From the
very moment of their first meeting—and one unforgettable night
of passion—he knew she was different. And when he received her
fateful entreaty, he knew he would not be able to stay away...

**Available wherever books are sold
or at penguin.com**

S0132

Also Available

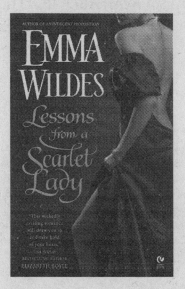

The Duke of Rolthven's new wife, Brianna, is the perfect aristocratic bride. So what would society say if they saw her with a copy of *Lady Rothburg's Advice*—a courtesan's lessons for the boudoir? When his innocent wife suddenly becomes a vixen in the bedroom, the proper Duke is truly astounded by her seductive powers. Following a courtesan's advice might lead to trouble—but will it lead to Brianna's ultimate desire: winning her husband's love?

"This wickedly exciting romance will draw you in and take hold of your heart."
—*USA Today* bestselling author Elizabeth Boyle

Available wherever books are sold
or at penguin.com

Also Available

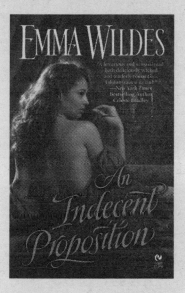

It's the talk of the town. London's two most notorious rakes have placed a public wager on which of them is the greater lover. But what woman of beauty, intelligence, and discernment would consent to judge such a contest? Lady Carolyn Wynn is the last woman anyone would expect to step forward. But if the men keep her identity a secret, she'll decide who has the most finesse between the sheets. To everyone's surprise, however, what begins as an immoral proposition turns into a shocking lesson in everlasting love…

"A spectacular and skillfully handled story that stands head and shoulders above the average historical romance."
—*Publishers Weekly* (starred review)

S0126